GREEN BAIZE ROAD

Alexandra Connor was born in Oldham, and still has strong connections to Lancashire. Apart from being a writer she is also a presenter on radio and television.

ALEXANDRA CONNOR

Green Baize Road

HarperCollins*Publishers*

This novel is a work of fiction. The names,
characters and incidents portrayed in it are the work of the
author's imagination. Any resemblance to actual persons,
living or dead, is entirely coincidental.

HarperCollins*Publishers*
77–85 Fulham Palace Road,
Hammersmith, London W6 8JB

The HarperCollins website address is:
www.harpercollins.co.uk

A Paperback Original 1999
1

A catalogue record for this book
is available from the British Library

ISBN 978-0-00-783348-1

Set in Sabon

Typeset by Rowland Phototypesetting Ltd,
Bury St Edmunds, Suffolk

Printed and bound in Great Britain by
Clays Ltd, St Ives plc

This book is for all the Oldham babies born in the 150th Anniversary Year of the town. May they be as proud of their heritage as the author.

Green Baize Road – a slang term for a billiards table

Prologue

1913

Well, she knew she shouldn't, but she couldn't help herself. He was so lovely. If you could use the word 'lovely' in regard to a man. She, Lily, managing to catch a man like Harold Browning. Wasn't possible, she thought incredulously; surely she was imagining it all. But she wasn't. The engagement had set tongues wagging, all right. She expected more than a few would be watching for her stomach showing at the wedding.

But it wasn't like that. Lily wasn't pregnant. Wasn't lying to snaffle Harold. He loved her.

'Soft bugger,' Ellen said under her breath, looking at a letter Harold had written to her younger sister the day before. 'I wonder what book he got this out of.'

But she was joking, pulling her sister's leg, tweaking at her good fortune, secretly delighted that the self-effacing Lily should have cocked a snook at Bolton by nabbing its best-looking son. Who would have thought it? Not her, not anyone. It was time Lily had some luck; she'd been a loser too long. Too shy, too timid, too careful of other people's feelings – to the extent that no one had ever considered hers. Until Harold. Oh yes, Ellen thought, it was time Lily had some good luck.

Their sister thought otherwise. Louise tried to look pleased, but she wasn't. Didn't understand how Lily had caught Harold Browning, her jealousy only partially assuaged by the fact that he was poor. Handsome, but poor. That helped. If Harold had been well off she would have imploded with envy.

Ellen smiled to herself. Poor Louise, the elder sister, hooked on marrying money like a fish hooked on catching a fly bobbing on the water overhead. Saw it as her way out of Bolton, desperate to leave the dark streets, the grim alleys, the overhang of sooty sky. Dreamed about far-off places, did Louise, sunshiny places with sea and beaches. God knows why, no one in their family had ever been further than Manchester.

Ellen's thoughts turned back to Lily. Her sister was facing the mirror over the black iron range, the dim light of the fire catching the line of her throat. She was thinking, preoccupied, her lips slightly parted, her eyes half closed. Beauty, at once unexpected and touching, made an angel of her.

PART ONE

A ministering angel shall my sister be . . .
                    (Shakespeare, *Hamlet*)

Some folk rail against other folks, because other folks have
what some folks would be glad of.
                    (Henry Fielding, *Joseph Andrews*)

Chapter One

February 1918

Derby Street, Bolton, was virtually empty, only the mills and shops busy, and the town seemingly occupied only by women. The men were away at war, and had been for the last three and a half years. The Great War they were calling it. Harold had been called up quickly; Ellen's husband, Reg Shawcross, following soon after. Only Reg's brother, Walter, had escaped.

Which wasn't a surprise to anyone. His nickname said it all – Disappearing Walter. He could leave any town, any woman, any war. Some said he had got off because of his feet – flat, they said. Lucky, Ellen thought, deciding meanly that Walter would have fed his lower regions through the mangle to avoid being called up.

Sighing, she swept the basement steps and then walked back into the billiards hall. A sign – 'Hot Pies are not to be eaten on the Premises' – stared down at her. The place was low-ceilinged, dim, the only light coming from the green shaded overhead gaslamps that crowned the billiards tables. If you didn't look too close the tables seemed in reasonable condition, but on keener inspection the shabby felt cloths were ripped in places and at a few corner pockets hungry war mice had grabbed a dry meal.

'SHAWCROSS'S BILLIARDS HALL' said the sign outside, with an arrow pointing down the steep stone steps to the basement. Reg had inherited the place from his late father, running it with Ellen before the war, the flat above providing them with living quarters. Nothing had been

5

changed for decades in those rooms. No carpet, only linoleum, an outside toilet giving cold comfort on a winter's night – except when the old cat came and sat on your knee seeking warmth.

Not that Ellen hadn't made some changes to the flat since her marriage. Flowers in vases and the odd rug gave a more homely look, and the kitchen range – always lit – sung with the sound of a humming kettle and smelled, every day, of new bread. But it was hard work running a home *and* a business, and the customers who frequented the billiards hall were a rough lot.

Not that Reg would ever have allowed the toughest characters in. He had the reputation of being a hard man and could outfight anyone who made trouble. And in general the place had been frequented by regulars and young lads, though not now, not since the outbreak of war. Now the hall was mostly empty, except for the old men and the wide boys who came in from the cold and pushed around a few balls to kill time.

Ellen was too astute not to realize that many deals were done in the semidark basement to the sound of the clacking billiards balls. The black market flourished in Bolton, and more than once there would be a woman waiting at the basement door when she opened up.

'Nice day,' one of her neighbours had said that morning as she swept the steps. 'I heard that Walter were back.'

'Came home yesterday.'

The woman nodded, looked round. 'He well?'

'Ever known Walter to be anything other than well?' Ellen countered.

'He busy?'

'Ever known Walter to be anything other than busy?'

'Oh, Ellen . . .'

She paused, stopped brushing. 'What d'you want?'

'I never thought I'd say it, but I need some coal.'

'You and everyone else round here.'

'I heard Walter could get it.'

Ellen leaned on the handle of her yard brush.

'You'll have to ask him. Call back later, he's not up yet.'

'It's nine thirty,' the woman said, aghast.

'Walter keeps his own hours.'

There was a long pause.

'How's your sister?'

'Which one?'

'Lily.'

People seldom asked about Louise since she had married Clem Whitley and moved to Australia. To the sea and the beaches and the warmth. Bloody hell, Ellen thought to herself, she'd certainly got what she wanted, like she knew from being a kid what the future held for her. Yet for all her good fortune, Louise's infrequent letters were always moaning. Even though she had the money she'd longed for, Louise wasn't happy.

'So, how *is* Lily?'

Ellen shrugged. 'Not too good.'

'He were a right bastard, doing what he did,' the woman went on vehemently. 'Harold Browning playing the field like that. I thought he were supposed to be out there fighting, not running around with some foreign bint.' Her voice fell suddenly, careful not to be overhead. After all, Lily, pregnant and abandoned, had moved from Little Lever and was now living with her sister, the windows of her bedroom only feet above where they were talking. '. . . And in her condition, too. How's she coping?'

Her heart's stopped, Ellen wanted to say. Oh, not really, her sister's heart was still pushing the blood round her body, but she was living by rote. Since Harold's blasting letter, Lily had gone into a state of rigid efficiency, tending toddler Bess and waiting for the new baby who was due next month. Harold's child, conceived on one of those breathless leaves he and Lily used to long for so much.

Ellen hadn't told Reg yet. There was time for that. If

7

the gossip was to be believed the war would be over by Christmas, and then she'd tell him. Have to. Tell him that her sister had been dumped by her husband and that Lily, with no income and in need of moral support, had moved in with them. With her child, and a baby, all of them crowded into the little flat above . . .

Ellen winced at the thought. Bloody hell, what would Reg say when he came home? What would he *do*?

'I betcha Reg'll sort the bugger out when he gets back.'

Frowning, Ellen glanced over to her neighbour. 'He won't be too pleased, and that's a fact.'

'I wouldn't want to be Harold Browning for a king's ransom. Reg'll kill him.'

He just might too, Ellen thought, when he sees his home invaded and his sister-in-law humiliated.

'I bet Reg –'

'I have to go,' Ellen said suddenly, turning away. 'Call back and have a word with Walter later, will you?'

Closing the door behind her, Ellen heard a sudden movement and, peering down the long dim length of the billiards hall, could just make out a wiry figure sitting up on one of the far tables. Walter had been sleeping there, covered with a blanket. He had had to. All the other beds were occupied.

'Someone want me?' Walter asked, his strange, rasping voice low.

'So you're awake,' Ellen replied briskly. 'I thought you'd be out for at least another three hours.'

'With the noise of that kid crying?' he asked. 'No man could sleep through that.'

'Bess is only a child. Children do cry.'

'I bet Reg'll have something to say about it when he comes home. You know he doesn't like children.'

Exasperated, Ellen walked over to her brother-in-law. Walter was grey from sleep and lack of fresh air, his cheekbones prominent, the flesh drawn tightly over them. But

8

his eyes were large and alert, his fingers bony as he reached for the half-smoked cigarette tucked behind his left ear, and lit up.

'My neighbour wants to know if you can get some coal –'

'It'll cost her.'

'I had a feeling you'd say that.'

Walter smiled slowly, showing his charm, the notorious charm that had women hanging all over him like a cheap suit.

'If I get money from her, I buy more coal and you get the benefit.'

'You're all heart, Walter, a real humanitarian.'

He pulled a face. 'Have I ever let you down?'

'You never *fail* to let me down, Walter, that's the only predictable thing about you,' Ellen retorted, walking past him into the kitchen beyond.

He followed noiselessly, the blanket wrapped round his thin frame.

'It's bloody cold.'

'That's because we've run out of coal,' Ellen said drily, 'and if you want to get warm and have a hot breakfast I suggest you get some fuel on this fire sharpish.' She glanced up as the child started crying again in the bedroom overhead. Lily would to be down soon, with Bess. 'Move yourself, Walter. I can't carry all of you.'

'But –'

Her temper flared up all at once. 'No buts!' she snapped. 'You get coal on this fire within half an hour or you sling your hook. I mean it, Walter. I'm going out and if that fire's not lit when I get back, God help you.'

Reg away fighting, Lily and her bairn to cope with – another on the way – shortages of everything and now Disappearing Walter turning up like the proverbial bad penny – what in God's name, Ellen thought, could Louise possibly have to moan about?

Chapter Two

Hearing the door bang below, Lily held on to Bess tightly, rocking her. She knew that Ellen wouldn't stay angry, she never did, but she realized what her sister's anger was about and knew what a difficult situation she had put her into. There wasn't room in the flat for her and Bess, and when the baby came it would be impossible. And then there was Reg to think of. It was his house, after all. If the situations had been reversed how would Harold have felt?

Harold . . . Lily's eyes closed against the name. To write and tell her that he had fallen for someone else – it was crazy. He had to be lying, didn't he? . . . Her eyes remained closed, hardly daring to open and focus on the shabby back bedroom, untidy with clothes, the water pitcher on the bedside table freezing to the touch.

The cold was what was making Bess cry; she hadn't been this cold before. At home Lily had always managed to keep the small flat in Little Lever warm, inviting. Her wages had seen to that, and there'd always been the money Harold sent her. Money that hadn't been forthcoming lately. And just when, unable to continue working at the bleach factory, she needed it so bad, for her and Bess and the baby.

Baby. Lily's eyes opened, her gaze resting on her swollen belly. Any time now. Her baby, not *their* baby any more. She would have to be brave. She could cope, she *could*. She had to, there was no other choice. But hopelessness overwhelmed her. How could she really have expected to hold on to a man like Harold Browning? It had been a miracle that he had married her in the first place. She was pretty, but nothing special, and not clever, like Louise, or funny and capable like Ellen. She had been mad to imagine that he would stay with her when he could have any woman.

But he loved her. Or said he did. But then he had probably been lying . . . Lily stared at her stomach and touched the distended bump. When the baby was born, she would have to go back to work, earn money. But then who would look after the baby? Who would look after Bess *and* the baby whilst she worked? She had paid a neighbour to mind Bess before, but that was in Little Lever, and although it was only a few miles away from Bolton it could have been another country. It was Lily's little world, populated by people and shops she knew, her timetable worked out, her status as Mrs Harold Browning secure. Lily was in control in Little Lever.

But no longer. She was in Bolton now, and it was too much to expect that Ellen could mind her kids, what with the billiards hall *and* Reg to tend to. Oh God, Reg, she thought suddenly. Her brother-in-law didn't know she was here; how would he take it when he found out? They had never been that close, and everyone knew that Reg Shawcross didn't like kids.

He didn't like cheats either, Lily thought, growing cold. He'd to be bound to go after Harold; he was that type. He wouldn't let his sister-in-law be humiliated. He'd go after him – and maybe he would bring Harold home, Lily thought, hope rising, force him to face up to his responsibilities.

Lily's hand moved over her belly, her depression momentarily lifting. Reg would bring Harold home. He would force him to come back to her, and when he was back he would love her again. Yes, Lily thought, Harold *would* love her again.

Ellen liked to pretend that she went to the library to learn, but it was a lie. She went there because it was the only bloody place where people couldn't get at her.

Slowly she pushed open the heavy front doors of Bolton Library and walked in. Heaven, the place was virtually empty. Not much call for a library in wartime, she thought walking between the fiction aisles and turning at the bottom towards the portion labelled 'Biography'. There she scanned the shelves and then lifted out a book about Lillie Langtry, taking a seat against the window and opening the first page.

Good-looking woman, Ellen thought, scanning the portrait on the frontispiece. But then looks always mattered, didn't they? Even though it was more important what a person did with her life, not how she decorated it. Ellen's fingers were numb with cold and she blew on them hurriedly, turning the next page. If Walter didn't have a fire burning when she got back, she'd bloody have him. *Lillie* Langtry – quite a name. Named after a flower.

She could have been named poetically. If she had chosen her husband more carefully she could have been Ellen Larch now, instead of Ellen Shawcross. She smiled to herself. Not that a pretty name made you automatically lucky, otherwise Lily would have been blessed from birth. Like Lillie Langtry.

Snapping the book shut, Ellen's thoughts slid back to the past. Her sister Louise had teased her once, saying that there was a ghost in the glory hole, the little attic storeroom upstairs – the room above their heads that they told each other stories about. Footsteps at night, unplaced shuffles, seemed to seep down from the dark hideaway, the three sisters equally afraid of the musty, unexplored hole.

Louise had dared Ellen to go and look, her eyes quick with mischief. Unable to back down, that night Ellen had crept up into the glory hole – coming face to face with a white figure, Louise slamming the door shut behind her, whilst she screamed and banged to get out.

It had only been a dressmaker's dummy, but the pulsing terror Ellen had experienced had made her forever suspicious of her elder sister. Because Louise had a cruel streak.

Lily, however, did not. Lily was the sweetest, prettiest one of the three girls. Not that she believed it. Thought good of everyone else, but herself. Some nasty nick in her personality forbade it. Everyone else could be good and beautiful, but not her. She'd had no confidence, Ellen thought ruefully, even as a child.

Pleased to be out of the cold, Ellen glanced out of the library window, the biography of Lillie Langtry lying on her lap, a child drawing a stick along the pavement outside. The kids used to draw sticks across the black iron railings, but they had long since been requisitioned for the war effort. Railings, Ellen thought, what the hell did you do with railings? Spear the Germans to death?

If Walter hadn't got that fire going, she thought absently, she would swing for him. A nice fire would be inviting, make the place home again ... Oh Reg, Ellen thought longingly, how I miss you. Big, hard man, dark red hair, broad faced, no beauty, but tough. Never backed down from anyone, did you? Courage in spades. She remembered the billiards hall before the war, when it was busy, humming with low voices, clacking balls, cigarette smoke curling and uncurling under the shaded lamps.

No one had imagined that she would marry Reg Shawcross, a rough arse from the wrong side of the tracks. A backstreet kid.

Ellen smiled. Rough, oh yes, but not when he needed to be gentle. He made love so tenderly, so carefully, watching her face, stroking her hair and asking, over and over: 'Is that nice? Is that good for you? I love you, Ellen, I want to make you happy.'

He had come courting with all his worldly goods – a billiards hall on Derby Street, a rough name, and a wide boy for a brother. Hardly the catch of Bolton. You could do better, people told Ellen, you don't want to end up running a dump in the backstreets. Besides, no one knows what *Walter* Shawcross gets up to. He'll end up in jail – and so might his brother.

Ellen listened, then joked about learning how to make cakes with files in them.

'If you two end up in jail, make sure it's the same one. It'll cut back on the travelling when I visit you.'

But she knew that Reg wasn't a criminal. He might have no respect for authority, but he was an honest man. Walter, on the other hand, was a natural crook. But then, she hadn't married Walter.

Sighing, Ellen glanced at her watch. Time to go home, she thought, getting to her feet and replacing the book on the shelf. For an instant her figures ran over the gold lettering of Lillie Langtry's name and then she turned, drew on her gloves and headed for the exit.

No point daydreaming, time to get on with reality again.

Chapter Three

Lily gave birth to her second daughter, Emma, on 12 March, the baby small and sickly, Bess fretful, Walter doing his usual trick and disappearing – but not without first filling the yard outside with coal and tossing a couple of sacks over it to keep it dry. For once reckless, Ellen banked up the grate and sat throughout the night with her sister whilst she was in labour. Nothing, Ellen thought to herself, would induce *her* to give birth. Thank God Reg didn't want children.

Over the past few weeks, she had watched the rapid deterioration in her sister and knew that Lily would never to be able to cope alone. She also knew that Lily would never return to her cramped, friendly flat in Little Lever, although she talked repeatedly about Harold's return. When Reg came home, wouldn't he talk sense into Harold? Well, *wouldn't* he?

Time would tell, Ellen replied, unwilling to commit her husband to what might prove impossible.

But time and Lily were not such easy companions, and the depression that had threatened, finally swallowed her whole in the summer. She no longer worked at anything and spent long hours up in the tiny back bedroom above the billiards hall, watching and listening to the Bolton world going past in the streets. She cared for the baby well enough, but when little Bess became ill, it was Ellen who sat up with her night after night.

Unused to being a mother and unsure if she wanted any further responsibility, Ellen was unprepared for the fierce bond that grew between her and Bess. She had become fond of the little girl and found her amusing, so to see her listless and flu-ridden soon brought out her protective instinct. And, oddly, Bess turned to her aunt – not her mother – for comfort, as though she knew instinctively that Lily had no resources left.

After the cold weather, the heat came in fierce and unremitting; the narrow streets smouldering, dogs fighting, the flat stifling, oppressive, the basement billiards hall the only cool spot in the town. Unable to lower Bess's temperature, Ellen moved her downstairs, making up a bed for them both on one of the billiards tables at night and curling up beside her, rocking her in the small hours. Banked up with pillows and cool under the sheets, she whispered to Bess and told her stories, stroking the little girl's overheated forehead with the palm of her cool hand.

And upstairs Lily lay with her baby daughter and listened to the nights passing and the days beginning, and soon the bleach works and the memory of Harold began to dance in front of her eyes like a sickly dream, half remembered. She no longer thought about the war, nor about Harold's hoped-for return; she no longer believed it. It was over, her marriage was spent. As she was.

So when the tragic news came, Ellen kept it to herself for the time being. Reg wouldn't have to take issue with Harold Browning, and Lily wouldn't have to spend the rest of her days wondering what she had done for her husband to leave her. Because Harold wasn't coming back. Harold was staying in France permanently. Not with his mistress, but with a bullet in his chest.

The only person in whom Ellen confided was Walter, appearing intermittently but never staying long. Otherwise she kept everything out of her letters to Reg and lied, bold-faced, to her sister. She had to; there was no choice. Lily was unable to cope with the shock of Harold's desertion; the shock of his death would be too much.

By August it was clear to everyone that Lily could no

longer look after her baby, and Ellen – tired and over-worked with the billiards hall and Bess – had more than enough to cope with. So when Louise wrote and asked after the baby, Ellen eagerly wrote back and told her everything about her new niece. Yes, she was very blonde, lovely, quite a golden child. Very pretty, very good. And quite well now, not sickly at all, although the Northern air wasn't that good for her. She needed a garden and fresh air, space to grow. She was hampered in Bolton with Ellen and Lily; it was no place for a child. Not a special child – and Emma was certainly that.

> Tell me about her, *Louise wrote back*. I'd like to know more. The weather here is mild, and the house is all finished. Clem says we should start a family, but nothing's happening. You don't know what that's like, Ellen, you never wanted children. But we do. We could give a child a real start in life. We've got the money, and the house, got everything any child could want . . .

Who thought of it first, Ellen wondered afterwards, herself or Louise? Or was it something inevitable, something bound to happen? She remembered her sister and the glory hole and wondered. The incident had been a pointer to her – they might have been inevitably close as sisters, but there was that nick of spite in Louise, that competitiveness, which she had never lost.

Yet since that night Louise had never shown any other cruelty of nature, or maybe she just had locked that part of her character away, shelved it in her own mental glory hole. But things hidden, Ellen knew, never remained hidden for ever. So had Louise really changed? Ellen hoped so. Oh, her elder sister was a whiner, of that there was no doubt, and she was a snob, but her good points still out-weighed her bad, Ellen was sure of that.

Louise was lonely, rich, indulged. And Clem adored her, endlessly pliable to her every whim. If Louise wanted anything, she got it. He could see no wrong in her. Descriptions of the house in Australia, just outside Sydney, came through in glowing colour. Huge skies, beaches, space. Fresh, sweet air, unpolluted by smoke and coal soot. Just the place for a delicate child to flourish.

Soon the letters between the sisters became more frequent. 'How is Emma thriving?' Louise wrote to Ellen. 'Is she well? Is she happy? Does she need anything?'

Did she need anything? She needed everything. She needed a solid family background, stable parents, security. Because she had – Ellen realized at once – none of Bess's resilience, and was oddly out of place in Bolton. Fairhaired, fragile, silent, Emma stared from her mother's arms or from the second-hand pram in elegant resignation. She was, she seemed to imply, only marking time.

And meanwhile Lily deteriorated steadily, putting the baby down on the narrow bed upstairs and staring out of the window blindly. She forgot her child for minutes – later for hours – only Ellen's intervention reminding her of her responsibilities. Soon, Ellen was moving endlessly from her bed to the cramped back bedroom upstairs, up and down throughout the long summer nights, Bess crying for her, Emma listless, lying against her mother's side, Lily inert and hopeless.

It was wrong, Ellen realized, all horribly wrong. It was bad for everyone – for the children, for Lily, for the baby.

Then one morning an extraordinary letter came from Louise. Clinging to her sister's hand, Lily watched blankly as Ellen opened the letter and read it to her.

It said simply that she and Clem wanted to adopt the baby and bring her up as their own. They would love Emma and give her everything. Lily need no longer worry; her sister would take care of her child. Wasn't that the best thing for everyone? How could Lily worry knowing that she was giving her child the best chance in life? And also knowing that Emma would be going to family?

There was only one drawback – wasn't there always with Louise, Ellen thought. In order that Louise could, without restraint give Emma the best in life, she had to be brought up *as her own child*. It was to be a secret pact between the sisters. Emma would grow up believing that Louise and Clem Whitley were her real parents – Lily was no longer to be thought of as Emma's mother. In fact, Louise continued, it would be better all round if people in Bolton thought that Emma had died. It would avoid any complications later, Louise explained, or any division of loyalties. Emma could be adopted by Louise and Clem and brought up as their own. She would know nothing else. There would be no going back. It would be kinder to Emma in the long run. It made sense, surely. It was the only condition.

It was blackmail.

'Let people think Emma died!' Lily said blindly. 'But she's my baby. Not Louise's. She's *my* baby.'

'But can you look after her?' Ellen asked her sister quietly. 'Think about what she's saying, Lily. Think about it.'

Her voice was calm, but inside she was seething. So Louise hadn't changed that much, after all. What a caveat to add to the bargain. What a little pinch of cruelty to season the kindness. To ask Lily to say her child was dead, to expect her to wipe Emma out of her life completely. For ever. No longer a mother, just some distant aunt, in another country, without hope of reconciliation later.

But what was the option? To keep Emma here? To see Lily struggle mentally and physically to bring up her daughter, something she patently couldn't do? With Louise, Emma would have everything – money, education, affection.

But at what cost? a little voice picked at Ellen's conscience. Cautiously, she glanced at Lily. She still didn't know

19

about Harold. Thank God, Ellen thought, thank God for that.

'What should I do?' Lily asked helplessly. 'What should I do?'

She had lost weight, was older, tired, often listless, even occasionally confused. On the bed between them lay Emma, golden and charmed, but watchful. Aware.

'Louise would look after her, and Clem too. He's a very kind man –'

'But Emma is my baby. I can't give up my baby . . .' Lily said, her nose running, tears clinging to the edges of her long pale lashes. 'I would be giving up my own child. Harold's child . . .'

She trailed off, seemed suddenly to think, to consider. Ellen watched her curiously. Harold was no longer to be considered, Lily thought emptily. He had left her with this child, and she was unable to cope. Bess was older, and Ellen loved Bess, but the baby was a stranger, who had not shown her character yet. *Would* it be kinder to give Emma over to her sister? Would it, in fact, be selfish to cling on to her? After all, what had she to give her? Camped out with her sister over a billiards hall, no money, no future, no husband. She could manage Bess, but a baby . . . Perhaps it *was* the right thing to do, after all.

But could she deny her own child, sign her over, say to the world, 'My child died. I did not give birth to Emma, I am her aunt only, Louise is her mother'? And in later years, should they ever meet, Lily would have to act the aunt, not the mother . . .

Lily felt the tears dry around her eyes: tiredness, complete and fogging, dragged at her. What was the choice? Hold on to her baby and struggle? But how could she work when she could hardly haul herself out of bed? How could she run a house, a life, *how*? What future was there for a beautiful child here with nothing to look forward to, nothing to hope for?

So on that steaming morning, as the letter lay on the bed between the two sisters, the fate of Emma was decided. Yet until the last moment, Ellen expected her sister to retract, to fight to hold on to her child. But something about Lily's movements and expressions predicted disaster – and as the morning dipped into afternoon Ellen came to realize that the only security the baby would ever know was far away.

'Perhaps she *would* be better off with them . . .' Lily said quietly.

Ellen flinched at the words. 'Are you sure? Think about it.'

Slowly her sister looked over to her. A long strand of hair, once blonde, now faded, stuck to her cheek.

'Will I be punished?'

It took Ellen a moment to respond. 'What?'

Listlessly, Lily glanced at her baby on the bed next to them. After a moment she touched Emma's arm and then drew away her hand as though afraid.

'Will God punish me for giving her up?'

Ellen had no truck with religion. 'God isn't looking after her. We are,' she replied practically. 'Louise can give her everything. She'll want for nothing.'

'But she's *mine* . . .' Lily answered faintly.

There was a sudden noise from below, someone had come into the billiards hall for a game of snooker. They were racking the balls up, click, clack.

'Will she blame me?'

Will she ever know? Ellen wanted to counter, but knew she couldn't say the words. Below came the sound of balls being struck hurriedly, the scattering of colours flying across the dull baize of one of the tables.

'Will she hate me later?'

I don't know, Ellen wanted to say. How do I know? But looking at her sister she knew all too well what Lily wanted to hear. And she was more than willing to lie.

'If Emma ever found out, she'd be grateful to you,' she said softly, brushing away the strand of hair that had stuck to Lily's cheek.

At the moment Ellen's stomach felt bruised, as though she had been kicked, her chest emptied. She felt – and would feel for a long time to come – as though she had committed some awful, and unforgivable, crime.

Louise, desperate enough to brave the wartime seas, determined to acquire the baby as young as possible, had come for Emma and shortly afterwards she and Clem Whitley were declared the baby's legal parents. It was all so fast. Apparently Clem knew someone who could help, and used his money and influence to push through the necessary paperwork, and so soon, very soon, what had been an idea was a fact.

It was all so furtive, Louise and Clem taking the baby to Australia and then Ellen telling everyone soon after that Emma had caught influenza and died. It was a tragedy, she said, but maybe Louise would have a child of her own soon and it was, after all, better for Lily this way. So very carefully she planted the seed, laying the ground for Louise's phantom pregnancy – for the ghost child who would take Emma's place in the minds of the people in Bolton. And in such a way Emma became Louise's child. And in such a way Lily lost Emma.

It had been the hardest thing Ellen had ever had to do. Not the lying, but the negation of her niece's life. Should she have acted otherwise, she wondered, longing for Reg's return, for his reassurance. Should she have backed Lily, persuaded her to hold on to her child? As the sweltering summer turned to autumn, the answer was no clearer in Ellen's mind.

Snow was falling when the end of the war was announced, snow sweet and white, flattering the Northern ginnels and

the narrow terraced streets. The news travelled from news-
stands, radios, mouth to mouth, women coming out onto
their doorsteps, old men talking, children wondering what
the fuss was about. Your father's coming home, your father
. . . Wives and daughters hung about for news, clung on
to every bit of gossip, every syllable that told them when
their men were to come walking up their streets, into their
houses, and into their beds.

God, it was cold, Ellen thought, walking hurriedly
towards the corner, where she stopped, waiting for the
sight of her man . . . Oh, come on, Reg, she urged, come
on home. Let me hold you and take you to bed and tell
you all about what happened. Let me feel you and smell
you and taste you . . . She shivered, pulling her coat around
her, thinking of all the news she had to tell her husband,
and working through the best way to say it in her mind.

It's been rough, Reg. Bloody rough. The billiards hall's
just managed to stay open. I had Lily staying for a bit, just
till she got over the birth, but she's gone back to her flat
in Little Lever, and is now working at the bleach works
again. Harold's dead – I kept that from both of you – but
Lily knows about his death now, though I can't tell you
how she feels about it. She doesn't talk about him, or
about Emma. She lives, Reg. Just lives. You could say that
everything's back to how it was when you went away.

Only you'd be lying.

Breathing out hurriedly, Ellen clapped her hands
together to warm them. Time to explain later, she thought,
remembering how she had banked up the fire and made
a massive meal. He liked his food, did Reg. A regular
trencherman . . . Anxiety fluttered inside her and then
faded. Oh, she could get round him, she knew she could.
Once she got him into bed, she could convince him of
anything.

Oh come on, Reg, she thought impatiently, where are
you?

The light was fading, afternoon hard and cold, evening just waiting to pounce. I want you so much, she thought. God, I never knew how much I wanted you. She smiled at her own longing. Reg Shawcross, get yourself home. Now.

Her eyes closed. I'll count to five – no to ten. Then when I open my eyes he'll be there. One, two, three ... she peeked between half-opened lids, then pressed them closed again ... four, five, six ... Oh Reg, come on, *come on*.

He would be whistling, she knew it. He'd whistle and come up to her and pick her up and run up the stairs to the flat and they'd make love and laugh. Oh, she wanted to laugh, needed to laugh. There had been precious few light moments in the last months. Last years. Bloody war. Bloody life. Bloody hell, Reg, come on.

He'd want to see the billiards hall, of course. Check that she had kept his inheritance just so. Check the balls, racks, tables. Pretend he was looking at some palace, instead of a smoky backstreet place. It was his only delusion, Ellen thought smiling, her husband's one weakness. He thought Shawcross's Billiards Hall was Utopia, some dimly lit Valhalla. He'd used to stand watching the customers, smoking, letting the boys rack up, his voice louder than the rest.

'Oi, watch the cloth. You, Stan, I'm talking to you! Yes, watch it. The door opens both ways, you know.'

He was a master in his own tawdry kingdom, bets going down late at night when the closed sign was on the door. Ellen had seen men lose money, watches, and shoes on a bet, but nothing more valuable; Reg wouldn't have allowed that. 'A bet's a bet,' he'd say, 'but I'll not see any man ruined on my premises.'

In the first year of their marriage his old mother had taken the money, sitting in the tiny, carved wooden cubicle by the door, her black mittened hands shooting out under the black slat.

'That's sixpence.'

'That's steep.'

'That's the price, take it or leave it,' she'd croak. 'And don't cheek me. I knew you when you had nowt, and nothing's changed.'

Then Old Ma Shawcross died and Ellen gravitated to the cubicle, spraying perfume to drown the old lady smell, the black mittens hung up on a hook by her head, the door left open. When they were busy Reg would look over to her and wink, sometimes sidling behind the door and, unseen, putting his hand on her knee. A big hand, warm to the touch.

Ellen's eyes clicked open. The street was still empty. She'd count a bit longer and then go in. It was getting dark; maybe he'd missed his train. Reg could always miss a train. Never missed a trick, but a train, yes. One, two, three, she began again, four, five, six –

'Hey!'

He came behind her, lifted her up, buried his face in her neck, the snow falling on their faces. God, he was so sweet, so big, so much her man.

'I was waiting –'

He cut her off, his mouth over hers, his breath warm against her tongue.

'I missed you,' she said, laughing, as she pulled away. 'I've made food and lit a fire.'

'We don't need a fire in the bedroom,' Reg said, throwing her over his shoulder, a neighbour smiling as they passed.

Laughing still, Ellen banged her fists against his back. 'Put me down! Put me down!'

'When I'm ready,' he replied, whistling and unlocking the door of the flat and taking the stairs hurriedly.

Halfway up he stopped and slid her off his shoulder, taking her face in his hands and kissing her blindly, longingly. His hands moved over her body, unfastening her coat and dress, moving over her breasts hungrily, Ellen laughing and struggling to get free.

'Reg, hey, wait a minute –'

He didn't want to hear it. 'Wait? Are you mad?'

'I have –'

He had hold of her arm and was pushing, pulling her towards the bedroom, laughing, his mouth repeatedly finding hers, crushing out the words as she tried to speak. Finally he reached the door, fumbling with the handle, Ellen murmuring something as he continued to kiss her. Then suddenly the door fell back, Reg propelled forwards, Ellen falling to her knees beside him heavily.

Rubbing his elbow, Reg looked over to the bed – and stared, thunderstruck.

'What the hell is that?'

Ellen smiled wanly. 'A little girl.'

'I didn't think it was a rabbit,' he replied drily. '*Whose* little girl?'

'Ours.'

He stared at Ellen, then looked at the child, then looked back to her.

'*Ours?*'

'Well, not exactly.'

'Could you be exact?' Reg said evenly.

'She's ours now.'

'Why? Did you find her, or win her?'

'Reg –'

'I don't like children!' he said bluntly, getting to his feet and staring at the child. 'Anyway, she's deaf.'

'Huh?'

'She must be, or she'd have woken up with all the clatter we've made.'

'She's just tired.'

'I know how she feels.'

Sidling over to her husband, Ellen slid her arm through his.

'It's Lily's daughter.'

'Thank God for that! So when's your sister coming to pick her up?'

Ellen chose her next words carefully. 'Harold's dead.'

'What?'

'He left Lily when she was pregnant, then he was killed. She couldn't cope – when the baby was born Louise adopted it.'

'So why didn't Louise adopt this one too?'

'Reg, come on,' Ellen cajoled him. 'Lily's had a really hard time of it. I had to help her. I didn't want to tell you all this when you were away. I didn't want to worry you. Besides, it's all sorted now.'

His expression hardened. 'Like how?'

'Bess . . .' she gestured to the little girl in the bed, 'needed someone to look after her. Lily can't. She could hardly look after herself, so I've been looking after Bess.' She hurried on. 'She's a very good child, very quiet –'

'No.'

'No what?'

'No, we are *not* keeping her.'

Ellen shrugged her shoulders. 'Fine.'

'Yeah,' Reg said, wrong-footed, 'fine.'

'The council will find a home for her. Some orphanage.' Ellen kept her face averted. 'She's a pretty child; someone will want her. Of course, we won't know where she goes, or how they treat her. But I'm sure she'll be fine. After all, she's only our niece, why should we worry what happens to her?'

'This isn't what I expected –'

Angrily, Ellen rounded on him. 'It wasn't what I expected either! Nothing has been for years. Running this place, looking after my sister and her children and trying to keep tabs on that oily brother of yours – I didn't expect any of that, but I did it.' She dropped her voice as the child in the bed stirred. 'I never wanted children, I don't even like them – until she came along.'

Sighing, Reg looked away. 'I wanted it to be just the two of us.'

'I know . . . But she needs a home, Reg. She needs us.'

Slowly Ellen moved over to her husband and leaned her head against his shoulder.

'Look on the bright side. We could use her as a slave, get her to do all the housework and sleep in the outside lav.'

He laughed softly and slid his arm around her. 'And beat her regularly?'

'Of course, that goes without saying.'

He glanced over his shoulder. 'Does she always sleep in our bed?'

'Only when she's not tied up in the outside toilet.'

He smiled again and kissed her, leading her to the door and across the landing into the cramped back room beyond.

Chapter Four

'Are you trying to hypnotize that ball, or what?'

'Eh?' Stan Clark looked up from his crouch over the table.

'I said – are you going to hit that bloody ball before it gets a five o'clock shadow?' Gordon the Cuffs asked, tugging down the starched white cuffs for which he was famous. Thinks the girls like them, Ellen said drily; needs a cuff round the ear more like.

'It's my turn, and I'll take as long as I like,' Stan retorted, his voice picking up.

Reg materialized beside them instantly.

'Steady, lads.'

'I was just –'

'Cuffs, shut it. And Stan, hit the bloody ball, there are others want this table.'

'I –'

'Stan, just hit the ball –'

'He can't. He couldn't hit it if it was the size of a barn door.'

Reg's face darkened. 'Either hit it, or get out,' he said warningly. 'And you, Cuffs, stop winding him up.'

Reg moved over to the wooden cubicle where Ellen was counting the takings for the day. Over her head someone had pinned a note: 'DO NOT FEED THE ANIMALS', and a banana lay on the shelf in front of her.

'Very funny,' Reg said, turning round and then bending down towards the chair by the open door of the cubicle where a little girl sat patiently. 'So how are you, darling?'

Bess was sitting as she often did, watching the men playing billiards in front of her. She had been reading a rag book and by her feet a doll – well used – lay on its head.

'What happened to Dorothy?' Reg asked her.

'Poorly,' the little girl replied.

'Oh dear, that's a shame.'

'She's been working too hard,' Bess said sagely.

Reg exchanged an amused look with Ellen over the child's head.

He had come to accept Bess, then love her, then idolize her. There was no wrong she could do; and nothing she couldn't have. Hard up they might be, but Bess wanted for nothing – not clothes, nor attention. Only months after Reg had come back from the war he stopped shooing her out of the billiards hall, and soon she was a regular fixture there. She brought him luck, he said.

'It's her eyes,' he said simply; 'like a cat's they are.'

He was right; Bess had long, oblique eyes which were darkly brown – like her father's.

Not that anyone mentioned Harold Browning's name any more. It was lucky the Germans got the bugger before he had, Reg said. Both Lily and Bess were better off without him. But although Ellen might think he was right, Lily had never come to terms with the failure of her marriage, or the death of Harold. She had agreed to *pretend* to everyone that Emma had died, but when she heard of Harold's death Lily couldn't take it in. Was it real, or make-believe, like Emma?

On the surface, Lily had *appeared* to cope; had gone back to work, talked to the girls at Farnworth Bleach Factory, even seemed perfectly normal, but she wasn't. She talked too much about punishment, Ellen said, and started blaming herself, even once visiting the local Methodist church.

'Why Methodist?' Reg said when Ellen told him.

'They're serious, into damnation and all that.'

'It's not healthy,' Reg replied. 'She did the right thing for that kid at the time.'

But even if Reg could dismiss it so easily, Ellen couldn't. Having grown close to Bess she wondered how a mother – a *mother* – could give up her child. And then she recalled how great a part she had played in the passing over of Emma to Louise. Now that Ellen realized how much it would hurt her to part with her niece, she could hardly imagine parting with her own flesh and blood. But she hadn't known that then, had she? She had just wanted to give her sister the best advice possible. She had done the right thing, for the right reasons, surely.

And no good deed ever goes unpunished, she thought.

So she never spoke of Emma to her sister, and Lily seldom referred to her daughter, only mentioning her when letters came from Australia, then reading and rereading every word about her daughter. Correction, *Louise's* daughter. Because, to all intents and purposes, Emma was now Louise and Clem Whitley's child. They referred to her as their baby. Once Louise even wrote to Lily: 'Your little niece is sitting up and taking notice.'

Jesus, Ellen thought, has she no feelings? Angrily she had penned a letter back to Louise.

. . . For God's sake, have a thought for what Lily must be feeling. She gave up her child but you can't expect her to deny that she's Emma's mother to us. She may have to do it to the rest of the world, but not to her family.

A letter came back from Australia. It had been written weeks ago, but even so, must have been sent by return.

Dear Ellen,
  I don't know what I've done to cause such unpleasantness. God knows we are doing everything

we can to bring Emma up happy and well provided for. Clem and I both think that you are being unreasonable. Lily agreed that Emma would be adopted by us. The world thinks she is our child, and she *has* to think that, or there will be all kinds of ructions when she gets older. Surely even you can see that? . . .

Smouldering, Ellen showed the letter to Reg.

'Once a bitch, always a bitch,' he said simply. 'Louise has got what she wanted – as usual – and – as usual – everyone has to play by her rules.'

'But it's so hurtful for Lily –'

'Yeah, I know,' she sighed, 'but maybe it's better this way. A bit of pain now might save a lot of pain later.'

Glowering, Ellen rounded on him. 'And what's *that* supposed to mean?'

'Emma has a new life with new parents. She need never know that Harold buggered off and that Lily gave her up. Oh, don't look at me like that, Ellen! You know it's the best way. If that child grows up knowing the truth she would be forever pulled in two directions – tied to her mother here and the Whitleys out there. She would be torn, and later she might have to chose between them .'

Ellen frowned. 'How d'you make that out?'

'Because families argue, they fall out. And kids get in the firing line,' he said bluntly, slamming the tray of the till closed, the noise loud, even in the busy billiards hall. 'Why complicate her life with unnecessary problems? Life dishes out enough shit without adding to it.'

Sitting on the edge of her bed Lily took out the letter she had received that morning and reread it. Emma was nearly eighteen months old and walking, Louise said. She had described their house with a mixture of reserve and swank: she didn't have to remind her sister of the difference between a tired cramped flat over a hat shop in Little Lever and a bungalow outside Sydney. Clem's business was mining and property, and the rewards were evident. There was no need for her to point out that the air was sweet and sunny; that there was little rain and no soot. That there were no factory chimneys and whistles blowing the women to work on freezing winter mornings.

Emma would never know – Louise implied, without writing it – the feel of damp bedclothes or washing speckled with soot from open fires. The pet dog Emma had was not some mongrel who slept rough behind the UCP tripe shop, the clothes she wore were not cheap copies from Manchester sold up on Tommy Fields' market on a Saturday afternoon, the paraffin lamps spluttering on the sides of the stalls when the wind blew over cruel from the moors.

Christmas for Emma would come in high summer when it was possible to swim in the sea – not in streets choked with rubble, fruit hard to get, the oranges bitter, riddled with pips. In Australia Lily knew – without being told – that there were wide clean streets and windows that stayed shiny for weeks. There were no gaslamps there, no night-soil men.

It wasn't Paradise, Lily knew that. But it was close. She should be pleased, she thought, should be relieved to think of her baby being there ... but she wasn't. She wanted Emma back in her arms, wanted to smell her baby's skin and look into her eyes.

Louise and Clem had stolen her; taken away all the little sweetness of childhood that a mother waits for and treasures – the first word, the first smile, the first walk. Emma would call *Louise* Mother, she would walk to *her*, and talk like *her*. Posh, without the Bolton accent, the flat vowels. Emma would grow up seeing herself in Louise and Clem. She would grow to laugh like *them*, to think like *them*, to be like *them*.

She will never be here, Lily thought, never be here with

33

me again. Never again. The little time I had with her she
never knew, will never remember. I was her mother, Lily
thought. I was her *mother*... And then realized that for
the first time she had used the past tense.

'There's a woman looking for you,' Ellen said one morning
when she opened up the billiards hall.

Disappearing Walter was back. He had sidled in late the
previous night, trailing cigarette smoke and calling up the
stairs to the flat, his rasping voice loud.

'Oi, anything to eat?'

Reg, who had been washing, had run down to his
brother, punching Walter affectionately on the left shoulder. For a moment Ellen expected him to go down, but
Walter was stronger than he looked. Walter was never
what he appeared. And they were thick, those two, thick
as thieves.

But Walter looked pretty rough now, she thought as he
walked into the kitchen, cold and irritable.

'What d'you say?'

'There's some woman come looking for you, Walter.'

His pale eyes narrowed. 'What d'you say to her?'

'That you were expecting her,' Reg said mischievously,
his brother swinging round on him.

'Jesus, Reg! That's not funny.'

'Apparently she was a bit miffed, said you'd promised
to meet her outside the Town Hall,' Ellen went on, ladling
some eggs onto two plates and passing them over to the
brothers. 'Said something about you being a bastard
toerag.'

Reg laughed, shaking his head. 'Why don't you just get
married and settle down?'

Incredulous, Walter stared at him, pushed away the eggs
and lit up another cigarette.

'What's wrong with them?'

'Huh?'

'The eggs?' Ellen asked, spoon still in hand.

'Nothing.'

'So eat them.'

'I'm not hungry.'

'They cost money.'

'So I'll pay you!' Walter said shortly, turning to Reg. 'That's why I don't get married: women nag.'

'You don't get married because no women in her right mind would have you, Walter,' Ellen replied, 'not that this one looks all that easy to brush off. She had a very determined way about her. A kind of military bearing.'

Picking up the cue, Reg winked at his wife. 'Like how?'

'Oh well, she was of a certain age – you know what I mean – when a woman marries anything she can run to ground.' Ellen paused. Then: 'And she's bigger than Walter, could give him a good pounding if she took a mind to it. And she might. No woman likes to be made a fool of.'

'I hardly know her,' Walter said, blowing smoke up to the ceiling and trying to sound nonchalant. 'It's nothing serious –'

'Not to you, maybe,' Ellen provoked him, 'but I don't think she sees it that way.'

Reg frowned. 'Keen, hey?'

'As mustard.'

He glanced sidelong at his brother. 'So you won't be staying long then?'

'No woman's going to force me out of the town.'

Ellen turned away from the table, adding, under her breath, 'Someone's husband might, though.'

It was obvious that Walter hadn't heard her, and however much they might rag him about his latest conquest Walter was not seriously perturbed. He never was. About anything. His attitude to life was simple. No possessions, no ties. And if the worst came to the worst – and it sometimes did temporarily – he disappeared.

There was a rumour around Bolton that the two brothers weren't really brothers at all. After all, to look at them you'd be hard put to find any resemblance. Even their voices were dissimilar; Reg's hard Northern, Walter's hoarse, oddly accentless. There was no similarity in their bodies and faces, and their attitudes were as far apart as any two men's could be – and way too far apart for brothers.

But there was only one stumbling block to the rumour: Old Ma Shawcross. 'A cure for bad thoughts', she had been referred to locally. It was inconceivable that any man would dare to make love to Agnes, but *two* men similarly stoical – never. It would have been an understatement to say that Agnes wouldn't take anything from anyone. In fact, it had been her idea in the first place to set up the billiards hall, her husband having little say in the matter. Which was how things usually went with Bill. Whether he liked it or not, Agnes had told him, she was going ahead. He was out of work, so someone had to bring money into the house.

She'd found the premises and, God knows how, she'd bought up four worn tables from someone over Liverpool way. Billiards had been new to Bolton, something really different, and despite anyone's reservations, Agnes had soon had a winner on her hands. If it seemed odd that Agnes Shawcross – dressed in black ever since Bill died (an event no one could remember exactly; he was just there one day and gone the next) – should run a billiards hall, no one dared to mention it. She was from a family of six brothers and could scare the living bejesus out of anyone, a trait she passed on to Reg. But not to Walter.

Which was another reason why people wondered about her second son. Where Reg relied on brawn, Walter relied on charm and a kind of sneaking cunning. Had he applied himself, he could have been clever, but application was not Walter's strong suit. Women were. As were horses, dogs, and every kind of deal that required a quick mind and nerves of steel.

Walter didn't want a home life. Or a wife. Certainly not children. Walter even did without a house, stayed with 'friends' instead, usually women, and when he was back in Bolton, he stayed at the billiards hall. Why pay rent? he would ask. What the hell for, when he could live for free – or virtually free. He didn't escape scot-free, of course. There *were* some demands on him from his girlfriends. Sexual satisfaction – which he usually had no trouble providing; and promises – which he gave out like a bird gives out song. Unthinkingly.

'So what brings you back anyway?' Reg asked his brother.

'Business.'

'Like what?'

'You know,' Walter said evasively, 'this and that.'

'Oh yes,' Ellen replied, 'we heard there was a call for this and that.'

Reluctantly Reg rose to his feet and moved to the door that separated the back kitchen from the billiards hall. There was an old green curtain hanging over it, suspended from the top by a brass rail, Old Ma Shawcross's pride and joy. He pulled the curtain aside, but Walter was not taking the hint.

'Where's the little one?' asked Reg.

Ellen jerked her head upwards. 'Still asleep. Let her sleep in a bit; it's Saturday.'

'*Saturday* . . .' Walter repeated like a mantra.

They both ignored him.

'Get her to come in and say hello to her old dad when she gets up, will you?' Reg said, adding, 'You two going out today?'

Ellen nodded. 'Going over to see Lily. We always do on Saturdays.'

Reg was still hesitating by the door. 'Bess – does she . . . you know. Does she *ask* about Lily?'

For a long time Ellen had waited for this moment; had sensed its coming on many occasions; had even tried to work out in advance what she would say. But now the time had come and she was suddenly floundering, a fish on dry land.

'How d'you mean?'

Walter had lapsed into silence, intent on his own thoughts. They might have been alone in the dim kitchen.

'I was thinking . . .' Reg continued, '. . . you know, about Louise and Emma. Seems they've given the baby a good life. I never liked Clem, tight-lipped sod, but he's done right by Lily.' He paused, hoping Ellen would pick up the cue, but although she knew what he wanted her to say, she stayed silent. 'Lily must see how much better it is for Emma to be brought up by the Whitleys. It makes sense for a child to have two parents. They need that – a mum and dad.'

Still Ellen said nothing.

Walter coughed, rubbed his neck absently. It was like having a deaf mute in the place.

'. . . Ellen, I was thinking that we could . . . you know, we could do the same for Bess.'

The words were out. She *had* seen it coming, known they would one day leave his lips, the unspoken thought between them becoming real. But although she had longed for her husband to love Bess, now it seemed cruel. Wrong. At heart she wanted to agree with him, wanted to say – Yes, let's take Bess on as our own. We could adopt her, give her a secure life. We could make her happy. I agree – but something stopped her.

What would be the cost of such happiness? What would their pleasure mean to her sister? Lily had lost one child, had been forced to deny her motherhood once, how could she be expected – vulnerable and helpless as she was – to repeat such heartache? Didn't she live for the letters from

Australia, for every titbit of news about her daughter? Didn't she wash and press repeatedly the few baby clothes she had kept that Emma had worn? And keep a piece of her baby hair in a cheap locket round her neck?

Yes, Reg. I want Bess too, Ellen longed to say. I love her. She's given me more happiness than I ever thought possible. Yes, we could take her on as our own and have a proper family. We could go out and show her off, and hear her calling us Mum and Dad. She already calls you Dad, Reg, doesn't she? Well, I've longed for her to call me Mum, too. But I haven't let her.

Ellen turned to the sink and slowly began to pour some water over the dirty dishes. Love was one thing, but it wasn't an excuse to hurt someone else you loved. If she took Bess she would hurt her sister, *damage* her sister, irrevocably. Oh, people might think they had done the right thing, but she would know inside that it was a brutality, a body blow that no woman had the right to inflict on her own sister.

Louise might be able to do it, but Louise had always been emotionally elastic; pliable to her own needs, if not those of others. She could convince herself of anything if she told herself she was doing the right thing. But not Ellen. No, I can't lie to myself, she thought. I know better. I owe more to my sister than I do to myself.

Besides, hadn't her advice pushed Lily into letting Emma go? So how could Ellen now be so cruel as to profit from her sister's pain? Their parents were now dead, but both of them had instilled in Ellen a humanity she couldn't dodge. And never would.

'We can't, Reg.'

He stared at her, his face wiped of hope. In that moment she realized just how much he loved Bess.

'I'll be back this afternoon,' Walter said suddenly, standing up between them.

His body blocked them for an instant and seemed to

push them apart – but maybe Ellen's words had already done that.

'Don't say no, think about it,' Reg urged his wife.

As usual, Walter was oblivious to the strained atmosphere around him.

'. . . I'll see you around two –'

'Shut up!' Reg snapped suddenly.

'I was just –'

'Get out!' Reg shouted. 'Just get out.'

Unperturbed, Walter sidled to the door and left, the dark green curtain falling softly back into place behind him. For a moment Ellen and Reg listened to his footfall, then heard the basement door close and Walter whistling as he mounted the steep steps to the pavement. Rain was falling against the kitchen window, the daylight smudged with soot and sleet.

'It's getting late,' Ellen said at last. 'I have to get Bess ready to go out.'

'Ellen –'

She reached out and touched her husband's hand gently.

'No, she's Lily's child. She always will be. She needs us, but she needs her mother too, Reg. Don't take her away from Lily, don't even consider it, or dream about it. Trust me in this. If we did take Bess away from my sister there would be a tragedy that would ruin us all.'

Chapter Five

1921

Lily's hair was tied back severely, her clothes pressed and neat. She had worked hard, been promoted, no longer labouring on the floor of the Farnworth Bleach Works, but in the office. Her wages had improved too, the manager liking her efficiency, and – surprised by her skill with figures – he had even let her start doing the accounts. The responsibility had changed her, made her more stable, and out of the extra money she made, some was passed over to Ellen for the upkeep of Bess, and the rest was secreted away into a savings account.

She didn't tell anyone why, it was her secret, but at the back of her mind Lily had decided that before too long she would buy a little place and then ... the thought tingled against her heart ... then she would write to Louise and ask for Emma to be sent back home. She couldn't let Emma know that she was her daughter, but she could make a fuss of her niece, couldn't she? Spoil her? Take her out? Take her home? *Home*.

Lily's determination had paid off; she no longer suffered the depression that had hobbled her, she had a purpose now – to get her child back. Thank God it had been her sister who had adopted Emma. If it had been a stranger ... Lily shrugged off the damning thought. A stranger would have kept Emma, taken her away for ever. But not Louise. Louise would understand, would see that Lily had changed, would know that, in the end, the right place for Emma was with her mother. Even if that mother would always have to pretend to be her aunt.

She had told no one, until now, what she was planning, not even Ellen. Oh, her sister would understand, but she might worry, wonder silently if Lily was capable of raising Emma alone. After all, there was no man around. Never had been since Harold.

For which Lily was grateful; she didn't want to love again, didn't want to feel out of control, at the whim of her emotions, helpless, overeager to do anything to keep a husband. She had finished with that; had no longing for men, even though she was still only a young woman. She could cope alone; she *would* cope alone. She had her sister for support and soon she would have her child back.

The thought made Lily smile as she checked her reflection in the mirror. She dressed in a businesslike way now – long dark dress with starched white collars and cuffs, no jewellery, her blonde hair tied away from her face. Recovery had restored her prettiness, even Lily could see that, but she didn't want to use it – ignored it instead, underplayed it. She wasn't setting out to find a husband, but to be a breadwinner for her child.

She had to be very determined, very single-minded. There was a little way to go yet, but soon she should have the money she needed to buy the tiny terraced house she had seen in Little Lever. It wasn't grand, but she could make it nice. It even had a glory hole to store things in, a little attic room like the one her parents had had. And at the back of the house was a tiny bedroom that would be perfect for Emma. Emma's room, made ready and waiting for her daughter's return.

Besides, thought Lily, she wasn't being unreasonable, wasn't expecting to reclaim everything she had lost. She could see well enough how happy Bess was with her sister and brother-in-law. Bess might visit her and chat away happily, but she was Reg's child in everything but blood.

She thrived at the billiards hall . . . Lily sighed. It wasn't the place she would have chosen for her child, but Bess loved it, a little show-off already, fearless, the customers doting on her.

But Emma wouldn't have settled in an environment like that, Lily thought. Hadn't everyone known from her birth that she was special? That she was the golden child? Fragile, elegant even in her pram, a baby born to be extraordinary. Lily wasn't a snob, she was grateful to Ellen and Reg for what they had done for her elder daughter, but Emma was a different kind of child. A chosen child. A child who needed a special atmosphere to grow up in.

Which, to be fair, Louise and Clem had given to her for three years. But Lily could take over now. She was somebody at last, not a factory worker any more; she was office staff, a woman in her own right. She had earned her respect through grief and hard work. No one pitied her now. Lily Browning wasn't the sad, sick little woman she had been, she was strong again.

Strong enough to bring up her child. Strong enough to plan and wait a little longer, strong enough to buy her house and make it ready. She had a plan. She had a purpose. She had a role in life, that of a mother.

Idly she fingered the letter addressed to Mrs Clem Whitley. The post was forgotten. She had a reason to live.

She had a future again.

Restless, Ellen jerked herself awake and got up, careful not to disturb Reg sleeping beside her. It was too much, Walter had gone too far this time. And Reg should have had more sense. Their savings gone. Every bloody pound she had scraped together since the end of the war all gone. And to who? Some tupenny-ha'penny tart of Walter's. Reg had explained it all. She needed the money to get away from her husband and set up a business with Walter.

Ellen had stared at Reg incredulously.

43

'Since when do they pay men to sit on their arses, smoking?'

'He was going to open a shop –'

'And I'm Princess Alice,' Ellen had snapped. 'Walter's conned you, Reg.'

'Walter'll pay the money back –'

'Pay it back?' she'd countered. 'Where is it?'

'He lost it.'

'Down a drain or on a bus?' Her voice had been acid.

'A bet –'

'*A bet!*' Ellen had howled. 'It was my money, our money, Reg. It took some finding.' She'd shaken her head. 'You know what he's like – why the hell did you give it to him anyway?'

'Because he's my brother.'

'And does that put him before your wife, Reg?' she'd asked icily. 'You don't understand, do you? You don't see what a bloody white elephant this place is. We only just make enough money to support this dump. That's why I've been saving so hard. Not for treats, not for any bloody holiday, but to make sure we can meet the rent if times get even harder. That's what your brother's just lost us: twelve months' rent money.'

Now creeping past the back bedroom where Bess was asleep, Ellen pulled on her dressing gown and went downstairs into the kitchen. The fire had gone out and her hand shook as she lit the gas, the cold flame making the room seem hostile, unfriendly. Slowly she made herself some tea, jumping as the door from the billiards hall opened and Walter walked in.

'I wouldn't mind a cup,' he said simply.

'It'll cost you a year's rent money,' Ellen replied, relighting the fire and staring at the first cool flames.

'I'll get the money back.'

'Who knows, Walter?' Ellen asked without turning round to face him.

44

''Bout what?'

'The bet. Our money you lost. Who knows about it?'

'Well . . . a few people.'

She closed her eyes. 'That means all of Bolton now.'

'Why worry about what people think?'

'Well, you obviously don't, but I do,' Ellen replied shortly. 'I'm respectable, and this business is straight. What you do is your affair, but I don't want you coming here and messing on my doorstep.'

'I've told you, I'll get the money back,' Walter reassured her. 'Every penny.'

'Honestly?'

He nodded. 'Yeah, sure I will.'

Sighing, Ellen turned to him. 'I mean, will you *earn* it honestly?'

'Look, I was drunk, I didn't know what I was doing.'

Ellen stared at him. 'Well, that makes me feel a lot better.'

'You know I'm not mean. I always bring something when I visit,' he said, thinking back frantically. 'I bought you a set of pans the other month.'

'Which were probably ready warmed.'

'Aw, come on, Ellen, are you suggesting that they were stolen?'

'No,' she replied phlegmatically, 'I'm sure they were.'

Sitting down with her head bowed, Ellen could hear Walter make the tea and then lay a cup beside her. The one with the crack in it. Typical, she thought, men.

'So why are you up?'

'Couldn't sleep,' she replied sarcastically. 'I was worried for some reason . . . What about you? Guilty conscience?'

'Not tired.'

She sipped the tea: industrial strength.

'Look, I don't care if you're a crook, Walter, but I don't want Reg tarred with the same brush. We'll be a laughing stock round here, you gambling away our savings. What

45

the hell will people think?' Her voice hardened. 'I warn you, Walter, I want no more trouble coming to this house. Especially not to Bess.'

'I wouldn't do anything to hurt that girl –'

'You're breathing, aren't you?'

Smiling, Walter sipped his tea.

'I'll get the money back to you,' he said simply. 'You're not just mad about the bet, anyway, you're worried about something else. You have been for days. What's up?'

He was right, she had been worrying.

'I can't stop thinking about all kinds of things,' Ellen admitted finally. 'The past . . .'

'Ah.'

She shot him a wry look. '. . . Louise and Emma . . .'

Walter lit up a cigarette and pulled on his gloves.

'Going somewhere?'

'Nah, just got cold hands.'

'Go with your cold feet,' she said coolly. 'Are you sleeping on one of the tables?'

He nodded. Come morning he would throw the bed-clothes into a cupboard and rack up in time for the first punters. No one realized that where they were lining up a shot Walter had been happily snoring only an hour before. It was like that when you were poor, Ellen thought, you had to make do. Make do with what clothes, fuel, food, even what bed you could manage. Make do. Not that Louise had ever had to do that . . .

'I was thinking of going abroad,' Walter said suddenly.

'Not without paying me back first, you're not.'

'It would be a change.'

'So which woman is it this time, Walter? Your so-called business partner? Although the only business you could run is funny business.'

Angry as she was, Ellen couldn't stop herself smiling. It was all so messy, but so predictable. The woman – or her husband – would come to the billiards hall looking for

46

Walter. Disappearing Walter, who had by that time lived up to his nickname. There would be tears, if it was the woman, or threats, if it was the man. And then Reg would step in and suddenly the threats would peter out. Because Reg Shawcross would sort it out for his brother – as he always did.

'Why don't you get a job and settle down?'

Walter's face set like cement. 'I'm not that type, Ellen, you know that.'

She leaned across the kitchen table towards him, her chin cupped in her hand. Curiosity came suddenly. She wanted to talk, wanted to do anything to lift the feeling of unplaced anxiety, because Walter was right, she *was* worried, unsettled.

'Why does Reg always stand up for a toerag like you?'

'He's bigger than I am. And older.'

That was true.

'Did he always stick up for you when you were kids?'

'I used to thieve off the market stalls and then run off, and he would block anyone who tried to follow me.'

'But Reg doesn't hold with stealing.'

'He didn't then either. He used to see I was off clear and then give me a right thrashing later when he caught up with me.'

She laughed, sipped at the bitter brew.

'What about your mother?'

'She never stole anything.'

'I don't mean that, Walter! I mean, what was Old Ma Shawcross like when you were kids?'

'Like she was when she was here – a right old bitch.'

'She spoke well of you, too,' Ellen said drily.

A silence fell between them, no one stirred overhead, and the streets outside were silent. A newspaper lay on the scrubbed top of the kitchen table trailing an advertisement for the latest hairstyle – the Eton crop. Thoughtfully Ellen fingered her own long brown hair, Walter blowing smoke

47

rings into the stillness. She might have her hair cut and think about chucking out her corset and shortening her skirt. Cause a stir in Bolton and no mistake. Well, why not? she thought. She had the legs for it and it would be nice to have short hair when the summer came. They could even go to Blackpool for a few days – it was the fiftieth anniversary of the first Bank Holiday – and it would be hot then.

What was she talking about? she thought suddenly. There would be no trips to Blackpool this year, no treats of any sort. And why? Because of Walter. Because somebody always buggered things up, Ellen thought. That was life. Well, her life anyway. But not Louise's.

It would be like being on permanent holiday, living in Australia, Ellen mused enviously, remembering the few blurry photographs sent by Louise, one of Emma standing in the garden and another of her as a baby lying on a rug. This photograph Lily treasured and had had framed long ago. All the other news about Australia Ellen had gleaned from the library, long ago working out just where Emma was, and reading avidly about the climate and the animals out there.

It had seemed not just like another country, but another planet, it was so remote in distance, even tone. Ellen smiled grimly. Louise would be a snob out there, certainly no mention of Bolton, or the billiards hall. And Clem would be bragging away, buying up his property, developing his tin mines, and showing off their indoor bathroom. *An indoor bathroom*, Ellen thought wonderingly. They didn't even have electricity yet, and the lav was still outside and freezing when you sat there with the winter gales coming under the gap in the door.

Walter, who had gone back into the billiards hall, now returned with something in his hand: a package, badly wrapped.

'For the little one,' he said, shamefaced.

Reluctantly Ellen took it. Walter was crazy about Bess. Funny that. Like his brother, Walter didn't like kids, but he loved her.

'Thanks,' Ellen said, unwrapping it. Her breath caught. It was a tiny golden bear with a red satin ribbon round its neck. Expensive. 'God, Walter, this is a beauty.'

'Well, just as long as Bess likes it.'

'She couldn't help but like it,' she said, then narrowed her eyes. 'Whose money did you buy it with?'

'Aw, Ellen, leave off.' Walter looked suddenly serious. 'I've been thinking about Bess lately, wondering what her sister's like.'

This was some admission, coming from Walter.

'Emma's doing well. You remember, I read some of the letters to you and showed you the photograph.'

The kitchen was very still. Quiet morning hours.

'Must be odd, living out there,' he mused. 'Not like here at all. Wonder if she remembers Bolton?'

'Emma was a baby when she left. I doubt she can remember anything about England.'

'Seems funny – you know, pretending she died. Must be hard that, on Lily. One thing's for certain, though; that bloody sister of yours won't be reminding her of home. If you ask me, Louise Whitley will be doing everything in her power to put as much distance as she can between this family and that kid.'

Without realizing it, Ellen's hands had tightened around the cup she held. She was suddenly afraid, guilty, and in need of comfort – even from Walter.

'Did I do right? The advice I gave Lily. Was it right?'

So, thought Walter, this was what was on her mind – the reason she was sitting in the kitchen in the dead of night.

The question tingled for a long moment between them before he answered.

'Yeah, it was. And even if it wasn't, there's nothing you can do about it now.'

Chapter Six

A dishevelled Lily wrenched open the door and walked hurriedly through the billiards hall, ignoring the comments of the customers as she passed, a letter clenched in her hand. Leaning against a far wall, in the semidark, Walter saw her and shrank back out of sight, watching as Lily rushed towards the door that led out into the back kitchen, her hair untidy, her eyes bloated with crying.

Ellen was ironing as her sister hurried in and, seeing her face, froze.

'Lily, what it is?'

Lily was unable to speak, just passed her the letter.

It was addressed to Mrs Clem Whitley in Australia, but the address had been scored out and another hand had written next to it: *The Whitleys have moved. No longer here. Sorry, no forwarding address.*

Stunned, Ellen read it and then reread it, at first unable to comprehend fully what she was seeing. The Whitleys had moved – without telling anyone. They had left their home and gone away. With Emma. *With Louise's sister's child!*

'Emma's gone . . .' Lily said, her eyes blank.

'There must be a mistake,' Ellen said firmly. 'They'll write and tell us where they've moved to. They'll be a letter in the post now, don't worry.'

But even as she said it, she knew there wouldn't be. Louise had played her trump card and made sure that she would never lose Emma. With that ruthless cruelty she had never lost, she had stolen her sister's child.

'Emma's gone,' Lily repeated helplessly, 'she's gone.'

'We'll find her,' her sister replied. 'Listen to me. We'll find her. They'll write and tell us where they've gone.'

But Lily was blind with terror, her voice faltering, the old instability returning fast and furious.

'I have to go out there –'

'You can't,' Ellen said practically. 'You haven't the money.'

'I'll make the money!' Lily shouted. 'I'll borrow it. Walter must know someone who'll lend it to me.'

Panic was making her frantic, her movements staccato.

'You don't know where to look for Emma,' her sister remonstrated with her. 'Australia's huge; you can't just go out there on a wild-goose chase.'

'I have to go!' Lily shouted. 'I HAVE TO GO!'

Her scream came unexpected and terrifying. Reg ran down the stairs from the flat above and hurried into the kitchen.

'What the hell –' He stopped, staring at the two sisters. 'What's happened?'

Without saying a word, Ellen passed him the letter, then took hold of her sister's hands. They were icy.

'But she can't do this!' Reg said vehemently. 'Louise can't do this.' He turned to Lily. 'We'll sort it out, don't worry. That bugger Whitley's not getting away with it.'

But Lily wasn't listening.

'I was going to buy a house for us . . .'

Reg and Ellen exchanged baffled looks.

'. . . I nearly had enough money to buy it. A little house, up Market Street. Emma was going to come back and live with me.'

Firmly Ellen held on to her sister's hands, squeezing them.

'Lily, calm down. Did you tell Louise this?'

'No, it was a secret,' Lily replied. Then shook her head, frowning. 'Well, yes, yes, I told Louise what I was planning in my last letter. I told her how excited I was . . .'

Ellen could hear Reg take in a deep breath. So *that* was what had happened: Lily had confided her wish to get her daughter back and Louise had panicked, responding not with reason, but with drastic and cruel measures. No one was going to take the beautiful Emma away from her – not even her rightful mother.

'I had it all worked out . . .' Lily went on blindly. 'The house, the job . . . I was going to tell you about it next week, when things were settled. I was even up for a raise, Mr Simpson said. My work's good, I'm going to be . . .' she trailed off, brushing away Ellen's hands and pacing the kitchen like a trapped animal. 'Where is my daughter? WHERE IS SHE?'

She's gone, Ellen wanted to say. Your daughter's gone for good. You won't find her, because Louise doesn't want you to, and she has the money and the guile to cover her tracks well. If you looked for years, Lily, you still wouldn't find her. And what's worse is that your daughter doesn't even know you. She never did. Emma doesn't know the future you planned for her with you, nor that you loved her so much. She doesn't remember to whom she was born, or where she came from. She doesn't even know that you are her mother. If she knows anything about you, it's that you're some distant aunt. Your daughter doesn't know you, Lily. Dear God, she won't even miss you.

'Be calm, love,' Ellen said, trying to hold her sister as Lily brushed her off. 'Please, try and be calm.'

'I want her back!' Lily shouted, her eyes brilliant with terror. 'She's not coming back, is she?'

Unblinking, Ellen stared into her sister's face. Was a lie a kindness now, or was it better to tell her the truth, to snap any useless hope? Oh God, she thought, why me? Why do I have to tell her?

'Lily, you have to be brave –'

'Emma's gone, hasn't she?'

Reg had held his breath, his heart thumping as he

watched his wife. Tell her, he willed Ellen, tell her. Be strong enough to tell her the truth.

'Yes, Lily, Emma's gone. She's not coming back.'

There was no sound from any of them for a long time. Outside a tram passed, footfalls sounded on the pavement. Somewhere a woman laughed and at the end of the street the rag-and-bone man called out hoarsely into the cold air. Somewhere else it was warm and sunny. Somewhere under different skies a beautiful child had been moved to another safe home, with parents who adored her. She would be breathing and moving, running and talking, Ellen thought – but not here, not now, not ever.

Reg and Ellen had expected hysterics, but instead Lily seemed to shake herself awake. She picked up the letter and walked over to the kitchen range. There she dropped the blue envelope into the hot bank of coals and then took the cheap locket from around her neck, with Emma's baby hair in it. For a moment she weighed it in her hand and then let it fall, circling and curling before it fell into the hot flames, her dream of happiness melting into dull smoke.

Chapter Seven

Florence Trent was playing the piano by the side of the dais – badly, some said in the audience, but then that could have been because the instrument needed tuning. Not that it mattered anyway; people didn't come to hear Florence playing, but to listen to Josiah Wake, a newcomer to Bolton who had arrived trailing stories and glory like one of the new-fangled film stars. In fact, Josiah had even managed to lure people away from Charlie Chaplin at the Empire – an unheard of feat, especially for Ellen, who had been reluctantly dragged along by an enthusiastic Lily.

Wake had been to America, they gathered, and India . . . India, all that way away, and he'd worked with the poor. In that case he should feel at home in bloody Bolton, Reg had retorted drily when Lily told him about Wake. It was seven months since they had learned of Emma's disappearance; seven months in which Lily had given up hope of her house in Little Lever. No word came from Australia, no change of address, nothing. The Whitleys and Emma had, to all intents and purposes, disappeared.

Not surprisingly, Lily couldn't bear to be reminded of her plans, so she stayed on at the bleach factory, working long hours and coming home to a minute house she now rented on Fletcher Street, only a hundred yards from the billiards hall.

Sandwiched between a cantankerous old couple and a family of seven, Lily was the only woman living alone in the terrace. Quite an achievement, in its way. After all, not many men could find the bloody rent every week, let alone a woman on her own. But Lily did. It was a matter of honour to her. And honour was just about all she had left.

Daily Monday to Friday she did the books for Mr Simpson, returning home every night around seven. At the weekends she went round to Ellen's – and sometimes her sister called by at night for a chat, to see how she was.

Which was impossible to judge. No depression, no anger, no reaction of any kind seemed to affect Lily. Just a sweet kindness, constant and heartbreaking. When Ellen went round there was always a tray laid out for them with matching cups and saucers and a cake Lily had made fresh. There were napkins, too, starched and crisp, and with her increased wages Lily had bought some second-hand – but sound – pieces of furniture.

The house, with its narrow blue painted front door, was like a flower on a dung heap, its neighbours slovenly and unkempt, their windows hung with washing and sheets flapping in the sooty air like lolling giants' tongues. There might be battered prams outside next door, and slops thrown haphazardly onto the pavement, but Lily's doorstep was donkey-stoned – the only one in the street.

She lived by rote and seldom referred to her lost daughter. But on Emma's birthday, she and Ellen had laid an extra place at the table and pretended – as children do – that the stranger was amongst them. And all the while Ellen tried to come to terms with her guilt and Lily tried to come to terms with her grief.

It had done Ellen no good trying to introduce her sister to eligible men, and when Walter had suggested that they all go out for an evening, the remark had been greeted by muted horror. Walter's intentions, although kind, were exactly what Lily dreaded. She had her life under control now, but to break her routine, to allow other people in, was to risk losing that hard-won control.

In the same way, Lily was afraid of getting too close to Bess in case some wicked fate took her away too. Her daughter was safe with Ellen and Reg – best to let her stay with them. Better to let them gradually assume the role Louise had snatched for herself so violently.

Ellen's attention was reluctantly and only momentarily dragged back to Josiah Wake's sermon. 'Hey, Lily –'

'Sssh!' Lily replied, her eyes fixed on Josiah Wake. 'Listen.'

Before Lily had thought that Church was dour, religion serious, cold. In her bleakest moments she had once looked for religious comfort but found none. But all that changed when Josiah came to Bolton touting his own view of God. His preaching and hymn singing were a revelation, his imposing, barrel-chested presence, with his booming voice and patrician features, came sweeping into the dark Northern town like an Old Testament prophet. And his conviction, his confidence, his *strength*, reached Lily as nothing else had done for years.

Impatiently Ellen nudged Lily's arm. 'How long does this go on?'

'Ssssh!' Lily said again under her breath. 'Be quiet.'

Sighing, Ellen settled back in her seat, avoiding the glance of a woman staring at her from across the hall. One of Walter's women, no doubt. Not that anyone had seen Walter lately.

Josiah was crescending to his final points: '. . . and we have to believe. *Believe*. Or we are nothing, if we have no faith, we have nothing. God is in each one of us, making us all strong . . .'

Ellen was wondering about supper. What she would make for Reg? . . . Her thoughts were suddenly disturbed by Josiah's diatribe, his voice echoing round the Hall Street Chapel. Why the hell does he shout? she wondered. He could say just the same things in a normal voice. Her gaze wandered round the audience, amazed to find that – apart from Walter's ex-girlfriend – everyone was fixated.

Well, Josiah Wake *was* a striking man, you had to hand it to him. Big and smart, in his long dark frock coat. But then what kind of a woman could live with all that shouting? Ellen doubted if he was any good in a fight either, or the type of man to get coal in the middle of a war.

Josiah was leaning over the pulpit towards his audience.

'. . . just confess your sins and all will be forgiven you . . .'

Ellen doubted that. Wondered why Lily was staring at him. What sins had her sister committed that deserved her bad luck? Marrying the wrong man? Trusting her sister?

'. . . God sees everything . . .'

God help Walter then, Ellen mused.

'. . . and hears us when we call on Him. He gives us what we need to make us happy. Not what *we* think we need, but what He *knows* we need . . .'

It was a good thing someone knew what they were doing, Ellen thought idly, glancing over to her sister.

Clearly Lily was fascinated by Josiah Wake, her eyes following his every movement, her lips slightly parted as though she might taste his words, as well as hear them. Curious, Ellen glanced at the other women in the audience and then smiled to herself. Oh dear, she thought, Walter had better look out. We have another lady-killer amongst us.

'If you ask me –'

'Which no one did.'

'– that Wake bloke is a fake.' Reg glanced up from the paper he was reading. 'Wake the Fake.'

Wincing, Ellen began to count up the takings in the cubicle. In front of her the tables were all busy, even though it was past ten at night, the players mostly husbands wanting to escape their wives, as usual Cuffs leaning on the furthest table, waiting for Stan Clark to take his shot. He was fiddling with his sleeves, the starched white cuffs gleaming out of the semidark.

'I think Lily's keen on him.'

Reg stared into the cubicle at his wife. 'Wake? Nah.'

'She is. I know the signs,' Ellen assured him. 'I was worried at first, thought he was a ladies' man, but although the women all dither around him, apparently he only chases God.'

'That chapel's busy every service,' Reg mused. 'The bloke must have something.'

'Charisma.'

'Huh?'

Ellen looked up from the takings and smiled. 'I heard the word on the wireless. They were talking about Valentino. Saying he has charisma.'

'Valentino is a movie star.'

'And our Josiah is a star in his own right. At least in Bolton,' Ellen countered. 'I have a hunch that Lily's going to set her cap at him.'

'I thought she was off men.'

'Josiah doesn't count as a man,' she replied deftly. 'He's God-fearing, moral. He's not threatening.'

'He would be if he fell on you,' Reg said. 'He's a hell of a size.'

'Ah, but Josiah wouldn't fall on you, he'd support you, and that's the difference. You wouldn't see Josiah pulling a stunt like Walter. He's a man who takes his responsibilities seriously.'

Leering, Reg leaned over and squeezed his wife's knee.

'Like me, you mean?'

'You don't believe in God!'

'I could – if there was something in it for me.'

Suddenly a commotion started up on the third table, a couple of newcomers starting to argue about a shot. Immediately Reg walked over to them and exchanged a few words, the players on the surrounding tables stopping to listen. And then Ellen noticed a figure out of the corner of her eye, and turned to the door, shaking her head at Bess as the little girl approached.

'You should be in bed.'

'I couldn't sleep,' Bess replied, sneaking into the cubicle and sitting at Ellen's feet. 'Let me stay with you for a while.'

'Reg will be furious if he catches you,' Ellen said, stroking the child's hair.

'Dad won't mind, he never does.'

No, he didn't, Ellen thought, and that was the problem, whatever Bess did was all right by Reg. He could see no fault in the little girl, no shortcomings. And woe betide Ellen if she criticized·Bess, or even suggested that she was anything less than perfect. Bess this, Bess that ... if she had been the jealous kind she would have resented her niece.

But she wasn't the jealous kind, and she loved them both.

'You'll get cold down there.'

'Is it busy tonight?' Bess asked, unable to see the hall from where she was crouched.

'Full house.'

'Lots of money then.'

Ellen laughed.

'Enough.'

'Will we ever be rich?'

The question surprised Ellen. 'Do you want to be rich?'

'I dunno. I just wondered.'

'Being rich isn't that important. Being happy is what counts,' Ellen told her, thinking immediately of Louise.

Certainly *Louise* was rich. And greedy. Greedy with money and with people. Taking, always taking. Not like Lily, always giving. But now maybe, just maybe, Lily might have got her reward. Might at last have found someone. Ellen pushed aside the unwelcome notion that she had thought the very same thing when Lily got engaged to Harold. Maybe her luck really had changed this time.

For a while Ellen had watched Lily's metamorphosis: the

59

emergence of the smart little businesswoman, with her neat house and genteel ways. Not that Lily would ever have said it, but she loathed the billiards hall, loathed the punters and the smell and sight of the place, the chalk marks, the sawdust on the floor, the smell of old smoke and damp coats.

She had aspirations, Ellen realized suddenly. Louise wasn't the only one who had ambition. Perhaps Lily, in her sweet way, might also want something beyond the life she had been born into . . . The thought unsettled her. If she *did* go after Josiah Wake, how would Lily fare? He had travelled; who was to say that after a while he wouldn't be off again? And how would Lily take another desertion?

On the other hand Josiah was hardly young. He must be forty at least, and he was unmarried. His work had been his life – but perhaps he was looking to settle down now, looking for some worthy wife to come home to at night. And why couldn't it be her sister? Ellen thought she would like to see Lily pull off another coup. Oh yes, she had been envied for marrying the handsome Harold, but too many people had been delighted at the failure of *that* marriage; their envy vindicated. Poor Lily, the deserted wife, then widow, then worse, to lose her child . . .

Oh yes, it was time Lily had another grab at happiness.

'Brr. I'm cold,' Bess said, shivering and breaking into her aunt's thoughts.

'Serves you right. I told you not to sit there,' Ellen replied, hauling the little girl to her feet and kissing her on the forehead. 'Go back to bed.'

'Will you send Dad in to say good night?'

Dad, always Dad.

'Don't worry, I'll send him in.'

'Promise?'

Taking Bess's palm, Ellen drew an X on it with her finger and kissed it. Then she shooed the little girl out of the hall, not realizing that Reg had been watching them all along.

* * *

Well, it was a cold place and uninviting, Josiah thought, but he had to go where God wanted him to go and Bolton was as good a place as any. Striding down Deansgate, he was fully aware of the attention he drew, and doffed his hat many times, his well-modulated voice exchanging numerous greetings. Not that he was a vain man, he thought, but he was pleased by the reaction to his arrival and by the full audiences who attended his sermons. He had been led to believe that the North of England was full of barbarians, ignorant drunks and womanizers, but there was, after all, good to be found in the people here too.

He wouldn't judge – that was God's duty – he would simply do what he could. Josiah paused at the end of Moor Lane and looked into a shop window. Passersby were surprised to find the preacher so wrapped up in the perusal of vegetables, not realizing that the glass gave Josiah an opportunity to check his reflection before he walked on. Perhaps, he thought, he might bring the United States of America into his next sermon. Would these people know about America? Maybe – and if not, it was his Godgiven job to educate them. Smiling to himself, Josiah walked on.

What he really needed was a housekeeper – some respectable, quiet woman. No one loud – he didn't care for the brash Northern voices and found them grating. No, he wanted someone pleasing and unassuming. A lady.

But there weren't that many ladies in Bolton. Women, yes, and very good women too, he was sure of that. But not ladies. Not educated ladies who had intelligence. He was deep in thought, walking ahead without looking, when suddenly Josiah found himself face to face with a very angry woman blocking his path.

'Watch where you're going!'

'I beg your pardon?'

The woman was pointing downwards. Slowly Josiah followed the direction of her finger. He had inadvertently brushed her newly stoned step with his foot.

61

'You should trying cleaning that and find out how you'd like it if some clumsy sod walked all over it.'

There is good in everyone, Josiah told himself, you just have to look for it.

'My apologies, madam –'

'All morning that took me,' the woman went on. 'I've got a houseful of kids and a week's washing and I don't need people holding me up.'

Josiah was all mortified embarrassment. 'As I said –'

'Bloody preachers! You want to get down off the bloody pulpit and see how the real world lives,' she snapped, turning away and bending down to stone the step again. 'Words are cheap; it's hard work makes the world go round.'

Seething, Josiah regarded the kneeling woman and felt a sudden, and unchristian, desire to kick her backside. But, aware that he was being scrutinized, he merely apologized again and walked off – certain that everyone was watching him and admiring his control.

Oh yes, Josiah Wake was no ordinary man, It was going to be difficult to find a woman to come up to his standards.

Chapter Eight

It wasn't so much a church as a tin mission. Certainly it went by the name of church, but it was nothing like the stern, dark spired cathedrals of Manchester and Salford. Hall Street Chapel was poked away on the corner of Trinity Street, behind the railway line and under the viaduct, the sounds of passing trains making noisy inroads into the huge empty hall and shaking the window panes. Around the distempered walls were pictures of figures from the Gospels, and Bible tracts – together with a poster proclaiming the arrival and subsequent preachings of Josiah Wake.

Lily stared at the autocratic profile and told herself again that she wasn't interested in Josiah as a man. She liked his preachings, that was all, liked to hear all that energy and certainty belted out at night when the trains passed less frequently on the half-hour, going over to Manchester. Even the way Josiah dealt with those interruptions was impressive. He simply ignored them – just raised his voice above the shuddering, rattling commotion as though the disturbance was merely something Godgiven, to test him. Lily was sure that *nothing* had ever discomfited Josiah; after all, hadn't been all over the world? To America and back?

Maybe even Australia . . . no, she hadn't to think about that . . . Josiah Wake had shown her the future; his preachings telling her that there was a new life waiting for her. If Lily just believed.

But it was difficult to believe when she was on her own, not one of the rapt congregation. The hall was bleak, draughts coming under the door, the smell of the rain

63

unwelcome and depressing. Even the pews looked uninviting, empty; sad and scratched, old school and church pews cobbled together from various places; the hymn books dog-eared, smeared with old ink.

He must be used to so much better, Lily thought. It was a measure of his faith and compassion that he could come to Bolton and preach his hellfire sermons when he had preached the same in exotic places that she could only guess at.

She had tried very hard not to reveal her admiration, but Ellen had caught on fast, as had Reg. They teased her about Josiah mercilessly; not unkindly, but it still embarrassed Lily, who was timid by nature. Half the women of Bolton seemed suddenly to have taken a new interest in religion. As had their men – sick to death of hearing about the preacher.

'Not again,' Ellen said good-naturedly, one evening when Lily had gone round to ask her sister if she would like to accompany her to Hall Street Chapel. 'I don't want to go to another sermon, Lily. I've had enough religion to last a lifetime.'

Reg looked up from the billiards table he was brushing. His shirtsleeves were rolled up, his well-muscled arms overtly masculine. Josiah was always fully dressed in black. Respectable.

'I heard that Wake was leaving town soon.'

Lily paled, Ellen laughing at her husband.

'Don't be mean to her, Reg! You don't know anything of the sort.' She turned to the shaken Lily. 'Don't listen to him. We'll go over and see Josiah later.'

They weren't the only ones who turned up, Hall Street Chapel was full. Halfway through Josiah's sermon there was an unexpected interruption at the back. Someone had come in late, and although no one looked round, it was difficult to ignore the disturbance as the person took his seat.

'. . . God knows what is in our hearts . . .'

'How d'you know?'

A hushed silence fell over the congregation, every head turning to the source of the voice: Walter sitting, impassive, in his seat.

Surprised, Josiah stared towards the back of the hall.

'Brother, why do you doubt?'

'I wondered how you knew so much about God,' Walter replied evenly, his arms crossed, his hoarse voice deliberately provoking. He had heard enough about Wake to want to see this paragon, and after several beers his curiosity had finally got the better of him.

'I didn't know Walter was back,' Lily said, horrified.

Ellen shrugged.

'Neither did I. Looks like he's had a skinful too,' she replied bluntly. 'Nothing changes.'

'Friend,' Josiah bellowed, 'tell me what troubles you. God forgives all sinners.'

'You too?' Walter replied lazily.

There was a shocked hush, followed by a shuffle of embarrassed female feet. Everyone knew Walter Shawcross, and his reputation. How could he come to the hall and heckle the saintly Josiah?

'. . . I forgive you your doubts, brother, and love you as God does.'

This was too much for Walter. In his book love meant women, not some unseen deity.

'Bloody hell,' he said simply, lighting up.

Josiah was losing patience, and although he was well used to hecklers, to the unbelievers who always sat at the back and unsettled everyone, he was not about to see his reputation flattened by some smart-mouthed thug.

'Are you a believer, brother?'

Walter's expression was glassy. 'Nah.'

'May I ask why?'

65

'I can't trust someone I haven't met, and I haven't met God. And neither have you.'

It was a good point, Ellen thought, stealing a quick glance at Lily. Her sister was blushing, mortified.

'I know God in my heart –'

'How come?'

Josiah stared at Walter with something approaching loathing, his smile as welcoming as a gin trap.

'God is in all of us – if we just listen to Him talking to us.'

'Where I come from you get put away if you hear voices,' Walter continued, taking a long drag from his cigarette.

'You're talking blasphemy!' Josiah roared, his voice thumping off the walls of the chapel.

But Walter was unperturbed.

'I'm talking bloody sense, which is something you don't,' he replied, getting to his feet and walking down the aisle to the dais.

Every pair of eyes was fixed on him. He might be several stones lighter and years younger than Josiah, but with a few beers inside him Walter would take on anyone – the grander, the better.

'Perhaps you should leave,' Josiah said stonily.

'I thought God loved a sinner –'

'Aye, that's true,' some other man mumbled from the congregation, laughing. 'You should be all right then, Shawcross.'

Joshua hadn't expected any further insurrection in the ranks and was eager to undermine Walter before anyone else started stealing his thunder.

'Brother –'

'You're not my brother,' Walter said flatly, pausing at the foot of the dais and staring up at Josiah. 'I heard about you, over Leeds way. The social-climbing preacher. You're a snob, and no mistake, Wake . . .'

Dumbly Josiah stared at him.

'. . . You weren't too well received there, were you?'

Helplessly, Lily stared at Josiah and willed him to turn the appalling Walter into a pillar of salt. How *could* he come here and heckle a man like Josiah Wake? Walter Shawcross, of all people. And he was drunk, that was obvious; she had seen that flinty expression on his face too many times before to mistake it.

'I have preached in Leeds, that's true,' Josiah said, but his tone was a little less certain than it had been.

'And they were glad to see you out of town,' Walter replied, finishing his cigarette and stubbing it out on the floor.

'I left of my own choice. My mission was over. I had stayed a long time there, given my best.'

Doggedly, Walter stared up at Josiah, who was suddenly very pale against his black suit.

'Some said you were more interested in tea parties, than preaching –'

Lily was up on her feet in an instant. Lily, of all people, standing up to Walter.

'Brother Wake does a lot of good, Walter Shawcross. You should take a leaf out of his book.'

Turning his head slowly, Josiah studied the young woman who had come to his defence. She was flushed with annoyance, her pretty face unsoftened by the severe hairdo, her slim frame tiny in a smart suit. Hadn't she been here before? He remembered her vaguely, his dark eyes now taking in every detail of her appearance, his smile winning.

'Dear sister, don't worry. I am questioned many times –'

'Not without bloody cause, I'll be bound,' Walter said bluntly.

'– there's no need to upset yourself.'

'You're drunk, Walter,' Lily said, flustered.

She wasn't the first one to notice.

'I might be drunk, but I can see more in this condition than you bloody lot can see dead sober,' he replied, staring

67

at Josiah for a long moment. 'Well, preacher, get on with it. *Preach*.'

'I have to ask you to leave,' Josiah said calmly.

'Are you going to make me?' Walter countered, Ellen raising her eyes heavenwards.

'Your shame should force you to do the right thing.'

'You're talking to Walter Shawcross,' someone shouted. 'Shame and him are strangers.'

But Walter hadn't finished. 'Just remember that not everyone's taken in by you, Wake.'

'God knows my true intentions –'

'If He does, He's a bigger fool than you are,' Walter replied deftly. 'You're not the sort to stay in Bolton.'

Grimly, Josiah held his ground. 'I'm sincere and I'll prove it to you.'

'You prove that,' Walter said smoothly, 'and I'll kiss your arse on the Town Hall steps.'

A laugh went round the congregation, Walter smiling and weaving slightly on his feet.

'Walter, sit down!' Lily said icily, her voice cutting through the laughter abruptly. 'You're making a fool of yourself.'

Silence fell in an instant.

Suddenly aware of all the eyes upon her, Lily blushed, her face on fire. What *was* she doing? People would talk about her and wonder why she had defended Josiah Wake . . . Slowly she slid back into her seat, her face averted from Ellen. She had shown her hand, made herself ridiculous. God, would she *never* learn?

Smiling winningly at his saviour, Josiah continued, but nothing he said after that had quite the same effect as it had before Walter's arrival, and twenty minutes later the sermon drew to a close. Lily gathered together the hymn sheets as the congregation walked out, gossiping and throwing amused glances over to her.

Well, people said afterwards, it was better than any

sermon, and no mistake. Timid little Lily Browning standing up to Walter Shawcross, the latter wearing his familiar expression of mischief, Josiah Wake glowing with triumph. Better entertainment than the movies.

Ellen was impatient to leave.

'Come on, Lily, let's get home.'

'You go. I'll see you tomorrow.'

Hesitating, Ellen took the books from her sister's hands.

'Don't worry about Walter, he was just stirring it. You know him.'

'I'm not worrying about Walter,' Lily said honestly, 'I just wonder why he did it.'

'Entertainment.'

'But Josiah's a good man –'

'I think you've already made your feelings clear, Lily, to most of Bolton.'

Her sister glanced away. 'Josiah's a good –'

'How do you know?' Ellen interrupted her. 'No one knows anything much about him.'

Lily's eyes were wide with certainty. 'I just *know*,' she said firmly, then embarrassed, took the hymn books back from her sister.

'Well, just be careful –'

'What's that supposed to mean?'

'Don't be fooled,' Ellen said softly. 'I don't want you to get hurt. You've been hurt too much already.'

Flushing, Lily turned away.

Up on the dais, Josiah waited until he saw Ellen leave and then walked over to Lily. When shadow fell over the hymn books she looked up, her mouth drying.

'I should thank you for coming to my defence, sister,' Josiah said, assessing Lily and finding himself well pleased. 'But I can look after myself, you know. God protects me.'

'I was just –'

'Being Christian,' he said, smiling.

She hadn't been prepared for the smile and felt her neck

69

flame, her hands suddenly sticky. Oh no, Lily thought, not again. Hadn't she reacted the same way when she first met Harold, and what good had that done her? She couldn't fall in love again; it wasn't right, it was bad for her.

Picking up the hymn books and then putting them down again, Lily hesitated, uncertain of what to do next. She felt stupid, clumsy, close to tears.

'Can I walk you home?' Josiah asked her, fully aware of the effect he was having.

'I can manage. It's . . . it's not far.'

'But it's dark and you're on your own,' he countered. 'I would like to see you home safely.'

Keeping her head down, Lily paused to think. If she accepted she would fall in love, she knew that, but if she rejected the offer she might live to regret it. Wasn't it time for her to think of living again? This was a Christian man, a good man, surely she would be safe with him?

'You have an advantage over me,' Josiah said gently.

Surprised, Lily looked up. 'How?'

'You know my name, but I don't know yours.'

A moment tingled between them before she replied. 'Lily . . . My name is Lily, Lily Browning.'

'You're a right bugger, Walter,' Ellen said when she got back to the billiards hall.

He was leaning against a table, a cue in his hand, his face impassive.

'And Wake's a bloody sycophant.'

'I'm surprised you can pronounce that, with all you've had to drink.'

'Drunk or sober, Wake's still a crawler. From what I heard, he thinks he's a nob, tried to smarm up to all the Leeds widows.'

'You mean the ones you missed?' Ellen retorted smartly.

'Oi,' Walter's billiards partner said suddenly, 'it's your shot.'

Deftly, he bent down and took his aim. The ball went into the top right-hand pocket as though it was on elastic.

'I can't be that drunk,' Walter said smoothly, straightening up and turning back to Ellen.

'You embarrassed Lily.'

'Hey?'

'Don't come the innocent, Walter! You know that Lily's keen on Josiah Wake.'

He let out a slow whistle. 'More fool her. She ought to chose her men more carefully.'

'And pick someone like you, I suppose?' Ellen replied coldly.

'She could do worse.'

'No. No, she couldn't . . . Got my money yet?'

'Your shot again, Walter,' Stan Clark said, interrupting them.

Patiently Ellen watched her brother-in-law take the shot. 'You missed.'

'I never miss a thing,' Walter said, winking at her.

'As the man said when he got struck by the bus,' Ellen retorted. 'Just tell me – was there a purpose behind tonight's fiasco with Wake? Apart from just causing trouble?'

'I told you, I heard about Wake over Leeds way. I thought the congregation should know about him.'

'*What* did you hear?'

'That he'd done a runner.'

Ellen frowned. 'A woman?'

'Nope.'

'Bad debt?'

'Nope.'

'Oh, for God's Sake, Walter, tell me!'

'Jesus, Stan!' he replied, rounding on his partner. 'You're supposed to aim for the *pockets*.'

Ellen took in a deep breath. 'So what *did* you hear about Wake?'

'Nothing *exactly*,' Walter answered her. 'Just rumours, you know, that Wake had made himself real unpopular throwing his weight around. Pompous fart. He tried to get into Leeds society and failed, so he moved on. He used to be an actor.'

'Oh God,' Ellen moaned.

'Yep, a two-bit actor. But apparently the work dried up, so he changed tack. Now he's got a double act with God.'

This was unwelcome news. Lily needed someone reliable, steady.

'But Wake might have changed,' Ellen said hopefully; 'he might have settled down, found his calling.'

'Yeah,' her brother-in-law replied phlegmatically, 'and I might be a monkey.'

'Some say you already are, Walter,' Ellen replied evenly, 'some say you already are.'

It felt good to Lily to be walking next to a man again; especially a man like Josiah Wake. How kind of him to see her home. How gentlemanly.

'I'm sorry for Walter's interruption,' she said apologetically. 'I can't think what came over him.'

Surprised, Josiah looked down at her.

'You know him?'

Lily nodded.

'He's my sister's brother-in-law.'

The news wasn't welcome to Josiah and he walked on in silence for a moment, Lily lengthening her stride to keep up.

'What he said about Leeds,' Josiah said carefully, 'wasn't true . . .'

'I never thought it would be!' Lily interjected.

'. . . I did my best there. People can be so judgmental.'

'Oh, you don't have to explain to me,' Lily said hurriedly. 'Honestly, honestly, you don't.'

He was uncomfortable! she thought, mortified. And she

72

had done that to him, bringing up Walter and the embarrassing scene at the hall. What was she thinking of? Why hadn't she just let the matter rest? Well, she would now. She didn't want to hear any more. What did Walter know anyway? He was always causing mischief. Josiah Wake was a gentleman, anyone could see that. Lily hesitated, uncertain of what to say next.

'Are you staying in Bolton?'

Was that too forward? she wondered, blushing.

But Josiah merely smiled, pausing at the street corner to cross over, his hand resting momentarily on her arm as a tram passed.

'I think I may well settle here,' he replied lightly. 'The town has many delightful things to offer.'

Lily was flushing again as he looked at her, and he was flattered by her obvious interest in him. Carefully he appraised her appearance and concluded that she might well do – even with the appalling relatives. He wouldn't jump to any conclusions about Lily Browning though: he would ask around a little, and talk to her, ease her out. But he liked her. Thought her sweet. Benign.

'I would like you to come to the service on Wednesday,' he said suddenly, smiling again, his hand reaching out to take hers. 'It would matter to me.'

Her flesh burnt against his.

'I . . . I would like that,' Lily stammered, surprised as he withdrew his hand abruptly and said: 'Well, here you are. Delivered safe and sound to your door.'

She blinked like a sleepwalker. Home so soon? Where had the time gone?

Flustered, Lily rummaged for her key.

'It was so nice of you to walk me home,' she said quickly, wanting to keep him there for a moment longer. Hoping that someone might see her with him. 'It was so –'

''Til Wednesday then,' Josiah said kindly, tipping his hat to her. 'Goodnight, Lily.'

73

'Goodnight . . . thank you . . .' she replied, watching his tall figure move away and then round the corner. A moment passed, allowing her to savour the sight and sound of him, and then she sighed and turned back to her door.

It was only after she closed it behind her that she realized she was smiling.

Chapter Nine

Funny how life works out, Ellen thought. She and Reg had never wanted children, until Bess came to them, and then they had tried to extend their own family. But nothing happened. No babies, no false alarms. It was no good mentioning it to Reg, he would have been on the defensive immediately, taking even the mildest comment Ellen might make as some kind of slur on his manhood. So she kept quiet and when people asked her when they were starting a family of their own, she told them that one child was enough.

But it wasn't ... Ellen emptied the pail of dirty water down the outside drain and glanced up as she heard footsteps passing on the street overhead. In Old Ma Shawcross's time there had been two entrances, one in the basement and the other on the ground floor, leading to the flat. But the latter entrance had been damaged repeatedly, in brawls and by vandalism, so they had boarded up the door and now the only way into the flat was through the billiards hall.

It hadn't seem to matter much in the old days, but now Bess had to walk through the hall to get to the flat and that meant walking past all the players. Ellen wrung out the mop in her hand and coughed. It was coming cold – how did it get round to winter again so fast? As the days shortened and the streets chilled, more and more men would come down to the billiards hall for a game – and for some warmth and company. There was no licence, but Reg turned a blind eye to the hip flasks, the odd snifters of bargain whisky, which hung on the air with the odour of cheap smokes. He didn't mind if the players took a drink – he only minded if it made them argumentative.

Ellen thought back to an incident only the previous month. Two strangers had come in for a game and laid a bet – Reg wasn't in and she couldn't stop them. The game lasted for nearly three hours, every point contested, until finally one man won. Simple. Or it should have been, but booze had made the men scratchy and the loser took it bad. So bad that he had struck out at his partner – and Ellen had been in the way.

She had lied about it to Reg, of course, said that she had bumped her cheek on the side of the kitchen range, but it worried Ellen. She might be able to cope, she *had* to cope, but she didn't want Bess to face the same rough treatment – accidental or not.

She would have to think about it very carefully, Ellen decided. Oh, it was early days yet, but Bess would soon grow up and she didn't want some tupenny-ha'penny lout sweeping her niece off her feet, tying her into some dead-end marriage and a rented house by the railway line. Bess deserved something better. An education, for one thing. She was bright enough to warrant good schooling, she might even have a career one day.

The thought pleased Ellen. She didn't mind struggling to keep the billiards hall afloat, didn't mind Bolton and the stinging little knot of streets that held her in its sooty cat's cradle. It was her town, the library, the shops, the chemist where she had bought her first lipstick, baby dummies swinging from a hook behind the door. She had no ambition to *better herself*.

Not like Lily, and certainly not like Louise ... Ellen paused on the thought, then put the mop and pail under the outside basement steps. They had heard nothing from Louise, not one word about her or Emma. To all intents and purposes they had disappeared off the face of the earth. They might be dead ... Ellen took in her breath. They had lied about Emma's death and now the lie had come true. To all intents and purposes, Emma Browning was no more.

Then suddenly Ellen realized that Louise *couldn't* get in touch. What could she say after so long? How could she excuse her actions? And besides, if she contacted Lily the inevitable would happen – Lily would want her daughter back.

God, Ellen thought, what a mess, what a bloody awful mess. Sighing, she walked back into the kitchen and poked the fire, the flames starting up brightly, the sound of Bess laughing upstairs with Reg coming sweet down the stairwell. It wasn't fair on Lily, Ellen knew that, but she couldn't help but be glad that fate had given her child into their care. And though Bess was not truly theirs by blood, she was as close as their own. Nature had cheated Ellen in one way, but blessed her in another.

Besides, she knew that Lily was more than happy with the arrangement. Bess knew that Lily was her mother, but the bond wasn't really there. That bond was between the Shawcrosses and Bess, so much so that Bess had been given the surname Shawcross, Browning cast off easily. She had never known Harold and the name meant little to her. In fact, to all intents and purposes, Reg was her father. So Bess might go out with her mother and sit politely listening to Lily, but she was always glad to leave, to return to the billiards hall and Reg. And recently the arrangement had seemed to bother Lily less and less.

Why? The answer was obvious – Josiah Wake. In the few months since Lily had met the preacher she had finally seen a way to restore her fortunes. Her job was respectable and she was growing more confident, and if Josiah married her, Lily wouldn't be pitied any longer. People would forget her failures; she would have the status again that a woman alone could never have.

But when Josiah was around – Ellen had to admit it – Lily seemed slightly cowed. Hanging on every word he

uttered, she made it obvious by every sentence and manner-
ism that she worshipped him. Not that she said anything
directly, but the expression on her face when Josiah was
out walking with her said it all: *I have a man again, a
preacher. A fine, good man.*

Before, Lily had scuttled around the Bolton streets, only
truly confident at work or in her little rented house on
Fletcher Street. But gradually, and skilfully, she had edged
herself into Josiah life's. Before his sermons she organized
the books and music, and afterwards she listened to him
as he dissected his words and the congregation's response.
She was his emotional barometer, his gauge, his uncritical
supporter.

But what did Josiah think of her, Ellen wondered. It was
so hard to tell. Oh yes, he liked Lily, anyone could see
that. He was kind, too, taking her arm when they walked,
and reading to her from the Bible. A trip to the pictures
would have been more romantic, Ellen thought, but maybe
that wasn't his way. After all, Lily had told her, Josiah had
never been married. He wasn't a charmer, his religion was
all his life now.

So was there room in that life for a wife, Ellen thought,
pulling on her crossover apron and getting out the washing.
Or was Lily putting her hopes on a man who wasn't about
to settle down? On a man who might leave town at any
time? Was she – Ellen winced at the idea – riding for
another fall?

'The flowers are beautiful,' Josiah said admiringly as he
walked round Hall Street Chapel. 'Thank you, Lily.'

She blushed at the compliment. It had been worth it –
even though the blooms had cost her half her wage packet
– just to see the pleasure on Josiah's face. They had been
growing closer, she thought happily. He was attentive,
kindly, almost paternal – and she had never had that
before. He was different, not a bit like Harold.

Which was a shame in a way, because Lily had loved Harold passionately and found herself unexpectedly responsive when they had made love. If she thought about it now, it seemed wrong, almost unladylike, but she couldn't deny it – she and Harold had spent many happy hours in their narrow double bed, curtains drawn against the Bolton sky, their bodies hot under the sheets. She had found herself longing for him, and after a while she had even initiated their lovemaking – a memory that now made her burn with shame.

So when Harold left her she missed her husband and the father of her child and unborn baby, just as she missed her status. But most of all – although she would never tell anyone – she missed those blind white hours of pleasure that she had never known previously and had thought never to know again.

Stealing a glance at Josiah, Lily studied the dark frock coat and the thick brown hair. His hands were large, the nails oval and well tended. What would they feel like on her body, Lily wondered suddenly, flushing as he turned to look at her.

'What is it?'

'Nothing.'

Josiah frowned. 'Are you feverish? You look pink in the face, Lily.'

Her hands went up to her cheeks. What *had* she been thinking of? Dear God, what would he think of her if he knew?

'It's warm in here.'

Josiah stared at her in amazement. 'I thought it was very cool myself,' he replied, staring up at the windows where a chilling shower pelted the glass. 'Are you sure you're quite well?'

Her face was burning up.

'I'm fine, Josiah, fine.'

'Well, if you're sure,' he said reluctantly, picking up his

79

notes for the evening sermon. 'I'm preaching about the sins of the flesh, Lily,' he told her. 'I apologize for being so blunt, but the matter has to be handled.'

She was scarlet. Rigid.

'Are you *sure* you feel all right?' he queried again, then sighed. 'Forgive me, Lily, I should have realized that I was embarrassing you. This is not a matter I should have brought up with you.'

Why? she thought desperately. Why not? Don't you think of me as a woman? As someone you want? Desire? . . . God, Lily thought, turning away. She had to control herself.

'The devil tempts us in various ways . . .' Josiah went on.

She could hear him moving around behind her and longed for him to *be* tempted, to lay his hand on her shoulder, her neck.

'. . . but we have to resist.'

Why? she thought agonizingly. I've resisted for a long time, and I miss a man's body. Yes, who would have thought it of timid little Lily Browning? But I miss a man lying next to me. I'm not what you think, Josiah. Not what you think, at all.

'. . . The influence of the American moving pictures, the new fashions, make-up . . .' 'Times are changing, Lily, the world is changing. People want different things. The old morals are breaking down . . .'

She hoped he was right, hoped he might undergo some breaking down himself.

'. . . we have to set an example.'

Smiling uncertainly, Lily glanced up at him. 'I don't understand.'

'Lily, I have been watching you for a while. I enjoy our talks together, I admire the way you have made a life for yourself with your limited advantages . . .'

Is that a compliment, or a criticism? she wondered.

'. . . I, too, have had to struggle, often facing up to unpleasant truths and difficulties.' He moved closer; Lily's heart speeded up. '. . . and I have been lonely. Just as you have. You're a fine woman, Lily, not like the rest of your family.' He winced at the thought of Walter Shawcross, gambler, and worse if the gossip was true. 'And I know how you must have felt about your husband's unfortunate death . . .'

That wasn't all, Lily thought uncomfortably. I could have remained a deserted wife, unable ever to consider marrying again. At least Harold was kind enough to get shot.

'. . . but you've got over your loss, and now it's time to think of the future . . .'

Is he always so long-winded? she wondered.

'Could you think – perhaps – I don't ask for an answer now. But if you would think about it. If you *could* perhaps think about it . . .'

This was too much. 'Think about *what*, Josiah?'

'Marrying me.'

The words were out, no romance, no tenderness – but no unkindness either. It was just his way.

It would do.

'Yes,' Lily said eagerly, 'I'll marry you, Josiah.'

Then she smiled and tipped up her face towards him. But instead of kissing her on the mouth, he merely brushed his lips against her forehead hurriedly.

'Josiah, we have to talk about something,' Lily said, surprised to see him move away and begin shuffling with his sermon notes. 'You know about Bess. My daughter.'

His back was turned to her. Did he really stiffen as she said her child's name, or did she imagine it? Nervously Lily stared at the man in front of her. She had what she wanted, a proposal, a marriage to come, security. But she knew that she had to tell him about her past or he would never be able to trust her. He had to know about Emma, about the lie surrounding her death, and the way she had been taken away by Louise. Much as she might dread it, she had to tell him everything. It was only fair; there could be no secrets between them.

'As you know, Bess lives with my sister Ellen –'

'At Shawcross's Billiards Hall,' Josiah said coolly, turning back to Lily and then smiling. His chill had vanished; maybe she had only imagined it.

'They – Ellen and Reg – have been very good to me, and they love Bess –'

He cut her off in mid-flow.

'Let's not talk about Reg Shawcross,' he said curtly, 'or his brother, who caused such a scene that time at my sermon.'

'Walter's not around much. He travels . . .' Lily said softly.

'Thank God for small mercies,' Josiah replied.

'I want to talk about Bess, Josiah. I'm her mother. I couldn't even think it, living on my own, but maybe there could be a way of having her back, of having a real family again –'

He smiled warmly at her and she relaxed, suddenly lightheaded. Obviously he knew what she was going to say, and approved. She'd have to negotiate with Ellen and Reg, of course, tread carefully as they'd been so good to her and to Bess, but here was the opportunity to begin easing Bess back into her life, and in time, who knew . . . ? She could have her daughter home. Now all she had to do was to tell him about Emma. Maybe with Josiah's help she could find her daughter. The little child she had had stolen from her could be found and brought home. Her dream – which she had kept to herself since that terrible day when the letter had been returned from Australia, leading her even to disguise her feelings for Bess, so hopeless did the possibility of being part of a proper family seem – would finally come to fruition. After all the humiliation, loss, and pain, she might finally be able to reclaim her children, to have her babies back.

'Josiah –' she said softly, Emma's name tingling on her lips.

But he interrupted her at once. 'Dearest Lily, you mustn't worry. You really mustn't,' he said kindly. 'I won't come between you and Bess. I understand the bond of motherly love. Things will continue exactly as they are. I promise.'

Lily's mouth dried, words hard to find. How could she mention Emma when it seemed as though he didn't even want Bess?

'But . . . but . . . I wondered if, after we're married, Bess could come and live with us?'

His expression faltered, like a man about to lose his footing. 'With us?'

'Why not?'

'Lily,' he said, his tone suddenly cooler, 'I have never wanted children. The congregation is my family –'

Her hand went out to him without thinking, resting gently on his sleeve. 'But Josiah, Bess is my *child*.'

'Have I ever lied to you, Lily?'

She shook her head.

'I have only ever told you the truth,' he went on. 'Lies are impossible between people who love each other. If I lied and agreed to something I would regret, how could you respect me if I went back on my word? How could you look up to me? Trust me? Don't you see how it is kinder this way – for us to talk things out and understand the situation before we marry?'

Lily was unsure if she really understood the argument, it sounded so bizarre. Was Josiah really trying to take *credit* for refusing to grant her wish? Was he expecting his righteous honesty to obliterate the fact that he had just rejected her daughter? Blindly she stared at him, locked into immobility.

She knew she should walk out now, turn away, reject

him. But if she did, what was there? Another proposal? Unlikely. She would never make herself vulnerable again. So what was her future? To see Bess grow up with the Shawcrosses, whilst she continued at the Farnworth Bleach Works until she retired? Always on the outside, looking in on other people's good fortune?

If she rejected Josiah she rejected her only chance. If she accepted him life would improve for her and change very little for Bess. Her daughter would stay with her sister and be happy. And Emma would remain forever out of reach ... Lily stared hard at the bare floorboards, trying to decide what to do.

Josiah glanced at his fob watch. Time was moving on, coming up to his sermon. The actor in him was getting nervous before his performance.

Suddenly she didn't love him as much as she had done only a little while ago. How odd, Lily thought, within minutes her feelings had halved. What had he been saying? She struggled to remember. Oh yes, about lies. About how there could be no trust in a relationship without honesty ... But she hadn't got around to telling him about Emma, had she? Obviously that would have been the death knell to his proposal. He didn't want Bess, so how would he ever condone the idea of trying to recover a supposedly *dead* child, a child about whom he knew nothing?

Silently, Lily continued to stare at the floor, at a knot in the wood, which looked suddenly like a coiled snake. Josiah Wake had let her down, disappointed her. He had shattered her dream – as others had done before. Slowly Lily took in her breath. She had no anger towards him, no spite, only disappointment, but in that instant something changed radically within her.

She knew then that she would never tell Josiah about her lost child. It would be a secret – one of those secrets he hated so much. Someday he might find out, but it was unlikely. No one but the Shawcrosses in Bolton knew that

Emma was alive. So how could Josiah discover the truth? Lily kept her head down, thinking quickly. His proposal was her last chance, her only chance. She had to take it.

So she did. It might feel that she had lost her child all over again – but she wouldn't lose everything . . . Slowly Lily looked up at Josiah. He smiled warmly, kindly, at her. And she smiled back.

Not for one instant did he suspect the unspoken lie, or the injury he had done to her.

Chapter Ten

Josiah came round to see Lily the week before they were due to be married and told her he had a surprise, asking her to walk with him through the town, and stopping outside the door of number 187 Church Street, the right address for a preacher and – deliberately? Lily wondered – some distance from Derby Street and the Shawcrosses. Next door a woman was just leaving and nodded to them, Josiah smiling and tipping his hat. The house Josiah had chosen for them was narrow and dark-fronted, the entrance decorated by a heavy brass knocker, his name on a brass plaque beside it: *The Rev. Josiah Wake*. Unlocking the door, he ushered Lily in.

'So what do you think of it?' he asked, turning on the gaslights, the room coming into its own.

Lily stared at the stranger furniture, the heavy dark wood standing like a domestic congregation in front of her. This was no house for children. It didn't seem to care for noise, was stiff-backed, righteously erect. And large – roomy enough for Josiah's books and furniture – which had appeared from nowhere. He had used his savings, Josiah told Lily, and wanted to make a fine house. But oddly enough she hadn't been asked to go with him when he'd chosen the dinner table or the drawing-room pieces.

'Are you happy?' he pressed her.

And what could she say? Tell Josiah that she was disappointed? That the house didn't feel like hers? That she had longed to share the buying with him, that her pleasure would have been to push and pull the pieces into place? To wonder if she wanted the table under the window, or by the door? What about *her* choice of colours, curtains? What about the female absorption in cushions and china ware? What about her possessions, for which there now appeared to be no room left? What about *her*?

'It's lovely,' she said dully. She had no choice but to go along with it – it was all already done.

He was lyrical with pleasure.

'I wanted to please you, to do everything for you.' He patted her shoulder, her eyes closing momentarily to his touch. 'I didn't want you to have to worry, my dear.'

He took her hand and led her into another room with stacked shelves of books and a desk busy with notes. So he was living here already! He had moved in before her! It was – Lily realized then with real misgiving – as though Josiah had laid siege to the house; won it over, before she could. Mastered it, before she could make it a home.

'Are you pleased?' he asked her again.

'Of course, thank you, Josiah,' Lily replied, glancing round.

It was a man's house, no trace of a woman here. It could have been a bachelor's home. There was no imprint of a female in anything. And after their marriage, would there *ever* be any trace of her?

His pens were lined up on his desk, next to a pile of papers, his strangely small handwriting drilled into the white sheet. Gingerly she touched it, then turned round. A religious print faced her, hanging oppressively over the fireplace.

'It was my father's,' Josiah said, following her gaze.

She was surprised. 'Was he religious?'

'In his own way,' Josiah replied. 'It's a pity my parents didn't live to see my marriage. They would have been pleased at my choice.'

It was a pretty compliment, but – or was Lily being suspicious? – contrived. Any real tenderness and warmth had been measured out over the previous months, Josiah giving verbal affection, but little physical contact. He was shy, Lily thought, he would change when they were married. When they were living together he would be different.

But it worried her enough to confide in Ellen. So on the Saturday before the wedding, Lily called at the billiards hall and asked Ellen to go for a walk with her up to Winter Hill.

'It's a bit cold, isn't it?'

'Put on something warm,' Lily countered. 'It's sunny up there.'

They caught a tram halfway and then walked the rest of the distance out to Winter Hill, pausing when they reached the summit. There they looked down on the mill chimneys and the curl of the River Irwell, razor bright in the low sun. Pulling her collar up around her neck Ellen blew on her hands and watched her sister, wondering what she was thinking about. Far away, the sound of a Salvation Army band came thin and tuneless on the Northern air.

'Are you nervous about the wedding?'

Lily glanced at her sister, smiling half-heartedly. 'A little.'

'But you love Josiah?'

'Yes, I love him.'

The answer was curiously passionless and confirmed what Ellen had been thinking for a while.

'But not like you loved Harold?'

Lily hung her head. 'It is so obvious?'

'Only to me.' Ellen linked arms with Lily and stared out over the town.

Above them a cloud shielded the sun, the shade chilling them for an instant before it passed on.

'He's very kind to me,' Lily said softly.

'I know he is.'

'And courteous.'

'Passionate?'

'Ellen!'

'Oh, Lily,' her sister chided her gently, 'no one can hear

us up here. We can say what we like. I know something's the matter, so you might as well spit it out.'

But what her sister said next was not what Ellen expected.

'I've been thinking about Emma.'

The name froze on the air, Ellen taking a moment to recover.

'*Emma* . . . ? Why now?'

'Josiah's against children –'

'I know.'

' – and I made my choice when I decided to marry him. I decided to keep her a secret.'

Ellen frowned. 'We've already talked about this, Lily, and you know I'm behind you all the way. Josiah will never know about Emma from me. And who else could tell him? No one round here; everyone in these parts thinks Emma died a long time ago. You don't have to worry about anything coming out about the past. It'll stay a secret.'

A burst of chill wind blew a strand of hair across Lily's face. Impatiently she brushed it away.

'But it feels as though by marrying Josiah I've given her up again,' she said. 'I've really given her up now. Can't ever hope to see her, to get her back. Can't even talk about her to him –'

'But you can to me.'

Nodding, Lily linked arms with her sister. 'I know, I know . . . Oh, Ellen, do you think I'm right marrying Josiah?'

'Why the doubts now?'

Lily's eyes were watery with the cold. She was so pretty, Ellen thought, so vulnerable.

'I want to know if Josiah's worth losing my child for.'

It was a blunt question, which left Ellen floundering for an instant.

'Lily, look at the facts,' she replied briskly. 'Emma isn't

going to come home if you *don't* marry Josiah.'

'But I feel as though I've made a bargain.'

'What bargain?' Ellen snapped. 'Lily, listen to me. I don't want to be cruel, but you have to face up to the fact that you might never see Emma again.' She brushed her sister's cheek with the back of her hand. 'I'm sorry, but you can't put your life on hold for her. You have to make your own happiness without her. It's not what you want to hear, but it's been a long time and we've heard nothing from Louise. And to be honest I don't think we ever will.' She saw Lily flinch. 'Are you sure that Emma is the real reason you've got second thoughts?'

'He's cold,' Lily said suddenly.

A crow landed only a few yards away from them, a black shape against the dry grass.

'You mean that Josiah's not loving?'

Lily winced. You weren't supposed to talk about things like this, she thought. Even to your sister.

'He doesn't . . .'

Ellen pushed her cold hands deep in her pockets and turned away from the wind.

'What?'

'He doesn't kiss me.'

'What!'

'Oh, he kisses me, but he doesn't . . .' Lily trailed off, regretting that she had ever started the conversation.

'*Really* kiss you?' Ellen finished for her, well aware of her sister's embarrassment.

'Yes, that's right,' Lily agreed, her voice hardly above a whisper, 'and he never seems to want to hug or get close to me.'

When she had been going out with Reg, Ellen thought, she was forever slapping him down. He was crazy about her from the first, adored her – even now their lovemaking was intense. And funny. And easy, comfortable – but never, never, without passion. He would come up behind her in the kitchen and slide his hands under her apron, his fingers stroking her nipples . . .

Hellfire! Ellen thought, shivering next to her sister. Life was hard enough, you needed a warm body at night to make you forget your worries. If she and Reg hadn't had so much fun in bed they might never have pulled through the rough times – especially when Old Ma Shawcross lived with them. Or more recently, when Walter had gambled away their savings.

So how would the fragile Lily fare with a man like Josiah Wake?

'You could call the wedding off, Lily. Reg and I would stand up for you, make –'

'No, I can't do that!' her sister replied, horrified.

'You could. Better that than get yourself into a mess.'

She didn't say *again*, but both of them thought it.

'No,' Lily repeated. 'I'll marry Josiah and I'll be grateful that he's looking after me. He's got many good qualities.'

'I know,' Ellen said seriously, 'but has he got enough?'

Yet whatever Lily thought, she *did* marry Josiah Wake and they *did* go to live in Church Street. But within weeks invitations for Ellen to visit Lily decreased, and soon Lily was making excuses not to visit the billiards hall either. Bess was invited to visit her mother alone at the weekends – Lily was evidently embarrassed at excluding her sister – but at least, Ellen comforted herself as she dropped the child off on Saturday afternoons, Lily was continuing to see her daughter.

Reg had seen it coming.

'Bloody Wake,' he said scornfully, one evening, when the Shawcross family, Walter included, were gathered in the kitchen. 'Trust a Christian to break up a family.'

'Oh, come on, Reg, he might just want Lily to himself,' Ellen reasoned.

'For what? His handmaid?'

Idly she stirred the soup she had made, glancing over

her shoulder towards Bess. The little girl was preoccupied, playing with a doll that Walter had brought her on his last fleeting visit – a visit he had cut short when Ellen started asking about the money he had lost. Still, it hadn't stopped him turning up again. Oddly enough, Bess hadn't seemed to miss her mother or to long for the weekend visits, and that worried Ellen. Don't let *this* child suffer for a man, Ellen thought. Please, Lily, don't let anyone come between you and your daughter. Not again. Not again.

With her head bent low, Bess's hair had half fallen over her face, the unusual eyes shielded. She had little of her mother in her, and less of Harold Browning. In fact, she seemed more like Reg than anyone else. Funny, outspoken, resilient. Was that because she had grown up under his influence, Ellen wondered. Because she loved him and wanted to emulate him? Whatever it was, it was good for the child.

Perhaps – after the first months of marriage – Lily might go back to her old ways. Ellen hoped so; missed her sister and their talks, worried about her. Only the other day she had seen her pass on the street, her clothes businesslike as always, her little face set. So serious, Ellen thought, so unlike a new bride.

And by contrast Josiah was flourishing, pounding his Bible and roaring out his sermons, working his way up to being a town worthy. The previous week he had been quoted in the *Evening News*, his photograph beside his words. Impressive – if you liked that kind of thing. He had turned the Church Street house into a rectory almost; people calling to talk to him at all times of the day and night to tell him their troubles, Josiah willing to listen, and even more willing to talk.

'If someone paid that bugger by the word,' Walter said brusquely, 'he'd be as rich as an Arab.'

'People rely on him,' Ellen replied, standing up for her new brother-in-law.

'People are bloody fools. They'd rely on a talking horse if it told them what they wanted to hear.'

Putting her finger to her lips, Ellen turned to Bess, who was now sitting at the kitchen table.

'Shall we go and visit your mum on Saturday, love?'

The oblique eyes fixed steadily on hers. 'If you like.'

'No, Bess, not if *I* like, if *you* like. Do you *want* to go?'

Immediately she shook her head. 'No.'

Reg grimaced. 'From the mouths of babes –'

'Oh, shut up!' Ellen snapped, turning back to her niece. 'Don't you want to see your mum?'

'You're my mum.'

She wanted to say no, no, I'm not. But she hesitated, and in that moment of hesitation realized that she was – to her shame – pleased by the words.

'Bess, you know better than that –'

'I don't want to go!' the child replied heatedly. 'And you can't make me!'

She had never been prone to tantrums, so the outburst was shocking.

'Why don't you want to go?' Ellen asked carefully, without anger. If Bess was upset, she had a reason to be.

'She doesn't want me there.'

'Where?'

'At that house,' Bess said, turning back to her plate. 'I hate it there.'

Disappearing behind the sporting pages of the newspaper, Reg backed off, Ellen sitting down next to the child.

'What's wrong with the house?'

'It's cold, and I don't like him.'

'Who? Josiah?'

Bess nodded, her heavy hair falling over her shoulders. In time, Bess would be a stunning woman.

'He's a bully.'

There was a sharp intake of breath from behind the *Evening News*. Then Reg lowered the paper, his eyes hard.

'He's not cruel to you, is he, love?'

'Oh no,' Bess replied, looking from Reg to Ellen. 'But he's ... you know, frightening.'

Ellen frowned. Perhaps Josiah *was* frightening to a child – those dark clothes, his height, his heavy features and that ringing voice. Yes, she could see how he might appear terrifying.

'What do you talk about when you go over there?'

'He *never* talks to me,' Bess replied.

'But he must say something.'

'He says hello and goodbye, but nothing else. He just sits there.'

Ellen was curious. Leaning towards her niece, she said, 'How d'you mean, he just sits there?'

'When I go to visit Lily –'

'When you go to visit your *mother*,' Ellen corrected her. 'Go on, what happens?'

'He sits in a chair in the room all the time I'm there. Just watching us.'

This was news, Ellen thought, and not good news either. She could imagine Lily in that dark house, sitting uncomfortably in the parlour Josiah had created for her, trying to hold a conversation with her daughter. No wonder Bess didn't like going. Which child would, with the spectre of a silent, judgmental preacher watching every move and listening to every word she uttered?

But why didn't Lily stop it, Ellen wondered, knowing the answer already. She wouldn't dare. She could never stand up to Josiah before they married, and now – as his wife – she was well and truly cowed. He had even put pressure on her to give up her job at the Farnworth Bleach Works.

It made sense – Lily didn't have to work any more – but she couldn't face a total curtailing of her freedom, couldn't live every twenty-four hours in that cold narrow house full of Josiah's things. The Farnworth Bleach Works was no place for a preacher's wife, Josiah told her. If she cared about what people thought, and if she loved him, she would resign.

Defiantly, Lily had refused. But when she told Ellen about it her sister knew that it was only a matter of time before she gave in to Josiah's wishes. He was taking her over, piece by piece, and Lily, being vulnerable, would cave in. She would believe that he was right, and reassure herself by counting his good points – that kindness she quoted so often.

That kindness which was killing her.

PART TWO

Deserves to be preached to death by wild curates
(Sydney Smith 1771–1845)

Beware the Prodigal
(Anon)

Chapter Eleven

1940

Being an industrial city Manchester was – along with
London and other major centres – a likely target for bombing. The mills were still flourishing, driving out the fabrics
and silks for parachutes, women undertaking engineering
jobs as their men were called up. Ellen and Reg had continued with the billiards hall, but at the outset of war the
customers had dwindled to a trickle. Most men were gone,
only the old and those too young to fight remained behind.

Oh, and Walter. This time he was too old to be called
up – But not too old to run a black market. He had started
almost as soon as war was declared, knowing from experience that there would be shortages, and people desperate
to get food and clothing and all manner of essentials. His
figure, still razor thin, was soon a familiar sight around
Bolton, in alleys, around the dark streets, haunting his old
stamping grounds. He was the only one who relished the
war. It brought out the best in him, he said.

As for Reg and Ellen's savings Walter had lost so many
years before, they never materialized in the same form – not
as notes or coins. But there was food, furniture, presents for
Bess and clothing for Ellen. Rumour had it that the woman
who had caused all the trouble in the first place had 'managed to set herself up in a little shop' over Oldham way.
A shop which closed after six months. She obviously wasn't
used to working upright, Ellen had said acidly when she'd
heard.

But although Ellen had never let Walter or Reg forget

the matter, she'd adjusted, saved again, and she and Reg somehow kept the white elephant of a billiards hall running. It was a matter of pride to her, especially after Walter's fecklessness had kept Bolton gossiping for far too long. And unless she was very mistaken, he was due more trouble now. Wars were always a profitable, if dodgy, playground for the likes of Walter Shawcross.

In the years since Lily's marriage Ellen had grown fatter, heavier, slower, fifty, facing up to hard work and her role as mother to Bess. Because, to all intents and purposes, that was what she had become: Bess's mother.

Banging the door closed, then banging it again until the lock caught, Ellen pulled the old green curtain across to keep out the draughts and turned on the electric light, having checked the windows were blacked out and no light could escape through any chinks in the curtains. *Curtains*, she thought, that was pushing it. Thin things they were, well used, but then she and Reg had never had the money to replace them. Other things had taken precedence: like food – and Walter's little present to his brother.

The car had been Walter's way of repaying Reg for his brotherly solidarity. And an apology – not that he could just come out and say it. Instead Walter had come up with some cock-and-bull story about some man over Rochdale way who knew someone who knew someone else who had a car. Reg's eyes had come out like chapel hat pegs when he'd heard.

A car, a bloody car! Jesus, no one had a car round their way – except for the doctor and that Miller bloke, but he didn't count because everyone knew he was a bleeding crook.

Reg had said nothing to Ellen until the vehicle arrived and then he'd guided her out onto the street with her eyes closed. Agog, the neighbours had gathered round, Reg finally telling his wife to open her eyes and look. Oh, she'd looked all right, looked like she might faint.

Walter had been standing smiling a little way off.

Ellen had called over to him, 'Was this your idea?'

'You don't have to thank me,' he'd said, sidling over. 'I owe you –'

'You *still* owe me, Walter, but I'd like the money in cash, not metal.'

Then she'd noticed Reg's face and suddenly realized that he wanted that blasted car so much and, after all, he'd had so little. So Reg had got to keep it and no one asked Walter where it had come from because ignorance with Walter was always bliss.

Then the following week it had been Ellen and Reg's wedding anniversary and that morning she had got up and stretched and glanced over to Reg, lying fast asleep with his mouth open, snoring. Across the landing Bess had also been asleep. The promise of her beauty had blossomed in her teens, catching everyone like a heat wave in November. Pulling on her dressing gown Ellen had gone downstairs, hoping to find a card or a little parcel on the table, but there'd been nothing. Only a couple of apples going brown.

Glancing round the room now she thought how little had changed since that day, but then, what had she wanted really? Only to be happy and she had to admit that wish had been granted. Poor, certainly, but content, yes. Money would have been nice, perhaps a move out of the town – but the billiards hall (albatross that it was) happened to be Reg's baby and it was their living too, so how could she even dream of leaving? It all came down to accepting your lot in life.

Not that Louise ever had, Ellen thought. But then how could she be so sure? Ellen didn't know *what* Louise's lot in life was any more. Since her sister's betrayal so many years before there had been no word. She could, Ellen realized with a shock, be dead for all anyone knew. Certainly well over fifty. What the hell would Louise look like now? Fat? No, not Louise. Thin and mean then? Maybe. Certainly posh, in a big house with Clem grown sleek on his money. With Clem – and *Emma*.

How had she grown up? A beauty, like her sister? Emma would be a young woman now, blonde, willowy. Did she have the same oblique eyes as her sister? The same full, smiling mouth? The same friendly sexuality which had the men reeling?

Was Louise still happily married to Clem? It mattered to Ellen that her own marriage had survived, that she and Reg still made love eagerly, that for every argument and every slammed door, they could both turn away and know, always know, that there was someone around who would never stab them in the back.

Not like Walter. Who could *he* trust? Especially after his spell in prison. That had been about the time of their anniversary, the year the car had appeared . . . He'd been caught handling stolen goods, the police tipped off by a jealous husband. That got Walter put away well and good. It had to happen; Walter had been lucky too long. And dishonest. Word had gone round Bolton within hours, Ellen bold-faced, but secretly mortified, Reg defending his brother as ever. And as for Bess – she wouldn't hear a word said against her uncle.

But the news had shattered Lily. She'd wondered at first if she could hide it, but realized that Josiah would be bound to find out. And he did, walking in with a sanctimonious expression on his face, which said – *Do you see? I was right all along. You can't mix with the likes of the Shawcrosses.*

The whole episode had been a real facer, Ellen remembered grimly. It was bound to happen sooner or later, but although it seemed to have little effect on Walter, it had turned the family inside out, like a worn pocket. Reg had been outraged with his brother, but Lily, poor sweet Lily, had really suffered, blackmailed by Josiah into finally cutting off all ties with the Shawcrosses. He had waited for his chance and it had finally come – via Walter, of all people.

Lily had told Josiah that she had broken off all contact, naturally. But nothing on earth could separate the sisters for long and so since then she'd crept round to see Ellen when Josiah was at church, slipping down the basement steps and past the billiards players like a terrified ghost. She had to be back before Josiah got home, back to the dark house on Church Street. To the kindness that had every condition of cruelty.

The thought of Lily and Josiah took Ellen back to that wedding anniversary. A simple pleasure it had turned out to be, one of the last really good days before war broke out, yet it had not started promisingly!

'You look awful,' Reg had said, walking into the kitchen.

'Thanks, Reg,' she'd replied sarcastically, turning on the gas and reaching for the frying pan.

'Yeah, bloody awful. You should take a break . . .' he'd gone on, picking up the paper and beginning to read.

She had had a fleeting desire to set fire to the bottom of the page with the lighted match she was still holding.

'. . . a holiday would do you good.'

'And who would run this place and take care of you?'

'Bess. She's more than capable.'

'She's at work.' Ellen had pointed out, with a glow of pride.

Bess had qualified as a secretary and was working for the *Evening News*. She was going to be a journalist, she'd told them. You watch, I'll do it. Ellen believed her.

'Maybe Bess needs a break too,' Reg had murmured idly. 'She's been working really hard.'

'Maybe we all need a bloody break!' Ellen had snapped, banging down the pan on the table top. 'Why don't we all pack up and go on holiday!'

Reg had been on his feet in a moment, grinning.

'Which is just what we're going to do,' he'd told her,

kissing her roughly, his morning beard catching her skin. 'Happy Anniversary, Ellen. Happy, happy, anniversary.'

So they'd gone in Reg's car and been stranded when it broke down, but it hadn't mattered. It hadn't mattered that it rained every day in the Lake District either, or that they had to hide under a canopy of trees to keep dry when there was a cloudburst. Sandwiches in soggy paper, wet clothes, tea in flasks, tasting of tannin – none of it mattered. And when the windows of the car steamed up Ellen only remembered Reg leaning forward and drawing a heart in the condensation – with their names inside.

Which was why it seemed so unbelievable when war had broken out again, Bess, promoted already, writing up the news in the paper daily. The few punters who'd remained in the billiards hall had all teased her about it; offering their own opinions on the state of the world. Chamberlain was an ass, they'd said, a bloody coward, everyone could see what that bloke Hitler was up to. It did her little good trying to talk politics to the likes of Stan Clark or Shooting Cuffs.

But no one had really expected the war. They had thought Chamberlain would stop it at the eleventh hour. But when he didn't, there were the usual patriotic rushings to fight. Yet for all the enthusiasm on the part of the younger generation, the older people felt only a sense of something ominous; something achingly familiar and hideously well known.

'Morning.'

Ellen turned at the sound of Bess's voice. She was dressed in a navy suit, her hair pinned up. Her impact, as ever, caught her aunt by surprise.

''Lo, darling.'

Why wasn't she married yet, Ellen wondered. There had been so many boys hanging round. Admittedly most of them were useless, too stupid or too dull for Bess. But there had been others, and, unless she was very much mistaken, there was now someone at the paper. A man called Geoffrey Tyler. But for how long? Who knew how long it would be before he was called up?

'I might be back late,' Bess told her. 'I said I'd go and do an interview in Manchester.'

'Be careful –'

'I will. The trains are still running. Even if it's not to a timetable any more.'

'I worry about you.'

Bess pulled a face. 'Why? What will happen, will happen. Bolton's a small place. Say they asked me to go somewhere else –'

'You think they might?'

'I don't know. But if they did, I'd have to go,' Bess said firmly. 'It would help my career no end.'

And there it was: the steel. The look of Harold Browning and the steel of God knows who. Certainly not Lily. Poor Lily had no guts left, thanks to Josiah. So, Ellen wondered, where had her niece's physical and mental courage come from? Oh yes, *she* was tough enough, but not like Bess. Bess simply had no fear. None at all. Life was hers for the taking. If you didn't live it you were cheating yourself, and that was a crime in Bess's book.

Was it because of her mother's example? Seeing Lily cowed by Josiah Wake, did Bess subconsciously make a decision to be her own master? Is that why she hadn't married? To escape a man's control? It was obvious to Ellen that times had changed, but it was still a novelty for a young woman to have chosen a career over marriage. Things hadn't changed *that* much. The world wasn't that ready. Yet.

'I think,' Bess said suddenly, without preamble, 'that Geoffrey will soon be going off to fight.'

Ellen glanced over to her niece, remembering how Geoffrey had once come to the billiards hall to pick Bess up for an evening out. They had been going to a dance at the town hall, some big do for the newspaper. He had arrived early – stocky with a huge laugh – and watched as Bess fussed about her lipstick, pulling faces behind her in the mirror. They had been so comfortable together, like kids. But were they in love? Ellen wasn't sure. She hoped so, would have enjoyed seeing the friendship between them develop – but if Geoffrey was going off to fight, what chance was there?

'You'll miss him.' Ellen said gently.

'He's going to report from the front. Some paper in Manchester's read his work and hired him.' Bess hesitated, pulling on her gloves. 'God, I hate this war.'

'All wars are hateful,' Ellen replied.

'Did you worry when Reg was away during the last war?'

Did I worry? Ellen thought. Only every day, every hour, every minute.

'Geoffrey will be fine, honestly, he'll be fine.'

Bess held her look for a long moment then turned away.

'No one knows,' she said simply, 'no one really knows.'

Of course she didn't mean to irritate him, Josiah thought, watching Lily as she made breakfast. She was moving around very quietly, her hair drawn back, going grey, if she looked close, around her surprisingly ageless face. Behind her the clock on the kitchen mantel said nine fifteen; there was the sound of several letters dropping on the mat in the vestibule. He watched as Lily went to pick them up, returning a moment later and passing them to him.

She should have more spirit, he thought. Surely she had more life in her when we first married? Then she had seemed sweet, and anxious for his comfort, the house tidy, the fire always laid in the grate in the front room, ready for callers, fruit in a bowl on the windowledge, a photograph of his dead parents on the sideboard. Dusted, always dusted.

But in the last couple of years Lily had ceased to attend his sermons, keeping to the house instead. Perhaps she blamed him for his stand over Walter Shawcross – but in all honesty how could he (a man of standing) approve of his wife's continued association with such a family? He was looking after her best interests, surely she could see that? Surely she understood that he was only protecting her?

It wasn't as though he had ever forbidden her daughter to visit. In all the years that Bess was growing up she had been welcomed, and he had always been there for her calls, keeping a benevolent eye on his wife and his stepdaughter. A man could hardly be expected to do more. And yet, if he was honest, Josiah had felt a chill between the girl and himself even at the start, and as she got older Bess had made little effort to hide her dislike of him. It was too bad really, Josiah thought, slicing open the first letter and then glancing at the envelope as an afterthought. A bill, what else?

His gaze lifted from the letter and rested for a moment on his wife. Surprised, he noticed that Lily was standing rigidly with an unopened letter in her hand, colour flushing around her neck.

'What is it?'

She heard him, but did not reply.

Josiah raised his voice: 'Lily – what is it?'

His voice sung in her head and then pooled amongst several other voices, long ago remembered. Tightly, Lily's fingers closed around the envelope, her eyes fixing on the black cooking range in front of her. For years she had leaded that range, kept the fire going, shone the kettle on the hob. Cakes had been made there, for Josiah's parishioners, careful little buns laid out in rows to feed the faces of the whining visitors.

Oh, and how they had come, in all weathers, arriving at the door on Church Street and expecting immediate admission. It had never been a real home, Lily thought, more like a doctor's surgery, and she might just as well have been a housekeeper, not the mistress of the place. Resentment had set in after the first few years of marriage, when every suggestion Lily had made about changing the furniture or redecorating a room was pooh-poohed. It would cost money, Josiah had said, it would cause a lot of disturbance. And work for her.

But he hadn't meant it, he'd meant that it would disturb *him*. He hadn't even been lying directly, he'd believed what he was saying; he was that self-deluding . . . Lily had been surprised by the animosity she'd began to feel, the undying bitterness. Her husband was not what he appeared, she'd realized; he was selfish, egocentric, arrogant.

She'd begun to loathe listening to Josiah practise his sermons, the words high blown and empty. How could he talk about love, she'd wondered, when he knew so little about it? Their lovemaking had been perfunctory, half-hearted, even embarrassing. Josiah hadn't really wanted a wife, he had wanted a cook, a cleaner and an assistant.

But Lily had stuck by him because she couldn't admit another mistake to anyone – even Ellen. She had made her choice, given up on ever claiming Emma, on her job, and even her independence for Josiah Wake – and if he wasn't worth it no one would ever know.

Sometimes though, she wondered if fate would take a hand. If that secret between them might suddenly stretch and come to life, biting him savagely, making him see that his wife had lied, deceived him. The secret Lily had with-held, so afraid to lose him, was now the only way she could see of escaping Josiah.

So she waited, knowing that nothing ever stayed hidden for long. You could hide things away in dusty little glory holes, but in the end someone discovered them. One day someone would mention Lily's second child, remembering only vaguely something about a daughter who had died. And then Josiah would start asking questions, demanding the truth. It would be down to her then whether she perpetuated the deception or confessed. Said – I lied, Josiah, I pretended Emma was dead when all along I had given her to my sister. I did it for you. For you.

Then Josiah would know that his meek little wife had lied to him. That she had deceived him, that the one person he believed he had had totally and completely under his thumb had betrayed him. He would burn with humiliation to realize that his dowdy, cowed wife had duped him. He would be outraged, sanctimonious – and then he would wonder what other huge secrets she had kept from him.

Then he would leave her.

Funny, but the thought didn't seem so frightening to Lily any more. She knew that she lacked the courage actually to confess, but more than once the secret had burned her tongue, and once or twice she had almost told him – then thought better of it.

But someone, or some event, would expose her in time. One day Emma's existence would be slapped in front of Josiah like an unappetizing meal. And when it was, Lily would be free of him.

'So what does the letter say?' Josiah asked her again.

Lily smiled distantly and pushed the envelope into her pocket.

'Nothing important, Josiah.'

He watched her and knew that she was lying. The realization was startling. Suddenly the Lily he knew was gone and he, for once, was left floundering.

'Ellen, Ellen!'

She rushed out to the sound of her name being called, to find Lily at the kitchen door.

''Lo there,' she said, then frowned. 'What's the matter?'

In reply, her sister handed her the letter. Ellen sat down at the table to read it. The envelope had been addressed to Lily's old home in Little Lever and then forwarded to the house in Church Street. And the writing was agonizingly familiar.

Dear Lily,
   This is a very difficult letter to write . . .

Louise had written at last! After all these years, their sister had renewed contact.

   . . . and I hope you can forgive me for what I did. Not that it was meant to hurt you. I thought at the time that it was the best thing for everyone concerned.
   But times change and so do circumstances. Clem lost his business. He took some bad advice and lost all our money . . .

Ellen paused and glanced to her sister.
   'Go on, read it,' Lily said quietly.

   . . . and now he's left me. I suppose it's funny. But you must know how I feel, Lily. Harold left you, after all.
   I can't stay here now and I want to come home. With Emma. You see – it's so difficult to ask you this – but we need help. And she is your child, after all . . .

'Bloody hell!' Ellen said shortly. 'She conveniently forgot whose child Emma was when everything was going well.'
   Slowly Lily sat down next to her sister. Her colour was high, cheating her age. She looked, Ellen thought incredulously, invigorated.
   'Go on, Ellen, finish it.'

   . . . I've thought about it for a long time and talked to Emma. Arrangements have been made and we're coming back to Bolton. It will be a dangerous trip and I wouldn't undertake it lightly unless I thought it was the right thing to do. But there's no future here in Australia now, and Emma's finally seen things my way. I thought of sending her to England alone, but she's been very protected, very sheltered, so I've decided to come with her.

We'll need somewhere to stay. I know I'm asking a lot, but I can make it up to you, Lily. I know I can.

Emma's a beautiful girl, really beautiful, and clever. We brought her up with everything, and she's a credit to anyone. I've told her that we have to return to England and she's not keen, but when she gets home I'm sure she'll settle.

But I haven't told her that you are her mother. She thinks that you're her aunt, Lily, as she always has done. Surely you can understand? She's grown to *be* my child, and so far away from England it was easy to pretend that she really was. Besides, we did agree that she would think I was her mother, didn't we? I wasn't too wicked, not really.

I'll get back on my feet, Lily. I just need some help now. Will you tell Ellen that I'm coming home, although I suppose she'll be furious with me . . .

'She's right there,' Ellen said heatedly. 'So now she comes home, when everything's gone belly up for her.'

. . . but I know you'll understand, Lily.

If all goes according to plan and the journey's safe, we should be back at the end of the month. Please can you put us up?

Sorry, Lily. Sorry.

Yours,

Louise

Angrily Ellen rose to her feet and lit the gas under the kettle, putting out two cups and saucers and ladling some tea into a pot. Well, this was a turn-up, and no mistake. Louise coming back to Bolton – what a nerve! What a bloody nerve.

'She sounds sorry –'

'Sorry!' Ellen snapped. 'She bloody should be, the bitch.'

'Oh, Ellen –'

Amazed, she stared at her sister. Lily, what *is* the matter with you?'

'My daughter's coming home,' she replied, her voice perfectly calm. 'What I dreamed about for years is coming true at last.'

Is she thinking straight? Ellen wondered. Hadn't it dawned on her sister that Emma's return would beg a thousand questions? Even if Lily didn't tell Josiah the truth, Emma's presence would be bound to excite questions. Besides, Ellen thought frowning, the letter didn't ring true. Why would anyone in the middle of a war, with the threat of U-boats and God knew what else, undertake such a long journey? Just to get away from a broken marriage? Hardly. Australia was a big country – why sever all ties and come back to England? And then there were those phrases – *she's not keen ... Emma's finally seen things my way ... I thought of sending her to England alone* – which sounded ominous to Ellen. It simply didn't add up.

Anyway, she thought, why had the marriage broken up? She didn't trust Louise, hadn't for years, and she could smell a lie coming off the paper like an odour. Emma was nearly twenty-two – why didn't she make a life for herself in Australia? Why did her parents' failed marriage mean that she had to come to England with her mother? Because she was so sheltered, protected, that she couldn't fend for herself? No, Ellen thought, there's something else going on. Something altogether more complicated.

'Lily, what are you going to do?'

'Write to Louise and tell her that they're welcome.'

'What about Josiah?'

'*What* about him?' Lily countered, taking the teapot from her sister and filling both cups. Slowly she added the milk and a sprinkle of rationed sugar, then pushed one towards Ellen.

'Drink it whilst it's hot.'

'Are you mad?' Ellen snapped. 'What are you going to tell Josiah?'

'That my sister's come home with her daughter,' Lily replied, as though it was obvious. 'That my niece is back in England.'

'But the truth will come out,' Ellen said anxiously. 'You've got away with it for years, Lily, but can you honestly say that if you see that girl you won't want to tell Josiah the truth? Or Emma? Imagine it, seeing your daughter every day, pretending, lying . . . Oh, come on, Lily, you couldn't keep it up.'

'If it has to come out, then so be it,' Lily replied, sipping at her tea, her hair working lose from its tight bun.

She seemed unnaturally animated.

'Lily, Josiah will find out –'

'I don't care.'

'*You don't care!*' Ellen said incredulously. 'You have to care. You know what kind of man Josiah is. He'd never forgive you if he knew the truth; if he knew that you lied to him. He's always thought he owned you body and soul – how the hell do you think he'll react? Hiding the existence of a daughter is no small matter.'

'He didn't want Bess,' Lily replied coldly, 'so why should he have wanted Emma?'

'That's not the point, and you know it!' Ellen replied, exasperated. 'He'll want to know why you didn't tell him. Why you lied.'

'If I'd have told him about Emma he would never have married me,' Lily replied simply. 'We both know that. He didn't want children, he never has. Besides, at that time being married was so important that I felt I couldn't risk losing him. You know how things were then, Ellen. I wasn't well, I couldn't cope . . .' she trailed off. 'I never thought that Emma would come home.'

Frowning, Ellen sipped her tea and watched her sister over the rim of the cup. Lily's attitude was astounding. Didn't she care about her marriage any more? Was that the reason for her unexpected recklessness? Or maybe her long-held dream about Emma's return was blinding her to reason. Or maybe, just maybe, the loss of Josiah was *worth* risking.

Understanding struck her with all the accuracy of a punch. *Lily no longer loved Josiah*. Security and marriage had proved to be a sham. She had grown to dislike him, and when that happened a woman stopped worrying about what her man thought. Not that Ellen could blame her sister. She couldn't have endured Josiah for a month, let alone years. His confidence had turned to conceit, bordering arrogance. His presence pompous, not commanding; his mannerisms forced. Now Josiah Wake's sermons were parodies; an actor reciting the same lines to the same audience in perpetuity.

But his audiences never dwindled, especially now that there was a war on. And there were so many lonely women wanting comfort. Ellen frowned. There were always women devoted to Josiah, the ones who visited Church Street constantly, bringing him presents – something which must have infuriated Lily over the years – but she had never suspected him of adultery. That wasn't Josiah's style. He might like the adoration, but not the mess of affairs.

Poor Josiah, Ellen thought wryly, he was really struggling now, aware of his own bombast. Not that he would have admitted it to anyone, but Lily was vital to his existence. He needed his wife to make him feel powerful, to make him believe that there was one person over whom he had total control. The adoring parishioners went away each evening; possibly one day they might see through him and stay away for good, but Lily was permanent. He told Lily what to do, to eat, to wear, to say, commanding his little army of one rigorously. Lily made him feel like a big man, and as long as he believed his wife was totally cowed by him, Josiah was secure.

Which was why, Ellen realized, Josiah would never forgive her for lying to him.

Chapter Twelve

Lily telegraphed Louise and – on the insistence of Ellen – suggested that her sister and Emma come to Shawcross's Billiards Hall for the reunion. There was no allotted day of arrival as travel was hazardous, so when the last week of the month came and went, no one was unduly surprised when they hadn't arrived.

'It's the war,' Lily said quietly. 'They'll be here. Maybe tomorrow, or the day after.'

Reg and Bess had been told of the imminent visit, but reserved judgement, keeping out of the way as every day Ellen laid a table in the front room. It was seldom used and smelled of damp, the wallpaper faded, the curtains tired in the weak winter sun. What would Louise think after Australia, Ellen wondered one evening in the week after Louise and Emma had first been expected, remembering the photographs she had seen in the library, of houses filled with light Then she wondered why she was bothered *what* Louise thought. Snobbish, ambitious Louise – so critical, so ready to find fault – had been deserted by her husband. Ellen might have a mean little home, but she still had Reg.

But she still couldn't stop fiddling with the plates and tea service, turning the chipped cup away from the centre of table and making a mental note to keep it for herself. Then she glanced into the fly-blown mirror over the fire and checked her reflection. So she was fatter, but she had worn well, considering all the hard work, and as for Lily – she glanced at her sister reflected in the room behind her – if a stranger had passed Lily quickly on the street they would think her no more than thirty-five.

Thirty-five ... Emma was nearly twenty-two now. Hardly a child any more, hardly in need of looking after. I mean, Ellen thought, Bess could look after herself and there was only three years between the girls, so Emma must be pretty cosseted. And what about Louise? Was Louise really wanting to come back to Bolton and make a life for herself and her daughter in the town where she was born?

Hardly. Not Louise. She couldn't take the stares, the gossip. *There goes that stuck-up Louise Whitley, not so stuck now that her husband's upped and left her* ... How could she possibly fit back into her old life, the one she so despised? And as for Emma, what possible common ground was there between Australia and Bolton?

Oh God, Ellen thought, I smell trouble ... She glanced over to her sister cautiously. Lily had been sneaking off to the Shawcrosses daily, telling Josiah that she needed to get out of the house. He was suspicious, but nervous of confronting her. Ellen sighed to herself. How would Lily take seeing her daughter at last, yearning to tell Emma the truth, to usurp her sister once and for all? Could she contain herself as time passed? Could she seriously imagine that she could hold her tongue? Ellen doubted it, uneasy with Lily's uncharacteristic recklessness.

Another hour passed, Ellen reading the evening paper and checking the blackout at eleven. At twelve fifteen she was just about to wake a dozing Lily when the doorbell rang. Gingerly, Ellen pulled back the edge of the curtain and glanced up through the kitchen window. Two pairs of feet stood on the pavement. Strangers' feet.

'I'll go,' she said, hurrying to the door, a flustered Lily following her into the empty billiards hall.

Her heels clacking on the bare floor, Ellen strode to the outer door and opened it. Two women stood on the step outside. The moonlight slanted downwards unkindly, making unflattering shadows under her sister's cheeks, Emma's face turned away.

'Louise,' Ellen said simply, staring at her sister.

God, she had aged, grown weedy thin, her mouth down-turned, lips thin with bitterness. Her make-up and clothes were immaculate, though – no coupons there – one gloved hand gesturing towards the young woman who stood next to her.

'This is Emma . . . your niece.'

No emotion, no plea for forgiveness, no kiss to the cheek. Nothing, just a statement of fact.

And then Emma turned and looked into Ellen's face.

She was fairly tall, her skin tanned, her eyes deeply blue, her hair sun blonde. Around her long, fine neck was a fur-collared coat, and the tiny pearl earrings she wore blinked in the patchy light. She had no immediate look of Bess, but there was *some* resemblance – the same stunning impact of beauty. Only with Bess it was a smiling loveliness; in Emma there was a coldness, a winter look about her eyes. But then, perhaps that was the moonlight, nothing more.

'It's so good to see you,' Ellen said to the young woman. 'Come in, come in.'

Catching hold of Emma's arm, Louise guided her into the dimness of the billiards hall. In that instant Ellen could sense the shock register in her niece and suddenly saw the place as it looked to a stranger's eyes. The long bare tables, the cues hung up, or resting against the walls. Posters and notices – 'NO BETTING' – adorned the distempered walls, the old odour of chalk and stale cigarettes coming strong.

Ellen had never minded any of it before, but something in her niece's expression made her feel unexpectedly defensive.

'Nothing much changes here.'

'You can say that again,' Louise murmured.

'If you don't like it, you can go now,' Ellen snapped back. 'You invited yourself, if you remember.'

Tugging at her sleeve Louise affected a hurt look. When

118

she was young and attractive she could pull it off, but now she looked ridiculous.

'Oh, Ellen, don't nag.'

'Is this where we're going to stay?' Emma asked suddenly.

Ellen looked at her niece with astonishment. Where *had* that voice come from? A sound so melodious, so lazily seductive that no one, on hearing it, could ever forget it. It had no accent, no Australian twang, it was simply a voice which no one else had ever owned – drowsy, laced with sex appeal. Oh God, Ellen thought again, this is trouble.

But just as she was about to answer Emma, Ellen noticed Louise looking over her shoulder into the hall beyond. Her expression was odd, something between ingratiation and hostility.

Turning, Ellen saw Lily. For all her troubles, Lily had kept something sweetly childlike in her expression. She came up to them and smiled briefly at Louise, then turned to Emma. For the rest of her life Ellen would remember the moment that her sister saw her daughter for the first time in twenty-two years.

Emma was standing perfectly still; what light there was trained on her face like a spotlight searching out the crowd for the star attraction. In the dim bleakness of the billiards hall, she glowed, and Lily saw that glow, searching her daughter's features, inspecting her, reading her, remembering that this – *this* was her daughter. This was Emma.

Slightly intimidated by Lily's scrutiny, Emma's hand went up to her throat.

'What's happened to your finger?' Lily asked, her voice quick.

Emma glanced down, pulling on her glove to cover the scar on her little finger.

'She had an accident.'

'She had an accident!' Lily replied, her colour rising. 'When? When did it happen?'

'A long time ago,' Louise answered, smiling awkwardly, aware that Emma didn't know who Lily was. Jesus, she thought, this could be embarrassing.

'What happened to her?'

'It was a shooting accident –'

'Shooting!' Lily repeated, horrified. 'What was she shooting?'

'Elephants,' Louise replied sarcastically, unfastening her coat and glancing back to Ellen. 'We're been travelling a long time, I think a cup of tea would be welcome.'

Her sister's cheek nearly winded her, but Ellen bit her tongue, too aware of the subtext going on between Lily and Emma to retaliate. Her sister was going to give everything away, she thought, ushering everyone into the front room: Lily was going to open up a can of worms which would have been better left shut.

'Oh,' Louise said simply as they walked into the front parlour, 'it's . . . just as I remembered it.'

'Which is more than can be said for you,' Ellen replied, catching her niece's smile out of the corner of her eye. Maybe Emma wasn't so bad, after all. Maybe it was just Louise's presence which brought out the worst in her.

Slowly, Louise dusted a chair with her handkerchief and sat down. Ellen's palm itched with the desire to hit her. She was worse than she had imagined. All her snobbery, her social climbing, had done her no good at all: in the end Louise was just another deserted wife. Only Louise hadn't the humility to adjust her attitude. No, her fall in status had merely enforced her ego, her conceit a carapace.

'We cleared out the rats last week,' Ellen said, folding her arms as she looked down at her sister.

'Rats!' Emma said hoarsely.

'It's just a joke,' Lily assured her, 'Ellen and your . . . Ellen and Louise have always pulled each other's legs.'

She had nearly said it! Ellen thought, reaching for the sandwiches and laying them on the table in front of them. She had nearly said *your mother* and then checked herself. Oh God, Ellen moaned inwardly, this was going to be dangerous.

Delicately Louise took a sandwich and placed it on her plate with the air of someone handling a dead mackerel.

'Salmon paste,' said Ellen.

'*Paste?*' echoed Louise. 'We have fresh fish at home.'

'So go back.'

Lily winced. 'Ellen!'

'Don't round on me! This is my house and I won't have anyone coming in here and making me feel uncomfortable.'

'I'm your sister!' wailed Louise.

'A fact you conveniently forgot until you needed help –'

'How could you talk to me like that, after all I've gone through?' Louise replied, lifting up the top of the sandwich and then replacing it, untasted. 'Emma and I have been through hell, haven't we, sweetheart?'

'Yes, Mother,' the drowsy voice intoned, Emma glancing round the parlour and avoiding Lily's scrutiny.

'Clem was a . . .' Louise dropped her voice conspiratorially, '. . . *bastard*.'

'What?' Ellen asked.

'My father was a bastard.'

'Emma!' Louise said, horrified. 'How could you say such a thing?'

'I didn't. You did.'

Louise smiled awkwardly at her sisters, tugging at her collar and taking off her hat. Her hair, once so abundant, was now dyed auburn, thin and overpermed.

'So,' she said, in what was a ghastly parody of small talk, 'how have you been, Lily?'

Wincing, Ellen began to pour out the tea. For a long moment Lily said nothing – no one could have guessed what was going on in her mind at that moment – then she coughed and smiled. *Smiled*, Ellen thought incredulously. Why didn't she smack Louise in the mouth?

'I married again –'

'What!'

Ellen turned away, trying not to laugh. That was one up on Louise and no mistake.

'I married a Methodist minister. Josiah Wake.'

Louise was luminous with spite. To find her sister – the one she had cheated, the hopeless, depressed, struggling Lily – to find her remarried. It was too much.

'Any children?' Louise croaked.

'Just the four,' Ellen replied, pouring tea.

'Four!'

Lily's smile was beatific.

'No, Louise, no children. Apart from Bess. You *do* remember Bess, don't you?'

Louise was struggling to remember anything. 'Yes, oh yes. Bess . . .'

'She's going to be a journalist –'

'I take mine without milk,' Emma said suddenly, staring at the teacup Ellen had passed to her.

Like mother, like daughter.

'Drink it for once, darling,' Louise urged.

'But I don't like milk,' Emma countered, defiantly staring at her aunt. 'Sorry.'

Oh, yes, she was sorry, Ellen thought. She didn't know just how sorry she was going to be. This was no timid girl who couldn't stand up for herself.

Grudgingly she filled another cup and passed it to her niece.

'No milk.'

'Thank you.'

'Think nothing of it.'

The temperature in the parlour had dropped several degrees. It could have been the cold night, but Ellen doubted it.

'And how is Ron?' Louise asked.

'*Reg*,' Ellen corrected her, thankful that he was upstairs asleep.

'Oh yes, Reg . . .' Louise replied, trying a smile. 'How is he?'

'Fine.'

'He's been marvellous,' Lily chimed in, 'a wonderful husband to Ellen. And like a father to Bess . . .'

Was she doing it deliberately, Ellen wondered. Or was Lily just guileless, unaware of the effect her words were having?

'. . . He's been a tower of strength. A really good man.'

Louise was having trouble speaking. This was not what she had expected. She had thought to return – if not in triumph – at least able to score some points. So what if her marriage had failed? She had lived, been abroad, had clothes that no one in Bolton could even dream about. She was someone to be reckoned with. All she had to do was to stick to her guns, to her master plan. It would take a little cunning, but she could pull it off. She wasn't going to be reduced to the role of poor relation.

Her lips pursed, Louise turned to Emma.

'I'd like to talk to my sisters alone, sweetheart.'

'But I haven't finished –'

'*Now*, sweetheart,' Louise insisted, steel melting through the honeyed tones.

Angrily, Emma got to her feet. 'I'll go for a walk.'

'You can lie down upstairs, if you like,' Ellen offered, suddenly sorry for her.

'No, I'm fine,' Emma replied, picking up her coat. 'I'll leave you to it.'

In silence, Louise waited until she heard Emma's feet mount the steps outside to the pavement, and then she leaned back in her seat, staring at her sisters. The pretence had all gone; her little childhood cruelty fully blown.

'Lily, you have to take Emma back.'

'What!' Ellen replied, slamming down her teacup. It broke on impact.

'You have to,' Louise repeated. 'I can't stay here, I have to go home. Back to Australia.'

Lily stared at her sister blindly. 'But I thought you were coming back to Bolton to stay.'

'*Here*!' Louise laughed, bright with malice. 'Oh no, I don't think so. Clem will take me back, he has to. I know too much about that man to let him cheat me.' She tugged at the hem of her skirt sharply. 'I've done enough for you, Lily –'

She didn't see the slap coming, only felt the back of Ellen's hand as she struck her.

'What the hell!' Louise said, cupping her face and cringing.

'You bitch!' Ellen hissed. 'You selfish, vain, cold-hearted bitch –'

Immediately Lily was on her feet, moving between her sisters.

'Ellen, don't.'

'*Don't*?' Ellen countered. 'Don't do *what*? Tackle her for what she did to you? Someone has to: Louise has got away with too much for too long.' Angrily she turned to Louise. 'You stole your sister's child. You took Emma. You moved house and never let Lily know where her child was. You let years pass and never even had the kindness to send a note and tell us Emma was alive. No photographs, no news, nothing. You nearly ruined your own sister . . .'

Louise slumped back into her seat, her cheek scarlet where she had been struck.

'Emma was well looked after. No one could have looked after her as well as we did.'

'You wanted her then because it suited you, not because you loved her,' Ellen snapped. 'And now you want to get rid of her, dump her back with her mother, because it no longer suits you to have her around.' Her eyes narrowed.

'Oh, I get it. You want to get back with Clem, don't you? And Emma would cramp your style. So now you've brought her back here for us to take care of.'

'Ellen,' Lily pleaded, 'it doesn't matter –'

'Yes it does!' she replied heatedly. 'I saw what she did to you, Lily. I watched how you suffered. If you don't remember what you went through, I do. No one on earth should hurt another person that much – certainly not their own sister.' She turned back to Louise. 'Have you ever thought what it might do to Lily if she took Emma back now?'

Louise glanced from Ellen to Lily, and then she folded her arms.

'I thought you'd be pleased.'

'How could she be.' Ellen snapped. 'We agreed to a story a long time ago, Louise. It's been the lie we've all lived. To all intents and purposes the daughter Lily gave birth to died. How can she suddenly produce Emma like a rabbit out of a hat?'

Stung, Louise stared at her sister. 'You have to stick to the story,' she said flatly. 'Just say Emma is your niece.' Pleadingly she turned to Lily. 'You can do that, can't you?'

'Why should she?' Ellen retorted, answering for her sister. 'Maybe Lily doesn't want that now. Maybe it would cause problems –'

'How could it?' Louise replied sharply. 'Say Emma's my child, that she was named after your dead daughter. People wouldn't find it surprising that you're looking after your niece –'

'She's not a child,' Ellen cut in. 'Emma is old enough to look after herself.'

A closed look came over Louise's eyes. Ellen saw it and registered it.

'Why did you bring Emma to England?' she asked Louise coldly. 'To keep her well away? Why?' She glanced over to the door. 'She's a handful, isn't she?'

'Emma's just high-spirited –'

'Oh no!' Ellen replied shortly. 'What has she done?'

'For God's sake! You make her sound like a criminal!' Louise replied heatedly. 'I just thought that she needed to be away from certain people.'

Certain men more like, Ellen thought.

'Emma's a grown woman now,' she went on firmly. 'Not a child. We can't control her or tell her what to do. I have my own life and so does Lily –'

Louise looked from one sister to the other, confusion clearing.

'Oh, I see ... Your preacher husband doesn't know about your little girl, does he?'

Lily was speechless, Ellen momentarily stunned.

'Perhaps it wasn't such an unkindness I inflicted on you, after all, Lily? Perhaps it was convenient for you to have Emma out of the way.'

Rising to her feet suddenly, Louise walked to the fire-place and rested one arm along the mantelpiece. She was no longer cowed, no longer intimidated. Just confident, sure of herself again.

'A preacher, hey? Well, well, well, I never thought you were interested in religion, Lily. But they can be very serious, those people, can't they? Very single-minded. Very honest . . .' Her tone was coaxing, mock sympathy. 'Didn't he want children?'

She saw Lily flinch and knew she had scored.

'I'm right, aren't I?' Louise crowed. 'The preacher didn't want to have to look after someone else's brat. Or maybe that wasn't it at all. Maybe he thinks of you as a poor widow who lost her child. It would be terrible for him to find out that you had been lying all these years. Things like that can ruin a marriage –'

'Louise, I'm warning you,' Ellen said.

Hurriedly, her sister put up her hands to ward her off. 'Oh no, Ellen, you can't bully me now. Not now I know the truth. You'll have to be very careful how you talk to me, or I could find myself blurting something embarrassing out, just like that!' She clicked her manicured fingers. 'If I got nervous, that is. But if I was treated well, then I might not find myself saying anything much at all.'

There is was, Ellen realized, the threat. The ghost was about to leave the glory hole. If Louise got what she wanted, she would keep quiet. If not, she would tell Josiah about Emma. It was acidly simple. In uneasy silence, Ellen watched her sister as Louise poured herself some tea and sipped at it. What was she planning now?

'Ellen, it's all right. I want to take Emma back,' Lily said defiantly, fired up with unexpected confidence. 'She's my daughter, I want her back.'

Louise raised her eyebrows. 'What about the preacher? He wouldn't take it well, and you don't want to be dumped by two husbands, do you?'

'I don't care, I want my daughter back –'

'Lily, think about it,' Ellen said warningly.

But her sister was adamant. 'I want Emma back.'

'But you can never admit who she is,' Ellen went on. 'She can't be your daughter, only your niece. Lily, you can't admit that you lied to Josiah. You can't risk it, you know you can't. You think you don't care about him any more, but I know you. You couldn't take any more unpleasantness. You need that man –'

'I need my daughter.'

'She never will be your daughter!' Ellen snapped. 'Emma's grown up, she's not the baby who left. She'll make her own life and move on – and if you told the truth, where would that leave you? You need Josiah. You need the security he can give you. If you really want to leave him, Lily, then do it in your own time, not under pressure. And don't do it thinking that Emma would fill the space he left. That would be a disaster.'

Lily shook her head. 'But she's my daughter.'

'Technically, yes,' Ellen said, her voice icy. 'But most people believe that she's Louise's child . . .'

'Well *I* can't keep her!'

Ignoring her, Ellen continued to Lily: '. . . which is exactly what they are going to *continue* to believe.'

Louise's voice was hard. 'I've told you –'

'*You* don't have any say in the matter any more!' Ellen snapped, turning away.

God knows how Reg would react, but there was no real choice, was there? And besides, he had always detested Louise. It would have been better if Ellen could have talked to him about it first, but there was no time; this had to be sorted out here and now. If it wasn't Louise might change her mind, create all kinds of mischief. There was no option. None at all.

'Emma can come to live here.'

'*Here!*' Lily said, aghast.

'Yes, here,' Ellen replied. 'There's room now. Thanks to one of Walter's little schemes coming off we've an extra bedroom, and she'll be company for Bess.'

'But this is a dump,' Louise said scornfully.

'So take her back with you, and see how Clem would like that,' Ellen replied flatly. 'I dare say you can blackmail him into keeping the marriage afloat, but I don't see him wanting to keep Emma as well. Not now she's grown up. I know you, Louise. You want a free rein and you can't have that if Emma's around. You need your husband back far more than you need your supposed daughter.' She paused. Then: 'Clem's been playing away from home, hasn't he?'

It was a direct hit, Ellen realized as she saw the stung expression on Louise's face. Clem was having affairs . . . Well, who could blame him?

'You shouldn't really waste time, Louise. Some younger, prettier woman might be moving in on your patch already.'

Her vanity was the only thing keeping Louise upright.

'Clem loves me.'

'I doubt it,' Ellen replied, standing up. 'And I don't care. I'll tell you frankly, I don't like this. I think Emma's trouble – sorry, Lily – but I've a hunch there's more to all of this than Louise is telling.' She walked over to her sister and stared at her. 'For years I've watched Lily suffer for what you did, and that's the only reason I'm helping you out. It's not for Emma, or for you – it's for Lily. But I tell you now, if Emma comes under my roof, she lives by my rules. That's my final offer – take it or leave it.'

An hour later, Lily let herself into the house on Church Street. Josiah was away preaching, unaware of her nocturnal comings and goings. Exhausted, Lily leaned heavily against the front door, letting the latch key fall from her hand. Ellen was right about her. Ellen always was ... Slowly she walked from the vestibule into the kitchen and sat down heavily, too tired to go to bed.

She thought of her sister and found herself almost admiring Louise. It was an unwelcome thought, but *she* could never have travelled alone, gone back to Australia to save her marriage. She hadn't even had the courage to go out there to try to find her lost child. Louise was a bitch, but she was strong. Lily thought she herself could never have lied and blackmailed people to get what she wanted. She could never stand up to anyone.

Which was why she was still married to a preacher she didn't really love. She had thought she was brave, but she wasn't really. She might kid herself, but she couldn't really live without Josiah. Ellen had been right: Emma was grown up, no longer a baby. Lily would never be able to turn back time and reclaim the years she had lost with her daughter. It had been a dream, and now it was time to wake up.

The best she could hope for was a friendship with the girl everyone thought was her niece. The girl who would go to live with Ellen would never know the truth because – the thought made Lily wince – it wouldn't matter to her. Emma didn't need her mother, she was an adult, beautiful and rather awe-inspiring – so far removed from Lily that she probably wouldn't even believe the truth if it was told to her. Better to let Ellen take her in, as she had done with Bess. Better to watch from the sidelines. The time for motherhood had come – and gone.

It was sad the way things were going to work out, but it was probably for the best. She would stay with Josiah and keep her secret – but not for ever.

She had changed. She was no longer serving time, but marking it.

Chapter Thirteen

Bess was trying not to cry as she walked along. No one must see her crying; she couldn't show herself up. Carefully she skirted the main streets and then turned into Derby Street, seeing the sign of the billiards hall and a huge red arrow pointing down the stone steps. The paint was wearing off the sign, neglected. Well, who needed a billiards hall in wartime?

She wanted to run the last few yards, but forced herself to walk, taking the steps calmly and pushing open the door to the billiards hall. But once inside – without being able to stop it – Bess began crying and slid to the floor, the door locked behind her.

It didn't matter that she hadn't loved him, she had been fond of Geoffrey as a friend, liked his ways, his humour. Liked *him*. He had only been called up a few weeks ago, hardly enough time to get into trouble, let alone die ... Bess willed herself to get up, but stayed where she was, her heels drumming furiously on the floor. It was stupid, useless, it made no sense – the bombings, the demolition of people's homes, the news coming daily of countries invaded, places no one had even heard of before. They talked about boundaries and nations and people no one knew in Bolton, discussed tactics, listed losses ...

Losses ... the word slammed into her head as Bess pulled her knees up and sobbed.

Feet materialized in front of her.

'Hey, kiddo,' Walter said, lighting up two cigarettes and giving Bess one. As though it was perfectly normal, he sat down on the floor next to her and blew smoke rings into the cold hall.

'Geoffrey was killed,' Bess said, biting back tears.

Gently Walter slid his arm around her shoulders and she leaned gratefully against him. She would have loved Walter Shawcross whatever he was like, being her beloved Reg's brother, but over the years they had formed their own special bond. When she had been naughty as a child, it was Walter who had covered for her, lying, his snake's eyes unblinking; when she had had arguments with Ellen, he had taken her side, even when she was wrong. *Especially* when she was wrong. And it was Walter – Disappearing Walter – who had brought home tales of life beyond the Northern town of Bolton.

Ill-educated and naturally dishonest, Walter had God's gift for adventure, and had known from childhood that life was always over the next wall, beyond the next town. Although not as physically brave as Reg, Walter was an emotional giant. He simply had no fear – of love, poverty, disgrace or happiness. Bouncing from love affair to love affair, from petty thieving to prison, from youth to middle age, Walter remained constantly inconstant. His visits unannounced, sometimes staying a day, sometimes a month. No one knew – because Walter didn't. He went where he wanted, when he wanted.

And Bess loved him for the example he had set her: for the courage to live. Ellen might still remind Walter of the loss of her savings; she might despair of his prison record and womanizing, but Bess adored him. He never paid back the debt, of course, but he had had the extra bedroom made, and after a good patch, he'd had a bathroom put in the flat above the billiards hall. No more sitting on the outside lav, he said, lounging in a hot bath with a fag in one hand and the racing pages in the other.

And then he'd be off again, God only knew where, Reg defending him to Ellen, Bess missing that all-too-familiar rasping voice calling for her.

'Sorry about your boyfriend,' Walter said quietly now, blowing smoke between his lips.

'He wasn't a boyfriend, just a friend.'

'I'm still sorry.'

His shoulder was bony against her cheek, but the cheap cloth of his jacket smelled familiar and safe.

'Why did it happen, Walter?'

'Because it did.'

A moment passed, someone moving overhead.

'It's not the same now, is it?'

Walter inhaled deeply and then let the smoke out slow. 'With that girl being here, you mean?'

'Yes, with Emma here.'

'It's different.'

'I don't like her.'

'I don't blame you.'

She laughed, her tears already drying as she flicked the ash off her cigarette.

'I can't believe she's my cousin. She doesn't seem like anyone in this family.'

She's not your cousin, she's your sister, love, he wanted to say. Your *sister*. And no, she's not like anyone in this part of the family, but she *is* like your bloody aunt.

'She's beautiful, though.'

Walter nodded. 'She is that. But then so are you.'

'I'm not in the same league, Walter,' Bess replied honestly. 'What makes her so beautiful?'

'She has all the right parts in all the right places . . .'

Bess laughed again.

'. . . and she has a voice which would make steel melt.' He paused. 'But she'll never amount to anything.'

'Rubbish!'

'Listen, I know women, and that one will end up unhappy – for all her looks.'

Silence settled for an instant between them.

'You should have married.'

'Nah, I like playing the field.'

Bess smiled. 'You'll get old one day, and *want* to settle down.'

Walter's face was thoughtful as he looked at her.

'I'll never settle down, kiddo. And I'll never get old.'

Ellen was wringing out the washing, her back to Reg, up to her elbows in water. On the radio some man was talking about Germany, but she wasn't listening; she knew all about it already, read the papers, heard the gossip. War gossip, war news. Wars everywhere – at home and abroad. Rationing: butter, four ounces; sugar, twelve ounces; meat scarce.

'Is Emma going to get a job?' Reg asked suddenly. He was too old for the services, but that didn't stop him from volunteering for war work.

'Where could she work, she's no experience?' Ellen asked her husband.

'She could get training at the munitions factory. God knows there are enough around here. Other women are working there.'

But Emma didn't want to do that, it was beneath her.

Ellen had tried to be patient, to put down her niece's sulks as reaction to her being so unceremoniously dumped by Louise – the woman she thought of as her mother. But there was no way of getting through to Emma. She was prickly, defensive, almost embarrassed. At one point she had told Ellen that she was expecting Louise to come back for her, but when Ellen told her that Louise wouldn't be coming back she looked so vulnerable; so suddenly childlike.

It was obvious that Emma had been spoiled, petted like a pedigree animal, beautiful and highly strung. It was obvious too that she had seldom been corrected; manners did not come naturally to Emma. And yet although she was sure of her beauty and often sounded very mature, there was some insecurity about her which showed in her eyes at times – a fear, a hard realization of rejection. Her mother had dumped her. Her parents had separated and neither of them wanted her. Instead she had been left far away, with people she didn't know, in some Godforsaken dump. All her familiar surroundings and possessions had gone; everything Emma owned had been crammed into an initialled suitcase. She had been dismissed, thrown out from the warmth into the cold. And it frightened her.

On many occasions Ellen had wanted to tell her the truth, to make the unbearable, bearable, but she couldn't, the bloody secret that had dogged them all for so long still clanking behind Emma like the chain after Marley's ghost.

Ellen genuinely believed that it would make Emma's situation easier to bear if she knew that Louise wasn't her real mother. But then what? Then Emma would have to be told who her real mother was – and Lily hadn't taken her on now that she'd returned to Bolton. She'd been rejected not once, but twice. There was no solution – Emma was going to be hurt either way.

As she was hurting now. And yet Ellen wondered just *what* Emma was missing. The woman she thought was her mother? Or the man she thought was her father? Or her old lifestyle? Who knew? No one, because her niece confided in no one, just kept to herself and became sullen if asked to do anything.

'Spoiled rotten,' Reg said bluntly, 'that's what she is, spoiled rotten.'

'It's difficult for her,' Ellen replied. 'You have to give her time to settle down. Things are so different here. She must feel it – away from the Whitleys and all her friends.'

'You think she had friends?' Reg asked. 'I'd say she had Judas's talent for friendship.'

She could have a friend here, Ellen thought. If only Emma knew that she had a sister; if only Bess knew . . .

They would have a bond then, a person to whom each could always turn. Like her and Lily.

But not like her and Louise . . .

It was strange to think that in the end Emma had more of Louise in her than Lily. Try as she might, Ellen could see nothing of Lily in her niece. It wasn't that Emma was cruel – she didn't have that spiteful streak of Louise's – but she was cold, without feeling. She felt rejected, and that made her defensive.

Could normal affection and warmth have been drummed out of her as a child? Or had it never been there? But it must have been, Ellen thought. Harold had been the friendly type – too bloody friendly, in fact – and Lily was always sweet-natured. So surely there must be *something* of her parents in Emma. Or maybe her upbringing with the Whitleys had obliterated every trace of Browning influence. Watching her niece, Ellen wondered to what sunny paradise they had sent the child that had left her as cold as a wilderness inside.

'Tea, Josiah?'

He glanced up at his wife, one finger resting on his place in the Bible.

'We had tea only an hour ago, Lily. We must be more frugal. There's a war on.'

She wanted to ask him then about the First World War when he had been an army chaplain. It was getting difficult to think of Josiah as he had been: full of fire, yet autocratic; an actor, through and through, playing out his role with sublime confidence. He would have taken care of his uniform, made sure the soldiers knew that he was there to offer them comfort. A hero. Almost.

He was too old to see service this time round, stayed home instead and preached to whoever wanted to hear him . . . Lily studied her husband. He had gained weight, heavy round the middle and the jowls, the full head of hair iron grey. His looks – once so distinguished, had failed and he knew it, his vanity bruised, his temperament uncertain now that his heyday had passed.

Nothing had turned out as she had expected – not one thing in her whole life. And as for Emma . . . Lily sat down beside Josiah in front of the small fire, smouldering under its load of cheap coal. How had she managed to give birth to two such beautiful children? Oh yes, Harold had been a handsome man, but both Emma and Bess were remarkably attractive. She should have been proud – and she was. Of Bess. Not of Emma, not of the spoiled, sullen young woman who treated her with such obvious disdain. Even for an aunt.

Lily folded her hands on her lap and watched Josiah read. They had never had much money. Every penny had been stretched, every item scrutinized, a cheaper version bought if possible. No lights were ever left burning, coal cheap and soap cheaper. Every household detail was overseen by Josiah; another mark of his control. Like affection. Lovemaking had ceased, comfort eked out intermittently, and only after Lily requested it. A ritual humiliation to go alongside all the other humiliations heaped up over the years.

But it was easier to give way to Josiah than to fight him. She had no desire to do that; so she just watched him and waited. Besides, to all intents and purposes, Lily had no real reason to leave. Josiah wasn't violent, or even verbally abusive. He was always kind, and believed that he had gained complete control over her by that wicked kindness. And his pity, his pompous, misplaced pity.

She didn't feel the same patronizing pity from Bess, though. They were not particularly close; that privilege was reserved for Ellen and Reg. But her elder daughter came to see her on a regular basis and told her about her job, Lily marvelling at her intelligence and confidence.

They never talked about her father though; Harold

Browning was off limits, as thoroughly dismissed by Bess as his surname. In Reg Bess had found the father she wanted, and no shadow of a natural father could be permitted to impinge on that relationship.

At first, stupidly, Lily had expected Emma to call and see her as Bess did. Surely they would become friends and visit her together. But soon it became apparent that her younger daughter felt no tie to the woman she believed to be her aunt. When they were parted it had been easier to imagine their reunion and the relationship that would follow. Lily had realized that it could never be one of mother and daughter, but aunt and niece would be something, she had thought, and then maybe – just maybe – they might grow to like each other and become close.

But that had been just another fantasy, Lily thought, looking down at her hands. Emma obviously thought that Lily was just a weak-willed, insignificant woman who was bullied by her husband – certainly no one to admire or respect. But did Emma respect anyone, Lily wondered. It was patently obvious that she loathed the Shawcrosses and had all of Louise's worst traits: vanity, selfishness and a pounding lack of compassion.

'Lily?'

She looked over to Josiah.

'What is it?'

'I was just thinking . . .' he paused, she held her breath hopefully, wondering if he had somehow picked up on her mood, tuned into her sadness. '. . . that perhaps another cup of tea *would* be nice, after all.'

She couldn't possibly stay here, Emma thought, glancing round the tiny makeshift bedroom. It was so dismal, so poor. Outside a cat mewled to be let in. Condensation ran down the windows. Louise had stayed in Bolton for only a few weeks, long enough to make sure that Emma was firmly ensconced in Derby Street, and then she left.

She never thought Louise would really go through with it, but she had. Reason and persuasion had failed, Emma's day in the sun was over ... Biting her lip, Emma turned to look out of the window, the sound of Lord Haw-Haw droning on over the radio downstairs. It was a punishment, Emma realized, a way of curtailing her adventures. And all because of a man. Jerry Tolas. *You just don't go around breaking up marriages*, Louise had shouted to her, *You're acting like a cheap tart.*

So when Jerry told Emma had he wasn't going to leave his wife, Emma had played the field a bit and people had gossiped, and that, together with her father leaving Louise, had put the cap on things. She was out of control, so she had been sent to England either to cool down, or to bring trouble to someone else's doorstep ...

And now she was stuck, no money, no chance of escape. Just stuck in some freezing hole ... Emma closed her eyes, near to tears. She had to be tough, she was strong, she could cope. There was a way of getting out of here, she just had to find it, that was all.

What really hurt was that there was no one here she could talk to. Not the dreadful Reg, or Walter ... Emma shuddered. Hadn't someone said that Walter Shawcross had been in jail? *Jail*. It didn't bear thinking about. She thought of his long narrow hands, with the nicotined fingers, and his rasping voice. His skin was white, colourless, like everyone else's in Bolton, the sun never shining for long and never making an impression on the slate-dark streets.

To make matters worse there was a war on. Blackouts at every window, Ellen annoyed if she stayed out late, asking her where she had been, Reg disapproving, telling her she'd get a reputation.

'No decent girl hangs around the streets –'

'I was walking.'

'Walk indoors next time.' Reg countered. 'I don't want any trouble. Act like a lady, can't you?'

It had all been so different in Australia, before the war. She had been so admired there, and there'd been so many young men around. But not here. Here the only men Emma saw were the ones who came to the billiards hall: boys who stood open-mouthed gaping at her, or old men, too ancient to be called up, smoking and chatting in the semidark.

What a place to end up! Emma thought incredulously. She had foreseen her future as a good marriage to some businessman in Sydney, a fine house, children one day. Certainly plenty of social life – but not here. Here they wanted her to go out to work in a munitions factory with girls who came from the cramped streets that surrounded her.

She couldn't do it, she simply couldn't. There had to be some way she could get out of it. But there wasn't . . . Louise had left Emma with no money, no means, just passed her on to her sister – who was a stranger. Which was hardly surprising as in all the years that Emma had been growing up her relations in England had seldom been mentioned.

Now and then her mother had made reference to Ellen and her husband *being in business*. Business! What kind of a business was running a billiards hall? And as for her other aunt – married to a preacher, and as timid as a child. Fretfully, Emma wrote her name in the moisture on the window – *Emma Whitley* – and then rubbed it out furiously.

She had to find a way to get out of Bolton. Fast . . . Her forehead rested against the cold glass of the window, her hands tucked into the sleeves of her cardigan. Homesickness welled up in her all at once, her sullen reserve suddenly cracking, hopelessness settling over her. She felt unwelcome. Unloved.

'Hi,' a voice said suddenly behind her.

Emma stiffened, her expression hardening as she turned and saw Bess.

'It's freezing up here.'

'Put some more clothes on then,' Bess replied, hovering by the door. 'I just wondered if you wanted to go out.'

'Where?' Emma replied, her tone sarcastic. 'Where *is* there to go in this dump?'

'We could go to the pictures –'

'I'm tired,' Emma said, cutting her off and lying down on the bed.

Hesitating by the door, Bess could imagine how she would have felt if the situations were reversed, and much as she disliked her cousin, she felt sorry for her.

'Look, Emma, you have to try and settle down here.'

Dismissively, Emma put one arm across her face, covering her eyes.

'Why?'

'Because you live here now.'

There was a long pause, Emma never moving.

'Did you hear me?'

'Oh, leave me alone!' Emma snapped, sitting up, her eyes brilliant.

She was close to tears, Bess realized; the tough front was only an act.

'Come on, do let's go to the pictures. There's a Humphrey Bogart film on –'

'I don't want to!' Emma snapped, swinging her legs over the side of the bed and gazing out of the window. 'How can you bear living here?'

'Because I'm happy here,' Bess replied, her tone cold. 'This is my home –'

'God help you then.'

Bess's patience cracked at the words. 'All right, so it's not what you expected! Sorry. It's not a palace –'

'Hah!'

'– but it's not a slum either. Besides, you should realize that we're all doing our best for you.'

'Who asked you to?' Emma replied hotly, her beautiful

voice hardening. 'I never asked anything from any of you. It's not my fault I'm here. I never wanted to come here.'

'But now you are here, you could try harder,' Bess countered, her face colouring. 'Ellen and Reg are doing their best, but it's difficult supporting another member of the family. It's obvious that they've no money. We all have to work —'

'So that's it!' Emma cut in spitefully. 'They've sent you to plead their cause — *go and tell your cousin to get a job.*'

'They never said anything,' Bess replied, walking over to the bed and staring down at Emma. 'It isn't like that here. No one talks behind anyone else's back. If we have something to say, we come out and say it.'

'Well, bully for you,' Emma responded bitterly, staring up at Bess. 'Anyway, Lily doesn't work.'

'My mother's married —'

'Oh, so maybe I should get married instead of getting a job,' Emma smiled winningly. 'That shouldn't be too difficult.'

'You don't marry for convenience.'

'Why not? I bet that was what Lily did.'

Stunned, Bess stared at the young woman facing her. It was one thing to have a go at her, but not her mother. Bess might not be that close to Lily, but she had grown up feeling more that a little protective towards her.

'What the hell would you know about my mother?'

'It's not difficult to guess that her marriage wasn't a love match,' Emma went on unperturbed. 'She hardly seems infatuated with the preacher.'

'She's had a hard time,' Bess said warningly, 'and you can't judge her.'

'I can, and I will,' Emma replied, the golden voice metallic. 'She's weak. You all are.'

To her astonishment, Bess suddenly burst out laughing.

'What the hell is so funny?'

'You are,' she said finally. 'Who d'you think you are?

Someone special? Someone we should all be in awe of?'
Bess was still smiling mockingly. 'I don't know what you
were like in Australia – maybe you were thought of a bit
of a catch – but you're a no one here, Emma. No one has
time to be impressed by you. There's a war on, in case you
hadn't noticed, and too many good people are getting hurt.
No one has time for your little tantrums.' She walked to
the door and turned. 'I'm more than willing to get on with
you. I'd have liked a friend, and you could certainly do
with someone to talk to. But it's up to you. Just remember
one thing – when you've got over feeling so sorry for yourself. You *need* us, Emma. We don't need you.'

'I don't need anyone!'

'You do,' Bess said quietly. 'Everyone needs help. Just
be grateful there are people here who are willing to give
it.'

'And what if I don't take it?' Emma challenged her, the
lovely face white with spite.

'Then it's your loss. Not ours.'

Chapter Fourteen

He had to admit that he had never expected to feel this way about anyone, Peter Holding thought, walking through Bolton and pausing at the entrance to Derby Street. Maybe it was because of the war, that uneasy sensation that life could be over any day, that made everything so precious. Or maybe it was the madness of a forty-eight-hour leave. Or maybe, just maybe, it was because Bess was beautiful and he couldn't imagine living without her.

They had been so secret about the whole romance. She had said nothing to anyone, and neither had he. Perhaps she just felt the way he did – that by making their love public it might be threatened, taken away. Spoiled. He had not told her that he was coming home on leave, had wanted to surprise her, arriving in Bolton with sufficient time to call in on his father first.

Arthur Holding lived on the respectable outskirts of the town, in a good solid house which unfortunately had seen better days, neglected now since his wife died. Only photographs reminded him of Dorothy, photographs of her on the mantelpiece and, by his bed, next to the one of his son in uniform. First a private, but quickly an officer, which was only to be expected from the son of a businessman.

From the first Peter had been born to do well, in a modest way. Born to inherit the small engineering works by the River Irwell, his future assured, security certain. He would never be wealthy, but he would never want, and he had something solid to offer a wife when he found the right girl.

But then just after the war had begun Peter had found

himself sitting next to a young woman on a bus going slow and steady through the town. He had just signed up for the army, his papers in his pocket, the bright uncharacteristic sun making the evil of war seem ludicrous.

Bess had smelled faintly of soap. Her profile had been turned to him, the slight upturn of her eyes fascinating. Obviously deep in thought, she had not noticed his scrutiny but when she'd got up at her stop Peter had felt a sudden urge to follow her. It is madness, he thought, as he walked behind her. What am I doing? She might be married, spoken for. But he didn't believe it. Something about her – something indefinable – told him that this was the woman he had waited for.

She walked quickly, almost outpacing him, then disappeared into the building that housed the *Bolton Evening News*. A reporter? Or just someone coming to tell a story? Peter favoured the former; she had been too purposeful, too sure of her surroundings to be on unfamiliar territory.

He waited there for two hours until Bess materialized again and when she did it was going dark. It was crazy, but he couldn't stop himself falling into step behind her and following her all the way to Derby Street. He saw her go down the basement steps of Shawcross's Billiards Hall. The wrong side of town, his late mother would have said, obviously a girl from the rough side of the tracks.

Frowning, Peter wondered why she had gone in there. It wasn't the kind of place he expected a young woman to go alone, but then suddenly he remembered something he had heard a long, long while back, about the Shawcrosses, something his mother had once said. Walter Shawcross was a rogue, she'd explained, Reg a hard man, but honest, and he and his wife had taken over the care of their niece and brought her up as their own. Peter struggled with the memory. It had been a long time ago, but he was certain that that was what his mother had said. And then something about the girl's real mother marrying a preacher . . .

Not that it mattered. The young woman he had followed was, he guessed, the same girl his mother had spoken about. He stared at the grim building. How could someone who looked like her come from a dismal place like that? Then as he stood there, a light came on suddenly in the basement, quickly hidden by the drawing of a blind.

Well, so what did he do now? He wanted to speak to her, it was *urgent* that he speak to her. But what could he say? I've been following you. I've been waiting for you for years ... Oh God, Peter thought. He had fallen in love. Love at first sight. It was enough to make a cat laugh.

But the next day Peter was back, waiting to catch sight of Bess, and the next, and the next. And on the fourth day, entering the newspaper office, Bess finally noticed a stocky, dark-haired man at the street corner and thought he looked familiar. She thought he looked even more familiar a few hours later when she went out to get some lunch and he was standing on the pavement.

Embarrassed, Peter glanced away.

'Excuse me.'

He turned at the sound of her voice, her dark blonde hair glossy under the one o'clock sun.

'Yes?'

'Are you following me?'

Her voice wasn't from the wrong side of the tracks, and her confidence wasn't commonplace either.

'I ... I ...' he hesitated, dark brows drawn together, hands deep in his pockets. 'Yes,' he said at last, looking her full in the face. 'Yes, I was following you.'

She raised her eyebrows. 'Why?'

'I know you ... I mean, I think I know you.' He was blundering, foolish. 'I saw you the other day on the bus.'

'And?' She wasn't being rude, just curious.

'I wanted to know you better.'

There was a flicker behind her eyes and then Bess turned on her heel and walked off.

Mortified, Peter ran after her. 'Listen, I didn't mean anything by it –'

'I don't know you. Please go away.'

'I didn't want to offend you.'

She was walking briskly, crossing Deansgate.

'Well, you have offended me. Now go away.'

'Please,' he pleaded, 'let me explain.'

Turning suddenly, Bess nearly took him off balance.

'Explain what? You've admitted that you followed me. I don't think there is anything left to say.'

'I just –'

'If you don't stop it, I'll call a policeman.'

Immediately Peter stopped walking.

'I think you're beautiful,' he said recklessly.

'I'm not surprised,' she replied, walking on without looking back.

From that moment Peter Holding was determined to have Bess Shawcross, and set about finding out everything he could about her, pressing his father for information. Her mother *was* still alive, he discovered, and married to Josiah Wake, a well-known figure in Bolton, a cantankerous, arrogant man who belted out his hellfire sermons three times a week and twice on Sundays.

But Arthur Holding could tell his son precious little about Lily. No one knew much about her; she had simply retired into the vast shadow of her husband's ego and never re-emerged. Though Peter pushed him, his father could remember little else. Except something about Ellen Shawcross's sister going to Australia.

'Now Louise *was* a real snob,' Arthur told his son, laughing. 'Bragged about what she had and where she was going.'

'What happened to her?'

Arthur shrugged. 'I don't know. They weren't our type, we never mixed with the Shawcrosses.' The old man paused. 'Your mother thought they were common.'

Common. . . the word lingered like a miasma over Bess.

147

Common, no match for a respectable young man with a future. Or so everyone would have said – if they had known. Not that there was anything *to* know for months, Bess refusing to speak to Peter, before he went to training camp and never replying to the letters he wrote after that.

She kept them though, Bess told him later, all tucked up the unused chimney in the bedroom, to guard her privacy. Then finally – one day in early October – he received a letter where he was stationed in Kent.

> Dear Peter,
>
> Well, I don't really know what to write, except that I thought I should after all your letters. We still haven't been introduced, but I've found out all about you – and it seems that you're quite respectable.

He smiled at that; she had been checking him just as he had been asking about her.

> As you know I work for the paper, war correspondent – in Bolton! But otherwise there's not much to tell you. You know where I live and so you must know about Ellen and Reg – and Walter. If you don't, Disappearing Walter is my uncle. Ask round, people will tell you *all* about him. Everyone knows Walter.
>
> And I know about you now, a man of substance, with your own family firm. Not quite a billiards hall though, is it?

Was she mocking him?

> The rationing makes things hard at home, but we manage, as I hope you do. I imagine things are a lot more difficult where you are. If you want to, you can write to me again.
> Bess.

So he did, every day. Sometime only a couple of lines, sometimes pages. He wrote about the conditions, and about his fellow soldiers, making clever drawings in the margins. Sometimes he would talk about when he would see her again, soon he asked her for a photograph, and many months after Peter Holding began writing to Bess, he told her he loved her.

Carefully arranging to cover a story in Manchester to coincide with Peter's twenty-four-hour leave, Bess hurried to St Anne's Square. Evening was falling, the church in darkness behind her as she waited. Her excitement was intense. This was the third time they had met up, always hurriedly, always greedy for more time to talk, to plan, to look ahead. There were kisses and they held each other, but nothing more. That would have been wrong for both of them. This was to be nothing tawdry. They had their whole lives to make love. But for all of that, Bess realized how much she was attracted to Peter and knew he adored her, always touching her face, her hair, and laughing in that way lovers do. At nothing, and everything.

Hurry up, Bess willed him. Hurry up . . . He was late. Delayed, the bitch time biting into the twenty-four hours and making it too short, too hurried. Bess paced the street and pulled her coat tightly around her. She was cold, chilled, her skin longing for him.

Then suddenly he came around the corner from Deansgate. Was he so handsome? God, she hadn't remembered that. And so tall? . . . Her feet began to move, to hurry towards him. This was her man, *her man*. He had seen her too and had broken into a run, both of them almost colliding as they flung their arms around each other, Bess resting her head on Peter's shoulder, her lips against his neck.

'God, you're beautiful,' he said, drawing away to look at her. 'New hairstyle?'

She raised her eyes heavenwards.

'Same as it always is.'

'Adorable,' he replied, sliding his arm around her shoulder. 'We don't have much time.'

'I love you.'

He hugged her tightly against him.

'I love you too,' he said, kissing her mouth and neck. 'I can't believe I'm here, and that you're with me. I was worried that you wouldn't be able to get away.'

'I'm on a job here,' Bess replied, 'a story –'

'You don't have to go –'

She laughed. 'No, I've done it already. The time's ours now.'

They ate little, and then sat for a long while talking in a small hotel foyer in the middle of town. Blackouts covered the windows, there were servicemen checking in and out, a few girlfriends and wives coming to meet up with them. Bess knew that some of them would book rooms for a few snatched hours but, although tempted, she never suggested it. And neither did Peter. So they talked and held hands and let the greetings and departures take place behind them, an owlish clock watching from the wall. Hurry, hurry, it reminded them, time's passing, say what you want to say. But hurry.

'I've missed you so much,' Peter said for the twentieth time, taking her hand and looking into the palm. 'Oh . . .'

Bess leaned forwards.

'What do you see?'

'I see a wonderful life, with a man who adores you, and children.'

She smiled, feeling his finger stroke her palm.

'What about a career?'

He frowned and leaned further forwards, as though he really was reading the lines.

'You'll be editor of the *Manchester Evening News*!'

Laughing, Bess swotted him on the head.

'It's true!' Peter insisted. 'Look at that line there, it distinctly says – editor of the *Manchester Evening News*.'

'Does it say when?' Bess asked, winking at him.

'After your marriage,' he replied seriously, a woman suddenly bumping into the back of his chair.

Startled, Peter let go of Bess's hand as the woman apologized – and then he glanced up at the clock.

'Oh God!' he exclaimed. 'Look at the time.'

Flustered, Bess stared at him.

Had he just proposed to her? Was it really a proposal or a joke? Damn that woman for interrupting him! Frustrated, she rose to her feet, wondering how to ask him. But it was too late, the moment had gone. He was preoccupied, hurried, anxious about missing his train.

Together they hurried down the streets towards the station, Peter holding her hand tightly, Bess silent. Oh God, let him mention it again, let the train be late, let us have just five more minutes . . . But when they got to the station it was crowded, the train was getting ready to leave, Peter hurrying them both through the barrier. Flinging his bag on to the train, he jumped on board and then pushed a space for himself at the window. His head was suddenly one of many heads, his hand among many as Bess reached for it.

'Be careful,' she said quietly, her voice breaking.

'*What!*' he shouted.

'*I said, be careful!*' Bess called back, the train starting to move, Peter's fingers gripping hers, neither of them able to say another word as they looked into each other's eyes. Then the train suddenly picked up speed and pulled away, Bess running down the platform to keep up as Peter's fingers were drawn slowly, but firmly, out of her outstretched hand.

My darling,
    I never got the chance to say what I wanted to –

and now I've run out of nerve. When I see you it seems
so simple, but when I'm away, things seem so different.
I know you love me, and you know I love you. Oh
Bess . . .

Peter stared at the letter he was writing. Why hadn't he
asked her there and then? Annoyed, he picked up his pen,
then paused. It was impossible to say it on paper, he would
have to wait for another month. He had another leave
coming up, one Bess didn't know about. He would surprise
her then. That was the thing to do. That was what he *had*
to do.

Decided, Peter put the letter back in his wallet and
sighed. He would wait, it would be worth it in the end.

Which was why he was now standing at the end of Derby
Street and savouring the moments before he saw Bess again.
Would she find him changed? Or, God forbid, would she
be disappointed? His palms were suddenly sweaty with
panic. What if she had met someone else? A girl as pretty
as Bess would be sure to have admirers.

No, no, he thought, she wouldn't cheat on me. She would
have told me, written to me and explained, she wasn't
short on courage, or honesty . . . And yet they had kept
their relationship secret. He from his father, she from her
family. No one knew about them. Was that caution, or
guile?

Oh God, Peter thought despairingly, what am I thinking?
What am I doing? Just walk over the road and knock on
the door and ask for her. Go on, do it!

But what if she wasn't there? Or if she didn't want to
see him? Peter's gaze fixed on the grim black-sooted billiards hall. What he most wanted in the world was inside,
like a diamond in a pile of coal dust. He loved her, she
loved him. There was no time for secrecy any longer.

But still he hesitated, only turning when someone tapped

him on the shoulder. Bess had seen him from the end of the street and run all the way to him. Her spectacular slanting eyes were moist, her lips warm when he took hold of her.

And there – in public, in the middle of Bolton, only yards from the Shawcross Billiards Hall – Peter Holding finally proposed.

Chapter Fifteen

The noise of feet clattering down the steps to the billiards hall made Ellen rush out.

'What's going on?' she asked Bess, turning to Peter. 'And who's this?'

'My fiancé,' she beamed. 'Meet Peter Holding.'

'Pleased to meet you,' he said, putting out his hand to Ellen. 'I've heard so much about you.'

'Well, I've heard nothing about you,' Ellen replied, shaking his hand and turning back to Bess. 'You're a dark horse and no mistake.'

'I just wanted to see if Peter felt the same way as I did,' she explained. 'I had to wait and see – and then if nothing had come of it, no one would be any the wiser. The war – it just makes everything so uncertain.'

Hurriedly, Ellen shooed them inside and closed the door, pushing a makeshift draught excluder at the bottom. Bess, engaged! She was stunned, wondering what she thought about it all. Peter – that was his name, wasn't it? – seemed nice enough. Well spoken, nice-looking in a underplayed way, and an officer. Quite a catch.

But that wasn't what was important, Ellen thought, what mattered was Bess and her happiness. She had never seemed to care much for anyone before – apart from Geoffrey Tyler – and she had always insisted that theirs was merely a friendship. So wasn't this exactly what she had hoped for? To see Bess settled? But who was this Peter Holding? A thought struck her suddenly, *Holding* – wasn't there an engineering works by that name on the outskirts of Bolton, near the old isolation hospital?

'Are you Arthur Holding's lad?' Ellen asked Peter.

He smiled. 'Yes, that's right.'

'I met your mother once,' Ellen said, without explaining just how she had met Dorothy Holding.

It had been such a long time ago, towards the end of the last war, when meat had been all but impossible to find. Giving up on her usual butcher in Spa Road, Ellen had walked for a long time, making for the better part of town. She'd known that whatever meat was available would be more expensive, but Bess had been little then, and Lily had needed building up after Emma's birth so Ellen had been determined to find something whatever it cost her in coupons.

Arriving at Thompson's Butchers, she began to queue, aware of her shabby coat and wool headscarf. The other women had been obviously more prosperous, but she'd ignored the stares and waited patiently for her turn. The butcher had been running out, Ellen had seen that, but she'd reckoned there should still be something left for her – even if those in the queue behind her would be disappointed.

Then when she'd finally reached the counter she'd been just about to speak, when a woman behind her had said, 'Mr Thompson, how are you today?'

Ellen had ignored the woman and asked, 'What have you got?'

But the butcher had been looking over her head to the person behind.

'Hello, there, madam, I think I've got something in the back.'

She was invisible, Ellen had realized. She had wandered onto unfamiliar territory and was being usurped, the woman from the wrong side of the tracks being reminded of her position.

'My husband was saying how nice it was to see you and Mrs Thompson the other day –'

155

Ellen had turned on the woman behind her. 'It's my turn.'

She'd stopped talking, studied Ellen with a patronizing look, and then had turned back to the butcher.

Ellen had got nothing that day. Only a bitter taste of class, and a sour reminder that war or no war, some things never changed. The woman had been Dorothy Holding, the mother of the man who was now wanting to marry Bess.

The billiards hall seemed even grimmer that evening as Ellen walked through, the couple following behind her. Smoke and beer lingered on the air, and damp was creeping in, making the basement smell. The tables would suffer for it, Ellen thought, but what could they do? There wasn't money to heat the place and anyway their customers weren't that particular.

But perhaps Peter Holding was.

Ellen could hear them laughing behind her as she pushed open the door to the kitchen, Reg looking up from his evening paper.

'Reg, Bess has something to tell you,' Ellen said simply, walking over to the fire and riddling it. Aware suddenly of how she looked, she took off her apron and tried to tidy her hair. 'Go on, love,' she urged her niece, 'tell him.'

'We're engaged,' Bess said, taking Peter's hand. 'You don't mind, do you? I mean, you're both pleased, aren't you?'

Reg was on his feet in a moment, studying the young man who had just walked in. God help you if you hurt his girl, Ellen thought. No amount of position or influence will count then.

'I wanted to ask your permission, Mr Shawcross.'

'Like hell,' Reg replied. 'You've already made up your mind.'

Hugging Bess, he smiled, but then drew back. His eyes had a faint expression of injury in them, of regret. He had known nothing of Peter Holding before that instant, his girl for once not confiding in him. And there was more to it than that – Bess married would mean Bess gone.

But generously he shook hands with Peter. 'So, what d'you do?'

Ellen winced, wondering how Peter Holding would take the question. Would he think it impertinent? Reg Shaw-cross, a billiards hall owner, asking about his prospects?

But apparently Peter wasn't bothered.

'I'm away at the war at the moment, sir,' he replied, 'but usually I help run the family business with my father.'

'You Holding Engineering?' Reg asked suddenly, his expression wary.

So he was thinking along the same lines as she was, Ellen thought, wondering if the difference between their backgrounds would prove awkward.

'That's right. It's a good firm, not that big, but success-ful.' Peter turned to Bess. 'I can provide well for Bess, honestly I can.'

'I don't doubt it,' Reg replied, studying him. 'How long have you two you known each other?'

'A few months.'

'That's not long,' Reg said, suddenly protective. 'Are you sure about getting married?'

'As sure as I am of anything,' Peter replied.

Reg studied him carefully. 'She's special –'

'I know that, sir.'

'– and smart.'

'Oh, Dad . . .'

Peter heard the word and mentally filed it. So Bess called him, Dad – but wasn't Reg Shawcross her uncle?

'It's the truth,' Reg went on. 'I want the best for her. She deserves the best.'

Peter was about to reply when someone walked in, coming down the stairs from the flat overhead. Walking in yawning, Emma paused at the doorway and then smiled, her tremendous face shifting from sullenness to interest in an instant.

'Oh, hello.'

Peter smiled in return. 'Hello.'

'I'm Emma,' she said, her voice mesmeric. 'Who are you.'

'Bess's fiancé.' Peter replied, Ellen smiling at the choice of words.

'Fiancé?' Emma echoed, turning to Bess. 'You never said anything.'

She was on the defensive immediately. 'We've just got engaged –'

'But you're in the army,' Emma replied, studying Peter's uniform. 'Surely you won't be getting married until the war is over?'

There was a momentary pause.

'I want us to get married straight away,' Peter replied, turning back to Bess.

Caught off guard, she floundered. Surely this should be something they discussed privately – whether to marry now or wait. It was all well and good that Peter loved her, she loved him, but they needed time and space to plan their lives together, not be forced to make decisions immediately.

Irritated that she had been put on the spot, Bess took Peter's arm.

'Let's go for a walk.'

He picked up the cue immediately, then turned to Reg, who was all too aware of the shift in atmosphere.

'So we have your permission, sir?'

Sir, Ellen thought. What did that mean? Just good manners, or respect?

'We'll have to have a talk,' Reg replied, 'but you've got our permission, yes.'

It was dark when they walked outside, Bess holding Peter's hand, the streets almost deserted. He was unusually quiet, she thought. What was he thinking about?

'Don't you want to get married now, Bess?'

She squeezed his hand. 'I hadn't thought about so quick a wedding. Can't we just enjoy being engaged for a bit?'

'But we *could* marry now,' he went on enthusiastically, 'get a special licence.'

'Peter, there are so many things to think about,' Bess replied, 'so many things to arrange.'

'Not for a quiet wedding.'

'I think Ellen and Reg might like to have a bit of a do. I don't want us to go sneaking off,' Bess responded patiently. 'They've done a lot for me.'

It was all such a rush, she thought. The engagement had been what she wanted, but to get married immediately – now that was something altogether different. She hadn't even met Peter's father.

'Have you told your father about us?'

'Not yet.'

'But shouldn't you?'

'He'll be pleased. How could he not be?'

But she wasn't as sure. Perhaps the founder of Holding Engineering might not be so delighted to hear that his only son was going to marry into the Shawcross clan. It was unsettling just how suddenly her happiness had turned to apprehension – and all because of what Emma had said.

And maybe Emma was right. Maybe they *were* rushing into things. After all, how much did they really know about each other? There was a war on; that made people react differently, made them impulsive. The world was no longer as safe as it had once seemed to her, what with the bombing, women called up for war work, some mutilated soldiers already invalided home. Horrors which would once have seemed incredible were now commonplace. What kind of time *was* it to talk about marriage?

The only time, she realized. Love came whether it was wartime or not, and if she loved Peter that love had to be treasured – and made public.

'So *shall* we?'

159

Frowning, she turned to him. 'What?'

'Shall we get married now?'

'No, not now, Peter . . .' she said after a moment. 'I'd like to meet your father first.'

'So he can give his stamp of approval?' he teased her, taking her hand and pulling her towards a doorway. Tenderly he kissed her cheeks and then her forehead, his lips warm, comforting.

'I just want everyone to be happy about it,' Bess murmured. '. . . and I want to tell my mother.'

Surprised, he drew away, looking into her face.

'You've hardly mentioned her before. Does it matter to you what she thinks?'

'Yes, it does. Lily's not had an easy life; it would be nice for her to feel involved in this.' She laid Peter's hand against her cheek. 'Does that seem silly?'

'No,' he replied, kissing her palm, the night cold around them. 'It seems kind . . .' he kissed each finger of her hand gently, '. . . just like you.'

Oh, she had seen *that* look before, Ellen thought, staring as Emma began to brush her hair in the mirror over the black-leaded range. Jealousy, that was what it was. Pure, unadulterated, jealousy. Bess had a fiancé. Bess was going to get married. Not her. Why not? Emma was thinking, why not her?

She was so like Louise that it seemed more and more believable that Louise was her *real* mother, not Lily. Intermittent letters came from Australia addressed to Emma, which she took to her room and read alone; letters that were never shared, or gossiped over. Secrets . . .

Like so many other secrets, Ellen thought, knowing that Emma would write to Louise that night, scribbling furiously about Bess's engagement. God knows how long it would take the missive to reach Australia, but that didn't matter, the news would be dynamite. And how envious

Louise would be – Bess to marry Peter Holding – Why wasn't it Emma who had captured him, she would think. Probably she would write back to Emma saying as much – you should be getting married, find yourself a good catch like Bess. You've got to settle down, forget the past.

Slowly, Emma brushed her hair, her eyes fixed on her reflection. Later she would go out, hanging around with her one and only friend, Joan Williams, a girl with a reputation. And not a good one. Reg had tried to tackle Emma about it, but she had simply shrugged, telling him that it was none of his business. After all, he wasn't her father, was he?

They had never got on, Ellen realized regretfully. The bond between Lily's first child had never extended to the second. Reg was always guarded, as though he could never trust Emma and had to keep her at a distance. Ellen knew that many times her husband had had to bite his tongue, resisting the temptation to lash out at his niece.

Just as he was doing now.

'It's quite a turn-up,' Emma said, that dark voice low, 'Bess getting married.'

'She's a great girl; any man would be proud to marry her,' Reg replied coldly. 'How's your job going?'

He had finally managed to bully Emma into work, but only weeks after she started at Crowthorn Mill she had been moved from the factory floor to the offices of Mr Leonard Crowthorn. His secretary, no less. Reg didn't like to think about how Emma had manufactured a promotion so fast, but was sure it had more to do with his niece's looks, than her ability.

'Fine,' Emma told him, 'old Crowthorn's sweet.'

He wasn't. He was a bastard, Reg thought, immoral and lecherous, the bane of most of the women who had ever worked for him. His wife had died years before and since then his *modus operandi* had never changed. Hiring a woman, he would flatter her into believing that she was going to be the next Mrs Crowthorn and then, after he had bedded her, Crowthorn would move on.

So when Reg heard that Emma had been moved from the safety of the factory floor to Crowthorn's office, he had tried to warn her.

'Oh, I can look after myself,' Emma had laughed in reply, her mouth wide, red-lipped.

'That's what a lot of other women have said before,' Reg countered. 'I'm just warning you, that's all. He's no good, a womanizer.'

'Like Walter?' she had asked, deliberately provoking him.

Needled, Reg's face had set. 'Did you have to take lessons to get this stupid?'

'But I –'

'You might think you're really smart, but you're not,' Reg had gone on, his voice low, angry. 'If you want to play with fire, Emma, fine – but if you get into trouble, you're not bringing it home. Remember that.'

But she hadn't got into trouble, had she, Emma thought slyly, still brushing her hair as she glanced at her uncle's reflection over her shoulder. Crowthorn was an old lecher, but she was smart enough to keep him on his toes . . . Her hair crackled with static as she increased the brushing . . . So Bess had nabbed Peter Holding, had she? Well, her cousin wasn't the only one who could get married. They could all look so smug now, but she would wipe the grins off their faces.

Peter Holding wasn't that much of a catch; Leonard Crowthorn was a lot richer, and he had a big house on the park. So he wasn't good-looking, or young – what did that matter? He was wealthy. Emma's lips parted. She wasn't going to have her face rubbed in Bess's good fortune. After all, *she* was the one who had come from Australia, *she* was the best-looking one, a good marriage was hers by rights, not her tupenny-ha'penny cousin's.

Laying down the brush on the mantelpiece, Emma then kneeled down and poked the fire, her mind whirling. She couldn't bare the indignity of having to write home and tell her mother the news; Louise would be so furious. Not that she should care about what she thought.

It had been pretend, all that petting when she was a child. All that – *You're my darling baby, your Mummy loves you more than life itself*... Her mother didn't give a damn about her, Emma thought coldly. She'd only stayed in England long enough to check that the Shawcrosses would keep to their word. So eager to escape back to Australia had she been that she'd risked a dangerous, protracted voyage. Rather be bombed, than Boltonized.

Angered, Emma keep her head down and her feelings hidden as she began to stroke the cat. She would show them all! Louise, the Shawcrosses, everyone. She wasn't going to let Bess triumph over her, and she wasn't going to be left alone in the billiards hall with old Ellen and Reg. God, what a life that would be, what a grim, Godforsaken fate.

'Ouch!' she snapped, as the cat suddenly scratched her.

'What happened?' Ellen asked, surprised.

Guileless, her niece looked up. 'I was just stroking her, that was all.'

'But she never scratches,' Ellen went on. 'You must have done something.'

'Or perhaps the cat knows more then we do,' Reg said coolly, from behind his paper.

Chapter Sixteen

Heaving himself up out of his chair, Josiah rose to his feet and struck a pose in the mirror. One hand held high, the other clasping the Bible, his head tipped upwards to lengthen the sagging jowls. He could – if he tried hard enough – imagine that he was little changed, that the impressive figure of years ago was still looking back at him from the mirror. And if he *did* admit that he had aged, he had done so with *gravitas*.

No one could doubt the value of the work he did; preaching to the women left behind and the men he could reach when they came home on leave. Although, oddly enough, few of them seemed to want to talk of spiritual matters when they returned for those few brief days. It was the *time* to talk of God, Josiah thought, what better time was there? This should be his finest hour, counselling, helping the poor soldiers to find strength.

But they didn't seem to want it. Instead far more of them found their way to Shawcross's Billiards Hall instead of the Hall Street Chapel. Dropping his pose, Josiah began to brood. The Shawcrosses had been a thorn in his flesh for years. He had tried to understand them in a Christian way, but they seemed way beyond redemption. Even Lily was showing her true colours now; rarely attending his sermons, spending more and more time in the house. And she could be very cool with his parishioners, very cool indeed.

He also thought that she might be seeing her sister secretly – even after all that he'd said. No, Josiah thought, his wife would never disobey him, not after all that he had done for her. Given her his name, a home, the status of a minister's wife. She couldn't betray him, go behind his back.

But he wasn't sure. In fact, he was getting more and more suspicious of Lily's actions as the months passed. Their love making had ceased long ago, and although they still shared a bed, there was always a cold portion of cotton between them which was never breached. Not that it worried Josiah, he had little sex drive and reserved all his energy for preaching, but there was something about his wife's attitude he found alarming. A distance, a look about the eyes that seemed horribly like distaste.

Josiah coughed and turned from the mirror. He must be wrong; it was nothing. He was just imagining things, that was all. Lily needed him, relied on him. Everyone knew she was dependent, vulnerable, weak. Without him she would be nothing . . .

But then suddenly Josiah found himself panicked, unease gripping him. He needed *her*, he admitted reluctantly. Without Lily he couldn't go on, couldn't maintain his status, his poise. Her quiet admiration had bolstered him up for years; and now, seeing it lessen, he realized that his wife was his bolt hole. He had to find out just what was bothering her, what wicked thing had come between them. Who had turned her away from him? What devil had sneaked into their life and reduced him in her eyes?

He would find out, Josiah determined, full of the fire of righteousness. He would find out and stop it. It was his duty as a husband and as a Christian. It was his duty to Lily.

And to himself.

Winter Hill. Aptly named, Lily thought as they walked to the top and stood looking down over Bolton. The cold was chilling, cutting into her, the clouds low hung and muffled with snow. Beside her stood Bess, her hair covered by a hood, the collar of her winter coat turned up, her nose pink from the chill.

'I wanted you to know about the engagement right away,' she said kindly. 'I wanted you to approve.' She turned to look at her mother. 'You do, don't you?'

Lily stared at her daughter. *My daughter*, she thought wonderingly, you are my daughter. How odd that seems now; I've seen you for so long with Reg and Ellen, in the billiards hall, going off to work, independent, happy that I passed you over to them. Secure. She studied Bess's features in the high chill air. Her face was remarkable, her eyes slightly slanted, the full curve of her lips reminding Lily so much of Harold.

Harold – he had managed one thing well: given her this lovely child, and memories. They had held her in good stead; memories of their making love, of the sweet happiness of their mumbled affections, the pride she had felt in marrying him. She, of all people, marrying the handsome Harold Browning ... The triumph still registered in Lily and she realized that for all the pain of his leaving and subsequent death, marrying Harold had been the greatest triumph of her life.

Having her daughters should have been, but that had been coloured too much by circumstance, and besides, Lily realized honestly, she had been a poor mother. Well, we get what we deserve, she thought. Ellen was more a mother to you, Bess, than I ever was. So how can I resent the bond between you two? Rather I should be grateful that you love me even a little.

'I'm so happy for you,' Lily said, reaching out towards her daughter, but then resisting.

Bess saw the hesitation and immediately took her mother's hand in her own.

'I want you to like him,' she said simply. 'Peter's a good man, a happy one.'

Happy, that was good, Lily thought. Happiness was the one thing on earth that you could never have too much of. No one ever complained – *I'm too happy.*

'And he's got a good position?' she asked, feeling the kindness of her daughter's hand in hers, longing to hold on for ever, as she should have done all those years before.

'His father's Arthur Holding – they own Holding Engineering . . .'

Lily raised her eyebrows. This was good news. Bess had made a fine match.

'. . . When Peter gets back from the war, he's going to run the business with his father. Then in time Mr Holding says he wants to retire and Peter will take over. His father's running the works alone for the time being – until the war's over and Peter gets home.'

There was a firmness about Bess's voice which Lily instinctively picked up on. The way she kept repeating, *when Peter gets back from the war . . . when Peter gets home . . .* never allowing any doubt to colour the future she was so assiduously planning.

'Bess . . .'

'What is it?'

'I wanted to ask you something,' Lily went on cautiously. Was she brave enough? Well, why not? She had been frightened for so long and it had got her nowhere. 'Do you blame me?'

Bess's eyebrows rose. 'For what?'

'For giving you over to Ellen and Reg?' Lily asked, turning her head away, her eyes fixing on a horizon. 'I had to, I was ill and couldn't cope . . .'

Her daughter's fingers curled around hers and tightened. For the first time – the *only* time in their lives – Lily felt a closeness beyond words.

'. . . I don't want you to think that I didn't love you, Bess. I did. I always did and I still do. I think about you all the time.' Lily couldn't seem to stop talking, now she had finally begun. 'I'm so proud of your career and how you've turned out. And now this engagement . . .' Her eyes remained fixed on the horizon; the last sunlight of the cold day was dipping, slipping into twilight. 'I want you to know that I love you, Bess. I always have. Even if I wasn't there, even if I didn't seem to bother about you, I loved you. You were never more than a thought away.'

'Oh, Mum . . .' Bess said brokenly, holding onto her mother's hand as a child might.

Mum, Lily thought. She called me *Mum*. And in that one word she had absolved everything. There was no bitterness, no recriminations. Her daughter had forgiven her by saying the one word Lily had despaired of ever hearing.

'Oh, bloody hell, you're back!' Reg said, straightening up from the till and glancing at his brother. 'I thought you'd buggered off once and for all.'

'Fat chance,' Walter said, walking towards the doorway and pausing.

'Are you staying?'

'For a while. I've got business in this area.'

Reg grimaced. 'Nothing dodgy, is it? Just tell me it's nothing dodgy. Ellen'll go mad if it is.'

Grinning, Walter passed his brother some tobacco. Under the light he looked grey, overtired.

'Are you all right?'

Walter reached for the dimp behind his ear and lit it.

'Fine.'

'You look knackered.'

'It's my lifestyle,' Walter replied, the hoarse voice amused.

Dragging deeply on the cigarette, he sat down and picked up the evening paper as though he had never been away. London had been a diversion, but he liked Bolton and had been whistling as he walked into Derby Street, taking the basement steps two at a time.

'Can I stay for a while?'

'Do you need to ask?' Reg replied, studying his brother's face and remembering the kid who had stolen from the market stall decades before; the young man who had worked the black market, the thief put away for two years over at Strangeways. Then he remembered all the women who had come looking for Walter. *Tell that bloody brother of yours that I'm waiting for him. Tell him he can't treat me like this. Toerag . . .*

'You should give those up,' Reg said flatly, as Walter started to cough.

'I like my ciggies.'

'You like anything that's not good for you,' Reg replied, walking over to the range and putting the kettle on to boil.

'I thought I heard voices,' Ellen said, coming into the kitchen. 'Oh, look who's here.'

''Lo there, Ellen.'

''Lo, Walter.' she replied smoothly. 'Should we expect a visit from the men in blue soon? Do let me know, I'll set a tray.'

'My life's above reproach,' Walter answered her, smiling. 'I was framed.'

'Like the *Mona Lisa*,' Ellen retorted, laying an extra place at the table. 'You can sleep on the kitchen couch, Walter.'

'The billiards hall will do for me – it always has done before.'

'Nah,' Ellen said simply, 'too bloody cold even for the mice. We'll make up a bed on the couch and you can kip down here at night.'

He nodded, pushing some tinned food over the table to her.

'I brought you these.' Rationing had made luxuries almost impossible to find – for anyone but Walter. 'Is that girl still with you?'

'Bess, or Emma?'

'I heard our Bess had got herself a man.'

'How did you hear that?' Ellen asked. 'She only told *us* the news the other day.'

169

'Word travels,' Walter said, tapping the side of his nose. 'And I hear everything. Arthur Holding's boy – not bad, not bad at all.' He picked up the mug of tea in front of him. 'What about the other one – Emma?'

'She's doesn't change,' Reg said, his tone guarded.

'Working for old Crowthorn, I heard.'

'The War Office could use you, Walter. You get the news fastest than Reuters.'

'So – *is* she working for Crowthorn?'

Reg stiffened. The news was all over town and he didn't like it. Emma was getting a reputation for herself – something he was sure she had had in Australia. No wonder Louise dumped her with us, he thought bitterly. She must have been glad to be rid of her.

'She's been with him for a while.'

'As what?'

'His secretary.'

'Ah . . .' Walter said simply, looking into his mug.

'What's that supposed to mean?'

'Nothing, Reg. Just *ah*.'

'She's a handful,' Ellen said sharply, beginning to peel some potatoes.

'I suspect she always has been,' Walter replied. 'No good will come of her.'

'You don't know that for sure.'

'Yes I do,' he said flatly. 'She was seen the other day out to lunch with him.'

Ellen put down the knife she was holding. 'Out to lunch? With Crowthorn?'

Walter nodded. 'Rumour has it that she fancies herself as his next wife.'

'So did every other woman he . . .' Reg trailed off, the unspoken words clanging in everyone's ears.

Dear God, is Emma having an affair with Leonard Crowthorn? Ellen thought, swallowing hard. Oh no, not that. She couldn't, she had to have more self-respect. But then self-respect wasn't Emma's strong suit. And why was that? Because of the way she had been brought up, or because the woman she took to be her mother had rejected her? All Emma really seemed to care about was money. And who had money? Crowthorn.

'I'm going to have a word with her when she gets home,' Reg said, his tone deadly. 'I won't have her bringing disgrace on this house.'

Walter laughed.

'What's so bloody funny?'

'I was just imagining what the beautiful Emma would say to that – *Me bring disgrace! What about your brother. He's a thief.*' Walter smiled. 'Of course the only difference between me and Crowthorn is that I'm an amateur and he's a professional.'

'I wish she'd never come here,' Reg said coldly. 'She's been nothing but trouble and she's been worse since Bess got engaged. I think she's jealous.'

Walter drained his mug. 'You should be glad she's taken up with Crowthorn and not some decent man.'

'It's not funny!' Ellen snapped. 'She's Lily's child, and my niece. I feel responsible for her. What would happen if she *didn't* hook Crowthorn? Oh, don't look at me like that, Reg! We have to face the truth, and you know it. This is no time to dodge the issue. If she *is* sleeping with that man . . .' Reg winced, '. . . and he dumps her, then what? Who would have her then? And what would it do to Lily to find out what her daughter's like? You know my sister, she'd think it was all her fault.'

'Emma would have turned out the way she has whoever brought her up,' Walter said flatly. 'She's too much of Harold Browning in her, and too little of Lily.'

'I still think I should have a word with her,' Reg replied, 'try to talk some sense into her.'

'She's a born whore,' Walter said flatly. 'Let her get on with it.'

Chapter Seventeen

It was past eleven when Emma finally got home that evening. Reg and Ellen had gone up to bed and only Walter was still up, sitting on the makeshift couch by the dampened-down fire, smoking. His face in the dim light was drawn, his hands white, liver-spotted, the bones prominent. He heard the door open and the soft footfall come across the billiards hall and then looked up as Emma walked in.

She was a beauty, no mistake about that. Her eyes widened as she saw Walter.

'Well, well, well.'

'I've been better,' he said calmly.

'You look a bit sickly and no mistake,' Emma replied, walking past him towards the kettle. Her right hand touched its side and then she reached for a mug. 'Want a cup of tea?'

'You should have more sense.'

She turned, amused. 'What *are* you talking about?'

'Crowthorn.'

Languidly, she made the tea, poured herself a cup and added milk. Over the rim, she stared at Walter, her eyes unblinking.

'I do what I like.'

'I heard.'

'You should talk! You always do what you want.' She paused, stared at him. 'Are you here to make trouble for me?'

'Could I?'

She shrugged. 'I bet you'd like to.'

Walter thought she would leave him then and go

upstairs, but instead she sat down on the old rocker by the
fire, putting her feet up on the fender.

'Did you know my father?'

Surprised, Walter balked. He had to remind himself that
Emma was talking about Clem Whitley, not Harold
Browning.

'No.'

'What about my mother?'

Louise, not Lily. 'I never liked her.'

'Why not?'

'Louise was – *is* – a snob. Thought she was better than
everyone else. Had ideas way above her station, though
God knows why. All hat and no knickers, that's Louise.'

Emma listened, but said nothing.

'Why all the questions, Emma? Are you two in contact?'

'Not really . . . I mean, we write, but you know how it
is in wartime – the letters don't always get through.'

She was on the defensive, trying to appear nonchalant
to cover the hurt.

'Did she manage to get Clem to come to heel?'

'Oh yes, she got Dad back,' Emma replied, as though it
had been a foregone conclusion.

'So you must be planning to go back to Australia as
soon as the war's over?'

Her gaze was level, met his without flinching. She's a
tough one, he thought, real tough.

'Things aren't much better out there than they are here
now. The war's changed everything.' Her right foot tapped
on the fender. She was irritated, suspecting that Walter
had guessed that Louise didn't want her back; that she
hadn't mentioned her daughter's returning once, just said
that she hoped Emma had settled down in Bolton . . .

'Mind you,' Walter went on smoothly, 'why should you
go back, now that you think you've nabbed old
Crowthorn?'

Although Walter expected it, Emma didn't turn to look

at him, just kept staring into the last remnants of the fire. She had a luminous quality about her, he thought, something sexual, feral. It was obvious, underlined by her voice, and the way she moved. Had she been more willing to apply herself she could have utilized her beauty more profitably. But she was lazy, too ready to take the easy way.

'So, what about Crowthorn?'

'What about him?' Her tone was challenging.

'He'll never marry you. You know that, don't you?'

She blinked, then laughed harshly and stood up, towering over him. Walter had the distinct impression that she might lash out, her temper barely controlled. God, he thought, it would take a strong man to master her.

'What makes you think he won't marry me?'

'He never married any of the others,' Walter replied.

'They weren't me.'

'True . . .' Walter stretched his legs out in front of him and crossed his ankles. 'but don't you think you owe something to Reg and Ellen?'

'Like what?'

'Loyalty, dignity. They took you in.'

'So? They took Bess in too. They *like* taking in strays.'

Her bitterness winded him for an instant. She was very young, yet chock-full of spite.

'Don't hurt them,' Walter said quietly.

'They're not children –'

'I'll repeat it. Don't hurt them. If you do, Emma,' he continued coldly, 'I want you to know that you'll have me to answer to.'

She knew that he meant it. Emma knew that in Walter Shawcross she had met her match. He was her real enemy. They were two of a kind. She was so transparent to him, she could have been a pane of glass.

'You can't do anything to hurt me –'

'I can do more than you think, Emma. And I *will*.'

Then she struck out with all the force of Louise's practised cruelty.

'I doubt it. You're just a common little thief, Walter. No more, no less.'

Over the following months, Peter's letters came regularly, Bess reading and rereading them, then writing back, pouring out her feelings, just as he did. Nothing would go wrong, she said repeatedly, nothing. They were going to be happy. Bugger the war, nothing was going to stop them being together – when he got back. After all, she wrote, how long could the fighting last? It had been going on for nearly three years now, it had to stop soon. Everyone said so, especially with the Americans involved. God, didn't everyone see what a waste of time it was? What a waste of time, and men?

Peter wrote back and reassured her. They would be fine. Darling, I love you, I love you. Just hold on. I think of you all the time and carry your photograph. It's summer now, he wrote, things never seem so bad in the summertime. Perhaps it would be over by Christmas. OK, so they had said it before, but maybe *this* Christmas would bring the end of the war.

Don't forget me, Bess wrote. Don't stop loving me, Peter wrote back. Take care, they both wrote, we have the rest of our lives together. Take care, Peter. Remember to duck, there's no bullet with your name on it.

Stay careful, stay safe. Stay mine.

Josiah could hardly believe it. Tears poured from his eyes, making a fool of him, his tight little congregation watching him in embarrassment. Outside a siren wailed, the parishioners quickly hurrying to their feet, eager to get away from the bombs and the crying man in front of them.

Staggering off the pulpit, Josiah followed them blindly, then turned outside the door and walked out onto the main street instead. It was past five, the autumn night coming in slow. But not the planes, humming in the sky overhead, making for Manchester and the River Irwell and the industry in the valley. Stumbling, Josiah ignored someone calling his name as he lurched away down Trinity Street.

He couldn't go home, not there of all places. His vision was blurred. How could he cry in public? What would people think? His nose ran, his mouth hanging open as he tried to pull himself together. He would walk, he would walk . . . where? Where would he walk? Where was he walking to? *What* was he walking to?

If only he hadn't taken that route this morning, if only he hadn't gone that way past the ginnel down Bury New Road. It wasn't his part of town, but he had been called out to visit a parishioner. It had been a bright start to the day, sun shining, hardly believable that there was a war on – until you saw the occasional bombed-out terrace or boarded-up shop. Josiah had been almost happy until he'd gone down Bury New Road, then taken the ginnel for a short cut.

The two women had been talking, headscarves on, wicker baskets over their arms, a child idling around the younger woman's feet. Neither of them had seen Josiah coming and as he drew near he could hear their conversation.

'. . . Look, I'm just telling you what I thought. I saw that Emma Whitley in town yesterday and it struck me there and then. Oh, it's such a long time ago – you won't remember it, I doubt that many would round here – but Lily Wake was married to a bloke called Harold Browning before she married that preacher.'

Josiah had stopped to listen, ducking behind a gate.

'I don't remember that.'

'Your mother would,' the older women went on. 'He died, did Browning. Got shot in the first war. But they had two children, Bess – who lives with the Shawcrosses, and another baby who died.'

Joshua frowned. *Lily had had another child?* Never! She

would have mentioned it to him. It wasn't the kind of thing you kept a secret from your husband.

'The baby died? Ooh, that's a shame.'

'It was that,' the women went on, 'and then I think Lily Browning had some kind of breakdown when Harold left her . . .'

'I thought you said he died?'

'He did, later in the war. But that was *after* he left her.'

Harold had left Lily. But, thought Josiah, he had only been told that Harold Browning had died. He hadn't been told anything about Browning deserting his wife . . . The woman was wrong obviously, confused, she didn't know what she was talking about. It was just old gossip, inaccurate gossip. Lily would have told him otherwise.

'. . . and Lily was so upset that she let her sister Louise adopt the baby and take it to Australia – but the baby died out there soon after.' The old woman shifted her shopping basket from one arm to the other. 'I can't remember how she died. Some illness. Anyway, a short while after Louise had her own baby and called it after the little one who'd died. Another Emma.'

'And that's the girl that lives with the Shawcrosses now?'

'Right. It makes you think, doesn't it?'

''Bout what?'

'How funny life turns out. I mean, Lily gave her child to her sister, and now Louise has brought her own child back here.' The woman nodded to herself. 'It was seeing Emma Whitley in town that made me think back. It's nothing important, just a memory.'

Slack-jawed, Josiah leaned heavily against the gate. His stocky figure buckled, his eyes were unfocused. Lily had lied to him! She had lied. She, so quiet, so needy, had lied to him! And for how long? For years, years and years. How could he trust her ever again? How could he believe anything she said? He had known, *known*, that something was wrong. He had felt it.

And here it was: the truth. Her husband had left her and she had had a 'breakdown'. He had known from the start that Lily was needy, vulnerable. But unstable? Never. Dear God, if he had known before he married her . . . And that wasn't the worst of it. She had lied to him, never mentioned her second child – a baby who had died. How could she hold so much back from him? He didn't know her, he didn't know her at all.

Then another thought occurred to Josiah. If his wife hadn't told him about Harold Browning or her daughter, what else had she kept quiet? Just *who* was he married to?

He had tried to pretend that nothing had happened, but when he got to the Hall Street Chapel as usual and had begun to preach – when he had stood there looking at the congregation – he had broken down.

Josiah Wake had broken down in public. That was what his wife had done to him. She had ruined him.

Now Josiah stared blindly down the darkening street. There was no point avoiding the truth any longer. He had to go home and face Lily, confront her. There was nothing else he could do. Taking out his handkerchief, Josiah wiped his eyes quickly, shame burning like a brand in his throat as he retraced his steps to Church Street and unlocked the front door of his house.

There were sounds coming from the kitchen; Lily was washing, the slop of water echoing in the still house. She would never go into the air-raid shelters, said she was afraid of being trapped in one, so instead she had stayed at home and taken her chances, washing as the planes wailed overhead.

Surprised, she looked up as the door opened.

'Josiah . . .' Her voice trailed off as she noticed her husband's reddened eyes.

'You never told me!' he snapped, walking over to her and snatching the damp sheet out of her hand. 'Why didn't you tell me?'

She knew at once what he meant; after all, she had waited for this confrontation for years. Yet she still played for time.

'Tell you *what*, Josiah?'

'About your daughter,' he blundered.

Your daughter. . . Her heart thumping, Lily wiped her hands on a tea towel. It was time now, wasn't it? The time she had waited for. But she was still afraid. Was she really ready to risk the security he had given her for so many years?

But what emotional security had there been? I paid a huge price for very little, Lily thought. If we had been happy, if we had shared good times, it would have been bearable, but now all I can think of is that – in pleasing you – I cheated myself. And my child.

'Well?' Josiah said sharply. 'Don't you think you should tell me about your daughter?'

Lily hung her head, the words sticking in her throat. 'Emma is my daughter, yes . . .'

He blinked slowly, baffled by the present tense – but Lily carried on before he had time to interrupt her.

'I gave her to Louise when she was a baby. I had to. We all agreed to stick to the same story. We would say that Emma had died soon after she was taken to Australia.' Lily's head was still lowered, otherwise she would have seen the shock on Josiah's face. 'Then after a few months passed we said that Louise had had her own daughter and called her after Emma.'

'What the –'

But there was no stopping her. 'I had to do it. I couldn't support my children on my own after my husband left me.'

'I thought Harold Browning died,' Josiah said, his voice hoarse.

'He did, but he left me first.' She still wasn't meeting her husband's eye. 'I was very low, so Ellen took Bess in and my other sister adopted Emma. I didn't want Louise to do it – to pretend she was Emma's real mother – but it was the only way she would agree to take care of her. I had no choice.' Lily studied Josiah's face for understanding. There was none. In fact, there was no expression at all, just uncomprehending blankness. 'Then one day, Louise and her husband disappeared with Emma. They just upped and left with her, no contact, nothing. I didn't hear anything for years.' She moved over to Josiah, but he stepped back. 'Can you understand how that felt? To lose all contact with your child? Wasn't it bad enough that I had had to let my sister pretend that she was her mother? To let everyone think my child was dead? But even that wasn't enough. Louise had to steal her from me. For years I didn't know if Emma was alive or dead. Can you imagine how difficult it was for me?'

He didn't care, and had suddenly found his voice. 'I suppose I should thank you for telling me all this.'

Lily blinked, understanding eluding her.

'But you knew,' she said. 'You asked me to explain about my daughter . . .'

Josiah smiled coldly, his voice righteous. 'It's strange how God works, His mysteries to perform.'

Panic made Lily bluster. 'What d'you mean, Josiah? What are you talking about?'

'I think you presumed that I knew more than I did. You see, I'd just overheard a bit of gossip – about your having a child who died a long time ago.' Josiah paused to let every word sink in. 'I didn't know that the child had lived and had come back as the town tart. I didn't know that Emma Whitley was your daughter. I didn't know,' his voice rose, 'that I was the stepfather to some little whore.'

Stepping back, Lily stared at him, horrified. She had waited for years for something, or someone, to expose her – but in the end she had given herself away.

'Josiah, let me explain –'

'You lied to me! You didn't tell me the truth!'

'I couldn't!' she snapped back. 'Would you have married me if I'd told you?'

Josiah face's hardened. 'So instead I've married a woman who was a liar.'

Defiance, long overdue, flared up in Lily. She had nothing to lose any more, she had damned herself from her own mouth and now she was reckless. All the times she had mollified Josiah, had listened to him, supported him ... All his petty tyrannies and pompous posturings suddenly seemed ridiculous to her. Why had she stayed with this man? Why had she been afraid of what *he* would think of her? The secret she had hidden for so long was out – she had nothing to fear any longer. She was free of it. And she could now be free of him.

'I can't deny it. Whether you like it or not, Josiah, Emma Whitley is my daughter.'

'She's a tart!'

Lily winced at the word. It was partially true. Emma had gained a murky reputation. Friendly with no one but the flighty Joan Williams, she had quickly become the town flirt, boys hanging around her, talking about her. Even Ellen's blunt tongue had had no effect. Emma did what Emma wanted to do – and the rest of the world could go to hell in a hand basket.

'She's no good. Like the rest of your family –'

'Don't criticize my family!' Lily said fiercely. 'They've always helped me. They never judged me –'

'The Shawcrosses are hardly in a position to judge anyone,' Josiah replied spitefully. 'You duped me, Lily. You fooled me. I thought we agreed when we married that there would be no secrets between us.'

'And have you always been truthful with me, Josiah?' Lily asked him, her eyes searching. 'You're such a good, Christian man, but have you never lied to me?'

He was wrong-footed, suddenly on the defensive.

'My conscience is clear –'

'I wonder about Vera Marshall's, or Sally Plumber's?' Lily replied, the names striking out at her husband and winding him.

Oh, she had kept quiet for a long time, but if Josiah was about to attack her family and remind her of his qualities as a husband, it was only fair that she nudge his memories about his shortcomings.

'I never loved you enough to make a fuss,' Lily added quietly. 'Never loved you enough to care – that's why I let you have your little flirtations.'

'Those women never meant anything to me!' he blustered.

'It doesn't matter,' Lily said. 'I really don't mind. But I wasn't the fool you thought I was, Josiah. I'm not really anything you thought I was.'

Staggered, Josiah blustered, 'We have to discuss this –'

'There's nothing left to discuss,' Lily said evenly. She might be afraid of the future, but she had to go. There was no reason to stay with Josiah now. 'Emma is my daughter. Maybe she turned out this way because of what happened to her. Maybe she would have been different if I'd fought to keep her.' Lily paused. 'I don't know. I just know that what she is, is partially due to me.'

Josiah had expected Lily to beg his forgiveness, to plead for mercy; more under his thumb than ever. But she hadn't, and now suddenly he was the one on the defensive. The realization made him crafty.

'Does Emma Whitley know you're her mother?'

'No,' Lily said simply. 'And I don't intend that she should ever find out.'

Turning away, Josiah sat down, tucking his handkerchief into his pocket and then staring blankly at the cooking range in front of him. Some part of him still expected Lily to ask for forgiveness. When she did, he would punish her, as she had punished him. He wouldn't say what he would do, just leave it hanging. Let his wife consider what she had done, let her feel some remorse, some shame. And then, after a while, he would forgive her. It was the Christian thing to do.

But to his surprise, Lily simply rolled down her sleeves and said: 'I shall leave in the morning.'

Surely he hadn't heard her correctly?

'What?'

'I said – I'll leave in the morning. It's all right, Josiah, I understand how you must feel, how betrayed. It was wrong of me to lie to you, to keep such a secret between us for so long, but I won't embarrass you any further. I have some savings, I'll manage.'

'You're my wife . . .' he said, his voice losing its bluster.

'But I deceived you,' Lily replied, folding the sheets and putting them neatly in a pile. 'I wouldn't expect you to forgive me.'

He watched her as though mesmerized. This wasn't what he had expected, not at all. The vulnerable, needy wife he had bullied for so long had suddenly changed. *Lily didn't need him any more.* Panic made him catch his breath. *She was leaving him.*

'Lily –'

'It's better this way.'

'I think you should calm down,' Josiah said fatuously, his own voice dry with panic.

'But I *am* calm. I'm calmer than I have been for years.'

Josiah's eyes narrowed. Lily wasn't going to leave him and make him look a fool in front of the whole town. Not after all he had done for her. Besides, he would miss her. He needed her . . . The realization of his vulnerability was pungent, and it made him peevish.

'You can't go –'

'I can, and I will,' Lily said firmly, her delicate frame walking towards the door.

'Lily, I'm warning you –'

'You can't warn me about anything any more, Josiah,' she replied, implacable.

Freedom was only a few yards away. She could almost touch it. Freedom from the house, the sermons, the bullying Christian hypocrisy. I can go, I'm strong enough now, she thought, I can get away at last.

'Lily, don't go another step,' he warned her.

But as he said it her hand fixed on the door handle and turned the knob, letting in the cool air from the vestibule. She would walk away, start again. She could do it, she *could*.

'I don't want to have to threaten you,' Josiah said, standing up, his shadow falling over her where she stood, 'but you leave me no choice.'

Immediately, Lily tensed. '*Threaten me?*' she repeated, without turning round.

'Yes.'

'With what?'

'It's for your own good, Lily. You need a home and the protection of a husband. You couldn't cope on your own, you're not that type of woman.'

She turned slowly, her eyes fixed on her husband's face, her voice hoarse. 'Threaten me – with *what*?'

'I would *have* to do it,' Josiah went on, holding his wife's gaze, morally unassailable.

'What!' Lily shouted. 'Do *what*?'

'Tell Emma who her mother is.'

Far away Lily could hear the old carriage clock ticking on the mantelpiece, seconds beating by. It would tick on and on, as it had done for years, marking time. Marking out *her* time spent here. It would be wound nightly, to continue to stamp out the next day, and week, and month. And then years.

The hands would keep clicking round and round, just as she would. Clicking round and round in the tall dark house on Church Street.

Chapter Eighteen

Autumn passed, the winter winding on relentlessly, short-ages pandemic, the weather the most brutal in many years. In Bolton the streets were hard with hoar frost, alleys slip-pery, cheap coal making sooty inroads into the dark sky. The war continued too, Bess and Peter deciding that they would wait until it was over to marry, a church wedding promised.

In Church Street Lily tended house and a few streets away Ellen kept the billiards hall running with Reg. During the autumn months Walter had been busy with the black market, coming and going at all times of night, his thin figure slinking like a wraith through the blackouts. Some-times he would stop for a game with Stan or Shooting Cuffs – getting a potted version of how to win the war.

'. . . I've said it before, they want to get in there and string up that bugger Hitler.'

Bess, helping Reg one evening, raised her eyes heavenwards.

'Cuffs, how can they do that? No one can get close enough to Hitler.'

'We showed them what we could do at Dunkirk.'

'Dunkirk was a –'

Hurriedly Walter caught hold of Bess's arm. 'Leave it alone, let them think what they want.'

'But they talk rubbish half the time.'

He tweaked her nose. 'Oh, hark at the reporter,' he teased her.

'I can't help it,' she replied. 'There's news coming over about the Jews in Warsaw. They're starving them out. They say Hitler wants to rid Germany of them.' She frowned. 'The more I hear, the worse it gets.'

Together they walked into the kitchen beyond, Bess then kicking off her shoes and warming her feet by the fire, Reg looking up from the takings he was counting on the table.

'I saw widow Thwaites this morning,' he said to Walter, winking at Bess. 'She said you looked like you'd lost some weight. Said she'd pop round with a casserole for you.'

'Horse meat.'

'Oh, go on!' Bess said, laughing.

'Women like the widow Thwaites catch you when you're down,' Walter went on. 'Many a man's been seduced by a hot meal. By the way, how's that lad of yours?'

'Fine. I had a letter from Peter this morning.'

'You have a letter every morning,' he replied. 'When's he coming home on leave again?'

'I'm waiting to hear,' she said, rubbing her cold feet and glancing over to the door as Ellen came in. 'I was just saying – Peter wants to be home for Christmas.'

Christmas, Ellen thought. What kind of a holiday would it be? At the sound of feet overhead on the street, she pulled back the blind, but the feet moved on. No sign of Emma, even at ten o'clock at night.

She would be with old Crowthorn, Ellen thought, wondering why her letter to Louise hadn't been answered – one that voiced all her anxieties about Emma. Maybe her sister hadn't got it yet, or maybe Louise just didn't want to be bothered with trouble – which was more likely. Louise wouldn't want to be reminded of her responsibility to Emma. So far away, Louise could duck the problems with Emma, pretend they weren't happening.

Ellen stretched upwards and undid the rope that held up the clothes rack, letting it down and hanging the washing on it: Walter's nightshirt, Reg's underwear, a cardigan of Emma's still bearing a trace of perfume. Expensive perfume which Ellen would never have been able to afford;

perfume which only someone like Crowthorn could buy on the black market.

She could throw the girl out, Ellen thought, she had reason enough. But she knew she never would. Emma was blood, and whatever Ellen thought of Louise, she loved Lily and would do anything to help her sister. Sighing, Ellen loaded the rack and then winched it back up to the ceiling, then banked up the fire and watched as the clothes began to steam.

Behind her, Walter coughed, Bess read the headlines, Reg swore as he struggled to make the takings add up. It would be better when Peter came home, Ellen thought, cheering up. Christmas would see happier times, the family all together and the promise of the wedding to come. There had been too much bloody heartache. It was time for some laughter. She would save up her coupons and get some decent food in, hide the canned stuff away in reserve and get a tree from somewhere. Walter could help with that – although she didn't want to know where he got it from. Yes, Ellen thought, a Christmas tree would be nice; remind them all of the good times.

Christmas would see changes, Ellen decided, rallying her spirits; the family would have a holiday like no other, something to remember for ever. A siren wailed overhead but it didn't shake her resolve. She would drag Lily, if necessary, from that house on Church Street and collect them all together for Christmas Day. Lily could meet Bess's fiancé and they could all drink to the future.

It all hung on Peter, Ellen realized. With Peter came happiness, and the future they all longed for.

'You took my dress!' Bess snapped, flinging open the door of Emma's bedroom and standing furiously in front of her.

'So what?'

'So what! That's my dress, that's so what. I had to save up my coupons for ages to get the fabric.'

Impatiently, Emma flung it across the bed towards her.
'Have it back then. I just borrowed it.'

'You never asked me,' Bess said heatedly. 'I don't like
you borrowing my things. And I don't like you going
through my wardrobe.'

'Afraid I'll find your love letters?' Emma asked her, raising her eyebrows. 'From lover boy?'

Why was she still here, Bess wondered. Why did everyone endure her? No one really liked Emma, they just put
up with her because she was family – and it was obvious
that they were just a convenience to her. It wasn't that
Bess hadn't tried to get close to Emma. She had attempted
to include her, to introduce her to her friends – but Emma
hadn't wanted that, she preferred the company of Joan
Williams and old man Crowthorn.

The thought of him made Bess shudder. If what people
said was true, her cousin was involved with Crowthorn.
No, she couldn't be! Not Emma. She was too beautiful,
she could have anyone, so why pick Crowthorn? Just
because he was rich?

'What are you staring at?'

Bess blinked. 'You. I was thinking about the rumours –'

Emma laughed. 'You should never listen to rumours.'

' – about you and Crowthorn. They're not true, are they?'

Slowly, Emma leaned towards the mirror and checked
her reflection. She had Crowthorn by the nose now, leading
him on, letting him think that she was just about to sleep
with him – but she wasn't, not until he had married her.
Let him pant, she thought, let him wait until I have what
I want, and then he can have what he wants. It seemed
fair.

She stole a glance at Bess in the mirror and seethed. It
was all right for her, she had Peter Holding. Peter Holding,
young and attractive and quite well off. Not in Crowthorn's league as far as money went, but not poor either.
Jealousy shuddered in Emma all at once. She had been

clever with Crowthorn, but her imminent triumph was sour in her mouth. Did she really want to marry him? To walk up the aisle with a podgy, middle-aged man, however rich?

But what choice did she have? No young man loved her like Peter Holding loved Bess. And she couldn't let her cousin best her, could she? Not Emma, not the lovely Emma being pipped at the altar by her cousin. Chewing her lip, Emma remembered the letters from Louise, the urges for her to find someone well off and settle down.

Money's the only thing that matters in the end, darling. Love's all well and good, but it doesn't pay the bills, and men are unreliable. You need security. Learn from my example, Emma, and get yourself some money behind you, then, whatever happens, you'll be in clover.

Don't listen to the Shawcrosses about Leonard Crowthorn – they're just jealous. Maybe he is a lot older than you, but it's security you're after, and he'll be sure to look after a wife who looks like you.

If I was nearer I could help you more, but you do understand, don't you, Emma? I have to be here to keep an eye on your father and protect our interests. Things are improving slowly, but steadily – you must come and visit when things have settled down.

When things have settled down. The phrase said it all, just as the letter did, the subtext reading; I can't help you, so help yourself. Stop dreaming about love matches and marry Crowthorn and you'll be set up for life.

But it wasn't what Emma had wanted to hear. She had longed for Louise to write back and say: no, no, you mustn't go near that man. Come home, I miss you – but her mother hadn't. She had effectively given over Emma all over again – not to her sister Ellen this time, but to old man Crowthorn.

The realization left Emma dry with distress, the new rejection chilling her and killing off any remaining soft notes in her character. Why didn't anyone want her? Why didn't her own mother and father want her? So when Emma looked at Bess and saw her happiness, she felt such envy that she could hardly breathe.

'So, *are* the rumours true?' Bess repeated.

For a long moment Emma was silent. She wanted to shake her head and tell Bess the truth, to talk it out, maybe call Ellen in and ask them to help her, to make everything all right again. She wanted to cry and let them hold her and make friends with them and feel at home, instead of feeling angry and defensive. But she couldn't, and when Emma finally spoke again, her lilting voice was hard.

'It's all true,' she said, watching Bess's face colour. 'Aren't you ashamed of me?'

In reply, Bess merely dropped the dress Emma had borrowed.

'Keep it,' she said coldly, 'I don't want to have anything you've touched.'

Emma laughed, but when the door closed she sat for a long time staring at the faded wallpaper, injured and frightened, and then she began to rock herself backwards and forwards, like a lonely child.

The following morning, woken by the sound of knocking, Emma struggled out of bed and went downstairs. It was Saturday, she thought irritably, who would come knocking so early on a Saturday morning? Surprised to find the kitchen empty, except for the sleeping Walter, Emma walked through the chilled billiards hall and opened the basement door.

'Telegram.'

She put out her hand automatically.

'Sign here,' the boy said, passing her a pad.

Blinking sleepily, Emma did so and then reclosed the

door, staring at the envelope. It was addressed to Bess. No doubt from the brave Peter, fighting at the front. Telling his beloved that he would be home for Christmas. Emma weighed the telegram in her hand. Everyone was so looking forward to seeing him, talking about it constantly: Peter this, Peter that. And talking about the future too. When Bess gets married ... when the wedding takes place ... on and on, without end. Peter Holding had become a saint in everyone's eyes, Bess his good little wife to be.

Pushing her tangled hair back from her face, Emma stared at the telegram, her fingers itching. No, she couldn't open it, they would know. But what if she did open it and then reseal it? Emma paused. No, they'd guess, and then there would be hell to pay. Dry-mouthed, she remembered what Bess had said to her, and the expression of disgust on her face. She hadn't forgiven her for it.

But could she open her mail ... ? What if it was bad news? News of Peter? That would scupper everything. No jolly Christmas then; no future to plan and gloat over.

Unable to resist any longer, Emma tore the envelope open, pulling out the telegram and reading the words:

WILL BE HOME FOR 24 HOUR LEAVE THIS
FRIDAY STOP CHRISTMAS TOO
PETER

So he *would* be home for Christmas, just as they had all planned. And more than that, he would be home this week-end too. She tapped her front tooth with her fingernail, thinking carefully as she pushed the crumpled telegram and envelope deep into her dressing-gown pocket. Bess would be so thrilled, so eager to discuss their plans, so happy to see her fiancé again. She would talk about him nonstop ...

But how could she, if she didn't know? Emma walked towards the lighted kitchen door. No one knew that Peter Holding was coming home except her, and when he did arrive and surprise everyone they would just presume that the telegram had been lost. They wouldn't suspect anything – why should they?

Silently, Emma walked into the kitchen, glancing over to the sleeping Walter. God knows where he had been the previous night, she thought, filling the kettle and putting it on the range to boil.

She would pay Bess back for what she had said. Oh yes, she would make Bess realize that she couldn't talk to her like that. She wasn't a rubbing rag; she had her pride too. She might have been dumped in this Godforsaken hole, but she hadn't asked to be here. She hadn't wanted it.

Carefully Emma pulled back the blinds and looked up to the street, remembering how Ellen and Reg had said they were going up to the market by Lark Hill. Idly, Emma made herself some tea and cut a slice of bread, leaning on the windowsill and looking up at the feet passing.

When she had been a child in Australia the houses had been detached with gardens. When she had been a child it had been warm in winter, sunshine at Christmas, no snow, except for up on the very peaks of the Blue Mountains.

Louise had bought her all kinds of dresses and presents, painting her room yellow and hanging frilled nets at the window. She had made Emma take piano lessons too, and when her father came home from work Emma used to play for him, and he'd clap, although she was never very good ... Emma stared at the feet passing overhead ... Her parents used to tease her, say that she would never have to work because she was so pretty, and her father had told her that she was his favourite girl in all the world.

Then, when she was in her teens, her father found another favourite girl, and then another, and Louise started to shout a lot and dye her hair, and the parties got fewer and fewer, the money tight ... Emma kept staring, waiting for the next feet to pass overhead on Derby Street ... Then suddenly, their pretty daughter became a nuisance. Louise was short-tempered with her, not wanting to have to think about anything except Clem. The shopping trips ceased, and the outings. Emma was told to keep quiet, keep out of the way.

So she started playing her parents up, looking for attention, trying to make Louise spend time with her – even if it was only to tell her off. As for her father, he was more and more distant, the one person she had adored above all others losing interest in her. Hurt and bewildered, Emma had gone on the search for affection, and when she couldn't get it at home, she got it from the town boys.

Then one night her father moved out. Distracted, Louise started making plans avidly. Emma was told that they were going to go back to England, that she would have to stay with her relatives there for a while. I can stay here, she had countered angrily. No, you bloody can't, Louise had replied. You've caused me enough trouble, my girl. You just stay in England for a while and when I've got things sorted out again, then you can come back . . .

They went by ship, the voyage dangerous, Clem having pulled strings to get them to England, hoping that Louise would stay there. It was so cold when they got to Bolton and so depressing, all those terraces, mill chimneys, back-streets. Emma had walked with her mother in silence, hardly believing her eyes, and never, never, suspecting that her mother would leave her there.

Biting her lip, Emma finished the tea she had made and turned – to find Walter watching her.

'Who was at the door?'

'Kids. They brought some wood. Offcuts.'

Wincing, Emma watched him sit up in his worn long johns.

'What did you say?'

'What?'

'To the kids.' Walter fixed his eyes on her.

'I gave them a penny.'

'You carry money in your dressing-gown pocket?'

He was quick, but she was quicker.

'I saw them from the window, before I came down.'

Walter smiled slowly. 'So where's the wood?'

'Under the basement steps. Why don't you go and take a look at it?'

Walter's expression was hostile. 'I don't believe you.'

She smiled thinly. 'No one ever does.'

Chapter Nineteen

Emma, having learned from the stolen telegram that Peter would be coming home that Friday night, waited outside the station on Trinity Street to catch sight of him. Around six, Peter's familiar figure came down the platform, an army bag over his shoulder, his uniform smart, impressive. Altogether a man more attractive than she remembered.

It had taken Emma some time to plan her strategy, but finally she had decided on what she would do and had prepared herself accordingly. No make-up, no glamorous clothes, just a plain dark suit, her hair drawn back from her face, the full impact of her beauty making passing men stare.

At the barrier, she waited until Peter was nearly level with her and then stepped out, calling his name.

'Peter?'

He turned, recognized her and smiled.

'Oh, hello there, Emma.' Then he looked anxious. 'Is everything all right? There's nothing wrong with Bess, is there?'

Bess, always Bess.

She hung her head, her voice low. 'Nothing, everyone's fine. I just had to speak to you.' She glanced up at him, then away.

He was immediately curious. 'What is it?'

'I need a friend,' Emma said, with a catch in her voice. 'Oh, Peter, I can't talk to anyone here. No one understands,' she glanced round uncertainly. 'I've behaved so badly.'

He took her arm, guiding her hurriedly towards the

station café. A headline on the newsstand said, 'BRITISH ADVANCE IN BURMA'. Inside the café there were a few soldiers talking and drinking, a couple sitting by one of the steamed-up windows. As Peter and Emma entered a goods train passed quickly, blowing its whistle into the night air.

'Here, drink this,' he said, passing her a glass, having found them a table and ordered at the counter. 'It's brandy.'

She took it willingly, staring down at the table. She could hear the waitress talking behind the counter and flinched as a trolley clattered past the window.

'So, what is it?'

'I've been seeing Leonard Crowthorn,' Emma said, avoiding Peter's glance. 'I'm his secretary, but everyone thinks ... everyone thinks ...' She broke off, sipped the brandy. It fired her inside. 'It's not what everyone thinks, really it's not.'

Taking a sip of his own drink, Peter stared at Emma's bowed head, surprised that he had never really noticed her beauty before. And she *was* beautiful, ethereally so. Blonde hair, blonde skin, and eyes – he couldn't see the colour because she was looking down – but they were large and thick-lashed.

His protective instinct was aroused. Surely Bess had been wrong about her cousin. Surely they all had. This wasn't some hard piece, this was a nice girl, an unhappy girl.

'I want to be friends with them – the Shawcrosses – but we got off on such a bad footing they don't trust me now.' Emma's voice cracked. 'I don't have anyone here to talk to.'

And then she glanced up, her expression catching Peter off balance. He blinked, caught in the full force of her gaze, suddenly aware that his mouth was dry and his hands were shaking.

'Emma,' he said at last, 'the Shawcrosses want to help you. They're kind people –'

'But they're not my parents . . . and I miss my parents,' Emma replied, her tone lost.

His heart turned. He knew about homesickness, about being away from everyone and everything familiar, about that low ache in the gut that nothing relieved. Emma had been sent away, just as he had been sent away to war, and he understood how she felt. But it was worse for her: her parents had rejected her.

Slowly Emma sipped her drink, tears just starting at the corners of her eyes.

Embarrassed, yet oddly stirred, Peter put out his hand to touch hers. 'Hey, come on, don't get upset.'

'I can't help it, it feels as though I've got no one to turn to.' Emma looked at Peter appealingly. 'You don't know how lucky you are, having Bess. You must feel so wanted, so loved.'

'You'll find someone,' Peter replied eagerly. 'Any man would be proud to have someone like you.'

'You think so?'

'Of course. 'You're very beautiful.'

Emma shook her head. 'No, I'm not.'

'Of course you are,' Peter assured her. 'A man would have to be blind not to see that.'

'Bess is prettier than me.'

He hesitated. 'No, she isn't. She's different from you.'

Emma held his gaze. 'In what way?'

'More ordinary.' He frowned. 'No, not ordinary, more girl-next-door type.'

'And I'm not?'

'You're glamorous,' Peter told her, relieved to have found the word he had been searching for. 'Like a film star.'

For a long instant Emma stared at him across the table, Peter finding it difficult to look away, yet his hand automatically moving from hers. There was something wrong about all of this, he thought suddenly; he shouldn't be here. He should be with Bess. It was all right to try to help Emma, but it wasn't his place to get involved. It was someone else's job, not his.

'We should go.'

She started crying at the words, and Peter leaned towards her anxiously.

'What's the matter?'

'No one wants to spend time with me,' she said brokenly. 'No one gives a damn.'

'Emma, come on,' he urged her. 'Don't cry.'

'I won't embarrass you any more,' she said, sitting upright and wiping her eyes. 'I'm sorry. It wasn't fair of me to come here. You want to be with Bess –'

'Bess is expecting me; I have to go.'

'No, she isn't,' Emma said quietly.

'She is, I sent a telegram.'

'I opened it,' Emma confessed, searching his face for his reaction. 'I know I shouldn't have! I know it, but I did. I wanted to meet you first, to talk to you before you saw them, before they poisoned your mind against me.' She paused. Then: 'Oh, go on, hate me! You have every right. Opening that telegram was a despicable thing to do.'

'You shouldn't have done it,' Peter said coldly.

'You're angry now!' Emma replied, her voice dipping, a sensual laziness creeping in. 'I'm sorry, really I am. But that's me, that's the way I am. Always doing the wrong things. I'm not like other girls, Peter, not like Bess. That's why you should walk away now, before you get involved. I can only bring trouble to you.' She leaned back, folded her arms, her eyes challenging. 'Go on, go back to where you're comfortable. You couldn't be expected to under-stand someone like me.'

He didn't recognize the bait, even when he was swallow-ing it. Instead he felt a sudden surge of something close to anger, followed by curiosity. Emma's beauty was almost frightening, too much for Bolton – too much for him? She had as much as said she was out of his league, and that irritated him. Who was she to dictate his limitations? Carefully Peter scrutinized her. She was beautiful, she was clever and she was dangerous.

And suddenly he found himself wanting her.

'Lily, I don't want to say it, but that girl of yours is trouble,' Ellen said reluctantly, sitting on a bench facing the deserted bandstand in the park, where they had agreed to meet. There had been a massive argument that morning between Walter and Emma, and feelings were running high, so high that Ellen hadn't noticed her sister's silence at first.

She had watched Lily walking up to the bench slowly, her head slightly bowed. The brief spurt of confidence she had enjoyed had been put out, and all that remained was the threat of some telltale darkness in her eyes.

'How's Josiah?' Ellen asked, aware of Lily's quietness.

In reply, she shrugged. The gardens were silent, bereft of people, the sun appearing over the bandstand suddenly and making a brief spotlight on the seated figures.

'He's been very kind since he found out about Emma,' she said. 'But he doesn't mean it. He just thinks he's won, that's all.'

'Does he talk about it?'

'Sometimes. He sounds wounded and asks me how I could have lied to him. "How could you not tell me about Emma?" he says, then calls her names.' Lily's voice quickened when she asked, 'Which are true, aren't they? I mean, Emma hasn't turned out well, has she?'

'She's seems hellbent on wrecking her reputation,' Ellen said quietly.

'I wonder how much of it is my fault. You know, all the years she was away I used to dream about her coming home, dream about how she'd be and how we could be a real mother and daughter again. I would have walked out on Josiah for that ... but she's not what I expected. Not at all. And you were right all along.'

Ellen frowned. 'About what?'

'I was looking for an excuse to leave him. I did still see Emma as a baby in my imagination, and I did want her to fill any gap he left.' She sighed. 'Emma's no good, is she? Like her father, like Harold. Only it doesn't matter if a man runs around, does it? But it matters for a woman.'

A pigeon landed on the grass in front of them, one leg caught up with twine. It stirred as Ellen moved.

'I try and reason with her, but it does no good.'

'If I had kept her,' Lily went on, not hearing her sister's words, 'if I had somehow managed to keep her, she wouldn't have turned out like this. It's my fault.'

'You want to make yourself a martyr, fine,' Ellen said shortly. 'That's your choice.'

Two spots of bright colour suddenly highlighted Lily's cheeks. She was, Ellen thought with amazement, angry for the first time in years.

'Don't call me a martyr!'

'Then don't act like one,' Ellen countered. 'Emma would have turned out this way whether Louise brought her up, or you. It's in her blood. She's too much of Harold Browning in her to be any different.'

'She is my child!'

'More's the pity!' Ellen snapped back. 'You've worried about Emma for years — where was she, how was she? Then you were over the moon when you thought she was coming back. Emma was coming home, all would be well. But it wasn't, was it? Emma turned out to be a bitch —'

'That's enough!' Lily was seething.

'Not nearly enough!' Ellen continued, standing up. 'Emma's no good — and you'd do well to realize that, Lily, before she causes you any more heartache. Leave her alone;

she'll come out on top. That one could fall down a sewer and come up with a gold watch.'

Now Lily was on her feet, standing up to her sister, her eyes sharp.

'She's my daughter. How can you hope to understand how that feels? You've never had a child.'

Sucking in her breath, Ellen stared incredulously at her sister.

'Oh, maybe I was wrong, maybe Emma *has* got some of her mother in her after all. That was a bloody cruel thing to say! Haven't I been a mother to Bess? Well, haven't I? And who took in Emma? Or have you forgotten?'

'Ellen —'

'No, hear me out! You didn't take here in, and neither did bloody Josiah. I did, me and Reg.' Her voice was hard with fury. 'You think you've had a hard life, well so you have, Lily. It hasn't been a cakewalk for me either. It took a lot to support Bess and now there's Emma to think about —'

'I give you all the money I can —'

'Which I'm grateful for!' Ellen snapped, 'but it's not just that, it's all the bad feeling. No one minded Bess around — Reg and I love her like our own — but Emma's another matter. She's difficult and . . .' She broke off.

'And *what*?'

'I don't trust her,' Ellen said flatly, then softened her voice, aware of the impact of her words. 'Look, Lily, let's not fight. We never fought before. But you see what I mean — we're fighting over Emma. She's causing problems. Just like she always does.'

Heavily, Ellen sat down again, Lily standing over her for an instant and then regaining her own seat. The sun had gone, white clouds chased by grey.

'Oh, Lily, you have to stop worrying about Emma now. Do what you want with your life instead. If you want to leave Josiah, then do it. But do it for yourself, not Emma. You're not happy with the man, so why stay? Get out, don't let him tell you what you can, and can't do any more. You're stronger than you were, you could manage without him now. We'd back you, you know that. Listen, Lily, you don't have to take any rubbish from him –'

'I do. You know what Josiah said – that if I left him he would tell Emma that I was her real mother.'

'Maybe he was bluffing.'

Patiently, Lily looked at her sister. 'Maybe he is, and maybe he isn't. The question is – *can I risk it?*'

Dear God, what would happen if Josiah *did* tell Emma, Ellen wondered. What would Emma do if she knew that *Lily* was her mother? How Emma would hate to think that the timid, dominated Lily, married to Josiah Wake, was her mother. How she had sneered about Wake, and poked fun at Lily's old-fashioned clothes, clothes Josiah chose for her. The funny couple that lived on Church Street were a joke to Emma – her pathetic aunt, a person of no importance whatsoever.

Her mother. Not Louise at all, but Lily. And after the first bolt of news, what question would be sure to follow? *Who was her real father?* Not Clem Whitley of the property and mining fortune, but Harold Browning, some dead soldier who had deserted his wife and never amounted to anything.

Ellen swallowed. If Emma was off the rails now, what would she do when she found out who her parents really were? To hear that she had been rejected by her real mother *and then by Louise* – that would be too much to bear. It couldn't be allowed to happen. Emma couldn't find out, she simply couldn't.

Slowly, Ellen shook her head. 'I don't know what to say to you.'

Unexpectedly, Lily smiled. 'That's a first.' Carefully she pulled a headscarf over her hair, tying a knot under her chin. 'Well, it's poetic justice, isn't it? I was so desperate to get married, so determined not to lose Josiah – and now the tables have turned. I couldn't lose him even if I wanted to.'

'Look on the bright side – he might die young,' Ellen said, as they rose to their feet and linked arms. 'Don't worry, we'll manage, Lily. We always do.'

'But for how long?' her sister replied.

He shouldn't be feeling this way, Peter thought, staring at the photograph Emma had sent him. She was incredible, so beautiful, so unbelievable. To have a woman like that, to have a *wife* like that ... Peter stared blindly at the picture. What was he saying? He was going to marry Bess, he loved Bess. It was all planned: when the war was over they would marry. Why rush? Bess had said. They had their whole lives together.

But if you really loved someone you would want to have them at once, today. No waiting. If Bess really loved him, she would have married him last year, when he wanted her to, when he wanted to get a special licence. But she had made him wait. Why? Frowning, Peter stared at the photograph of Emma and then reached for his wallet and took out another picture.

Bess was smiling into the camera. His heart turned, his stomach shifting. But what was the emotion – love or guilt? If Bess had really loved him she would have married him, would have hated the thought that he might be killed, would have been determined to take his name. Well, wouldn't she? There were so many war marriages, people snatching at what happiness came their way – what was wrong with it?

Peter's tongue ran over his lips as he looked from one photograph to the other. He knew that Bess loved him, he loved her, and yet there was something missing – or maybe he was imagining it. No, Peter thought, he wasn't. There was none of the dizzying rush of euphoria that he felt on seeing Emma's handwriting on an envelope or her picture.

He knew he was acting badly – knew that she was too – but he couldn't seem to stop himself, or stop her. Didn't want to, if the truth were known. He was flirting with danger. In the middle of a war he had found even more danger at home than abroad – and, what was more, he *liked* it.

He liked to read what Emma wrote in her letters about Australia, about the money there, the opportunities, about the climate, the difference between Bolton and Sydney. It was another world – something he would never have seen, nor even dreamed about, had she not told him. She filled his head with images, whispered to him in dreams – but not about the little house that he and Bess would buy in Bridgeport Street, and how she would continue to work at the newspaper and he would inherit his father's engineering business. Nothing like that. Emma wrote about a place where you could go swimming naked, where there were jobs galore, and clean air. It was the future, she wrote, no more being tied to Bolton, to England, to the dirt of the North – this was where they could run to, to be free, alive. In love. Together.

Together. . . Peter found his breathing quickening, excited by the thoughts, the ideas with which Emma had mesmerized him. But if he *did* ask her to marry him they would have to leave Bolton – how could they stay? How could they look anyone in the face? His father? The Shawcrosses? Reg Shawcross in particular?

Not that he worried about Emma that way; she was strong, much stronger than him – she could hold her own. So maybe he would be tough enough too. After all, if they really loved each other, what was there to be ashamed of?

He had to make up his mind, and fast. Emma had hinted as much in her last letter. Peter having hesitated when she suggested they had a future, Emma had retaliated with news about old man Crowthorn, about how he had bought her a watch, and taken her to dinner. It was such a transparent ploy that, even while Peter felt angry with himself for falling for it, his jealousy was rising, panic setting in. Someone would get her, if he wasn't careful; some other man would walk off with the prize. And it was then that he knew the depth of his feelings for Emma. Love was one thing, but obsession was quite another.

She would be difficult, demanding; she would cause problems – to himself, Bess, and to their respective families. Emma was no ordinary woman, and played by no ordinary set of rules. She had told him straight: I want this out of life, and if you can do it for me, I want you. If not, I'll find someone else.

Such ruthlessness should have warned him off, but it didn't. It simply made her more of a challenge. He was sure of Bess, of the love she had for him. It was good and honest – but there was no edge to it. And Peter wanted an edge. How much he hadn't realized until he met Emma and then all his deeply repressed feelings came to the surface.

In his heart he loathed Bolton, his father's oily engineering works, and the future all mapped out for him. He wanted to escape – and if he could get away with the most beautiful woman he had even seen, then it was worth risking anything for. Anything – other people's happiness, Bess's, or his own – none of it seemed to matter any more. What he was about to do he may well live to regret, but he had no choice.

That was the power Emma had over him.

Chapter Twenty

As the clock turned seven fifteen there was a short scream. Walter jerked awake on the couch in the kitchen, fumbling to get to the light. Footsteps clattered down the basement steps, the door slamming closed as Bess rushed in.

She stood shaking, her hands clenched, her face blank with shock.

'Jesus,' Walter murmured. 'Jesus, what is it?'

She sat down heavily on the couch beside him.

'Bess, what is it?'

'They've gone.'

'Who?'

'Peter and Emma.'

He blinked, heard the sound of footsteps overhead. Ellen had woken. Reg, a heavy sleeper, would sleep through the Last Judgment.

'*Where* have they gone?'

'Run away,' Bess replied, loosening the collar of her coat. 'To get married.' She began to shake again. 'They're *getting married*!'

Walter flinched. For the rest of his life he would remember the minutiae of those moments: his own cough in the cold morning air, the cat washing herself on the windowledge, the soft fall of coal slack as the fire shifted in the grate, and the stubborn ticking of the clock on the mantelpiece.

There were no sounds of war that morning. No sirens, no all-clears. Just a very cold morning, too sharp a frost even for smog, the window sheened with ice.

'When?'

'Last night. Peter wrote me a letter. I got it this morning.'
She was about to pass it to Walter and then stopped, pushing it back into her pocket. 'Why did she hate me that much?'

'She was jealous of you.'

'But she had everything,' Bess replied, trying not to cry. 'Everything – she didn't need to take my man. Not Peter. For God's sake, not Peter.'

She would cry later, in her room, cry when no one could see her. She had to toughen up to face the town and the gossip that was sure to come. By afternoon, everyone would know about it – her colleagues at the newspaper, the people in the shops, neighbours, friends. Everyone would pity her and point. She would be publicly humiliated . . .

Bess bit her lip hard, drawing blood. She had to be tough, had to be hard-faced. Had to find a way to go on, to work. She couldn't think about the house they had been about to buy, and the wedding, and the future they had all planned.

'Oh God, oh God,' she said, sobbing.

Walter pulled her towards him. 'I should have known something like this would happen. I should have done something,' he said coldly.

And it was then, as he rocked her, that Walter Shawcross made an oath. He would get even with that bitch Emma if it was the last thing he did. He would repay her for what she had done; would injure and humiliate her as she had injured and humiliated Bess. Wherever Emma went, however long it took, Walter promised himself, he would get his own back.

God help her, he would make it his reason to live.

Defiantly Ellen walked round to Church Street that morning. Josiah answered the door and stared at her, surprised. He had forbidden Lily to have any contact with her family and now her sister was on the doorstep! Hurriedly he looked around to see if anyone had witnessed her arrival.

'I want to talk to Lily.'

'She's not in.'

'Oh, get out of my way, Josiah,' Ellen snapped, pushing past him and walking into the kitchen. 'Lily, I've got some bad news.'

Lily was sewing, one hand poised in mid-air, waiting.

'Mrs Shawcross, I must ask you to leave –'

'Be quiet, Josiah, and let Ellen talk,' Lily said softly, her eyes fixed on her sister. 'What's happened?'

'This is my house!' Josiah blustered, his shirt collar undone, his puffy jowls reddening. 'I'm master here.'

'I want to talk to my sister,' Lily said calmly, 'alone.'

'You are my wife –'

Hurriedly, Ellen caught hold of her sister's arm and hustled her to the door.

'You're a fool, Josiah Wake. A puffed-up, pompous fool,' she said, sweeping past him with Lily. 'And if you say one more word, I swear I'll hit you.'

Ellen marched her sister in silence to Derby Street and down the steps to the billiards hall. Without asking any questions, Lily allowed herself to be led, fear tightening her chest. But she wouldn't ask what had happened – wanted to avoid the truth for as long as she could; to savour what little ignorance she had left.

'Go through,' Ellen said, holding back the old curtain, Lily dipping her head as she walked under it.

The kitchen was crowded, smoke rising from the fire and from Reg's cigarette. On the couch Walter was sitting, staring ahead, and on the old rocker by the fire Bess sat motionless. Frowning, Lily glanced at her sister, but Ellen said nothing. There was nothing she *could* say.

She had tried to get through to Bess but it was no good, not even Reg could help her this time. As for Walter, she sat with him, but said little. Bess was, Ellen realized, afraid.

Afraid to face the humiliation of her situation. Afraid to face the stares and the whispers and the laughs.

Haven't you heard? Peter Holding's run off with Emma – little tart. Left poor Bess in the lurch – would you believe it? What a showing-up. And she all keyed up about the wedding and what they were going to do, pleased as punch that she'd nabbed Holding's boy. Couldn't stop talking about it, could she? Should have upped and married him when he asked, and not waited. Not with that Emma piece around.

Taking Bess's arm, Ellen led her into the front room and then motioned for Lily to go in. Without speaking, she did so, hearing the door close behind her as she stared at her daughter. Heavily, Bess slid into a chair by the window and stared out.

'What is it, love? Lily said softly. 'Bess, what is it?' Gently, she touched her shoulder. 'Tell me, love, tell me what's happened. Is it Peter? Has he been hurt?'

Bess laughed.

'You're frightening me!' Lily said anxiously, 'Tell me what's going on. Please.'

'He's left me'

'Peter?' Lily said blankly. 'Where's he gone?'

'On his honeymoon,' Bess replied, glancing up to her mother, her face hard with distress. 'He and Emma have eloped.'

The years slid back in an instant. Lily was suddenly returned to the cramped back bedroom above, struggling with Bess and carrying Emma in the dark days after Harold had left her – deserted her, for another woman, the town talking, pitying her. She could feel the pain as though it was happening at that instant. Which it was – only not to her, this time, but to her daughter. And that made it worse.

She had seen Bess so happy, making plans, making a good match. Making sense of the past, the future looking good. She would have none of Lily's hardships, no traumas, no humiliation. She would be Peter Holding's wife, someone of whom she could be proud, and someone who would be proud of her.

But it had all disappeared, and the woman who had stolen Peter was not a distant cousin, but her sister. The sister Bess didn't even know she had.

'Bess,' Lily said, dropping to her knees beside her daughter's chair, 'I can help you.'

'No one can help me – unless you can stop them,' Bess replied, turning her eyes on her mother helplessly. 'Perhaps you could, if you hurried. Perhaps you could stop them and explain – make Peter come back. He's been stupid, that's all; he's besotted by her. He'd come back, he knows how much I love him. He'd come back if you could just find him . . .' She trailed off, staring blankly ahead. 'What am I talking about? He's gone off with her. He *chose* to go off with her, to marry her.'

It was absurd, Lily thought, incredible. She would wake up soon.

'Peter wrote me a letter – I got it this morning, too late to stop them. He said they were eloping, marrying on his next leave when he'd get a special licence.' Her voice rose, suddenly hysterical. 'He was going to marry me, not her! Not her!'

Lily gripped her daughter's hands tightly. She had felt the same rage, the same bewilderment of having lost her own man, but she still didn't know how to comfort Bess and struggled with the words.

'Bess, calm down. If he could do this to you he was no good –'

'Oh, how can you say that?' Bess snapped, pulling her hands away. 'You of all people know how it feels. Did it do you a bit of good people telling you my father wasn't worth crying over?'

'No, it didn't do me any good at all. Not on the day it happened, or the day afterwards. Or any other day that followed. It didn't stop me wanting him or missing him.'

Taking Bess's hand again, she saw the anguish in her daughter's face. She was in trouble, needing her mother. Wasn't that why Ellen had put them together? So that Lily could comfort her child? But what should she say to her? Be honest, Lily thought, that's all you can do.

'Bess, I'm not going to tell you that you'll find someone else. I wouldn't dare to say that, I know it was the last thing I needed to hear. Maybe you will, maybe you won't – all that is too far in the future to think about.' She held her daughter's gaze. 'I can only tell you that for once I can be of some real use to you –'

'How?'

'*Because I know how you feel*. Ellen doesn't, Reg doesn't, neither does Walter. They love you, but they don't know what you're going through. *I do*. I went through it too, remember. But I wasn't strong like you, Bess. I was weak, I caved in. Got depressed, afraid. Those days were terrible . . .'

'I remember them,' Bess said dully, 'the room upstairs, you crying. Sometimes I think I remember there being a baby about – but that was just my imagination, I suppose. I was very young – maybe I wanted a brother or sister to play with . . .'

Lily took in a breath. Should she confess now to the existence of a sister? No, she couldn't tell her Emma was her sister now. It would be too much, way too much to hear.

'I'm saying that I failed, Bess. But you won't. I couldn't cope, had to hand you over to Ellen, and then it took me years to find my feet again. I've made a mess of my life, Bess – and I won't let you do the same. One mistake, one stroke of bad luck – your father walking out – spoiled my life. Please,' Lily said, leaning towards her daughter and holding her gaze, 'please, Bess, don't let a man ruin your chances –'

'I don't care about my bloody chances!'

'You do. And you *will*,' Lily said firmly. 'Don't end up like me, please. For God's sake, let me do one good thing and show you how *not* to run your life. Don't let what's happened wreck everything, Bess. You've not lost your looks, your brain, your career, or your family. You've lost your man –'

'But I want him back!'

'I know! I wanted your father back too! I still do.'

Surprised, Bess stared at her mother.

'Yes, that's right. I still love him. I still miss him,' Lily confessed. 'But it's over for me now. It's not over for you. Losing Peter seems like the end of the world, but it's not. Believe me, it's not.'

'But I love him,' Bess said blindly. 'Oh God, I shouldn't, but I love him so much . . . I don't know what to do. What do I do now, what *do I do*?'

'You live,' Lily told her gently. 'You grasp your courage in both hands, and you live.'

'Is that all?'

'It's enough for now, believe me.'

Then Lily took hold of her daughter for the first time since Bess was a child, and held her and rocked her until she was quiet.

Chapter Twenty-one

Slowly he walked past the railway line and then turned into Moor Lane, leading to Deansgate. The windows were lighted for Christmas, but since the war, shortages had continued and both food and clothing were still rationed. He stopped and gazed into a dress shop window, looking at a mannequin wearing a red coat. The dummy's face was hard, red-lipped, the wig poor, the style outdated. It looked sad, especially under the dim window light.

Emma wouldn't be satisfied with that coat, Peter thought, moving off and jumping on a bus to take him over to visit his father. Alone. Emma never went with him. She blamed Arthur Holding for her thwarted ambitions, the old man's illness and subsequent early retirement being the reason why she was still in Bolton.

Peter – with all his talk of conscience and duty – had refused to go to Australia, saying he had to remain in England and carry on with the business. It was the right thing to do, he'd said, surprised that she objected. Emma had been so sure that they would get away, that she only had to sit out the war and her dreams would materialize: she and Peter in Sydney, away from bloody Derby Street, the smog, the factories and the billiards hall.

But her plan hadn't quite worked out as she had hoped. Oh yes, she *had* eloped with Peter. He'd found her rooms in nearby Rochdale and they'd married on his next leave, but instead of being able to leave for Australia immediately, Emma had had to wait – and wait in Lancashire. She hadn't thought it out clearly enough; her envy had just pushed her along. She had wanted to spite Bess and she had done. She had wanted to get out of Bolton and had convinced the vulnerable and besotted Peter that their future was in Australia.

Unfortunately she hadn't planned on the war lasting – certainly not for over two more years, years in which she had waited for her husband to come home, living in Rochdale – a town no better than Bolton – Peter coming home on leave to find his wife impatient, irritable, pleading with him constantly to reassure her that they would go back to Australia.

'Darling, you promise, don't you? Don't you?' she would ask, kissing his cheek, his neck, her lazy sexy voice intoxicating. 'I love you so much, we would be so happy in Australia, away from this dump.'

'When the war's over,' he'd told her, 'when it's over, we'll go. You just have to be patient, Emma, and bide your time.'

And to her credit, for a while, she did. They rented out a small terraced house on Colland Street on the outskirts of Rochdale and Emma tried to make friends with some of her neighbours, but her talk of Australia and her upbringing, and how she couldn't wait to get back, grated on them and soon she found herself isolated.

There was nowhere else to turn either. Certainly Emma couldn't show her face in Bolton, or run the risk of bumping into any of the Shawcrosses. The triumph she had felt at stealing Peter away from Bess had been short-lived; she was Mrs Holding all right, but the ring on her finger didn't quite compensate for the small house and the restriction to her lifestyle.

Obviously Peter didn't regret what he had done; he wanted Emma more than he wanted anything. But on one occasion he had suffered badly for his rejection of Bess, finding himself shadowed by Reg Shawcross on the first leave after his wedding. It was on Harland Street that he drew face to face with Reg, standing smoking a cigarette at the corner.

'Holding.'

Peter had tensed. 'Mr Shawcross.'

'I warned you,' Reg said, lashing out and catching Peter a blow to the cheek which felled him. 'You hurt my girl,' he went on, hauling Peter upright and holding him by the collar, 'you bastard.'

Struggling to free himself from Reg's grip, Peter took a swing at him, but missed, Reg pinning him to the wall and punching him several times in the stomach. Then suddenly he stopped, breathing heavily, and let go, Peter sliding, bleeding, onto the pavement.

'I could kill you, but I don't need to. Someone else will do it for me,' Reg said flatly. 'She'll ruin you. That bitch you married will bloody ruin you.'

When Peter finally managed to get home, Emma stared curiously at him, but wasn't interested in hearing his explanation. She didn't want to think of the Shawcrosses and didn't feel remotely guilty. After all, if Peter had really been so keen on Bess, he would have married her. Peter obviously loved her more.

But try as she might, Emma's conscience did start to nag at her and when Peter returned to the war she felt a guilt which was at once unexpected and frightening. Yet if she expected admonition from Louise, it wasn't forthcoming. If anything Louise was pleased to have the problem of Emma off her back once and for all, and the repeated mentions of Emma's return to Australia were met with half-hearted enthusiasm.

So Emma stayed alone in Colland Street, Rochdale, and Bess weathered the pity and the gossip that followed the betrayal she'd suffered. Yet nothing seemed to matter that much any more. Peter Holding had left her and chosen Emma – there was nothing she could do about it. It hurt, but life went on. Her dream had been usurped and Emma was living it. Now all Bess had to do was to start again.

Meanwhile sisters Ellen and Lily watched over the sisters of the next generation, Bess and Emma. In two different towns they kept tabs on each of them, Emma unusually low key, almost reserved, Bess still working on the Bolton paper. Anniversaries stung the whole Shawcross family. The mention of Christmas coming round again reminded them of the time when Peter had left Bess for Emma; and the fatal wedding day came and went without comment.

The wound that Emma had inflicted injured the whole family, and yet, at the same time, created an unbreakable bond. Lily would not even speak Emma's name. Her sympathy was entirely with Bess. Nothing Emma could ever say would excuse her actions. She was, to all intents and purposes, no longer a part of the family.

The isolation hit Emma hard, and she began to grow bitter, striking out at the only person who had stuck with her – Peter. And he couldn't strike back, couldn't stop loving her – because if he did, he would have to admit that he had made a mistake, that he had given up something of infinitely more value. And that he could never do. As Emma had once warned him, he had only himself to blame if he had taken up her challenge.

Peter got off the bus and walked the remainder of the way to his father's house. Since the war had ended he had run the engineering works and reported weekly to Arthur Holding, keeping him informed of what was going on. Arthur was grateful, but wary, seeing his son now in a different light: changed, cheapened, by his marriage.

He had approved of Bess, seen in her some spirit, some class. Yes, he had to call it that, class. She might – as Dorothy would have said – come from the wrong side of the tracks, but Bess was clever, honest, good-looking. A woman a man could be proud of. A woman Arthur would have liked as his daughter-in-law. It was true that she had grown up living over a billiards hall, and that her uncle was Walter Shawcross – but you couldn't hold that against her, and besides, her background didn't show.

But for Peter to marry Emma Whitley . . . anyone could see what she was: trouble. Oh, Arthur had seen women like that before, and they never made any man happy. Peter might be dazzled by her looks, but looks fade, and anyway, beauty wasn't enough – character was what you lived with, day after day. And how would Peter, trusting, fascinated Peter, cope with a woman who was flawed?

Was he a strong enough character? Arthur had thought Peter had shown some strength in picking Bess as his fiancée, but when he ran off with Emma what had that shown? Weakness? Or simply blind infatuation? Or some emotional death wish, which only a woman like Emma could fulfil?

Stirring as he heard the knock at the door, Arthur let Peter in.

'Hello, there.'

''Lo,' his son replied, walking in with a sheaf of papers. 'How are you today?'

Civility, no more. Emma had done that, driven a wedge between him and his son, splitting up not one family, but two.

'I get by,' Arthur replied, taking the papers and sitting down to read them.

He had lost weight, Arthur thought. Not surprising – he doubted if Emma was a good cook. And the return from the war had done Peter no good either. In uniform he had been a hero; in civvy street he was thrown back into managing an engineering works in a bleak Northern town.

Arthur knew that Emma longed to go back to Australia, knew how much she was pressurizing Peter to go with her. And yet Arthur – knowing full well what he was doing – kept his son in Bolton, pleading with him to stay.

Had Peter married Bess, Arthur would have sold the

works and waved them off happily to wherever they wanted to go. But he decided as soon as Emma came into the family that he would blackmail his son into staying. The reason was simple: the marriage would never last. Emma would tire of Peter and leave him. And then what? If his son was in Australia Peter would have nothing, but if he was in England he had security. The engineering works was not glamorous, but it was safe. And safety was something that Peter Holding was going to need.

Maybe not this year, or next. But before too long his son would be grateful for Arthur's stand. I don't want to see you hurt, Arthur thought. Although you've deserved it, I lay most of the blame at your wife's door and besides, whatever pain you've inflicted, Peter, you're going to get back. Twofold.

It was merely a question of time.

'What's wrong with Ted?'

'He's boring, and I don't want to go out with him,' Bess said flatly, turning away from the mirror and sitting down next to Walter. 'You know what I mean, don't you?'

He nodded. 'I'm going away next week –'

'No, don't.'

He smiled. 'Not for long. I've got some business over in Bradford.'

'Is she pretty?'

There were still women who fell for Walter, presents of pies and mufflers pressed on him – until someone got too close and then he was off again.

'You should get out more,' Walter said. 'I know this Ted bloke's not thrilling, but it's a change.'

A change, Bess thought. What kind of change was that when every man failed to match up to Peter? When every touch, and voice, and expression, reminded her of the one man she loved? Why go out? she wanted to shout at them, why bother? There had been only one man for her – and he had gone. She was a career woman now, thirty-two years of age, an old maid in everyone's eyes. And she didn't care. Didn't fret about the fact that all her friends were married and bringing up children. She had her job on the paper and she was doing well. She coped.

She didn't.

'You don't give them a chance,' Ellen said, eavesdropping. 'You shouldn't dismiss a man out of hand. Get to know them, let them show you what they're really like. Time's –'

'Running out?' Bess queried. 'Funny how often I hear that.'

'You know what I mean,' Ellen replied evenly. 'You need a man of your own, a companion.'

'Fine. I'll buy a dog.'

Walter laughed.

'It's not funny!' Ellen snapped. 'Bess should have a normal life, not still pining over that bloody Peter Holding.'

His name slapped down between them, Bess glancing down, Walter pulling his face at Ellen.

'It has to be said!' she retorted. 'The truth has to be faced. You're hanging on to a ghost, Bess, and there's no point in it. You have to get over it – Peter Holding's not coming back. He's gone.'

'Why don't you tell her how you really feel?' Walter asked sarcastically.

'I've held my peace for long enough,' Ellen replied firmly, 'and I've watched a beautiful girl get older and throw away too many chances. There are men out there who've wanted to marry you. There still are, Bess – but you can't push your luck too long.'

'I don't want to get married –'

'That's rubbish! You wanted to marry Peter Holding.'

'Yes I did!' Bess retorted hotly. 'And that's the point. No other man's matched up to him.'

'Then you should take those rose-tinted glasses off, my

girl,' Ellen hurled back. 'Holding was a nice enough man, but when it came to the crunch he acted like a right bastard. You know that, this family knows that, and the whole bloody town knows it. You do yourself no favours pining after him. You should have more respect for yourself. Everyone'll think you're still carrying a torch for him.'

'That's probably because I am!' Bess replied, getting to her feet and hurrying out.

Breathing heavily, Ellen glanced over to Walter.

'And you can shut up.'

'I never said a word.'

'I could hear what you were thinking,' Ellen replied, turning back to the sink and running some water. It was a moment before she spoke again. 'Am I being too hard on her?'

'Yes.'

'But I have to be, Walter. Someone has to shake her out of it, otherwise this will go on for ever. She'll never get married and never be happy if she doesn't put the past behind her.'

He sighed extravagantly. 'Be reasonable, Ellen. How can she? If they'd buggered off to Australia like Emma wanted, then she'd have had a chance to forget what happened –'

'But –'

'No buts,' Walter told her flatly. 'No one can forget the past. Not when it's only a town away.'

Chapter Twenty-two

Checking his reflection in the wing mirror of the car, he sat at the end of Colland Road, parked away from the street light, and waited. He would drive Emma out for dinner and then dancing, not that he danced much, but he liked to watch her take the floor with the many men who asked her, her feet in high heels moving rhythmically, her skirt flapping against her thighs, her eyes half closed. In a world of her own. She was good-looking enough and talented enough to have been a professional dancer, but that would have required effort and dedication. And Emma didn't like to work at anything.

Like marriage ... He had known from the start that her marriage to Peter Holding would never stand the test. Holding was attractive enough, and well set up with his father's business, but not the kind of man to keep hold of Emma. He was too predictable, wanting to settle down into marriage, his reckless gesture in ditching Bess and eloping with Emma, the one and only unpredictable thing he had ever done.

God knows how Peter Holding thought he could satisfy Emma. Didn't he know about her track record? Or hadn't he cared when he was lovesick? Or maybe he thought that she would settle down, be the little wife at home, looking after him and becoming a valuable member of the community.

He laughed to himself. If Peter Holding thought that he was a fool; should have stuck with his first choice and married Bess Shawcross instead. Now she would have made the right wife for him, and no mistake. A clever woman, smart, good to look at, too, and still holding a torch for Holding by the sound of things. What a joke! But then who ever married the right person? God makes them and the Devil joins them, he thought, and that's a fact.

Again he checked his reflection in the mirror and then pulled a white silk scarf around his neck. It didn't matter that he was no oil painting; no one cared what Leonard Crowthorn looked like – just that his wallet was full, and ready and willing to be pressed into service. Bit like Emma, in fact.

She should have married him, Crowthorn thought, but then again, the way it had turned out suited him just fine. A married woman was less of a drag to have around. Emma wanted money and fun, and he could give her that, without the bother of responsibility. Besides, it left him free to pursue anyone else he might fancy – just as Emma did, if the rumours were to be believed. They understood each other perfectly, a real marriage of minds.

Looking past his reflection in the mirror, Crowthorn could suddenly see the outline of a woman walking quickly towards the car. Emma's head was held high, her bag swinging against her side. Not hiding – she never did that.

'Hello, Leonard,' she said, her voice mesmerizing as she slid into the passenger seat.

'Hi there.'

She pecked him on the cheek, her skin smelling of the perfume he had brought her back from Paris.

'So, any problems?'

She raised her eyebrows. 'No, should there be?'

'Isn't he suspicious?'

Lazily she smiled. 'Peter? No, he trusts me.'

Crowthorn turned on the engine and pulled out into the road, the radio playing a Glenn Miller tune.

'I like this,' Emma said, turning up the volume and resting her head back against the seat.

'You should be more careful, you know,' Crowthorn warned her. 'People gossip.'

'So what? If Peter hears anything he won't believe it. Not if I tell him otherwise.' Her hand rested on Crowthorn's knee for a long instant. 'Miss me?'

'Every minute. I never had a secretary as good as you.'

She laughed, squeezed his thigh. 'That was a long time ago.'

'Before you married Holding. Before he dumped Bess Shawcross –'

'Why did you have to bring that up!' Emma snapped, taking her hand away and folding her arms.

'I was just take a trip down memory lane, darling,' he replied silkily, 'thinking about old times. Was it worth it?'

'Was *what* worth it?'

'Stealing Holding away from your cousin?'

Her voice took on a hard edge. 'She hardly put up a fight for him.'

'That wasn't the question,' Crowthorn answered, drawing up at some red lights. 'Are you glad you married Holding?'

'Peter's all right . . . oh, you know what he's like. Boring. Hard-working, devoted to me.'

'Poor Emma . . .'

Her eyes narrowed. She had come out for a good time, not for an interrogation.

'What's it got to do with you anyway? You're not interested in whether my marriage works or not.'

'That's true.'

'So why bring up Bess Shawcross?'

'I was just musing,' he said innocent. 'She's doing very well, you know; been promoted at the paper. Got her own page now, dealing with current affairs. Quite a coup for a woman.'

'I never thought career girls were your style, Leonard,'

Emma replied icily, as the lights changed and the car rolled forward.

'Why not? Times are changing. Women don't just have to be wives and mothers; they can go out into the world now and earn their own livings. Have their own careers. Be people in their own right.'

'Oh, do me a bloody favour!' Emma snapped, exasperated. 'There's only one thing you look for in a woman, Leonard, and that's not how well she types.'

'You misjudge me –'

'Yes, and you misjudge me. We both misjudge each other, that's why it works so well. Now are we going to have a good time tonight, or are we going to keep talking about Bess Shawcross?'

'I wonder if he ever regrets it,' Leonard went on, knowing that he was provoking her and enjoying it.

'What?'

'I wonder if your husband ever regrets ditching a woman like her? A woman who's going places.' He paused, letting the venom take effect. 'I wouldn't be surprised if Bess Shawcross doesn't up and out of the North, leave Bolton behind and go to London. I heard she'd been offered a job there.'

The words sunk into Emma's brain like grappling hooks. Her rival, her envied rival, might be the one to get out of the North! *She* might the one who escaped, who went to London, to have the pick of jobs and men! Staring ahead, Emma could feel the pulse thumping in her neck. She had been so stupid, so eager to score over Bess that she had never noticed how she had boxed herself into a corner. The dream had belly-flopped; Peter hadn't taken her away to Australia, and now *she* was the one stuck in the North whilst Bess Shawcross was free to go where she liked. God, Emma thought, she really was stuck well and truly. Not just with Peter, but she winced at the thought – possibly a child.

'Are you sure?' Emma asked, her voice husky.

Smiling, Leonard stroked her leg. The lie had done the trick; it had unsettled Emma, made her more pliable. She was easier to manage that way, less cocky, less likely to push her luck.

'It was just a rumour, darling. You know how people talk.' He jerked his head towards the back seat. 'Take a look, I've got a little something for you.'

For a long instant Emma hesitated, then she leaned over and lifted the dress box onto her lap.

'Don't worry, darling,' he said soothingly, 'you know that whatever happens you've got me.'

'Thanks, Leonard,' she replied, opening the box. 'Thanks a lot.'

There was absolute silence in the library, Ellen reading an article about Dior's New Look. The sound of heels tapping over to her broke unwelcome into her thoughts. Irritated, she looked up to find Bess standing over her.

'We have to talk.'

'SHHHHH!'

Ellen pointed to the sign on the opposite wall – 'Silence' – and raised her eyebrows.

'Can't we go outside?' Bess whispered.

Reluctantly, Ellen left her seat and followed her niece into the foyer. A huge poster of Shirley Temple was hanging over the staircase, and another of Humphrey Bogart facing them.

'I thought this was a library, not a cinema.'

'What is it?' Ellen asked. 'I was enjoying myself in there, getting some peace.'

'I've heard some gossip –'

'Oh, is that all?'

'– about Peter.'

As Ellen turned on her heel, Bess caught hold of her aunt's arm to stop her.

'Oh, come on, don't be like that.'

'I don't want to talk about him after what he did to you.'

'Emma's cheating on him.'

'And Hitler's dead,' Ellen replied sourly. 'Old news, Bess.'

'You *knew*?'

'Let's say it's no surprise.'

'But how could she?'

Ellen folded her arms, her expression incredulous. 'Just let me get something straight here. You were engaged to that man and he dumped you, ran off and married Emma, showing you up in front of the whole town. Now he's being cheated on and you're expecting me to be *sorry*?'

Bess's expression was sheepish. 'She was never right for him. I would never have cheated on him –'

'He got what he deserved, marrying her.'

'No one deserves that.'

'Oh God, Bess, for an intelligent woman you are such a bloody fool about men!'

A couple stared at them as they passed. Ellen lowered her voice.

'What worries me is why it *matters* to you any more. Surely to God you're not still hankering after him?'

Emma looked away. 'I just can't stop loving him,' she said quietly. 'Oh, go on, tell me what an idiot I am. I know: wish I could find someone else. But I can't. I still love Peter.'

'You'll waste your life, Bess,' Ellen told her seriously. 'Anyway, what about that job you were offered in London?'

'It wasn't a serious offer.'

'But you *could* get a job there?'

'If I wanted to,' Bess replied, 'but I don't. I like it here, with you and Reg. I know everyone here, this is my home.'

'And if Peter Holding was in London, would you be so keen to stay?'

The question hung on the air between them.

'I can't help the way I feel,' Bess said at last. 'It's as though I'm tied to him. I know how stupid that sounds, how childish. But it's true. I can't let go of him. I just can't.'

Gently, Ellen touched her hand, chosing her next words carefully. 'It's a fool's errand, Bess, a road going nowhere. Peter Holding loves Emma . . .'

The words stung.

'. . . he sees no wrong in her. If she stabbed him he would swear blind it was a love bite. But if she *is* cheating on him there will be trouble, big trouble. He'll find out and then God knows what'll happen. You don't want to be a part of that, Bess. You've got a good life going for you. Keep out of the mire.'

Blowing out his cheeks, Walter gingerly lowered himself into the back of the shiny Austin car and then sighed.

'Bloody hell. I'm feeling my age.'

'You all right?' Colin Porter asked him, staring anxiously into his face.

'Yeah, I'm fine.'

Nodding, Colin slid into the front seat and started the engine. He hadn't balked when Walter had beckoned him over at the billiards hall the previous week and asked for a lift. A lift where? Colin had asked. Up Rochdale way. I've a visit to make and I don't want my brother to know about it. I can't get there under my own steam, so I need you to take me. You on? Colin had agreed at once. He owed Walter Shawcross many favours and this was hardly taxing.

Glancing into the mirror Colin stared at Walter's reflection. Shit, he looked knackered.

'Are you sure you're up to this?'

'Oh, get on with it!' Walter snapped back good-naturedly.

Between giving Colin directions, Walter stared out of the window. He had never thought about being older, felt suddenly uncomfortable with the idea. He had spent so much of his life ducking and diving down these same alleys and ginnels they were passing, working the black market in the war and whistling for his women, every landlord within miles knowing him. Walter smiled to himself and wiped the condensation off the window to get a better look.

He'd been and done it all, hadn't he? And no one really knew just *how* much he done. God, what a lark it all was, what a game . . . The streets passed him by, one after another, their names known, remembered. He knew Bolton like a cat knows a country field – each place to hide, to go looking for trouble. He knew the stations too, all those trains which he had caught when he was bored. Trains going anywhere – what did it matter? Birmingham, Glasgow, London – Walter had seen them all.

Disappearing Walter. Disappearing once and for bloody all some day, he thought grimly. Only then he wouldn't know where the hell he'd be going . . . He winked suddenly, seeing Colin watching him through the driving mirror, and then turned his gaze back to the road. Out of Bolton, heading for Rochdale. Not a bad town, really, he thought, remembering a woman he had once spent a long weekend with. She had been very loving and he'd felt like a king. It didn't take money, Walter thought, or status, it was just how you felt in yourself. And he'd felt good.

'So where are we going?' Colin interrupted his thoughts.

'To see an old friend of mine.'

'Oh Jesus, Walter, not a woman!' he replied, panicked. 'Tell me it's not a woman. That always means a fight and I'm not up to it any more. And this car's new –'

'I'm passed all that, you daft bugger,' Walter replied, laughing, '. . . but it *is* a woman, yes.'

'Old flame?'

'Old sore.'

Colin reached for the heater dial. 'Are you warm enough?'

'I'm fine,' Walter said, looking round. 'Nice car.'

'I saved up.'

'You did well.'

But he wasn't envious. Walter had never wanted a car, or a house, never wanted anything but his freedom. And his brother. Liked to know he could always come back home to Reg and Ellen. In trouble or out of it. They'd been good to him, Walter thought, which was why he was going to return the favour the only way he knew how.

'D'you know the name of the street?'

'Colland Street. Turn next left and then third right,' Walter replied.

'Now where?' Colin asked when they arrived.

'Number 24. Stop on the opposite side of the street.'

The car drew to a halt, Colin turning to Walter in the back seat.

'Now what?'

'Now go and ring the doorbell.'

'What for?'

'So she'll know there's someone outside.'

'I know that! I mean, what do I say when the door's answered?'

'Ask for the lady of the house.'

'Yeah?'

'And then bring her over to the car.'

Colin frowned. 'There's nothing funny about this, is there? I mean, I'm not going to get into any rough stuff, am I?'

'No rough stuff, Colin. Now, go on, go and ring the bell.'

229

Straightening his coat, Colin walked over to number 24 and raised his hand to knock, then glanced over to the car. Impatiently, Walter waved his hand at him and then Colin rang the bell. There was a long pause, rain marking the shoulders of Colin's coat as he waited, the door finally opening a few inches.

From the car, Walter could hear nothing and merely watched as Colin said something and then leaned against the doorframe. The door opened wider, then wider still, and then finally Emma emerged, standing on the doorstep with her hands in her pockets, looking over to the car.

Colin was talking, but she shrugged him off, walking over to the Austin and wrenching open the back door.

'To what do I owe this honour, Walter?'

'Dumb luck,' he replied drily.

'You look peaky,' Emma said, her hair falling over her cheek, the heady drowsiness of her voice compelling. 'I'd take things a little easy, if I was you.' She could say *I want to kill you* with that voice, Walter realized, and make it sound like *I love you*.

'Climb in.'

She stared at the car. 'Not bad. Yours?'

'Just get in, Emma.'

Curious, she did so, sitting on the back seat next to Walter and staring at him. This was the man who had slept in the kitchen at the Shawcrosses', the man who had always stood up to her, disliked her. She thought of the cold kitchen and shivered.

'Someone walk over your grave?'

'Old memories. What d'you want, Walter?'

'I wanted a chat.'

Her expression was combative. 'About what? I'm busy.'

'I heard.'

'What's that supposed to mean?'

'You're running around, Emma. Cheating on your

husband.' Walter clicked his tongue. 'Not good. Not good at all.'

'Oh, spare me the sermons. What's it got to do with you?'

Walter continued smoothly, 'And it's beginning to show on you too. You look tired. A bit under the weather.'

Her expression shifted, suspicion coming in. 'I'm fine.'

'No stomach upsets? Nausea?'

Her face had paled, her tongue running over her lips. 'What are you talking about?'

'The child you're carrying,' Walter replied, his tone even.

'What the –'

'Don't bother denying it, Emma. I know you're pregnant. People talk.'

'People talk rubbish!' she snapped. 'I'm not pregnant.' She paused, her expression shifting. 'OK, so I was . . . But I'm not now. I got rid of it.'

There was a long moment of silence.

'You know something, Emma? When you've really been around like I have, you can tell a lie. Smell it, if you like. A sort of sickly odour.' He coughed suddenly, wound down the window an inch. 'You haven't got rid of the baby. You were too far gone to have the abortion.'

'How the hell would you know?'

'Because the woman you went to for help was an old girlfriend of mine,' Walter said, laughing and glancing out of the window. Across the street, Colin was scowling, stamping his feet on the pavement to warm them. 'Oh God, Emma, that was the wrong person to turn to. You really ran out of luck there.'

All the colour had gone out of her face. 'None of this has anything to do with you!'

'Is Peter Holding the father of the child?'

She reached for the door handle, but Walter grabbed her arm.

'Sit down!' he snapped. 'You've had things your own

way for long enough, Emma. Now it's time to bargain.'

Reluctantly she sank back in the car seat.

'You don't like it here, do you?'

'I love it,' she replied sarcastically.

'You want out, away from your boring husband and out of the North. But you're really stuck now, aren't you, Emma? You're going to be a mother, a regular housewife. You're *never* going to get away from here –'

'If you just came to gloat –'

'I came to offer you a way out,' Walter said deftly.

Her eyes narrowed. 'Why? You've always hated me.'

'That's true, but you should listen anyway. Now I'll ask you again – is this child Peter Holding's?'

'Who else's?'

'Old man Crowthorn's?'

She laughed. 'No, not Crowthorn's.'

'If you're lying to me –'

Impatiently Emma flicked back her hair away from her face. 'Oh, get on with it! If you've got something to say, say it.'

'Do you love your husband?'

'I'm fond of him.'

'But you could leave him?'

She raised her eyebrows. 'Sure I could leave him. Peter's a nice enough man, but he's boring. I thought he'd have more about him, thought he'd go to Australia with me. We could have made a real future out there. He could have got a good job and a nice house –'

'But he stayed home instead, didn't he?' Walter asked. 'Stayed to look after the family business, leaving you to play house.'

'OK, I don't expect you to feel sorry for me –'

'That's good, because I don't,' Walter replied shortly. 'I just want something from you.'

'Which is?'

'Your child.'

Emma stared at him for a long moment and then started to smile. 'You crazy old fool.'

'Think about it, Emma –'

'I have. This is *my* child.'

'Don't go all maternal on me. You didn't want it before, you wanted to get rid of it.'

'But I want it now!' she replied sharply. 'What do you want with it?'

'You'll never be a proper mother to that child, Emma. You know that, and I know that. Just like you'll never be a proper wife to that goon of a husband.' Walter let the words sink in. 'I'm offering you a way out, a way to rid yourself of the burden of a baby and leave the North. Think of it – you could go to London, or back home. You could find yourself a new man. New *men*. You couldn't do that with a kid in tow.'

Her eyes were fixed on his. She had spent many nights walking the floor, trying to work out what she would do. Stupidly, she had left it too late to get an abortion, and was now saddled with a baby she didn't want. Before long, her pregnancy would show – and then Peter would know. And how he would fuss her and fawn over her and imagine their life together for ever in the North, with their little family . . . Emma had loathed the idea and tried desperately to think of a way out. But there hadn't seemed to be one. Until now. And who of all people was offering it to her? Walter Shawcross.

But why?

'Why do you want the baby?'

'I don't want it for myself,' he replied evenly, 'but for Bess.'

'*Bess*!' Emma hissed furiously. 'What makes you think I'd give my child over to her?'

'Because you've no choice,' Walter replied, his tone hard. 'You can't stay here, you want out. And you can't live the life you want with a baby. So you have to get rid of it somehow, and I'm telling you how.'

'So I just hand it over to Bess Shawcross? Why her? Why not Peter? He's the father, after all.'

'Do you really think that he could look after a child when you've left him? He's besotted with you, Emma, can't imagine life without you – especially when he gave up so much for you. Believe me, when his dream of family life has been smashed, he'll be so shell-shocked, he won't be able to look after a cat. Peter Holding will fold when you leave him – and that'll leave the way clear for Bess. She can help him look after the baby.'

'Oh really? And why would she look after my child?'

'Because she still loves your husband,' Walter replied evenly. 'And because she'll love his child – even if you're its mother.'

Angrily, Emma glanced away, but she already knew she had lost. She would do what he said, hand over the child and run – get far away, as fast as she could. She could already imagine the freedom, the city, the men. It would be scary, frightening, she would be alone. But she would be free.

'What about Peter?' she asked. 'How am I supposed to explain all this to him? He's my husband, after all. You're talking about breaking up a marriage –'

Walter laughed hoarsely. 'Oh, grow up, Emma! This is me you're talking to. You don't give a damn about Peter Holding – he was just your ticket out of Bolton, that was all. You would have married a parrot if it had promised to get you back to Australia.'

She was suddenly panicky. 'But if I leave him and give up my baby, I'll have nothing left.'

There was a sliver of cruelty in Walter's voice when he answered her.

'That's right, you'll have nothing . . .' he leaned towards her, his eyes hard, '. . . which is exactly what you left Bess with.'

PART THREE

Funny how far we travel
Just to get back to the start

(Anon)

Chapter Twenty-three

As before, Walter had asked Colin to park the car opposite the house in Colland Street, Emma materializing a few minutes later carrying her new baby son, and a suitcase. She looked radiant in the daylight, as though she hadn't a care in the world, her eyes fixing on the Austin as it drew up at the entrance.

'Get in,' Walter said, opening the back door.

Obediently she did so, the baby fast asleep in her arms.

'God, he's a fine child,' Walter said, putting out his arms. 'Can I hold him?'

She passed him over without hesitation.

'So what happens now?'

'You're free to do what you want,' Walter replied, staring transfixed at the infant. 'Colin'll drop you at the station.' He nodded to an envelope lying on the seat between them. 'There's money in there. Just to see you all right.'

Carefully she picked up the envelope and then tucked it into her pocket.

'What about Peter? I wrote the letter, but he won't get it until he goes home at lunchtime.'

'Leave it to me,' Walter told her. 'I'll sort it out.'

'If you're sure –'

'Yeah, I'm sure.' Walter turned away from Emma as the car moved off towards the station. 'You got everything you need?'

She tapped the case by her feet.

'It's all in here.'

'Anything you want to say?'

Steadily she looked first at him and then at the sleeping child in his arms. Hers had been a relatively easy labour, but when the baby was brought to her she had been curiously detached. He was a pretty child, she could see that, but there was no tug, no emotional bonding to make her long to keep him. All she longed for was to leave, to get away as quickly as she could. They would look after him, she told herself, Peter and the Shawcrosses would see to it that the baby was cared for. He didn't need her – she was doing him a favour really.

'I was thinking –'

Walter cut her off. 'Don't think.'

She smiled, shook her head slightly.

'How d'you think he'll take it?'

'Peter?'

Emma nodded.

'Badly, he loves you. God knows why, but he does.' Walter coughed suddenly, turning his head away from the child.

'You sound rough.'

'Don't get your hopes up, I'm not pegging out yet.'

In silence they approached the station entrance, a soft drizzle falling as Colin parked the car. The concourse was busy with people, muffled announcements coming over the public address system. Through the driver's mirror, Emma could see Colin watching her as she opened the car door and stepped out.

'He's called Martin,' she said, reaching for her case, her voice faltering for an instant.

Walter nodded. 'Martin it is.'

Hesitating, Emma stood by the car. 'Look, Walter, it's the best thing for him,' she said, the public address system announcing the next train to London. 'I couldn't have stayed here.'

'I know,' he said simply, gazing into her eyes. 'Go on, close the door, there's a good girl. The baby's getting cold.'

Her bottom lip trembled for an instant and then hurriedly Emma closed the car door, picking up her case and walked into the station without looking back.

Reg was sweeping the floor of the billiards hall when he heard a car draw up outside. Walking up the basement steps, he was staggered to see his brother sitting in the back of Colin's car, holding a baby in his arms.

'Bloody hell, Walter, I thought you were past all that,' he said, opening the car door, Ellen following behind him.

'It's Emma's baby,' Walter replied, pulling the blanket around the child. 'Well, don't just stand there staring at me, give me a hand.'

'What the hell . . . ?' Ellen snapped, looking over her husband's shoulder. 'Walter, what *are* you doing? That's a baby you've got there.'

'I didn't think it was a bloody snooker cue,' he replied evenly, glancing up as a figure came down the street towards them.

Bess had seen the car first, then recognized Reg and Ellen talking to someone in the back seat. Walter? Was that Walter? Hurriedly she moved towards the parked Austin, Colin avoiding her gaze as she reached the car and bent down to look into the back seat.

'Walter . . .' Her eyes fixed on the baby. 'What are you doing with a *baby*?'

He smiled mysteriously. 'I'm not doing anything with it,' he replied, passing it over to Bess. 'It's Emma's child. Well, it was Emma's, now it's yours.'

Ellen leaned into the car, her voice sharp. 'What in God's hell are you talking about?'

'It's Emma's baby. Emma and Peter Holding's' he hurried on, before anyone could interrupt. 'Emma's gone, done a bunk. Didn't want the baby, so she gave it over to me. For Bess.'

Ellen's face was a study.

'Are you mad! Peter Holding'll have something to say about this. It's his child –'

'A man can't bring up a baby alone. Holding has a job, and,' Walter said hurriedly, 'besides, Emma's leaving will hit him hard – real hard. That child needs a good home, and a good mother. Unless I miss my guess, Bess loves Peter, so who better to look after the baby?'

Ellen's hand grasped the collar of Walter's jacket.

'You can't kidnap a child, it's against the law.'

Smiling smugly, her brother-in-law reached into his jacket and pulled out a letter.

'Emma explained everything in this,' he said. 'She's passed over the baby and wants Bess to look after it.'

'Give me that!' Ellen snatched the paper out of his hand as she turned to her husband. 'What d'you think about all of this?'

'He's a fine baby,' Reg replied, staring at Martin.

Sighing with exasperation, Ellen looked to her niece. 'You have to talk to Peter –'

'I can't.'

'Oh, Bess, get a grip!' Ellen retorted hotly. 'He'll need an explanation – and he'll want his baby back.'

Bess was standing with the baby in her arms, her face transformed, her eyes fixed on the sleeping child. Oh God, Ellen thought, this is going to be complicated.

'Holding'll never cope –'

'Walter, the baby belongs to its father. Besides,' Ellen went on, 'old man Holding will have something to say about this.'

'He's an old fart, and as deaf as a bloody post. He'd never even hear it crying,' Walter replied. 'What do men know about bringing up babies?'

'Not as much as they know about kidnapping them,' Ellen replied shortly. 'Walter, whatever possessed you?'

'It's the perfect solution,' he replied phlegmatically, reaching up for his brother's hand. 'Here, help me out,

Reg, will you? I've been sitting so long my legs are numb.'

'Match your head then,' he retorted, helping his brother out of the car and walking with him down the basement steps.

Shaking her head, Ellen took the baby from Bess.

'He's perfect. Quite perfect,' said Bess.

Ellen touched the baby's face gently and then sighed. 'Yes, he's good-looking, and that's a fact. Come on, bring him in, it's going to rain. And we've got some serious talking to do.'

Peter dropped the letter after he read it and sat down heavily. Outside the threat of rain had turned into a downpour. It wasn't true, Peter thought blindly, it couldn't be true. Emma had left him. But she had just brought home their son, how *could* she have left him? It didn't make sense. She had been fine the previous evening, a bit quiet but nothing worrying, and she'd not said a word then.

Now she'd run away . . . No, Peter thought, no, it wasn't true. He loved her, she knew that. He loved her, she would never leave him. Not him.

But the letter said . . . Oh, bugger the letter! Peter stared wildly around the front room. Was it the house that had made her go? Wasn't it big enough? Well, then he'd get a bigger one, and she'd come back. Or he'd sell up the engineering works and go off to Australia – that was what she wanted, wasn't it? Well, it wasn't too late, they could still go. He and Emma and the baby.

The baby . . . what had the letter said about the baby? That Emma had left him with the Shawcrosses and Bess. Bess . . . Peter stood up and then sat down again, almost laughing, nearly hysterical, his hands running through his hair, his heavy brows drawn together as he began walking the room. Backwards and forwards. His wife had left him, his wife had gone. Emma had gone.

Emma had gone . . . Her face came back to him in that

instant, that face that everyone looked at, turned to stare at when they were out together. And that voice, which made every word glorious. Jesus, how could he have imagined that *he* could keep a woman like that? Peter Holding – an attractive man, but not a millionaire, not an Adonis – how *could* he keep her? Oh God, Peter thought ... But I want her, I want her back. I don't care what she's done, I just want her back ... And then he thought of the baby – with the Shawcrosses, with Bess.

What would she be thinking now? He wondered, shame burning in his throat. After what he did to her, would Bess think that he had finally got what he deserved? And why, in God's name, would Emma give their child to Bess?

Because Bess once loved me, Peter thought, because once we planned to have children together. But it wasn't like her; Bess wasn't the type to interfere. It wouldn't have been her doing. It was that Walter Shawcross. He had done it to get revenge for Peter's hurting Bess. He was paying him back ... Heavily, Peter sat down again, his breathing quick, panicked. What could he do? Maybe someone knew where Emma had gone ... but he knew instinctively that his wife would have left no trace. No means by which to find her. Emma had gone and she wasn't coming home.

So this is what it feels like, Peter thought helplessly. This is how much it hurts to lose the person you love. This is despair, anguish – and this is what I inflicted on Bess. The humiliation, the grief – this is what *she* felt.

And yet even as he thought it, Peter still longed for the woman who had injured him, crying for Emma whilst knowing she would never come home.

Chapter Twenty-four

Lily jumped as Josiah's hand banged down on the pulpit. Bang, bang, driving the Bible words home. She wondered if God would approve, or if He would find it all a bit deafening, a bit theatrical. But then what could she expect? Josiah had been an actor once, and as he was growing older he was becoming more and more dramatic in his ways, a cartoon preacher, stuffed full of words.

She put it down to the influence of the cinema. No one would have expected a Methodist preacher to be such a fan, but Josiah was hooked, well and truly. He couldn't get enough of Spencer Tracy and Fredric March, even modelled himself on them. She knew that, although he would never admit it.

He was playing a role, Lily realized. Josiah wasn't really a preacher, he was just *acting* a preacher. And she had looked on with detached curiosity as gradually he had begun to expand his repertoire. His voice rose and fell, his mannerisms aping the Hollywood stars, his expressions dramatic, epic. Dear God, Lily thought, we have our very own Moses in Bolton. It was comic – to her. But the congregation loved it.

Bang went down his hand, bang again, the wooden eagle on the pulpit rocking drunkenly. It was all too absurd, she thought. How had she once loved this man? Looked up to him? How *could* she have done?

Josiah was working his sermon up to a climax, his words echoing round the hall. What a life, Lily thought idly, all bluster, all pretence, she tied to Josiah to protect a daughter who had turned out to be no good. It was like a film, Lily thought, like some silly overblown melodrama in which she just happened to have a bit part. Not a starring role, or even a character vignette, but just a walk on, an extra – who had never even managed to get a look at the script.

Minutes later they were walking home, Josiah grumbling, unhappy with his sermon, a knock on the door coming only seconds after they had walked in. It was Ellen.

'Hello, Lily,' she said, walking in and glancing over to Josiah. 'Hello there.'

Josiah stared at his sister-in-law mutely, fighting for words. Whatever he said, Ellen Shawcross just kept coming in and out these days with increasing frequency, as though it was her second home! And she knew she wasn't welcome. Barging in at all hours. He would have to speak to Lily again, to reason with her. Ellen Shawcross was taking liberties. This was his home, and what he said went.

Lily caught the inevitable glance of hostility between Ellen and her husband and, as usual, ignored it. She was seeing more of Ellen now and did not want to initiate a showdown.

'What is it, Ellen?'

'There's been a real turn-up for the book,' she began, delighted to note that although Josiah was turned away from her, he was listening avidly. 'Emma's run off and left the baby with Bess.'

The sisters would laugh about it for years afterwards. Josiah turned, goggle-eyed, at the news, the Bible dropping from his hand. His trump card had evaporated; the hold he had had over Lily had gone. Disappeared.

'What did you say?' Josiah couldn't help asking.

Lily caught hold of Ellen's sleeve. 'Gone? When?'

'This morning,' Ellen replied. 'She upped and left, and Walter took the baby off her and brought it back to us. Well, to Bess actually.'

'Emma left her baby with Bess?' Lily asked, incredulous.

Ellen nodded. 'History repeating itself, isn't it?' she said, turning back to her brother-in-law. 'You look a bad colour, you want to avoid shocks, Josiah.'

He tried to smile, but failed, his mind working and reworking the information, trying to assimilate it.

'You must know where the girl's gone?'

'No, no one does,' Ellen replied sharply. 'She doesn't want anyone to find her.'

'But the baby?' Lily said. 'What will Peter Holding say about all of this? It's his child; Walter can't just take it.'

'It's probably a criminal offence,' Josiah said meanly, 'taking a child from its rightful parent.'

Ellen ignored him. 'I went round to Peter's house a little while ago and there was no answer. I keep knocking, but no one was home. At least that was what he wanted me to believe.'

'You think he was in there?'

'Certain of it,' Ellen replied. 'I also think Peter Holding's in shock.'

He wasn't the only one.

'Are you *sure* the girl's gone?' Josiah said dumbly, bending down to pick up his Bible.

'Oh yes, Emma's gone. I know my daughter – despite what you think, I spent enough time at the Shawcrosses' before Emma was married to see what she's like – and I can tell you she won't be coming back,' Lily answered. 'The tables have turned now, haven't they? Now that Emma's gone, there's no reason for me to stay with you.'

'Now, Lily, let's be reasonable –'

'I've been reasonable for years,' Lily said pleasantly. 'But I don't feel like being reasonable any more.' Defiantly, she jabbed a finger into Josiah's paunch. 'You're nothing but a bully, a mean-spirited, pompous bully . . .'

Ellen and Josiah stared at her, open-mouthed.

'. . . I've waited for years to say that, for years and years. I think you're a joke, Josiah, and I hate your sermons, I think they're boring. I think *you're* boring.'

He backed away, suddenly intimidated. 'Now, Lily –'

'Marrying you was the biggest mistake I ever made, and I've made plenty. You're a windbag, Josiah, a laughing stock.' Shaking her head, Lily turned to her sister. 'What are you staring at? You've been thinking it for years, everyone has. Apart from his spinster harem –'

'Lily!'

She turned back to her husband. 'Oh, stop pretending, Josiah. It's over. You can't keep me here any longer. Get one of your church ladies to keep house for you – but not me. I've have enough.'

'Can I come and stay with you, Ellen, until I find somewhere to live?'

'Yes, yes . . .' Ellen replied, taking a breath. 'You can use Emma's old room.'

Nodding, Lily picked up her coat and moved to the door.

'I'm not taking anything, Josiah. I'll leave as I came, with nothing –'

Josiah's face had reddened, his bluster temporarily restored.

'I'm warning you, if you go out of that door now, I'll never let you in again. Our marriage will be over for ever.'

'Oh, Josiah,' Lily said quietly, 'didn't you notice that it already was?'

When Ellen and Lily returned to the billiards hall, Bess was sitting in front of the fire in the kitchen, holding the baby, who was crying.

'What do I do?' she said, her hair falling over her face. 'He won't stop crying . . . Did you go over to Peter's?'

Ellen nodded. 'No reply.'

'But he must be there!' Bess replied, rocking the baby, her colour rising. 'I'm not used to all of this. What's the matter with him?'

Gently Lily drew back the edge of the blanket to get a

clear look at her grandson's face and then glanced at Bess. A moment passed between mother and daughter.

'He looks like Peter. He's lovely.'

'I know,' Bess replied. 'He has his father's eyes.'

'I just hope he doesn't grow up to have Peter Holding's taste in women,' Ellen replied shortly, pulling on an apron and setting the kettle on the range. 'Or should I say wives?'

Still smiling at her grandson, Lily drew up a chair beside her daughter.

'Can I hold him?'

'Course you can,' Bess said with some relief. 'He cries with me.'

Ellen looked over her shoulder. 'You have to relax, don't be nervous. It's easy with kids – you keep them fed, warm and dry.'

'Easy – until he starts cutting his teeth,' Walter said drily, standing by the kitchen door.

'You should talk, Walter Shawcross. You've lost most of yours and it hasn't made you any the less trouble,' Ellen retorted, reaching for the teapot.

Busily she set out cups and saucers, but although she looked calm her mind was turning over and over. What in God's name would they do? They had to talk to Peter and get this sorted out. Oh yes, she thought, and who would end up looking after the baby? Not Peter surely? What Walter had said was true: Peter had the engineering works to run, and being an only child knew little or nothing about babies. Thoughtfully Ellen gazed at Bess and Lily, smiling to herself. Lily had really given that husband of hers a talking to! she thought gleefully. About bloody time.

'Lily's coming to stay here for a bit,' Ellen said, watching Bess's reaction. 'She can have the spare room.'

She didn't say *she can have Emma's room*, but that was what went through everyone's mind.

'You're staying here?' Bess asked curiously, but with no hint of reluctance.

Lily nodded. 'I've left Josiah.'

Laughing, Walter leaned against the door jamb.

'Jesus! I bet that hit the bugger hard,' he blustered. 'I bet old Josiah never thought his wife would up and leave him. Him being so God-fearing and all.'

'You *left* him?' Bess studied her mother's face. 'Why now?'

Why now? Because the reason for staying with him has upped and gone, Lily wanted to tell her. Your sister was Emma. The woman who stole your man, the woman who bore his child and then left that child. That was Emma. The girl who never knew I was her mother – just as you don't know you have a sister. That was the hold the godly minister had over me, Bess. He threatened to tell Emma the truth if I left him. So I stayed. But now she's gone I don't have to any more. That's why I can leave my husband now.

But she couldn't explain, so instead Lily kept her eyes fixed on the baby when she answered.

'Let's just say that Josiah wasn't what he appeared . . . None of us ever is.'

Chapter Twenty-five

The baby was crying as Walter coughed harshly, struggling for breath. Frowning, Bess glanced over to Ellen.

'He sounds worse than usual.'

'Maybe he'll choke to death and do us all a favour,' she replied, walking over to Walter and tapping him on the back. 'Cough it up, it could be a gold watch.' Gently, her hand rested on his forehead. 'You're hot.'

'I'm OK,' he muttered impatiently.

'No, you're not, Walter, you've got a fever,' she replied shortly. 'I hope it's not contagious, what with the baby. I bet that car of Colin's was draughty –'

'Oh, Ellen, don't go on.'

'It's not a question of going on,' she snapped. 'There's a baby to consider now. You'll have to get yourself better and be quick about it.'

But although her voice was light-hearted, when she turned away Ellen caught her daughter's eye and frowned. It was an infinitesimal gesture, but Bess caught it and, glancing over to Walter, studied his face, the harsh bark of his cough echoing in her head.

'Perhaps we should –'

But she was prevented from continuing by a sudden hammering outside.

'OPEN THIS BLOODY DOOR! OPEN THIS BLOODY DOOR!'

Hurriedly Reg got to his feet and moved through the billiards hall, the kitchen light giving only partial illumination. Business was over for the night, the faded Closed sign hanging on the outer door.

Violently, the fists kept banging on the glass.

'Hey, watch it!' Reg snapped, wrenching open the door, a man lurching towards him.

'I want him back!'

Catching the man by his collar Reg looked disgustedly into Peter Holding's face.

'You're drunk –'

'And you're a kidnapper!' Peter shouted hoarsely, weaving on his feet, his eyes unfocused. 'I want my baby back. That bloody brother of yours has taken my baby, I want my son back now –'

'In your condition?' Reg replied shortly. 'Do me a favour.'

Hurriedly he hauled Peter into the billiards hall and then pushed him into the wooden cubicle, looming over him.

'Keep your voice down, Holding. We've all had enough upset for one day.'

'It's Walter's fault! That brother of yours stole my child. The neighbours told me all about it. Described him, said he taken Emma and the baby away with him –'

'Shut up!' Reg said, holding Peter in his seat. 'Walter did you a favour. Emma ran off and left the baby with him, for safekeeping. We've been round your place and got no answer. If you were so bloody concerned about your kid why didn't you come here first before going to get a skinful?'

'Emma's gone . . .' Peter said blankly.

'It were always on the cards –'

'You didn't know her!'

'I knew her a lot longer than you, Peter,' Reg replied evenly. 'That's why I knew it were on the cards.'

A silence fell between them, Peter slumping in his seat, his arms limp by his side, his hair falling over his forehead. The expensive suit he was wearing had been mottled with rain, his shoes water-marked, his eyes puffy from booze and tears. He looked lost, pathetic.

'Listen to me, Holding,' Reg said, trying to cover his impatience. 'Oh, for God's sake, sober up and look at me! What d'you want to do?'

'I want Emma back.'

'It'll never happen.'

'But, if I could talk to her, bring her home.'

Reg's temper was thinning. 'She's gone, she won't come back and if she did, she wouldn't stay. You have to think about your son now, Holding. He's your first concern.'

'I'll . . . I'll look after him.'

'Really? What happens when you're at work?'

Peter shook his head, trying to clear his thoughts. 'I'll get someone to look after him.'

'Not with us here,' Reg countered. 'Let's get one thing clear, Holding. I'm not doing any of this to help you. I'm just trying to do what's right.' He paused. 'There's going to be three women living here from now on – my wife, Bess and Lily – that's three women who between them could help you to bring up a baby.'

'But –'

'Hear me out!' Reg snapped. 'The choice is yours – but if I were in your position I'd be glad of the offer. You could call at night and see your lad, and take him for weekends. Break yourself in easy, if you like. To be truthful, I don't like you, Holding. You were a bastard for what you did to Bess and I reckon you've finally got everything you had coming to you.' His big hands clenched. 'I don't like men who hurt women, I don't think it's smart to play around with a woman's feelings. And you did that, Holding. You ditched a prize like Bess, for a cheap piece like Emma.' He shook his head. 'But now I just look at you and I don't feel anything. Except pity. And that's a bloody awful thing to feel for any man.'

'I didn't mean –'

'Don't make excuses, I don't want to hear them!' Reg said shortly. 'The offer's there – we'll help you raise your kid, but only on one condition: forget Emma . . .' he leaned towards Peter, his size impressive, '. . . and if you ever – *ever* hurt Bess again, I will break your neck. D'you understand me? I will break your bloody neck.'

Cowed, Peter staggered to his feet.

'I better get home.'

'That's right, you go home,' Reg replied, walking to the door with him. 'Sober up and tomorrow we'll talk again.'

'I'm grateful . . .'

'Yeah,' Reg said dismissively, 'well, I tell you now I wish things were different. I wish my Bess was holding her own child and had her own husband, instead of picking up some other woman's castoffs.' Reg opened the basement door and watched a shamefaced Peter walk out into the night. 'You've a lot to make up for, Holding. Not to me, to Bess. You've got a second chance. Use it.'

He let the threat hang, unspoken, but like an unwelcome mongrel it followed Peter Holding down Derby Street and on the last train home to Rochdale.

Even after twenty-hours, Bess wasn't entirely sure *what* she felt as she sat looking at Martin lying on her bed, a blanket wrapped around him. Ellen had bottle-fed the baby earlier and burped him, and shown Bess exactly what to do with an infant which was only a week old, and yet now that Bess was left alone with Martin all she could do was stare.

He was so small, she thought, touching his fingers, his face restful in sleep, his hair blond, like Emma's. His skin was so fine it appeared translucent under his eyes, a tiny vein showing blue under the surface of his left temple. This was Peter's son, Bess thought incredulously, his child, his flesh and blood. Tentatively she touched Martin's cheek and felt a rush of panic – how could she look after something so small? She didn't know about babies, hadn't known the first thing to do. What if she dropped him?

252

Shall we bathe him? Ellen had said earlier, taking a plastic bowl out from under the sink. Horrified, Bess had stared at her aunt as she'd passed the baby to her. Bathe him? But surely he would drown, she would do something wrong . . . It had been Lily who had calmed her, showing Bess how to test the bath water with her elbow and lower Martin in gently, holding his head upright.

'It's just practice,' she'd told Bess, 'like everything else. You'll get the hang of it.' How? Bess wondered. Just what was she doing with a baby? What had Walter landed her with? And it was *Peter's* baby . . .

As if on cue, Peter, suffering a queasy hangover, arrived at that moment, as arranged, to see Reg. He was shamefaced, obviously shocked, unable even to mention Emma's name. In the cramped kitchen, he sat at the table with Reg and Ellen, his eyes averted from both of them.

'How can I expect you to help me?' he asked quietly.

'I've told you, it's not for you, it's for Bess,' Reg replied, lighting up a cigarette. 'Walter tells me that Emma wasn't against Bess looking after your child. Personally I think it's asking a lot of the woman you shamed publicly. Besides, Bess might not want to help you out. I wouldn't, in her shoes.'

For once Ellen did not intervene. Reg was holding court, putting Holding on trial.

'She has a good career now, Holding. Lots of men come asking for her – maybe she might not want to get saddled with a baby. I mean, Walter was acting in her best interests, but it seems to me that being a dogsbody for you might not be good for her . . .'

Surprised, Ellen stared at her husband as he continued.

'. . . Ellen and me, now we're getting on, but we're game, and as for Lily, she's got rid of that hopeless husband of hers and she's more than willing to help. But Bess, well now, that's another thing.'

'I've been thinking,' Peter said carefully. 'The offer you

253

made last night was very generous, Mr Shawcross, about the baby staying here during the weeks and me having him at the weekends.' His voice was humble, shamed. 'I'd like to take you up on it – I mean, I'll pay for the baby's food and clothes and anything else you see fit –'

'You'd have to. We've no money to waste,' Reg said solemnly.

' – and I'll call and see Martin after work every night and take him home weekends.'

'Could you cope with him on your own?' Ellen asked sensibly. 'I think maybe you should break yourself in a bit at a time, Peter.'

He nodded, dumbly grateful.

A footfall sounded overhead.

'That'll be Bess,' Reg said, getting to his feet. 'Now don't go running off this time, Holding. I think you should stay and have a proper talk with her, don't you?'

A few moments later Bess was standing in the kitchen looking at Peter Holding. She still had her crossover apron on, her glossy hair hurriedly held back with combs, her expression unreadable. They had not seen each other, or spoken, since Peter and Emma had eloped.

'Bess, I . . .' Peter's voice trailed off.

'Martin's fine,' she said simply. 'Reg said you'd come to some kind of arrangement.'

'Hasn't he discussed it with you?'

She smiled faintly. 'Of course. But I haven't really made my mind up yet, Peter.'

Discomforted, he glanced away. 'I'm so sorry about the way I treated you.'

Bess said nothing. She loved Peter, but was determined not to be hurt again. Emma had gone, leaving Martin behind. But where did that leave her? Should she be grateful, see it as a way of holding on to Peter, of forcing him back into her life? Say – look how well I look after your son, reward me, love me again.

She thought not. Peter Holding had to choose to come back to her, not merely for his son's sake . . . Besides, if she sacrificed herself to bring up Peter's son, what might happen? In time he might meet someone else and then where would she be – without a future *or* a career. No, she had been bitten once and was far too wily to be ripped apart again.

'I'll be honest with you, Peter, I don't know if I'm very maternal.'

'You always used to say you wanted lots of kids,' Peter replied, then flushed.

'I used to say a lot of things!' Bess snapped. 'Before you ran off with Emma and made a fool out of me.'

'I'm sorry –'

'Not as sorry as I am.'

'Bess, please, let me explain –'

'Forget it. It's over, Peter, passed,' Bess replied. 'I can't say it didn't hurt and I could have done without the humiliation, but I've survived.'

'You should have married.'

'No, I don't think so. I've made a very good career instead – there are others things in life, you know.'

'I was blinded by her,' Peter said suddenly. 'Emma was so . . . so incredible.'

Emma, Emma . . . Bess flinched at the name. Would she always be there, Bess wondered, her ghost standing between them? And what about Martin – would he grow up with his mother's ways, her mannerisms? Would Bess find herself, years on, having sacrificed her life for a replica of the person who had caused her such misery?

'Peter, will you do something for me?' Bess asked eventually.

'Anything.'

'Then go home . . .' Bess said quietly. 'Just go home.'

When she went back upstairs, Lily was sitting quietly with the baby.

'How is he?'

'Sleeping . . . How's Peter?'

'Missing Emma.'

Lily raised her eyebrows. 'He didn't say that, did he?'

'He didn't have to,' Bess replied, reaching forward and touching Martin's cheek. 'Do you think he'll ever forget her?'

There was a long pause before Lily finally answered, 'I don't know.'

To her amazement, Bess smiled. 'Thank you.'

'For what?'

'For being honest. For not saying what I wanted to hear.' Her gaze moved back to the baby. 'I know this sounds terrible, but I don't want to get close to him, because I'm scared of losing him. Stupid, isn't it? But I know if I let myself, I'll want this baby for ever and for ever. If I let myself love him I just know I could never part with him . . .' She trailed off, horrified by what she had said. 'Oh God, I'm sorry, Mum, I didn't mean –'

'I know,' Lily replied softly, 'and I understand what you're saying. You could be a good mother, Bess. The question is – is it what you want? Ellen and I'll back you whatever you decide. But don't think you owe Peter Holding anything. Do what you want, but make sure you do it for yourself. Don't tie yourself to anything, or anyone, or you'll learn to resent it . . . I'm giving you good advice, Bess, please take it.'

It was past two in the morning when Ellen woke Bess.

'What is it?'

'It's Walter,' she whispered. 'I can't wake him.'

Hurriedly, Bess got to her feet. 'He looked so tired earlier on,' she said urgently. 'I thought he wasn't well.'

'I have a hunch Walter's not been too well for a while,' Ellen replied, hurriedly knocking on Lily's door. 'Lily,' she called out softly. 'Go for the doctor on Royal Street. Quick as you can. We'll watch the baby.'

When Dr Young can back with an out-of-breath Lily he found Ellen wiping Walter's forehead with a damp face cloth, the cat watching from the window ledge, the fire humming under a bank of coal. The kitchen was warm, the light subdued, the evening paper, half read, lying by Walter's side.

Hurriedly, Dr Young kneeled down beside the couch.

'Walter? Walter, can you hear me?'

Mute, Ellen stood with her arms folded watching. She had made bread earlier and the smell of it filled the cramped room.

'Walter, can you hear me?'

Of course he can't bloody hear you! Ellen wanted to shout. If he could, he'd answer. He's sick, not dumb.

'How long he's been like this?' Dr Young asked her.

'He was fine earlier, tired, but all right. He had a bacon sandwich and a mug of tea.'

'Has he overstrained himself recently?'

'He was involved in some family upset,' Ellen replied. 'I think he got himself overtired. It was something that mattered a great deal to him. He went out with a friend of his – in a car – and got some things sorted. But he was shot when he came back. Real tired.'

'Didn't you notice he was ill –'

Ellen cut him off. 'Walter Shawcross is his own man. I can't tell him what to do, and neither could anyone else.'

Raising his eyebrows, Dr Young turned back to the patient and took Walter's blood pressure, then shone a torch into his eyes. Walter's breathing was laboured, slow, harsh in the small room. When the clock struck the half-hour suddenly, Bess jumped, glancing over to her aunt apologetically.

'So, how is he?' Ellen asked finally.

Dr Young stood up.

'He's dying.'

'No,' Bess said simply, her hand going up to her mouth.

'I hope he can't hear you say that,' Ellen said shortly.

'Walter can't hear anything any more,' Dr Young replied. 'He's slipping away.'

Ellen nodded. Her voice was controlled as she asked, 'How long?'

'I'll get him taken to the hospital –'

'You won't!' Ellen said hurriedly. 'Walter stays here. This is his home.'

Surprised, Dr Young looked into her face. 'Do you realize what you're suggesting?'

'Of course I do!' Ellen barked. 'My brother-in-law's dying, well, he's not dying in some place he doesn't know. This is his home, and here he stays.' She stared down at Walter's face. 'That man dragged himself over to Rochdale when he was on his last legs, when he hardly had a breath in him. He was thinking about *us*, not about himself. He deserves the best, and he'll not get less.'

Chapter Twenty-six

'I should close the hall,' Reg said the following evening, standing at the doorway of the small wooden cubicle and looking at the punters collected around the tables, cues in hand.

Collecting together the takings on the counter in front of her, Ellen looked up.

'Close? What for?'

'Walter,' Reg replied. 'It's not right that the place should be full when he's so sick.'

'Oh, come on, Reg, Walter would think you'd taken leave of your senses. He'd be the first to tell you we need the money.' Ellen stared down the hall to the furthest table. 'D'you remember when he used to kip down on that table? I used to get up sometimes and he'd be sleeping like a baby. Without a care in the world.'

'He was always like that,' Reg replied, 'never afraid of anything, or anyone. Tough little bugger . . .' He paused. 'I'll sit with him tonight.'

Ellen shook her head. 'He's not going anywhere just yet,' she lied, tapping the back of her husband's hand. 'Not for a little while.'

'I suppose it'll be like him to go off again, bloody Disappearing Walter.' Reg struggled to keep his voice steady. 'They always say that a death follows a birth.'

'Why don't you take a break?' Ellen said kindly. 'I'll do the takings and lock up if you like.'

Reg glanced over to the door that separated the billiards hall from the kitchen, then looked back to his wife.

'Walter never had kids, never wanted them – I wonder why that baby was so important to him?'

'He didn't do it for the baby,' Ellen replied quietly, 'he did it for Bess, and for us. It was a thank you. His way of paying us back.'

Throughout that long night Walter slept without waking. The cat curled on the window ledge, the fire kept banked up, the rack hanging empty overhead. Above, in the back bedroom, Bess sat with the baby and Lily, whilst Reg tossed and turned, unable to sleep. Only Ellen remained in the kitchen, dozing, then waking intermittently to check on Walter, the slow hours marking time through the night.

Wrapped in a thick dressing gown, she tried to read, but soon gave up, staring at Walter instead. His mouth seemed sunken, his breaths hardly stirring the blankets covering him. His hands, blue-veined and narrow, lay beside him, his feet intermittently twitching under the covers. Now and then he would move his head, only to settle again, his mouth and lips dry.

As quietly as she could, Ellen rose to her feet and moistened Walter's lips. His eyes opened.

'How do.'

'How do, Walter,' she said gently. 'You had a good sleep.'

'I were dreaming,' he replied, his voice rasping, forced. 'Thinking about your sister –'

'Lily?'

'Nah, that snob Louise. Always thought she was a cut above the rest of us.' He stirred, winced, then settled again, his head hardly making an imprint on the pillow. 'D'you reckon Emma went back to Australia?'

'Doubt it,' Ellen replied, drawing her chair up to the side of the couch. 'I bet she tried her luck nearer home.'

Walter nodded.

'How's Bess doing with the baby?'

'Oh, fine. Still a bit nervous, but she'll make a good mother.'

'More than Holding deserves.'

'She loves him.'

'More fool her ... I think I might be dying,' he said suddenly, without emotion.

'Don't do that, Walter, you still owe me money,' Ellen replied. Then, changing the subject: 'You hungry?'

'Nah, I just want to talk,' Walter replied, unexpectedly reaching for her hand. 'You've been a pal to me.'

'Likewise.'

A moment passed between them, the clock chiming the hour, an early bus passing on Derby Street.

'Soon be morning,' Walter said, holding on to his sister-in-law's hand. 'It's cold, isn't it?'

'Hang on, I'll get some more coal.'

'Nah, leave it,' Walter urged her. 'It's not that bad.'

Another moment passed between them, the thin dawn light creeping in through a gap in the curtains. Walter dozed, then woke, his eyes slow to focus.

'What time is it?'

'Nearly six.'

He smiled, squeezed her fingers. 'I should have married someone like you.'

'Oh, go on, I bet you say that to all the girls,' she teased him.

The clock ticked the minutes past.

He seemed to falter and sleep, but only for a few minutes. Outside, a man passed on the street, his footsteps echoing, milk bottles chinking in the cold morning. Blue dawn light settled on the window ledge. The cat, keeping the vigil with Ellen, jumped down and came over to the couch. But for once she didn't settle with Walter, and curled up by the fire instead.

'What time is it?' he asked when he woke again.

'Twenty past six.'

He nodded. Somewhere, far off, he could see himself as a boy running away from a market stall with a toy he had stolen. Reg was waiting for him at the corner . . . The image changed. Now Walter was calling on a lady friend, a girl he had once loved. She was turning to speak to him . . . Again the picture altered. Now Ellen, now Josiah Wake, now jail, now Bess.

Smiling, Walter allowed his thoughts to drift, his breaths catching. He was worried suddenly, struggling to remember something important. What was it? What was it that he had to do? Relaxing, he remembered – he had got the baby, and given it to Bess. He had done what he set out to do.

The kitchen door opened silently, Bess tiptoeing over to the couch.

'How is he?'

Ellen looked up at her.

'It won't be long now . . . Look, he's dreaming.'

Together they watched him, Bess by her aunt's side, the clock's hands turning round the hour, the dawn coming strong with the light.

And with the coming of that light, Walter Shawcross died.

Chapter Twenty-seven

'He's doing really well,' Bess said, lowering Martin in the pram and turning to Peter. 'Gaining weight just as he should.' She paused. 'Did you hear what I said?'

He looked up and smiled. 'Yes, yes, that's good,' he replied, getting to his feet and walking over to the pram. Carefully Peter touched his son's hand. 'I want to take him over to my father's at the weekend. D'you want to come with me?'

Why not? Bess thought. It would look odd, but then who cared any more? She had made her decision and the care of Martin Holding was now divided between the three women. During the day Lily and Ellen minded him, and in the evenings after work, Bess spent time with the child – and with Peter who called round every night. At first they were uncomfortable together; too much of the past blocked any familiarity. But now they were gradually getting used to one another again.

However, Bess still avoided being alone with Peter, until one evening when he asked her to go with him when he took Martin out in his pram. Nervously she accepted, well aware of the stares and gossip which followed them – *look, there goes Bess Shawcross, looking after Peter Holding's boy – makes you wonder, doesn't it? I mean, which self-respecting woman would do that? Unless she wants to get her hooks into him again, now that the coast is clear.*

Oh, yes, Bess knew how they gossiped, how Rochdale and Bolton whispered about her. She knew too that everyone expected Emma to return, to come back and claim her husband and her child. It was always in the back of their minds at home, too: the question – would Emma return?

She wondered, how much time Peter spent thinking about his wife, how many hours at night he longed for her, how many minutes in the day whilst he was at work he imagined her voice, her face. Not that he dared even to mention Emma's name.

But as the months passed, Bess allowed herself to relax a little. Maybe Emma *had* gone for good, disappeared out of their lives as Louise had done. It would be for the best, after all, wouldn't it?

Well, it would be the best for her, but what about Peter? He was grateful to her, Bess knew that, and he was thought-ful, good company – but the love, the attraction, was miss-ing. Emma was the woman he had left Bess for, and it was Emma he missed. He might loathe himself for it, and try constantly to restore the feeling between himself and Bess, but it wasn't there.

Yet time *had* been of some help. Now at least Peter could spend several hours a day without thinking of his wife – but when he did the impact was corrosive, leaving him limp as a glove. He knew he was a fool. He could see Bess, what she had done for his son, and what she did for him, but it made no difference. Whilst she loved him, he loved Emma; both of them dancing an eternal emotional waltz with the wrong partners.

'So,' Peter repeated, 'would you like to come with me to my father's on Sunday?'

'That would be nice,' Bess agreed. 'Your father's always saying he wants to see more of the baby.'

He wants to see more of you too, Peter thought. He hopes, like everyone else, that we'll end up together in the end.

'I was thinking,' he began, 'it's not very convenient for you to be looking after Martin in Derby Street. Maybe I could get a woman to come in to mind Martin here during the day.'

'What for?' Bess asked him, bemused. 'Why get a stranger in when everything's working so well at Derby Street?' Her voice cooled. 'Aren't you happy with the way Martin's being looked after?'

'Of course I am!' he replied, genuinely amazed by the question, 'I just want to make it easy for you.'

Then marry me, Bess thought, love me. Forget Emma ... She watched as Peter bent down over the pram, his hair falling over his dark brows. God, how I want you, she thought, the sensation an ache inside her. How long can I wait? How long? And what if you never want me again? What if you *never* forget Emma?

The thought made her take in a breath.

'Are you OK?' he asked.

'Fine,' Bess replied, glancing away from him and letting the brake off the pram. 'I have to get back now.'

Carefully she moved through the door and paused on the street outside. A neighbour saw her and smiled thinly.

'Is there anything you need? More money or anything?' Peter asked.

'It's fine, Martin wants for nothing,' she replied, still not looking at him.

The air was tense with their unease.

'Bess ...'

She didn't respond.

'Bess?'

'What?'

'I'm so grateful for everything you do,' Peter said, reaching out and touching her shoulder. 'I could never have managed without you.'

His touch seemed to burn through her coat and into her skin, and for an instant Bess hesitated, waiting for him to speak again. But when he didn't she shook back her hair and walked off, the pram casting a giant shadow before her.

*　　*　　*

'It's been months now,' Ellen said firmly, 'and no sign of Emma. I knew there wouldn't be. I even wrote to that sister of mine and asked if she'd gone back to Australia, but Louise wrote back and said she hadn't. Seemed bloody relieved, I might add. And not a word of criticism about Emma upping and leaving Peter and the baby.'

Reg looked up from the paper he was trying to read.

'You don't want Emma back, do you?'

'Of course not! It's just that . . . oh, things aren't right. They aren't right at all.' She turned away, picking up her coat and heading for the door. 'I'm off to the library. See you later.'

It was the only place she could think, in silence, with no one around to bother her. Not that Lily was being a nuisance, far from it. She had even gone out and found herself a flat nearby – but they had all pressed her to stay a bit longer. Funny that, Bess wanting her mother around so much, taking advice from Lily about Martin, listening to her mother as she had never done before.

And Lily had been giving her daughter some good advice lately. Encouraging Bess to get out more, to make a life for herself outside the billiards hall and the baby. She should be seeing people, meeting men. She should be living . . . Impatiently Ellen sat down and tried to read a book she had picked up off one of the shelves – a biography, usually a favourite of hers. But not today; she was preoccupied.

It was all well and good that Bess loved the baby, but what would the outcome be? All she needed was for Emma to turn up again and take Martin back, and where would that leave her? Without Peter *and* the baby. Because Peter would take Emma back in a second, Ellen knew that for a certainty. He might avoid talking about his wife, but her photographs were still dotted around the house and her clothes were still hanging in the wardrobe. Waiting.

It was no way to live, Ellen decided. Bess shouldn't be living in hope; she was worth more. A husband of her own, a child of her own. It wasn't enough just to borrow Emma's cast-offs ... Sighing, Ellen flicked through the book's pages. If the two girls had known that they were sisters, would things have been different? Would a bond have grown up between them? A tie that would have forbidden any treachery?

Could Emma honestly have cheated on her *sister*? And if she had known about Bess, wouldn't she have settled down better, found in her a confidante she had never had before? Ellen doubted it; Emma's problem was much deeper and of longer standing. When Louise and Clem rejected her the seeds were sown for the rest of Emma's life. From then onwards Emma mistrusted the world and hit out at everyone who came close.

Ellen sighed and closed the book on her lap. She didn't like the fact that there were so many loose ends, too much unfinished business – although no one else seemed as worried as she was, and Reg had ducked out. Well, he was a man, Ellen thought, and entitled to. After all, he'd never complained when his home was invaded by sundry children and adults. But she knew that he wanted some peace himself now, some time alone with his wife. Which looked pretty unlikely. He missed Walter too, and was afraid of growing old.

Times had changed, and they seemed set to change more. Ellen stared ahead at the barrel ceiling of the library and the new signs 'Exit' and 'No Smoking' hanging next to the old yellowed 'Silence' notice. There was even a children's area now, and a noticeboard with job advertisements pinned on it. Two evenings a weeks there were lectures, and more often than not schoolchildren would be milling about looking up books for projects.

It wasn't a bit like it used to be, Ellen thought. But then, what was? The war had changed everything, even the town was changing. Some of the smaller mills closing, the old bleach works in Farnworth boarded up. Old man

Crowthorn was still running his little empire, but he was bad on his legs now and mostly housebound. Shame Emma hadn't married him, Ellen thought, she'd have been well on the way to a fortune by now.

But then there wouldn't have been Martin. At least *he* was thriving, a big child, growing fast, Lily spoiling him and Bess spending every free moment with him. The miles they had all walked with that baby, round Bolton, then over to the moors, once even up to Winter Hill – a trek and a half, but it hadn't seemed that far, not when they'd packed a lunch and put it at the bottom of the pram to eat when they arrived.

It had been a fine summer afternoon, hot, with little cloud, Ellen walking beside Bess, Lily a little way ahead, her hair glowing gold in the sunlight. Martin had slept most of the way, but when they reached the top of Winter Hill and looked down over Bolton he had woken and begun to cry. Bess had lifted him out of the pram and rocked him. Her arms had been lightly tanned, her hair wavy and falling over her forehead as she crooned to him.

They had stayed for a couple of hours up on Winter Hill, the sun reddening Lily's nose and making freckles appear on the top of her arms. At one point Ellen had mentioned Josiah and Lily had rolled onto her back in the high grass, smiling up at the cloudless sky. Crickets had cheeped in the grass around them, and in the distance they had heard a train hooting as it passed through the drowsy town.

In Bolton there was still rationing, and grime, and men coming back from the war desperate for jobs. A change of Government had promised all kinds of new choices, but in reality life was hard and bitter in the Bolton streets. But that afternoon, up on Winter Hill, the three women had forgotten everything, playing with Martin, and laughing and talking. For those brief hours, Bess could have been Martin's mother, enjoying an afternoon out before going home to her own house and her own husband.

But instead they had all walked back to Derby Street, Peter calling round later to see the baby, Bess avoiding his gaze as though it hurt her to look at him. It was obvious that Peter was fond of Bess, and guilty for the way he had treated her – but what else? Was he guilty enough to forget Emma? Ellen doubted it.

A sudden noise in the library brought her thoughts back to the present. Ellen looked up to see a neighbour walking over to her. Groaning inwardly, she smiled half-heartedly at Nora Morris, the town gossip, as she slid into the seat next to hers.

'Hello there, Ellen.'

'Hello, Nora.' she replied, her voice low as she pointed to the 'Silence' sign.

Nora ignored it.

'I heard about what happened, such a shame. Fancy Emma running off and leaving her baby behind,' she tutted, luminous with pleasure. 'It's been a while now. I suppose she's not coming back – not if what I heard is true.'

Ellen's eyes fixed on the woman. '*What* did you hear?'

Nora touched her hair primly. 'Well, I'm not one to gossip . . .'

'Force yourself.'

'. . . but someone told me that your Emma had got herself very nicely set up in Stockport. With that Goldstein bloke –'

'The night-club owner?'

Nora nodded.

'I know it's not what you'd want for the girl,' she went on, her voice thick with mock sympathy, 'but apparently Emma's living with him in his place. Smitten, they say. She's absolutely bowled over by him. Wants to marry him – when he divorces his wife. Oh, and when she and Peter Holding are sorted out.'

Having expected to fell Ellen with the news, Nora was amazed to see her stand up, smiling.

'Well, it's been really good seeing you again, Nora,' she said, glowing. 'Be sure to keep me posted on any other developments.' Happily Ellen gathered up the books she had chosen and moved to the desk, humming under her breath.

Emma wasn't coming back; there was no way she would give up on Sydney Goldstein, owner of the largest casino in Manchester and several other clubs round the North West. He made old man Crowthorn look like a pauper, Ellen thought delightedly, still humming as she moved out into the street. Oh, Emma had hit the big time all right. Goldstein had a Rolls and a place abroad; she'd never leave him. Furs, jewels, and money were all hers now.

It took Ellen all her control not to break out singing. Emma had found her level, her perfect place in life. It didn't matter to Ellen that her niece was living in sin with a married man. Emma had never been respectable; it was inevitable how she would end up. The important thing was that Emma was in love – and she had everything she had ever wanted. Emma was set up.

Which meant that Emma would never come back for Peter or Martin. The way was clear for Bess at last.

Crossing at the traffic lights, Ellen jumped on a bus and watched as Bolton passed by the window, her heart soaring. All they had to do now was wait. In time Peter would see Emma for what she was and fall back in love with Bess, and meanwhile she would be bringing up his son, making an unbreakable bond between them. The future suddenly seemed clear. It wouldn't be easy, but in the end Peter Holding and Bess would be together. Nothing could stop it now. No one could stop it now.

It was meant.

Chapter Twenty-eight

It was Bess's birthday, Peter arriving at the billiards hall at lunchtime with a present and a bunch of flowers. Discreetly Ellen left them alone in the kitchen; Reg was out and Lily had long since moved to her own small flat round the corner in Fletcher Street.

'I didn't know if you'd be here,' Peter said, kissing Bess on the cheek, 'or at the paper.'

She smiled. 'I'm off soon. Got an interview to do this afternoon, some celebrity staying at the Midland.' She glanced at her watch. 'I should be back around six. Ellen's picking Martin up from school today.'

He nodded, watching Bess with something bordering on amazement. This was the woman who had stuck with him for years, long after anyone else would have given up. With the help of Ellen and Lily, she had brought up his child, allowing him to continue running the engineering works and open another branch in Bury. Let him immerse himself in work, the all-consuming passion which had kept him sane. Her devotion had been unconditional and unwavering – even when she must have constantly wondered if he would ever forget Emma.

But he had done, eventually. Not overnight, but slowly, as news came out about her liaison with Sydney Goldstein, and gossip came hot to Bolton about her activities. Her dancing at his clubs, her autocratic behaviour to her lover's staff, her constant reference to herself as *Mrs Goldstein*, although everyone knew that the real Mrs Goldstein was alive and well in Cheadle Hulme and not about to divorce her husband for any mistress.

It was painful, watching his wife humiliate herself – but as the injuries mounted some reality began finally to percolate through to Peter Holding. Emma had done worse than leave him; she had left their child, never even asking after Martin. She had never phoned, called by, written a note. Never enquired whether her son was even alive or dead. How could a mother behave that way, Peter wondered, finally judgmental. How could she forget that she had given birth?

Because Martin was an inconvenience, he realized. He himself had been dumped for being boring, small fry, but his son had been dismissed for being a burden. Emma wanted to get on – but Emma wanted to get on *alone*. So gradually, as Peter saw his wife for what she was, the scent of her, the sound of her, the sensation of her body lying next to his – all memories which had haunted him, digging their claws into him relentlessly – slowly began to fade.

Gradually, Peter noticed that when Bess came round he forgot Emma for a while, and then later, when they went out pushing Martin in the pram, Peter found himself laughing and talking easily with her – as they used to do. But it was all very slow, very cautious. He knew he wasn't over Emma completely, and he was not prepared to hurt Bess again.

At work, she had fulfilled all her promise. Not only had she helped to raise Martin but she'd also progressed at the *Bolton Evening News*. Her page had been expanded to take in Women's Issues, and her talent for sharp interviews had been spotted by the *Manchester Evening News*, which resulted in Bess doing freelance work for them. She was successful, in demand, attending parties, socially at ease, a woman who knew her own worth.

A woman who knew exactly what she wanted.

Peter knew that Bess had dated other men, a particular friend being Gordon Howell, another freelance journalist who travelled the country, writing about social changes since the war. Peter didn't like her seeing other men, but how could he protest? When he couldn't commit to her, how could he honestly scupper her chances elsewhere? But it rankled with him, and when Bess continued to see Gordon, and travel with him to London on a couple of trips, he found himself unexpectedly jealous.

'I thought we could go out for a meal on Saturday,' Peter said now, watching as Bess snapped the clasp closed on her handbag.

'I can't.'

'Why?'

'I'm going to a dinner. A journalist do,' she explained.

'Is Gordon Howell going to be there?'

Bess's voice was light when she answered. 'I suppose so. He usually is.' She turned to the sink and filled a vase with water, arranging his flowers carefully.

'I wanted to take you out for a birthday celebration,' Peter said quietly, 'somewhere special.'

'We can go another time,' Bess replied, putting the vase on the windowsill and turning back to him. 'One Saturday night's much the same as another.'

But it wasn't, Peter realized. This Saturday night he had wanted to talk to her about their future, finally putting into words what he should have said long ago. He wanted to tell her that he loved her and that he was grateful to her, that Martin was a splendid child because of her. That they could be a proper family, at last. His father had died the previous summer and Peter had inherited the engineering works. Everything was finally in place for them to settle down. He would divorce Emma and marry Bess.

But suddenly, unexpectedly, Peter was worried. Maybe Bess would no longer *want* to marry him. She had seemed so busy lately, so successful, this coming Saturday was typical. Perhaps she had finally grown tired of waiting. And who could blame her? Five years was a long time to wait for anyone; perhaps she had decided in the end that Peter Holding wasn't worth the wait. Perhaps Bess was no longer thinking of their being a couple. The thought made Peter clammy, scared. He had presumed so much, for so long. What if now he was to be proved horribly wrong? Maybe Bess *was* planning her future – but not with him, with someone else. Like Gordon Howell . . .

Anxiously Peter watched as Bess moved round the kitchen and made them a sandwich; she seemed very much in control, confident, her good looks refined, her poise almost formidable. This was not the Bess he had once dumped, this was a woman of standing, a woman who was respected, talked about – a woman who had the power to *choose*.

'Well, I have to hand it to her, she's got him thinking at last,' Ellen said, walking in at Lily's back door and taking off her coat. It was hot for early April, the sun high over the low terraces.

Lily was fanning herself by the cooker, her sleeves rolled up, her face flushed with the heat. She looked younger than ever; her hair cut and permed, her figure surprisingly trim in a waisted dress. Even the news that Josiah was becoming a tyrant in his church had no effect on her composure whatsoever.

'Who are you talking about?'

Ellen peered into the pan next to Lily.

'Bess. She's seeing that Gordon Howell bloke again. What *are* you making?'

'Soup,' Lily said flatly, banging the lid down on the pan. 'Is she serious about this man Howell?'

'Looks like it,' Ellen replied, sitting down and fanning herself with the midday paper. 'They've been seeing a lot of each other lately and they're going to a dinner on Saturday.' She glanced over to Lily. 'D'you think she's smitten, or just trying to force Peter's hand?'

'I hope she marries Gordon,' Lily replied unexpectedly. 'Peter's dragged his feet for far too long.'

'But what about Martin?' Ellen asked. 'How would Peter feel about Bess looking after Martin if she married someone else?'

'Well, *he's* not offered to marry her, has he?' Lily countered. 'So he can hardly act surprised if someone else does.'

Ellen studied her sister carefully. 'You're in a feisty mood today.'

Lily leaned towards her sister over the table. 'I heard from Josiah yesterday. He wants me back –'

'No!'

'That's what I said,' Lily replied curtly. 'And that's why I don't want my daughter wasting herself on someone who's not in love with her. It would only end in tears.'

'But what if Peter *did* love her again?' Ellen asked. 'I mean, he did once, before Emma.' She paused on the name, but Lily made no response. 'He might truly love her, and want to make it work out.'

'He might and he might not.'

'Either way,' Ellen went on, 'I still say that Bess is finally playing it clever. There's nothing like competition to make a man jump.'

The competition was at that moment sitting in the bar of the Midland Hotel in Manchester, sipping a gin and tonic. Gordon Howell, forty-three years of age, in demand for newspaper articles and dinner engagements. Slim, tall, with large dark eyes and a smooth unlined face, he was effortlessly clever and intensely private.

'You look wonderful,' he said, rising to his feet as Bess walked in.

She was wearing a dark red dress, her long slim legs elongated with high-heeled shoes, her hair piled on top of her head. In her maturity Bess Shawcross had found a sensuality and presence that turned heads.

Smiling, she kissed him on the cheek and took the seat next to him.

'How are you, Gordon?'

'Writing a piece on smog,' he replied, crossing his legs. 'Apparently we will all be issued smog masks by the end of the year.'

'You're joking?'

'Seriously, I heard a rumour that the Government was going to offer them to people with breathing difficulties in industrial areas. We'll be walking around like mummies by Christmas.' He paused. 'How's Peter?'

'Anxious.'

'Excellent,' Gordon replied, clinking glasses with her.

She smiled warmly at him. 'You know, I'm very grateful for the help.'

'If you want a decoy, I'm your man,' Gordon replied, tapping the back of her hand. 'I'll be your phantom lover as long as you need me.'

Sipping her drink, Bess glanced round the bar. No one there knew about Gordon Howell; it was a secret to which very few were privy. Because Gordon had no interest in her nor in any women. He had a friend in London, but it was not public knowledge; exposure would have been dangerous and ruinous to his career. So instead they had agreed – to their mutual benefit – that they would appear to be dating. The charade served both of them very well; it provoked jealousy in Peter, and threw suspicion off Gordon. Besides, they liked each other.

'So what about the trip to London next week?'

'I can't get away,' Bess said. 'It's the school holidays and I can't leave Martin entirely to Mum and Ellen, it wouldn't be fair.'

Gordon studied her for a moment. 'The boy knows you're not his real mother, doesn't he?'

'I told him a while ago, but he didn't seem to understand. Or maybe he didn't want to.'

'How did you explain about Emma?'

'I just said that his mother had had to go away when he was born,' Bess replied, her tone cold.

'Have you heard anything about her lately?'

'Not a word since last year.' Bess turned the stem of her glass round in her fingers. 'I suppose she's still with Goldstein. She wouldn't give up on that meal ticket easily.'

'I could ask around, see if anyone's heard anything –'

Hurriedly, Bess shook her head. 'No, don't bother, Gordon, let sleeping dogs lie. Emma's not in our lives and hasn't been for years now, and frankly that's the way I want it to stay. I don't even want to think about her any more.'

Suddenly Gordon leaned forward and kissed her on the cheek. Bess laughed in surprise.

'What was that for?'

'I just felt like it,' Gordon replied. 'Call it admiration – and a bit of good window-dressing.'

She leaned back to scrutinize him, smiling.

'Doesn't it strike you as odd, the ways things are?'

'No, nothing strikes me as odd – except the fact that you love Peter Holding so much.' He paused, curious. 'Just why *do* you love him, Bess?'

She sipped her drink and then laid the glass down on the table in front of them, her face flushed, the strange, oblique eyes calm and steady. She was, Gordon thought, remarkably impressive.

'Peter was once very impulsive, very alive. When we were together we had a kind of energy which I'd never felt before with any other man – and never have since. He was so loving, so kind. Very like Reg in a way. No side to him, no snobbery. It didn't matter a damn to Peter where I came from. Who cared if I was living over a billiards hall?' She smiled at the memory. 'He was easy, big hearted ... so when he left me for Emma I couldn't take the loss of him. No one ever filled it. I knew then, what I know now, that

Peter Holding is meant for me. It's as though I bought something very valuable a long time ago, and put a reserved sticker on it – "To Be Collected Later". She smiled apologetically. 'It's just that I haven't picked it up yet. Crazy, isn't it?'

Gordon was listening intently.

'Have you never been tempted by someone else?'

'Oh yes,' she laughed. 'I've thought about it. I've been lucky, you see, had my opportunities.'

'But you never followed through?'

'I never wanted to. Something always stopped me.'

Gordon lowered his voice. 'Does he know how much you love him?'

'I doubt it,' Bess replied honestly. 'He's not really that intelligent about emotions. So for the last few years I've had to make do with loving him by proxy – through Martin.'

'Rough.'

'Oh yes, all of that. And my family think I'm mad to still want him. But I do.'

'I hope he's worth it,' Gordon said quietly. 'Because you deserve a man who'll stand by you. What if he hurts you again?'

Bess flinched.

'I'm sorry –'

'It's OK, Gordon,' she said quickly, 'you just said what I've been wondering for a long time.' She finished her drink slowly. 'I don't know *what* I'd do if Peter hurt me again. Or if anyone tried to come between us.' Her voice hardened, pure steel. 'Yes, yes, I do know. I would fight for him, Gordon, that's what I'd do. I would fight for him – and I'd fight dirty this time. And believe me, I'd win.'

278

Chapter Twenty-nine

'Sit down, sweetheart,' Lily said, ushering Martin over to the couch in Ellen's kitchen and laying her hand on his forehead. 'Have you got a pain?'

His face was white, his blue eyes dark-circled, lips pale. 'My head,' Martin stammered, '. . . my head hurts.'

Lily glanced over her shoulder at Ellen as she walked in. 'Go for the doctor, will you? I think Martin's ill.'

Without hesitating, Ellen hurried off, Lily sitting down beside the little boy and holding his hand.

'Bess will be home soon, sweetheart,' she told him. 'She'll make it all better, you'll see.'

He clung to his grandmother's hand and Lily smiled, but she could feel his fingers clammy against her own and felt panic slide into her heart.

Dr Young spent nearly half an hour examining Martin and then gestured to Ellen and Lily that they all go into the front room. Pale, Lily closed the door and turned to him.

'What is it?'

'I want to take him into hospital –'

'What for?' Ellen asked shortly. 'I'm not a child, doctor, I want to know what's the matter with my grandson.'

'I think Martin has polio.'

Shaken, Lily sat down.

'*Polio?*' Ellen repeated. 'Dear God, that's serious.'

'It could be –'

'I saw some pictures in the paper of children in iron lungs,' Lily said brokenly. 'Oh, not Martin. Oh no . . .'

'It might not be that bad,' Dr Young said calmly. 'But

we have to take him into hospital straight away. There's been an outbreak recently – I've seen three cases in the last few weeks. We have to get him hospitalized and isolated.'

Hurriedly Ellen moved over to her sister and put her arm around her shoulder.

'We'll have to tell Bess.'

'She can go with him; that would be best,' the doctor said, walking to the door. 'I'll make all the arrangements. Just keep him calm and we'll do what we can.'

Within the hour Bess was called home from work, an ambulance taking her and Martin to hospital, Lily travelling by bus. Promising them that she would follow on, Ellen made a stop at the library, going to the reference section and reading what she could find on polio, which was very little. The medical books just said that it was known as *infantile paralysis*. The illness began with headache, fever and sometimes vomiting, and could be followed by a more severe headache and progressive muscular weakness and paralysis. The first week was vital, after which the patient might recover. Or not, death finally occurring from paralysis of the respiration.

Stunned, Ellen closed the textbook and stared blindly ahead. No, not Martin, not when everything looked to be finally working out. She had thought only yesterday that Bess and Peter would be reunited and that, with Martin, they would become a real family. But now Martin was in the Manchester Infirmary and Bess – white-faced and in shock – was with him.

Unsteadily, Ellen rose to her feet. Martin was critically ill, he might die . . . her hand went to her forehead. Peter had been told and was on his way to the hospital, but there was someone else who had to be informed. Martin's mother, Emma.

But why? Ellen wondered. Emma had never wanted to be a part of her son's life, she had made that plain. But this was different; her son might die. She had to be told . . .

In a daze Ellen walked to the library exit and then made her way back to Derby Street along the hot terraces, the sun wicked and relentless on the rooftops. To have Emma back, and to have her back under such circumstances – it was too cruel, too much to bear. But it had to be done.

The world was savage that day.

Alone in the hospital waiting room, Ellen turned to her sister.

'Reg has gone to find Emma.'

The name slammed into Lily's chest like a hammer blow. *'Emma!'*

'We have to tell her,' Ellen replied tightly. 'If the worst happened ... Oh, come on, don't look at me that way. You know we *have* to tell her, Lily; she's Martin's mother.'

Dumbly, her sister nodded. 'You don't think –'

'I don't know,' Ellen responded, the question obvious. 'No one knows how bad it is. Martin might pull through –'

'But he might not.'

'He'll live,' Ellen said forcefully. 'He's got Bess and us behind him – he'll live.' She stopped as the door at the end of the corridor opened and Peter walked towards them.

He moved like an older man, suddenly aged, his heavy brows drawn together, the lines around his mouth pronounced. Usually smart, his tie was off, his shirt collar undone, a five o'clock shadow darkening his cheeks. When he looked at Ellen his eyes were flat, without hope.

'How is he?'

'Bess is with him,' Ellen replied, taking hold of Peter's arm as he was about to move off. 'Reg has gone to find Emma.'

She could feel him tense under her grip.

'Why?' His voice was hoarse.

'She had to be told, she's his mother –'

'Bess is more a mother to Martin than Emma ever was!' he snapped. 'You should have asked me first.'

Ellen's expression was flinty. 'Now look here, Peter Holding, I'm not going to be spoken to like that! We've all done our best for you and your son, and we made the decision because we thought it was the right thing to do. Martin is very ill, he might die . . .' Peter's eyes fixed on her helplessly. '. . . Emma has to be told.'

'But I don't want her here!' he replied angrily. 'I don't want her near my son. I just want Bess to stay with him.'

'I know,' Ellen retorted calmly. 'I don't want her back either. None of us does. But we have no choice. She has to know, so you might as well prepare yourself.'

Oh, come on, Martin, Bess urged the little boy as she sat by his bedside. You can get out of this; you can recover. Nothing's going to keep you down . . . She took his hand and stroked the back of it, then turned it over and kissed the palm tenderly. I'm not going to let you be ill, and I'm not going to let you die . . . She leaned towards him and kissed his forehead, stroking back the damp hair.

The ward was cooling down as she sat in isolation with Martin, a nurse peering through the peephole in the door. It was all so silly, Bess thought as she wrung out a cloth and wiped Martin's face again. Everything had been going so well, everything working out and now this. It made no sense.

'Martin, sweetheart, listen to me. It's Bess. I'm here, I've come from the paper to be with you. And I'm not going away until you're better and you can come home . . .' She fought back tears. Oh, come on, Bess, she told herself, you can do better than this. He needs strength. So be strong. 'It's so busy at work, and your granddad's been making you a hutch for the rabbit. We'll get it just as soon as you come home . . .'

Deeply asleep, Martin never stirred, or gave any impression that he had heard her. But Bess didn't stop talking, telling him about his friends at school, and the rabbit, which was coming on his birthday. Come on, Martin, fight. No one will take you away from me. No person and no illness. You're going to live, she promised him, you're going to live.

'Bess?'

She looked up to see Peter standing by the bed.

'He's not well,' she said simply, 'But he'll be OK, I know he will. He must be.'

Silent, Peter stared at his sick child and then looked over to Bess. Her hair was untidy, strands falling over her face, and it was obvious she had been crying. Oh God, he thought suddenly, why did I wait so long? When you loved me so much, when you loved my child so much – why did I hold back? Who else would have done what you've done? Who else would have been here, praying for my child? Not his mother, but you. You, Bess Shawcross.

Impulsively he gripped her hand.

'I love you.'

She stared at him, one hand holding his, the other clasping Martin's.

'Dear God, Bess,' he went on brokenly, 'don't ever go away, will you? Don't ever leave us.' He leaned down, nuzzling her hair, his lips moving to her forehead, her cheek, her lips.

Crying, she kissed him, tears salt on their lips.

'Say you forgive me . . .' he murmured, 'forgive me.'

The night staggered on, Ellen and Lily in the waiting area outside, Peter sitting by the bedside with Bess. Now and again a nurse would pass but there were no messages, no bulletins on Martin's condition. No one knew how ill he really was, or if he would make it through the night. So they all waited and prayed.

'Where is he?'

'Who?'

'Reg,' Ellen replied. 'He should have been back by now.

After all, he knows where Emma is – with that Goldstein bloke.'

'Maybe she wouldn't come,' Lily offered.

'You think she'd refuse?' Ellen frowned.

'I don't know,' Lily replied quietly. 'It's just been a long time, that's all.'

Another hour passed, the heat lifting, moist rain coming, lashing against the windows, condensation trickling onto the sills inside. Pulling her coat around her, Ellen glanced over to her sister.

'You OK?'

'Fine,' Lily replied. 'Are you?'

'As good as I can be.'

'We've been through some things, haven't we?'

Ellen nodded.

'All the children, Emma, Bess . . . D'you remember when Louise took Emma away?'

'I'll never forget it.'

'I thought I'd lost her. It was like she really was dead.' Lily stared at the rain falling. 'I don't want Bess to ever feel that bad . . .'

Gently, Ellen took her sister's hand.

'. . . I wonder sometimes – if Emma had never come back, Bess would have married Peter and they would have had children of their own. We wouldn't be sitting here.'

'But we wouldn't have had Martin.' Ellen reminded her.

'No . . .'

A moment passed between them, silent but for the slap slap of the rain on the windows. And then suddenly the door at the end of the corridor opened again and Reg walked in, followed by a woman. A woman who was unfamiliar, a woman who hung back momentarily in the shadows.

'He'll be all right,' Bess said quietly, Peter's arm round her shoulder.

'How do you know?'

'Because I do,' she replied emphatically. 'Nothing can shake us now, Peter. Nothing, and no one.'

He nodded, but couldn't trust his voice. Where did she get the strength from? How could she carry on and not waver?

'Do you trust me, Peter?'

'With my life.'

'Then trust me now,' Bess told him. 'Martin will recover and we'll be together. Everything will work out for us – as it should have done a long time ago.' She looked from her beloved to his child. 'I won't lose either of you. I won't let you go. You're both mine for ever and always. Remember that.'

'Who on earth is that?' Ellen asked, rising to her feet and watching as the young woman standing behind Reg came towards them, her head lowered, her hair tied back, her clothes dowdy. '*Emma?*' she said disbelievingly.

'She wasn't with Goldstein,' Reg explained, his voice flat. 'She's wasn't in Stockport any more, either. She was in Salford, working in a pub.'

Lily was too shocked to move, just remained seated, staring up at her unrecognizable daughter, who hung back from all of them.

'A pub?' Ellen replied, walking towards Emma and staring at her incredulously. 'What happened?'

'Sydney Goldstein left me,' she whispered, her voice still mesmeric, but low. 'I found work where I could.'

Her head lifted, her eyes fixing on Ellen. But the expression of defiance was gone. She looked hopeless and very, very frail. Where was the arrogance, the person they could all dislike and resent? Where was the promiscuous wife, the mother who abandoned her child? There was no trace of that Emma. This one was downtrodden, beaten, cowed. Vulnerable. The rejected child again.

285

Oh God, Ellen thought, this is dangerous.

'Where's my son?'

Ellen jerked her head towards the isolation ward. 'Martin's in there.'

She didn't know what to say. For years she had chewed over the words she would heap on Emma's head when she saw her, but now she was numb, caught off balance.

She wanted to say – how could you treat Bess that way, and your husband, and worst of all, your son? How could you run off and enjoy yourself and leave them without a thought? ... But suddenly Ellen couldn't attack. Emma was on her uppers, that much was obvious, the glossy good-time girl had been reduced to a dim wreck. The beauty was still there, but played down so much that it seemed Emma no longer wanted anyone to look at her. Was she *that* changed, Ellen thought. And if she was, what did she need now? Security. And what did that mean? *A home and family*.

Which was exactly what they were giving her.

Oh no, Ellen thought, please don't let me be the one to hurt you, Bess. Please, not me.

'Can I see Martin?' Emma asked quietly.

Neither Reg nor Ellen moved.

Finally Lily struggled to her feet and, avoiding Ellen's gaze, guided her daughter to the door. 'He's in here.'

Bess would remember that moment for as long as she lived. The door of the isolation ward opened slowly, a shadowed figure standing in the entrance for an instant before moving inside. Bess was still holding Martin's hand and Peter's when she felt the latter tense as Emma's face came into the lamplight.

It seemed that everyone took in their breath, Bess holding – literally – holding on to her man and Martin, as her rival approached. Emma must have seen the closeness between

286

Bess and her family and yet she said nothing, merely dropped to her knees by the bed and began to sob.

And then Bess felt Peter's hand slide slowly from hers as he moved over to his wife and stood for a long moment behind her. Emma's face was obliterated by her hair, but when she finally turned and looked up at him the expression on Peter's face drove a wedge into Bess's heart that she thought would kill her.

Chapter Thirty

In silence, Reg sat in the tiny booth in the billiards hall watching the punters play snooker in front of him. The smoke was heavy, swirling under the lamps. Some men were laughing, others in deadly earnest as they lined up for a shot. But try as he might, he couldn't dislodge the image of Bess the previous night as she slipped out of the isolation ward and moved towards them, Lily handing her coat to her in silence.

'Where are you going?' Ellen had asked her.

'Home. Emma's with her son now, they don't need me at the moment.' Her voice had been controlled, but close, so close to breaking.

'Go back in,' Reg had told her. 'Your place is in there.'

She had hesitated, but then shaken her head. 'No, not now,' she replied, walking ahead of them towards the exit.

He had sat up with her that night, waiting for news, watching as Bess busied herself, Ellen talking to Lily in the front room. Many times he wanted to say something, but didn't know what, just felt her anguish as his own. Why had they gone looking for Emma, he wondered. Why hadn't she been the old Emma, hard-faced and uncaring? Not this down-trodden woman who evoked pity.

Was it genuine? Reg, always suspicious of Emma, doubted it, had even asked Emma how long she had been apart from Goldstein. But she had avoided the question, let it hang, so that everyone could draw their own inference. Maybe she had been thrown out a long time ago and struggled valiantly, too ashamed to come home. And then again, maybe it had happened recently and Emma was more than willing to play the helpless female to get her hooks back in the family.

Angered, Reg had made Bess a second cup of tea and passed it to her, banking up the fire.

'What are you thinking about?'

'Walter,' she'd said softly, glancing over to the couch. 'He was quite something, wasn't he?'

He brought Martin to you, Reg had thought, that's why you're thinking about him now; wondering what he would say . . . Wincing, Reg could imagine his brother's response all too well, and had tried his own brand of comfort.

'She'll up and go again –'

'Don't!' Bess had snapped. 'I don't want to talk about it.' He'd been clumsy with anguish.

'Bess, don't worry, Peter loves you –'

'When Emma's not around, yes,' she'd replied bitterly. 'When she was out of the picture he loved me. If she had just kept away he would have divorced her and married me. We would have been a family together, with Martin.' She had shaken back her hair, colour blazing on her cheeks. 'But no, she had to be called back, the heartbroken mother, who everyone will feel sorry for and forgive –'

He had put his hand out to her, but for once Bess had knocked it away.

'I don't want pity!' she'd shouted. 'I've had enough pity to last a lifetime. I want Peter! I want Martin! I want my family back!' And with that she had run off upstairs, leaving Reg sitting dumbly in front of the fire and wondering what the hell had happened within the space of one short day.

A soft rapping on the side of the cubicle brought his thoughts back to the present. Ellen looked in on him.

'We've just heard from the hospital. Martin's better. He's not out of the woods, but he's not going to be as bad as we first thought. He'll need treatment for a long time, and exercises, but we can manage.'

He stared at her.

'Will she go now?'

Ellen knew whom he meant. Hesitating, she glanced upwards. 'Is Bess still in bed?'

'No, she phoned the hospital first thing and then left for work.' He paused. 'That was the worst day's work we ever did, bringing Emma home.'

'We had to.'

'Why?' Reg countered angrily. 'You saw her, all pitiful and ashamed. Emma wants a safe house, someone to look after her – and who will that be, Ellen? Holding, of course.' He stalked out of the cubicle, so angry that for once he intimidated her. 'I can't look Bess in the face any more. I can't imagine the pain we've caused her.'

'We had no choice –'

'We had!' he snapped. 'We should have left it longer, waited to see how Martin faired.'

'And if he had died?'

'Then we should have told Emma afterwards!' he replied bluntly. 'Lied to her, said we couldn't find her. But no, we had to do the *right* thing. She never has, but we had to play right by her.' His voice was bitter. 'Well, I don't know if you can live with it, but I bloody can't. If we had killed Bess we couldn't have injured her more.'

Emma was listening attentively to Dr Young as he outlined Martin's condition. Her son would need a great deal of care and consideration. He would require exercises to be done three times daily, and many visits to hospital. His needs had to be put first until he was fully recovered. *If* he fully recovered. His legs were weak, and he would always walk with a limp. It would be a long haul, Dr Young told her, a very long haul.

'I can do it,' Emma replied firmly.

Well, she could, couldn't she? Luck had brought her back home to her husband and son, luck of a sort. Martin would be fine, he'd recover, he was a child, after all. And she would have a home again. The humiliation of being dumped by Sydney Goldstein had been catastrophic: from being a pampered mistress she had been ousted almost overnight, Sydney having her dismissed from the house like a member of staff. Humiliated she had begged him to take her back but he wouldn't relent and she had spent the next week trying to find work and somewhere to live. Unqualified, she had only managed to secure a position as a barmaid in some old-fashioned Salford pub by telling the landlord that her husband had deserted her.

Still smarting from Sydney's treatment, Emma thought back. She had been so sure that he would divorce his wife and marry her. After all, she was the best-looking woman in the area, the perfect companion for a man like that. But she had overplayed her hand, Emma knew that now. She had been too possessive, too demanding – and he had reacted by getting rid of her. God, what a humiliation, Emma thought, the rejection so public, so final. God knows what she would have done if Reg hadn't come along looking for her.

It was funny how things had turned out. Now she was back in Rochdale, Peter Holding's wife and Martin's mother. She would have to make a go of it, settle down, Emma thought. But it wouldn't be too bad; Peter obviously still loved her. Not that he hadn't been tempted, she thought, remembering Bess holding her husband's hand – but he *did* still loved her, she could see that. Anyone could see that. It was tough, but Bess had to find her own man and her own child. Emma was back and she was going to make a success of her life. No one was going to pity *her* any more.

So she assured the doctor that she would look after her son. She had to hand it to Bess, the little boy had turned out well – handsome, sweet-natured – and although he had hardly spoken two words to her, he would come round. She was his mother, after all.

Her life here could still be salvaged, Emma thought hopefully, though it had been a close-run thing. So maybe Peter wasn't exciting, but he had inherited his father's business now so they would never starve, and being a wife was much better than being the mistress of any man, no matter how glamorous.

Emma narrowed her eyes, thinking of how she would write triumphantly to Louise and tell her the news, pretend that she had come to her senses and chosen her family over Sydney Goldstein. Oh yes, Emma thought, everything would work out. She had nothing to worry about. Nothing at all. Her mother needn't know that Goldstein had dumped her. She could come out of this in triumph. Smelling of roses.

'That is your second gin and tonic,' Gordon said to Bess as they sat by the bar in the Monkey's Paw. 'It's not like you to drink.'

'I want to drink,' she said defiantly. 'I want to stop thinking.'

'But Martin needs you,' Gordon reasoned. 'He won't take to Emma, even if she is his mother. Besides, she won't stay –'

'Oh yes, she will,' Bess replied firmly. 'Emma found out just how hard it is in the real world and it scared her. Besides, she'll be out for revenge since Goldstein dumped her. She never got over her parents rejecting her, you know that. That's what makes her so spiteful and dangerous.' Bess sipped her drink. 'Emma wants to be safe again – and where safer than being a wife and mother?'

'What about Peter?'

'*What* about him?' Bess countered coldly. 'He loves her, he always has. He might try to fight it, but he'll give in. Besides, she's playing the ashamed card now. Sorry for what she did, eager to make amends – and he'll fall for it.' She paused, dry-mouthed with fury. 'I can't believe that this is happening! Can't anyone remember the past? Where was Emma when Martin was a baby? Who looked after him when he was teething, who took him to be weighed, who took him out in his pram? Emma didn't take Martin to school the first day, or look after him when he had measles. *We* did, Ellen, Lily and I – and Peter. Not her. She was never a part of it. But now she's back, and who can refuse a mother her child? No one.'

'Hold on –'

'Don't tell me to hold on!' Bess snapped. 'I've held on and on. I've held on to my hopes and held on to Martin and Peter. And where has it got me?'

'Peter cares about you –'

'Until Emma came back.'

'I think you're misjudging him,' Gordon replied, his tone even. 'I think that Peter Holding values you too much to be fooled by his wife.'

Hurriedly, Bess signalled for another drink.

'You're wrong, Gordon. He won't be able to help himself,' she replied bitterly. 'When I spoke to him last night he sounded different. Oh, he told me he loved me, but he was distracted, distant.'

'Emma coming back was a shock to him –'

'To everyone,' Bess said acidly. 'He talked about us – about us being together with Martin, telling me to be patient a bit longer. Emma would go away again, he said. But I'm not convinced. And I'm tired of being bloody patient.'

'So you're giving up on him?'

'Why not?'

Gordon shrugged. 'Personally I think you should have done that a long time ago. Holding was never that big a catch –'

Bess's face flushed with fury, just as Gordon knew it would.

'Peter is a good man!'

'But not worth fighting for?'

293

'Not worth fighting for?' Bess repeated. 'How do you make that out?'

'Because you told me only a few months ago that you wouldn't let anyone or anything come between you and your family – and now you're ditching them, giving up –'

Stung, Bess rounded on him. 'They aren't my family!'

'They are!' Gordon replied shortly. 'Legally Emma might be Peter's wife and Martin's mother, but she doesn't care about them. Before long, she'll revert to her old self, you know that. She won't be able to resist it. But if you give up now, Bess, you've lost them for ever. If there was ever a time to stand your corner, this is it.' He took the drink from her and laid his hand over the top of the glass. 'Go on, get out. Get back to that hospital and fight for what's yours.'

Bess bit her lip. 'Emma won't go. She'll stay, I know she will.'

'You're right, Emma *will* stay if you make it easy for her,' Gordon replied evenly. 'So go and make her life hell. You owe her that much.'

Ellen was adamant on one point: Martin was not going back to the Rochdale house in which Emma and Peter had once lived. However much Emma pushed for it. The child needed constant treatment and supervision – and Martin could only get that in Derby Street.

'How can we all stay here?' Emma countered, her tone controlled, reasonable. 'There isn't space.'

'There is. You can have your old room –'

'But what about Peter?'

Ellen stood her ground; Emma was being pleasant, suspiciously so.

'The first consideration is for Martin,' Ellen replied. 'The child has lived here all his life. When he gets out of hospital he doesn't want to be in less familiar surroundings. Besides,

you can't manage on your own. You'll need backup –
myself, Bess –'

'Bess!' Emma replied sharply, then softened her tone. 'I
can't ask her to do any more. She's done enough.'

'You can't ask her to do any less,' Ellen responded
evenly. 'She raised your son when you ran off. She's like
a mother to him.'

Ellen could see the flicker of irritation in Emma's eyes.
So Emma hasn't changed that much, she thought; still envious, still possessive – when it suits her.

'I suppose Bess *could* help.'

'And Lily would miss Martin too much if you took him
off to Rochdale full time. Remember, we all brought that
child up, and we all love him. You can't just come back
and get everything your own way, Emma. You're the one
who has to fit in now.'

Emma's jaw tightened. Who was Ellen Shawcross to tell
her what to do? She had been someone, lived in a beautiful
house, had servants – how dare some woman living over
a billiards hall order her around? But she decided to say
nothing, just bide her time. She would have her child back
and gradually move him and Peter away. You never know
what might happen; with Peter having more money they
just might emigrate, leave everyone behind. All she had to
do was to be patient.

But Emma wasn't a natural mother, nor was she patient
by nature. A week later, when Martin came home to Derby
Street, he was put in the upstairs bedroom, next to Bess's,
Emma deciding to sleep on the couch in the kitchen. Where
Walter had once sat watching her. To her amazement Peter
did not insist that she go and live with him in Rochdale.
Instead, her husband seemed more than willing for her to
stay at Derby Street. Stung by what she took as a another
rejection, Emma turned her attention to her son.

But Martin wasn't used to her and, being fretful and

poorly, cried for Bess or Ellen, never for his mother. Emma frequently got in the way, Reg watching the chaos with dismay. The house was too small for bad tempers, he thought, remembering how difficult it had been before when Emma was at home. But now there was a sick child here as well, and too many women.

'What the hell d'you expect me to do about it?' Ellen asked him one night. 'Emma wants to look after her son. What do you suggest I do – let her take Martin back to Rochdale?'

'Over my dead body!' Reg snapped. 'That child stays here. I don't trust her to look after him properly on her own. If anyone goes, it's Emma.'

Impatiently, Ellen cleared the table and piled the plates in the sink.

'She wants to make a go of it –'

'No she doesn't!' Reg snapped. 'She wants a breather, somewhere to play house.'

Angrily, Ellen slammed a saucer down on the table.

'*What can I do about it?*' she shouted at him. 'I don't want things to be like this. We have to make the best of it.'

'Try telling that to Bess!' Reg hurled back, throwing down his paper and walking out.

A few minutes later Lily arrived, walking in to find Ellen sitting in front of the fire with her crumpled apron in her hand. Her eyes were pink-rimmed.

'Have you been *crying*?'

'No!' Ellen barked, getting to her feet, embarrassed. 'It's just smoke, a down draught from the chimney.'

'I came round to see if I could help,' Lily said gingerly. 'Are you sure you're all right?'

'No, of course I'm not!' Ellen replied, throwing down her apron and turning on her sister. 'It's impossible here. Bess can hardly bring herself to talk to Emma – and I'm not surprised – and Emma wants to get Martin out and

296

be with Peter. I don't know why all of this had to happen. God knows, things should have settled down by now. We all need some bloody peace. This is Reg's house, and it's time we had it to ourselves. I never minded Bess and Martin being here, but Emma – she's another matter altogether. She caused trouble before, and she's doing so again.'

Ellen turned back to the sink and a subdued Lily slid out of the kitchen and walked upstairs. It wasn't fair; she knew it. Emma and Bess were her children, not Ellen's, and yet she had allowed her sister and brother-in-law to take the responsibility for years. And now they had all the trauma of Emma again.

When Lily entered Martin's bedroom, Bess was rubbing Martin's legs, Emma watching, her sleeves rolled up. The pitiful look she had worn the night she came to the hospital was lifting, her beauty coming back strong and powerful.

'You have to rub the calves like this,' Bess said patiently, 'thirty times on each leg to build up strength.'

'I can do that.'

'It's important –'

'I said I can do it.'

The atmosphere between the two women was electric, Martin mewling with pain.

'Can I help?' Lily asked from the doorway.

'There isn't enough room in here for anyone else!' Emma snapped.

'Hey, just a minute, it's not Lily's fault –' Bess began.

But Emma was hot, flustered, her patience strained. 'Why are you here anyway?' she asked Lily. 'What's any of this got to do with you?'

It was the tension of the moment that got to her: Martin whimpering, the room clammy, Bess massaging the little boy's legs, Emma snappy and thoughtless. If she had held her patience for a moment longer, Lily could have controlled herself – but it was too late.

'*What's it got to do with me?*' she said, gripping Emma's

arm and jerking her round. 'You're my *daughter*, that's what it's got to do with me!'

Immediately Bess stopped rubbing Martin's legs, her mouth opening. Emma shook off Lily's grip and stepped back against the wall. Her eyes had widened, fixed on Lily with disbelief. What was she talking about? *Louise* was her mother, the smart, snobbish Louise, who lived in detached splendour in Australia, not this little preacher's wife.

'You can't be my mother!'

But for Bess, understanding was coming fast. Emma was her *sister* – the woman who had stolen her man was her *sister*. She glanced down at Martin incredulously – so this child was her nephew, her sister's son. Suddenly dizzy, she sat down on the side of the bed.

'Emma is my *sister*?'

Lily nodded, seeing the two women stare at her in disbelief, the room oppressively hot around them, the little boy lying on the bed watching them silently.

'I don't believe that Bess is my sister,' Emma said, her voice faltering. 'I don't believe it! You're not my mother – Louise is my mother and Clem's my . . .' She trailed off, her face paling. 'So who *is* my father?'

Lily had gone too far to back off now.

'Harold Browning. The same man who's father to Bess,' she said quietly.

'So there *was* a baby,' Bess murmured, shaking her head. 'I thought I remembered there being a baby around when we first came to live here.' She stared at Emma. '*You* were the baby –'

'I don't believe it!' Emma repeated, pushing her hair away from her face.

Lily *couldn't* be her mother, she *couldn't* have been born here. Not in this dismal little town, to this dismal little woman. She was different from the Shawcrosses, better than them. She wasn't one of them . . . But suddenly it made sense to her now: Louise bringing her back to Bolton, back to Derby Street, leaving her with her sisters. But she hadn't left her with her sisters, she had returned Emma to the mother who had given her up as a baby.

'Things were so difficult, Emma. I had to give you to Louise –'

'You hypocrite!' Emma snapped violently. Lily reeled back. 'You've made me feel so bad about leaving my son, but you left me. You gave me up. You're as bad as I am.'

'It's not the same!' Lily replied, her face ashen. 'I didn't want to give you up, you ran off. It was easy for you, Emma, but it wasn't for me. Don't try and salve your conscience by tarring me with the same brush.'

Without another word, Emma turned and ran down the stairs. Bess covered Martin with a sheet and followed her, and Lily hurried after both of them.

'Emma, wait!'

'What for?' she snapped at her mother, turning as she reached the kitchen.

'I want to explain,' Lily said desperately. 'I've wanted to explain for years.'

'Explain what? That you didn't want me?' 'No one did, did they? Not you, nor Louise. No one ever wants me –'

'It wasn't like that,' Lily said plaintively.

'I don't even *like* you,' Emma replied cruelly 'I don't want to believe that you're my mother. You can't be!'

Bess caught her by the arm savagely. 'Mum must have had her reasons –'

'What reasons? There are no reasons for what she did –'

Lily was beside herself. 'Emma, listen to me! Your father was dead, I was ill. I couldn't keep you both –'

'So you chose to keep Bess!'

'It wasn't like that! It wasn't a question of choice. You were a baby, Emma, and my sister had no children. I knew Ellen and Reg would look after Bess, but Louise wanted you so much and I thought she'd give you everything I couldn't – a good life, money, everything. And she did. You've no idea how hard it was for me –'

'How *hard*!'

'Yes, how hard it was,' Lily insisted. 'I had to pretend to everyone that you had died, that you were in fact Louise's baby. It was heartbreaking. Louise kept in touch with us at first, but when you were only a few years old she moved and never let us know where you were. I didn't know if you were dead or alive –'

'That must have been convenient,' Emma retorted bitterly.

Stung, Lily moved over to her daughter. 'All right, I deserved that, but I loved you, Emma. I always have –'

'What do you want me to say? Thank you for the confession? I forgive you, Mother?' Emma wrenched open the back door and then turned. 'Well, I'll tell you one thing, history isn't going to repeat itself again. I'm not giving up my son . . .' she glared at Bess, '. . . or my husband. They're mine, and I intend to keep them.' Then she rushed out, the sound of her footsteps echoing down Derby Street.

Shaken, Lily stared after her. The heat was overpowering, making breathing difficult. Bess leaned heavily against the window ledge as she looked at her mother.

She had nothing left to say – couldn't even frame the words – *Why? Why did you tell her now?* Instead, she just stared at the linoleum on the floor and listened to the clock ticking.

Lily was the first to speak.

'I suppose you hate me?'

Bess shook her head. God, it was hot.

'No . . . I just can't believe that Emma's my sister. We could have been friends, like you and Ellen. Everything could have been so different . . .' She fought to find words. 'She won't go away now, Mum. You know that, don't you? That will be Emma's special punishment for you and me – to stay. To claim back what's hers – Martin and

Peter.' She laughed softly to herself. 'God, why did you do it?'

'I didn't think. I just lost my temper . . .'

Bess remained staring at the floor, incredulous, still trying to comprehend what she had heard, and what it would mean.

'Why didn't you tell Emma that you were her mother when Louise brought her back to England?' Her voice dropped. 'And why didn't you tell me?'

'I wanted to at first – but things got so complicated,' Lily replied hesitantly. 'It was a lie that took on a life of its own. I was terrified that Josiah would find out about Emma – he never wanted children and at the time we married she wasn't around. I needed him so much then.' She looked at her daughter imploringly. 'You can't understand, Bess, just *how* much I needed him. Then later, when I wanted to leave Josiah, he threatened to tell Emma the truth if I did. God, what a mess. One lie just spread and spread, hurting everyone . . . I never meant to hurt you.'

Bess was staring ahead blindly. 'But you did.'

Lily sat down on the couch heavily.

'I've been such a bad mother, such a bad wife –'

She had every reason to hate her mother, Bess thought bitterly. She could loathe her for ruining her chances, albeit inadvertently. But she knew too much about Lily to hate her. She had seen her struggle too often over the years, cowed by illness, depression, then by Josiah. Her life had been a series of routs, with only uneasy peace in between. She had had little happiness and now she was suffering again, knowing full well what one moment's loss of control had done.

Yet, even as Bess tried to sympathize, to accept, she found herself plotting.

Emma was her sister. Emma had taken her man and was now threatening to take over her life. Oh no, Bess thought, not this time. You might think you're going to win, but

301

you're wrong, Emma. I'm not going to miss out like my mother, I want what's mine, and I intend to get it.

And no one, especially you, is going to stand in my way.

Chapter Thirty-one

For three weeks Emma stayed at Derby Street and daily undertook Martin's exercises. Last thing at night she read to her son and slowly, very slowly, Martin responded.

'You wait,' Ellen said to Lily when she called round at her sister's in Fletcher Street. 'It won't be long now before Emma'll take Martin back to Rochdale.'

'She can't –'

'Oh, yes she can,' Ellen replied. 'Who can stop her? She's been looking after him as well as any mother could – who could fault her? Not the doctors, nor us. It's only right for a mother to take care of her child.' She frowned. 'Only not *this* mother, and not with *this* child.'

'It's my fault, isn't it?' Lily's voice faltered. 'If I hadn't blurted out the truth –'

'No, it's not your fault, Lily. What you said didn't help, but Emma wanted her family back anyway. She just feels righteous about it now, that's all.'

'And Bess?' Lily asked. 'I can't even look at her now, or Reg. He's furious with me.'

'Bess is being very quiet,' Ellen replied, 'very calm. She's plotting something. I don't know what, but she is. Trust me, she's not going to let her sister win this time.'

'But how can she stop it?' Lily countered, 'When Emma gets Martin back to Rochdale, she'll have won. And she won't let us have much to do with him then, I know that for a fact. She doesn't want me as a mother, so she certainly won't want me as a grandmother.'

Leaning back in her seat, Ellen folded her arms. 'But Peter's not playing her game, is he?'

'How do you mean?'

'When he's been round here visiting Martin, he's always made sure that he's not alone with Emma. Haven't you noticed that? He makes sure that Bess is there, or I am. He never wants to be alone with his wife.'

'He will be when Emma moves back to Rochdale. He'll have to, they'll be under the same roof.'

'*If* he goes with her.'

Lily glanced at her sister curiously. 'But if Martin goes, Peter will have to.'

'I'm not so sure,' Ellen replied thoughtfully. 'I never thought Peter Holding was up to much after he dumped Bess – but now I'm not so sure. He's a dark horse, not as gullible as I thought. Emma thinks he's still crazy about her, but I have a feeling that she might be a bit too cocky for her own good this time.'

Bess was sitting in a café on Bark Street, next to the Victoria Hall, her swing coat draped over the back of her seat, her elbows resting on the table in front of her. The freak weather had given way to the usual rainy May, chill winds blowing down from Winter Hill and the moors, passers-by hurrying against the cold. Deep in thought, Bess stared into her coffee.

As everyone had predicted, Emma was preparing to take Martin away from Derby Street within the next few days. She was a wonderful mother, Dr Young said, took her responsibilities very seriously and was obvious desperate to make up for her past actions. Besides, Martin was flourishing under her care. Which was true, Bess thought ruefully, her nephew was getting stronger, his walking improving steadily, although his right leg was wasted and he needed callipers to get about. Martin still smiled when Bess walked in to see him, but he clung to Emma when he was in pain and snuggled up to his mother when she read to him.

And oh, how Emma relished her triumph, Bess thought bitterly. How she looked over her child's head to her sister, her eyes challenging. But much as Bess might long to take Martin away from Emma, how could she? Emma was his legal mother and besides, Martin's happiness came first, not hers. So she let her sister steal him away, day by day, her kindness poisonous to watch. And after Martin, how soon would she take over Peter again?

The thought had galvanized Bess in action. Which was why she was sitting in the café, waiting . . .

She had been working longer hours at the paper as her maternal duties had been usurped. Several interviews had come up and Bess had gone off to Manchester and London to cover them, trying to pretend that her career was important, that it could make up for the aching gap in her life. She had also been seeing a lot of Gordon too, finding in him someone who would listen as she talked endlessly about Martin — searching, always searching for the one weak link, the one chink in Emma's defences. When she found that — she told Gordon — she would win.

Bess knew she was getting obsessive, but something drove her on. A hunch, an instinct that was equal to any mother's. She did not trust her sister; did not want Emma to take Martin away. In Derby Street he was safe, in Rochdale he was isolated. Alone. She couldn't allow that to happen.

But time was running out fast.

'I don't understand. Emma's been looking after him perfectly. Quite the little mother,' Gordon had said to Bess the previous evening.

'Emma is an actress, she can act any part. The perfect mistress, wife, mother — when she has an audience. I'm worried about when she *doesn't* have that audience.'

'Are you saying she'd hurt Martin?'

'I don't know,' Bess had answered honestly. 'She might. Or she might neglect him. Peter worries about that too; he

305

said at much yesterday. He wants Martin to stay at Derby Street with us, but he can't stop Emma taking him back to Rochdale. She keeps asking him to give her a chance, to make up for the past.'

Gordon had grimaced. 'And how does he feel about that?'

'He thinks she's trying to trap him, to turn back the clock.'

'So he's on to her?'

'It would seem so, but who knows? When Emma has Peter to herself again in Rochdale, how long can he resist her? She's his wife, she's beautiful. He's always been besotted. He might well fall back into the marriage.'

'So stop him.'

'No,' she'd said firmly. 'I've told Peter that Martin shouldn't be left alone with his mother.'

'But that means you're throwing him back into Emma's arms . . .' Gordon had trailed off, shaking his head in disbelief. 'Oh no, Bess, you can't.'

'I can, and I will,' she had replied. 'Martin has to be protected – whatever the cost.'

Draining her cup of coffee, Bess remembered the conversation and then waved as she spotted Peter across the road. Hurriedly he entered the café and sat down, taking off his wet coat and hanging it on a peg by the door.

'Am I late?' he asked, kissing her cheek.

His touch warmed her, made her heart ache. Oh God, she thought, what am I about to do?

'No, I was early,' Bess replied, signalling to the waitress. 'Can we have two more coffees, please?'

'You look wonderful,' Peter said seriously, touching the back of Bess's hand. She was dressed in a work suit, her hair lose around her shoulders, her eyes steady. 'How's Martin?'

She took in a deep breath. 'That's what I wanted to see you about –'

'Is he OK?'

'Fine, it's just that . . .' Bess paused, to let the waitress deliver the coffees and leave, '. . . Emma's taking him home this week.'

'*Home?*'

'To Rochdale. Back to Colland Street,' Bess said bitterly. 'I didn't think she would have told you. Probably wanted it to be a surprise.'

'She can't do it!' Peter said simply. 'I want Martin to stay at Derby Street with you.'

'But Emma's his mother, and Dr Young was telling us earlier that she could cope alone now. She isn't working – it's natural for a mother to look after her sick child.' Bess hurried on to prevent Peter interrupting her. 'No one can fault her care of Martin. She's done wonders with him.'

Peter took Bess's hand. 'I'm not staying in the house with her. I'll move out,' he said quickly. 'Don't worry, Bess, I don't want Emma any more.'

Helplessly, Bess held on to his hand. No, she thought, don't let me say it, let me keep him here, let me stay silent. But she couldn't hold back.

'I don't trust Emma,' she said simply. 'I don't want her to be alone with Martin. I don't think she's responsible enough . . . There has to be someone there who'll watch over Martin. I can't be there – but *you* could.'

He stared at her, momentarily dumbstruck. 'Are you serious?'

'Yes.'

'You're mad!' he said, tightening his grip on her hand again. 'I love you, Bess. I don't want to go back to Emma. I don't want to live with her –'

'But you have to look after your son.'

'No –'

'Peter, Martin is a child; we both love him too much to endanger him. I'm not saying that Emma would hurt him,

307

but she's not reliable, and someone has to be there to look out for him.'

'I can't –'

'Why?'

'Because I love you!' he snapped.

'Then if you really love me, you could do this.' Her voice softened. 'We don't have a leg to stand on. Emma is Martin's mother; she has every legal right to take him away from Derby Street –'

'But she left him once.'

'I know, but she came back and she's looked after him since. To outsiders, Emma looks like a reformed character. We can't make Martin stay at Derby Street.'

'I don't like this,' Peter said grimly.

'Look, I know you're worried, I understand, believe me. I wish I didn't. Emma is beautiful, and she's your wife. You think you might be tempted if you're living together again –'

'I don't want her,' he insisted.

'Just promise me one thing,' Bess said. 'I believe you when you say that you don't want her back. I think you truly mean it . . . But if you find that you fall in love with her again and if you sleep with her . . . don't tell me. Please, don't tell me.'

Incredulously Peter stared into her face. 'I couldn't do it to you, Bess. If I loved you before, I love you ten times more now. I won't cheat on you, and I won't sleep with Emma. She's not worth losing you for. She never was – it just took me years to realize it.'

Satisfied, Emma glanced over to Martin, sitting in the ambulance beside her. She had done it, no one could say she wasn't a good mother, and all those people who had had a down on her before would have to eat their words. Emma was back, restored to the bosom of her family. Anyway, it wasn't so bad being a mother. Martin might be a sickly child, but he was getting fond of her, and she needed someone of her own.

She would never give him up, Emma thought sanctimoniously. Her mother might give her up, but she'd show them ... Tenderly she took Martin's hand and was rewarded with a smile. When he was better she would be able to take him to school; when he was off his callipers she could take him out and about, show him off. He wasn't going to be puny all his life, surely.

As for Peter ... Emma frowned, he had been distant with her lately, but that was probably embarrassment, an uncertainty of how to behave in front of the Shawcrosses. After all, how could he show how he really felt when someone was always around? And as for Bess, her sister ...

Emma sighed and looked out of the ambulance window. It was a pity, but that was life. Besides, she and Bess had never got on; knowing she was her sister would hardly change that. And as for Bess loving Peter – well, it was doomed, wasn't it? She should have known that from the start, should have found someone else by now. Some other man, not her sister's husband.

Surprised to find that they had arrived so quickly, Emma climbed out of the ambulance and unlocked the front door on Colland Street. Several of her neighbours watched her. Gently one of the ambulance men carried Martin inside and took him upstairs, laying him on the bed in the room next to hers and Peters.

'Thank you for your help. We'll be fine now,' Emma said, showing them out and nodding curtly to her nearest neighbour.

But when she closed the front door there was silence. Stillness, memories hanging round her like old ghosts. The rooms were the same, unchanged over the years she had been away, and even her recent spring cleaning had not dislodged the aura of the place. Suddenly she could remember Walter Shawcross coming to see her, the Austin parked outside, and with a shudder Emma stood at the bottom of the stairs wondering what to do next.

Homesickness overwhelmed her, but she didn't rightly know for *which* home. Australia, or Sydney Goldstein's house? Not this one certainly . . . Disorientated, she wandered into the front room and fiddled with the curtains. She had done all this before, she realized, years before. Before leaving Rochdale, before Goldstein . . . Panic set in, sudden and overwhelming. What had she done? What on earth had she done? She didn't really want to be here, did she? This was the house from which she had run away so willingly, from these same walls, these neighbours, this furniture.

Breathing quickly, Emma turned and walked out of the room but stopped short at the bottom of the stairs. What was that? she thought surprised, what was that noise? Then she recognized the sound of her son's voice calling for her.

Numbly and unwilling, Emma began to climb the stairs.

Chapter Thirty-two

As Bess had taught him, Peter massaged his son's right leg, Martin squirming under his touch. The bed on which Martin lay was crumpled, the pillows flattened, uncomfortable. Below Peter could hear Emma talking on the telephone and tried to make out her words, but failed. Martin cried out suddenly.

'Sorry, lad.'

'OK, Daddy,' Martin said patiently, shifting his position.

'I have to do it to make you well. You know that, don't you?'

That day Peter had come home earlier than usual to find Emma sitting in front of the radio, listening to a play, Martin in his room upstairs. The volume had been turned up so that she would not hear her son crying for her.

Furious, he had snapped off the wireless and turned on her.

'What the hell are you doing?'

She stood up, her mouth sulky. 'What's the matter with you?'

'Martin's calling for you.'

She shrugged. 'I was only up there a little while ago,' she said impatiently. 'I can't spend every minute with him.'

'So bring him downstairs,' Peter countered. 'He was never left alone at Derby Street.'

'Oh, Derby Street!' she sneered. 'Of course everything was perfect there.'

'It was better than here,' Peter responded. 'I didn't worry about him there.'

Nothing had gone the way Emma had expected. Not

311

one thing. On the first evening, Peter had returned home from work to find her dressed in her best outfit, her hair brushed loose over her shoulders, a smile on her lips. Using the sensual lilt of her voice, Emma had ushered him into the front room and then curled up beside him on the sofa.

She was beautiful; at thirty-five coming into the full maturity of her looks, her body sensual, her movements lithe and intoxicating. For a moment he wanted her with every cell, then remembered what she had done, and remembered Bess.

'I have to go and look in on Martin.' he said, getting to his feet.

Wrong-footed, Emma stared at him.

'What!'

'I'm going to see my son.'

She reached for his hand.

'Later . . .' Her was voice low. 'We have a lot of catching up to do, Peter.'

His hesitation was short-lived as he pulled away and moved into the hall.

Furious, Emma followed him.

'What's the matter with you?'

'Nothing,' Peter said awkwardly.

'Nothing!' she parroted. 'I wouldn't call rejecting your wife *nothing*.' Her eyes narrowed. 'Oh, so that's it. My sister's got her claws into you, has she? Well, I suppose she hung around long enough to get something back for her trouble.'

He was so close to hitting her that it frightened him.

'I'll ignore that remark,' he said sharply, turning away and making for the stairs.

'Come back here!' Emma called after him. 'I want you. You're my husband,' but he kept moving away from her. Emma's voice was rising with spite. 'You were always useless! Always a loser. You never satisfied me once –'

Stunned Peter stopped short, then moved back down the stairs to face his wife.

'Lower your voice!' he snapped, taking Emma's arm. 'I won't have my son hear your filth –'

'It wasn't filth when you dumped Bess for me, then it was fun.'

Incensed, Peter shook her. 'Shut up!'

'Make me!' she shouted back, her lovely face turned up to his. 'Go on, prove you're a man that way – if you can't the other.'

Stunned, Peter stared at his wife and then brusquely let go of her arm. She was suddenly ugly to him. He wanted to shout at her, to throw her out of the house – but he couldn't. She was his wife, the mother of his child. Once, long ago, he had given up everything for her, and now he was reaping his reward.

'I'll sleep in the spare room,' he said icily.

Smiling, Emma folded her arms. 'I wonder how long you'll keep that up.'

'It'll be permanent,' he said coldly, turning away from her and moving up to his son's room.

Peter mistrusted Emma from that moment on and made excuses to leave the engineering works at lunchtime, just so he could check up on her. Sometimes he would find her talking on the phone, sometimes doing Martin's exercises – and sometimes she would be still in her dressing gown at twelve thirty.

'You should be dressed,' he told her the first time he discovered her like that.

She looked at her lazily. 'Why?'

'Because someone might call.'

'Like who?' she snapped. 'No one calls round here.'

'And who's fault is that?' he replied. 'You should make friends with the other mothers. When Martin's better he'll be back at school. He shouldn't lose touch with his friends. It's not good for him.'

'And how am I supposed to entertain a bunch of kids?'

'The same way other women do!' Peter replied angrily. 'Bess never had any trouble –'

'Oh, Saint Bess never had any trouble with anything, did she?' Emma sneered. 'Except keeping her man.'

They couldn't go on like this, Peter thought, turning away. The whole thing was too ugly. And it wasn't good for Martin to be shut away in his room for most of the day with only his mother for intermittent company. His thoughts hurdled on. He didn't have any real reason to take Martin away; Emma was clever enough to know that she had to look after her son, so she did what was necessary.

But Peter wondered how long *he* could bear being with her. He wanted out; wanted to take Martin with him back to Derby Street and collect Bess. They could buy another house somewhere, look after Martin together. Get married – in fact do what they had once planned to do all those years before. Before Emma.

But Peter knew he couldn't take his son back to Derby Street. If he did, Emma would take him to court and con everyone, the law would declare that Martin should be with his rightful mother and return him to Emma's care. So what other choice was there? He might be learning to hate Emma, and long to be away from her, but Peter realized only too well that he couldn't leave his son behind. Emma had him caught; just as she had planned. He was trapped – and he knew it.

'It's not good,' Bess said bluntly, standing by Walter's grave and staring at the headstone. 'Martin's gone back to Emma. And so has Peter.'

The Shawcrosses had decided to bury Walter in a church-yard up on Cocky Moor, away from the built-up terraces of Bolton. He would have liked to be able to see the countryside, Ellen had said; it would make him feel free.

'I don't know what to do,' Bess went on. 'If you were still alive, you'd know. You'd have some clever scheme all cooked up. I'm thirty-eight years old, Walter ... thirty-eight years old.'

Where had the years gone? What had happened to all her plans? Oh, she was successful, her career was doing well, but her private life was a disaster. Walter would never have ended up like her; he would have done something. But *how* could she do anything? And what *was* there to do?

Emma hadn't settled down – Peter had told her that much – and although Martin wasn't neglected, he was hardly flourishing. No one was happy, not the man she loved, or the child she adored. Not even Emma, if the truth be known.

So how could she force matters? How could she break up the make-believe family and bring them back home to her? There *had* to be a way, Bess thought, staring at Walter's grave stone for inspiration. There *had* to be a way.

Then suddenly the idea came to her. Old man Crowthorn ...

She could imagine Walter laughing at what she was about it do. *Leopards never change their spots,* he used to say, *and neither do people. They just repeat their mistakes over and over again.*

Bess just hoped that Emma repeated *her* mistakes ... It had been months now since her sister had taken Martin back to Rochdale, months in which Emma had made sure that the family hardly saw her child. She had effectively segregated him, supposedly to look after him, the caring, possessive mother – but Bess wasn't fooled.

She had lost her patience, and was ready to fight.

Summer was coming to its close, September bringing the first turn of the leaves, the weather still oppressive, clammy in the Rochdale house. The autumn term began at school, but Martin didn't attend on the first day or the second. He was too frail, his mother said. And meanwhile Peter left home later in the mornings and returned earlier in the evenings, always watching for some slip on Emma's part.

It was an impossible way to exist. The Shawcrosses knew it in Derby Street and Peter knew it. There was something in the air that September, some tragedy which was waiting its time.

When Lily was finally admitted to see him, Martin was quiet, Emma hanging around her son and never leaving her mother alone with him. The house was stuffy, the windows closed, Emma dressed in a pink blouse and pedal pushers, her hair newly washed. She looked radiant, almost smug.

'Say hello to your grandmother,' she told Martin.

He smiled wanly.

'How's your leg?' Lily asked.

'Better,' Martin replied hurriedly. 'I can go back to school soon –'

'Now you know that depends on how well you are,' Emma interrupted smoothly, 'You can't rush things, sweetheart.'

'But, Mum –'

She smiled at him, stroked his hair. 'I know best. I always know best.'

Lily glanced at daughter curiously. 'Martin does look a lot better, and his walking's really improved. He should get out more though, get some sunshine on his skin.' She could see Emma bridle.

'I know how to look after my child,' she said shortly. 'And Martin needs lots of rest.' Gently, she touched his cheek. 'Mum loves you and wants the best for you, doesn't she?'

316

Obediently, he nodded in the stuffy room, a bee humming drowsily behind the half-drawn curtains.

'She's suffocating him,' Lily told Ellen later. 'She's got Martin all bundled up like a china doll. He should be out and about, getting back on his feet. At this rate she'll make him into an invalid.'

'I can't even get in to see him,' Ellen replied curtly, 'When I call, Emma never answers the door. She thinks that child's a possession – and why? Because she knows that Martin is her only hold over Peter now.'

'I don't like it,' Lily said, unusually grave. 'Honestly, Ellen, there's a bad feeling in that house.'

Surprised, Ellen looked at her sister.

'You're worrying me, Lily –'

'That's because I *am* worried. It's not like a real home; more like a tomb.'

'Then we can't leave Martin there any longer,' Ellen replied firmly. 'We have to get him out – and we have to do it as soon as possible.'

'Why?' Emma said half-heartedly.

Irritated, Peter looked over to his wife. 'I have to go for work. It's an important conference –'

'So why can't I go with you?' she countered, sulky in a dressing gown, yet fully made up at nine in the morning. 'You owe me something, Peter. I have to get some excitement somewhere.'

Exasperated, he turned away from her. She had come to him frequently over the months, creeping into his room at night and sliding under the covers, her naked body pressed against his. Come on, you've been angry with me too long, she'd say, her hands expertly moving over his body and resting between his legs. Peter, show me you forgive me. This is Emma, your Emma . . .

She was stunning, and yet to Peter she seemed to have

lost every ounce of the beauty that once transfixed him. When he looked at her now all he could see was an image of his wife with old man Crowthorn or Sydney Goldstein and felt nothing of the mesmeric love he had once had for her. How *could* he have ever missed her? Had he been mad?

'I have to go to conference alone,' he said emphatically, turning away from Emma.

Irritated, she stepped between him and the front door, preventing him from leaving.

'I love you –'

'No, you don't.' he said wearily. 'And I don't love you.'

This was not what Emma had expected, the words slapping her as hard as the back of a hand.

'Then get out!' she snapped.

'I'll be back in three days. On Friday,' Peter said, picking up his briefcase.

'Don't hurry.'

He turned as he opened the door.

'Look after Martin –'

'MARTIN! MARTIN!' she shouted, 'Always Martin –'

Peter grabbed her arm tightly. 'If you don't look after my son, I'll make you pay for it,' he said darkly.

Unexpectedly frightened, Emma moderated her tone: 'All right, all right, Peter. You know I will. I always look after him,' she said, her tone silky. 'When you get back, promise me we'll talk. Please, say we'll talk.'

'Yes,' he replied, walking out onto the street. 'We'll talk.'

Chapter Thirty-three

Tuesday dragged by, Martin taken out by Emma to the park then returned to the top bedroom in the Rochdale house. As ever the lights stayed on as she moved around upstairs. Then the sound of a radio came clearly out on to the street, the silhouette of Emma dancing playing on the blinds. At eleven, the lights went out and at twelve the house was in darkness.

Wednesday passed in a similar way, nothing untoward, only the usual round of motherly duties, Martin wrapped up against the cold as he took his walk with Emma. He was pale, moving awkwardly on callipers, his mother beside him, occasionally helping him along, her eyes always scanning the street ahead. Her expression was blank, empty of feeling. Mother and son together, yet apart.

'It's Thursday,' Bess said quietly from the safety of the car parked a few doors down and on the opposite side of the road, a direction in which Emma had no need to walk. 'We've only got one day left. If she's going to do anything, it'll have to be today.'

Peter glanced over to her. The light was fading into night, the house on Colland Street lighted upstairs, Emma's figure moving around restlessly.

The two of them had been watching the house on Colland Street all week, in a last-ditch attempt to catch Emma out. They had hoped that she would do something that would finally damn her in everyone's eyes – but she hadn't. To all intents and purposes, Emma was a wife and mother waiting patiently for her husband to return after a business trip.

Exhausted, Bess leaned her head back against the car seat.

'Well, we tried, but it didn't work, did it?'

Peter stared at the house in silence, dreading having to return there, to play happy families with a woman he had come to despise.

'We'll watch the night out,' he said evenly.

'What for?' Bess countered, 'Emma's too clever to do anything.'

He shook his head.

'No, she's not that clever. That was always her weakness; she thought she was smarter than everyone else.'

'Maybe she is.'

His eyes remained fixed on the house. A man walked past slowly, but kept moving on.

Peter pulled his collar up around his neck.

'Are you all right?'

'Fine.'

His left hand reached out for Bess's, his touch warm, desperate.

Another hour passed, Bess dozing, Peter alert, ten o'clock sliding by – and then at eleven fifteen a dark car drove into Colland Street.

'Bess, look.'

She woke instantly, staring ahead.

The car had stopped opposite the house, and the head-lights were turned off. For a long moment no one moved and then a man got out of the car, crossed the road and knocked on the door hurriedly. An instant later Emma opened it, her figure a dark shape against the lighted interior. Peter held his breath, Bess staring as the man leaned forwards and kissed Emma on the mouth.

'Who is it?' Bess whispered.

'Does it matter?' Peter replied triumphantly. 'We've got her at last.'

'I think it's Sydney Goldstein.'

Expectantly, Peter turned to her. 'So now what – shall I go in?'

She caught his arm hurriedly. 'No.'

'But –'

Bess shook her head. 'Leave this to me, Peter. Please –'

'Emma is my wife.'

'Yes, and she's my sister,' Bess replied. 'If you go in there there'll just be a fight. No one will win. Confrontation is not the way to play it with Emma, you know that. Let me handle it.'

Reluctantly he agreed.

'So what are you going to do?'

'First I'm going home to get some sleep –'

'Sleep!' Peter echoed incredulously. 'Are you joking? What about Emma?'

'Emma can wait until tomorrow,' Bess replied, her tone composed. 'Let her have her moment of triumph tonight. After all, it's going to have to last her a lifetime.'

At eight fifteen the following morning, Bess arrived back at the Colland Street house. The car had gone, and the house was quiet. Abruptly she knocked twice, then again.

'Who is it?' Emma called downstairs sleepily.

Without answering, Bess knocked again.

'I'm coming! I'm coming!' Emma snapped, opening the door. She stared at her sister in disbelief. 'What the hell are you doing here?'

Pushing past her, Bess walked in.

'I've come for Martin –'

Emma pulled her dressing gown around her tightly, flicking her hair back from her face. She still smelled faintly of perfume and cigarette smoke.

'What are you talking about?' she snapped, struggling to come awake. 'Martin's not going anywhere.'

Slowly, Bess walked past her sister into the front room

and sat down. The early daylight was cold, blue shaded, the room chilly.

'Back to your old tricks, aren't you, Emma?'

'What?'

'Was it Goldstein last night? Or some new admirer?'

Emma's face paled, her eyes flickering with suspicion. 'What are you talking about?'

'We saw you,' Bess continued evenly. 'How many times has he been over here, Emma? Whilst Martin was in the house? How many times?'

Emma's voice took on an appealing tone: 'It's never happened before –'

'It was Walter who tipped me off,' Bess went on, ignoring her sister. 'I was thinking about him and about how he used to say that people never changed, just repeated their mistakes. That's when I remembered old man Crowthorn. He used to come here when you were first married, didn't he, Emma? It was convenient for both of you. He didn't want commitment and you were a safely married woman on the look out for a good time. I suppose it was inevitable that you'd revert to your old ways a few years down the line.'

'You can't come here –'

Bess cut her off again, her expression steely. 'One man has never been enough for you, has it? You can't really love, you see, Emma. Otherwise you couldn't hurt Peter so much. Or expose Martin to this.' Her eyes fixed on her sister relentlessly. 'At first, you just wanted to take Peter away from me to prove you could do it, then you got bored with him and started fooling around.' Bess paused. 'I knew you'd never stick it out. I knew you'd get bored again. It was just a matter of time.'

Defiantly, Emma folded her arms. 'This has nothing to do with you. It's between me and my husband –'

'Peter already knows. We were *both* watching you.'

For an instant Emma stared at her sister without

registering, then she sat down heavily, her dressing gown falling open, her long white legs exposed below the hem of her nightdress. Her face was expressionless, lovely, her eyes blank. It seemed for an instant that she tried to rally, but then she slumped back in her seat, defeated.

'Well done.'

Bess frowned. 'What?'

'You win,' Emma said. And for a fleeting moment Bess actually saw admiration in her sister's eyes. This is all she really understands, Bess realized, competition. Games. Winners and losers.

'So what d'you want to do now?'

Bess took in her breath. This was it, this was the moment for which she had waited for years.

'I want you to divorce Peter . . .'

Emma stared at her, but said nothing.

'. . . I want to marry him and I want Martin back.'

'Anything else?' Emma said acidly.

'I want you out of my life for ever. I want you well away from me and my family –'

'They're my family.'

'No,' Bess replied emphatically. 'They've never been yours. You left them once and you'd leave them again. I know that, and you do. I'm doing you a favour, Emma, letting you get away now instead of later. After all, why hang around? If you stay you'll just age and then you'll never get another man. If you go now, you've got a chance.'

'You're getting lines, Emma. Just a few around the eyes, but it's starting. You see, it doesn't matter if I age – I don't need to rely on my looks like you do. Peter loves me, he doesn't notice my faults –'

'Bully for you.' Emma said coldly.

'– but the men you want have their pick of women, and you've only got a short time left before you'll be thrown over for a younger model. You don't want this,' Bess said, gesturing to the room in which they sat. 'You want the big house, servants, money – Peter hasn't got enough for you. And besides, you'd never stay the pace with Martin.'

'He's my son.' Emma said, but her tone lacked conviction.

The picture Bess had painted was all too real. Emma knew that time was passing and that she had to make her move now, or never. Emma had thought that getting her family back would satisfy her, but it hadn't, and she had begun to long to get out. To escape. The house was choking her; how could she spend the rest of her life looking after Martin and trying to patch things up with Peter? Jesus, Emma thought, he didn't even want to make love to her any more. That had been the cruellest blow, one that had crucified her, the rejection of her sex, of the one thing she relied upon.

'Well?'

Emma looked at her sister coolly. 'What's in it for me?'

Bess had expected the question and merely smiled. 'Freedom, Emma. I give you permission to go. In return for your divorcing Peter I'll look after your son and I'll take on your responsibilities. You don't have to worry, or even look back. Your man and your child are no longer your concern; you're free to do what you want.' Bess stood up and pulled back the net curtain. 'Look out there, Emma. There's a world beyond these streets, the world you want. Why are you hanging on? To spite me? What for? We have the measure of each other now, no one has to prove anything.'

'That's easy for you to say, when you've won.'

And with those words Bess suddenly realized that she *had* won. That all the years of waiting, all the heartache and anguish she had suffered had served its purpose and equipped her to stand facing up to her sister and know that, in the end, she had defeated her.

'So we're agreed? I'll take over your responsibilities and

you can start again elsewhere?' Bess said, holding out her hand.

Amused, Emma took it. Their palms rested together, skin to skin, warmth to warmth, Bess staring at her sister, Emma's eyes searching her face. And then something astonishing happened. Both women suddenly moved towards each other and held each other for a long instant before breaking away.

For years afterwards Bess would remember the scent of her sister's skin and the puzzled lost look she had worn as a child.

Chapter Thirty-four

Almost twelve months to the day, Bess finally married Peter Holding at a private service in Bolton. Luminous with pride, Reg gave her away, Ellen and Lily watching. Josiah had died only months before, having had a stroke in his sleep. The house on Church Street had been left to Lily. Within days of inheriting it, she moved all the furniture out and sold every piece, keeping only Josiah's Bible. For luck, she said wryly.

The billiards hall on Derby Street continued to stay open, the sign a little more battered outside, the baize on the tables worn thin. There was talk of modernization, but Reg would have none of it, and hung on to the battered table at the far end of the hall where Walter had used to kip down when he came home from his travels. The couch in the kitchen stayed too, albeit reupholstered, and when she was tired Ellen sat on it and daydreamed about the past.

And about Louise, who had never been in touch ... Where was she now? In Australia? With Clem still? Who knew? Perhaps she was dead; it was possible – they were all older. Or perhaps she was still social climbing, as superficial and thoughtless as ever.

Look, there's a ghost in the glory hole.

Ellen balked at the memory. Ghosts in glory holes. There were no such things as ghosts, only secrets. Smiling, she thought about Bess, and then she thought about Emma. News had come that she was living in London, then later in France. Someone even sent Ellen a newspaper cutting of Emma, accompanying some important businessman at a race meeting. She looked sleek and beautifully dressed, her face as spectacular as ever.

She had never written to Ellen nor to her mother, and then, long after she left the North, Emma finally wrote a short note home. It was not addressed to her son, or her ex-husband – but to her sister, Bess. No one knew what was in that letter, and no one asked, but from then on, for the rest of their lives, the two women corresponded, searching for some mutual understanding.

And finding it.